UNHOLY INNOCENTS

UNHOLY INNOCENTS

Christine Heagerty Marton

Copyright © 2015 Christine Heagerty
All rights reserved.

ISBN 10: 0996364404
ISBN 13: 9780996364409
Library of Congress Control Number: 2015907718
Chris Heagerty, Round Rock, TX

For my husband Laszlo
and my sons Matthew and Michael

Table of Contents

Prologue ·ix

Book One

Chapter 1	The Owl Looking Backward · · · · · · · · · · · ·	3
Chapter 2	An End and a Beginning · · · · · · · · · · · · · ·	11
Chapter 3	The Lie ·	17
Chapter 4	The Hardest Test ·	26
Chapter 5	A Liar and a Thief · · · · · · · · · · · · · · · · · · ·	32
Chapter 6	Confess and Covet · · · · · · · · · · · · · · · · · · ·	41
Chapter 7	The Baptism ·	49
Chapter 8	Process of Elimination · · · · · · · · · · · · · · ·	58
Chapter 9	Reconciliation ·	66
Chapter 10	Extrication ·	78

Book Two

Chapter 11	Murder of Innocents · · · · · · · · · · · · · · · · · ·	89
Chapter 12	Ingenuity ·	98
Chapter 13	The Vigil ·	108
Chapter 14	Without a Trace ·	119
Chapter 15	Crumbs Along the Trail · · · · · · · · · · · · · · ·	131
Chapter 16	Sole Focus ·	142

Chapter 17	Despair and Revelation	151
Chapter 18	Ashara's Conundrum	163
Chapter 19	The Hawk of Qureish	174

Book Three

Chapter 20	Desert Bloom	189
Chapter 21	Saeed Adrift	207
Chapter 22	Damascus Plan	216
Chapter 23	Danel's Conflict	225
Chapter 24	The Lie Revisited	236
Chapter 25	Darkness	243
Chapter 26	Unwilling Complicity	254
Chapter 27	Protocol and Desperation	267
Chapter 28	Discovery Strategy	277

Book Four

Chapter 29	Snake in the Shadows	291
Chapter 30	Discarded Habit	300
Chapter 31	Scolopendra	310
Chapter 32	Beirut Inquiry	321
Chapter 33	Suspicions	330
Chapter 34	Documents	339
Chapter 35	Anonymity Unraveling	354
Chapter 36	The Snare	372
Chapter 37	The Noose Tightens	382
Chapter 38	Desperate Grief	395
Chapter 39	Apprehensions	405

| Acknowledgements | 419 |
| About the Author | 421 |

Prologue

Over a millennium ago, a religious schism within the Muslim faith occurred, encouraged by the preacher Adullah al-Khasibi, proclaiming the divinity of the Prophet Muhammad's cousin and son-in-law, Iman Ali. This schismatic sect became known as the Nusayris. Their followers were mountain peasants living in extreme poverty, earning their subsistence as sharecroppers for their Sunni landlords. Over the centuries, the Nusayris held a deep-seated grudge against the city-dwelling Sunnis, who persecuted them, all the while enjoying great wealth and unshared power. Early in the 20th century, the Nusayris changed their name to become known as the Alawis, taking their names from Ali ibn Abi Talib, Muhammad's cousin.

In 1925, the League of Nations placed Syria under French colonial rule. The French, desperate for soldiers and officers for their Troupes Speciales du Oevant, recruited and trained the Alawi minority in military affairs. With this maneuver, the French offered the Alawis a path out of poverty as military officers and ultimately the means to usurp power from the elitist Sunnis.

The Alawis had never been under the jurisdiction of the cities or the Sunni bureaucracy. In 1936, the Alawis petitioned the French for their independence, but their petition was never granted. The petition had six signatories, one of which was Sulayman al-Assad. That same year, Syria negotiated its independence from France, and in the agreement the Alawi became part of the Syrian state. Two decades later, the Alawi military would overtake the Sunni-held state and take revenge on the Sunnis, assuming what they considered their rightful place in Syrian leadership.

Sulayman al-Assad had a son named Hafez, an activist who attended the military academy in Latakia. Hafez al-Assad was a peasant but also a shrewd, ruthless politician and conspirator. In the chaos that emerged from Syria's independence from France, Hafez was able to offer Syria stability in the leadership guise of a strict and rigid military officer. He excelled in the removal of political rivals and reward for loyal followers. He intimidated the Sunni bureaucracy and utilized horrific torture and imprisonment to quell any dissention. Hafez successfully marshaled the solidarity of the Alawite community, the security establishment, the army and the Baath Party under his control and influence. Under the mantle of fear, he imposed a peace which did not tolerate dissention.

Hafez had two sons. The older, Bassel, destined to take over the reins from his father, was killed in an automobile accident in 1994. That left Bashar, an ophthalmologist by training, to fulfill his father's dynastic dreams for Syrian rule. When Hafez died in 2000, an inexperienced Bashar al-Assad ascended to take his father's place. His legacy was that of a crown prince, privileged and spoiled, who had been handed a kingdom yet had been given no training or experience in how to rule. Gone were his father's cronies, eliminated through exile or execution, who had helped his father rise. They had waited patiently for their turn at power, only to watch Bassel and then Bashar groomed to succeed their father.

Bashar regarded his presidency as birthright, a kingdom handed down from his grandfather Sulayman to his father Hafez, and finally to him. Bashar's rule became a reign of torture and imprisonment, so much more fierce than his father's that the balance between fear and peace was finally tipped. Fear could no longer contain the populace. They had had enough. Bashar was an irrelevant crown prince, in denial that the wave of democratic fervor sweeping the Arab world could touch him or his subjects. He was ready to fight at any cost for what was rightfully his.[1] In 2011, Syria became the stage for one of the bloodiest and longest uprisings in the Arab Spring. This story take place in the summer of 2012 at the infancy of Syria's Arab Spring.

---

[1] Ajami, Fouad. The Syrian Rebellion. Stanford, California: Hoover Instituion Press, 2012

Book One

1

The Owl Looking Backward

The hot stuffy air in the small apartment was the better of two poor choices. Ashara had alternately opened and closed the windows all day. Electricity had been intermittent, so neither the fan nor the air conditioning could offer relief. Right now, closed worked, but soon the lack of fresh air would force her to open up to the acrid smell of munitions and the hazy dust of destruction that would coat her tongue, film her eyes, and layer over her kitchen counter. Worse were the high-pitched lead-ins before the boom of the shell bursts, which were close earlier but had seemed to move off toward north Damascus over the last two hours. Danel would be home soon with the fish from the market and they would have dinner together, the antidote to her vulnerability and confinement this last month of her pregnancy. Finally, Danel's key sounded in the door, and the lock slipped open.

"You're late tonight. Two hours," she said.

"I'm sorry. I was in surgery. Would you've had me leave my patient wide open so I could be home on time for dinner?"

"Did you get the fish?" she asked, spying his empty hands.

"They were out of fish." Danel's fingers mechanically brushed his thick black bangs out of his eyes.

"A fish monger out of fish?" she said, right arm akimbo, foot a-tapping and her left hand raised heavenward. Danel's casual relationship with the truth always infuriated her. "You really expect me to believe that? In my four years in this neighborhood, the fish monger has never been out of fish."

"You win, Ashara. I forgot the fish. Do you want to fight?" he said.

"No. But you're lying makes me crazy. Now all you'll have is hummus and roasted peppers. What kind of wife offers only hummus and roasted peppers?" Her hands repositioned chest level, open palmed, waiting for his response.

"What makes you crazy, Ashara, is being pregnant, cooped up in the middle of a war zone. You know what makes me crazy?" His pitch raised up. "What makes me crazy is the senseless mutilation that I'm expected to repair day in and day out. If we're going to fight, let's not make it about fish."

Danel sized her up wearily to judge if he were sparring with his wife or her hormones. Dropping his leather satchel stuffed with patient charts, he walked in measured paces to his wife. With his hands on her shoulders, he squared her to him, focusing the confrontation. "And a wife who serves hummus and roasted peppers to a husband, who forgot the fish, is my beautiful and precious wife." He enfolded her in a protective embrace, rocking her gently. Ashara tilted her head to meet his gaze, her eyes glassed over with tears threatening to spill over the dam of her thick black lashes. "Now, let's have dinner," he said, "and thank Allah that we even have hummus and peppers, and each other." He dabbed the corners of her eyes with his folded handkerchief. "I have much to tell you about the day."

Their small, yellow Formica-topped table in the tiny apartment kitchen had been set hours ago. Growing weary of the scramble for light in the evenings when the power went off, Ashara stationed lit candles about the apartment to fill the lumen gap when the lights failed. She busied herself to deliver the fishless repast to the table.

"I have a small amount of wine." Her small frame waddled to the pantry to fetch it, filling a glass with water for herself. She carried her baby heavily in this ninth month, all out in front and riding low, yet from the rear she still appeared slim.

"No, better not. I'm on call."

"You were at the hospital for twelve hours, and they have you on call?" She reached for another tumbler and filled it with water. Her innate directness rarely filtered her feelings, especially when it involved Danel being overworked. Somehow she felt the hospital owed him some consideration for staying on while other staff fled. Every day, more and more, already 200,000 Syrians by the summer of 2012, traded the illusion of a normal life for a minimal existence in another country to save their lives.

Warming in the oven for some time, the peppers were slightly scorched and limp. Eyeing them as a personal failure, she transferred the pan to a hot pad on the table.

Rolling his shirt sleeves up to his elbow, Danel slid into his seat with an exhausted plop, his lanky legs stretched out resting on his heels. "Three more doctors and seven nurses failed to show up today. No one ever says goodbye; they just disappear." He traced his finger around a yellow swirl in the table top. "We're down to a skeleton crew. Everyone's trying to make do, but it's impossible."

"Staff departures have been going on for months. What really happened today?"

Sighing, he paused. "Unbelievable. Four soldiers burst into the emergency room with rifles, shouting and waving them around. I wasn't there, but Sister Helen was, and she told me about it later."

"What was Sister Helen doing in the emergency room? I thought non-government personnel were there purely for administrative work." Already the NGOs in Syria approached 1,500 and were incorporated into civil and charitable work.

"They are. Emergency was so shorthanded they asked her to help since she was a nurse." He scooped some hummus onto his plate and reached for some flatbread while Ashara served the peppers. "The soldiers were from the army, not government security men this time. They were looking for insurgents disloyal to Assad's regime. The waiting room was crowded." He dipped his flatbread into the hummus and centered a limp pepper on top. "There was an old man there with his grandson. The grandfather had shrapnel wounds in his thigh. The soldiers started yelling, accusing him of waging war on the regime." Still in disbelief hours later, he shook his head.

"The old man was trembling, denying it. The boy, who was about twelve, told the soldiers that his grandfather wasn't a fighter. They had been on the way to the market when his grandfather got hit." He paused to swallow some water. "The old man was 73 years old. Anyone could see he was incapable of fighting heavily armed soldiers."

Mesmerized, she clasped her hands tightly under her chin.

"Then the soldiers called him a liar. When the boy protested, they shot the grandfather in the head and then fired at the boy. Everyone started screaming, terrified. It was total chaos."

Ashara covered her mouth, her normally quick tongue silenced.

Danel's voice cracked, so he took a long deep breath to gather his composure. "Then they went to the charge nurse and put the rifle to her head. They told her that insurgents were terrorists and deserved to die. If they caught any more insurgents being treated in the emergency room, she'd be the next to die." He idly pushed a pepper across his plate. Many evenings of late he was too exhausted to eat, and his retelling of the murders left him little appetite.

"How can you not treat the wounded? That's an impossible order."

"Other hospitals called, warning us of the raids. We'd moved the wounded to the basement to hide them. The grandfather was so old, I guess the charge nurse didn't think he was a fighter. It was all so senseless."

He pushed his plate aside, staring blankly at Ashara. Laying his folded arms on the table, he lowered his head, his shoulders shaking as sobs escaped. She rose to comfort him, cradling his head against her chest. His arms wrapped around her and their unborn child. She'd only seen him weep once, when his father died five years ago.

"Up until now I have been able to look past such senseless cruelty. But at some point, it shakes your faith in mankind. I feel so powerless. I'm sorry. I didn't mean to burden you."

"Shhh. Shhh. It's alright."

"I should have gotten us out of here months ago. What was I thinking, putting you and our baby in harm's way? Ashara, I'm so sorry. I should've taken better care of you both. If this insurgency continues, and Assad is defeated, there will be retribution taken. As Alawites we are particularly vulnerable."

"Shhh. It wasn't just your decision." Touching his chin, she tilted his head up. "We made the decision together to remain not knowing what would happen here."

"Yes, but seeing so many casualties at the hospital, I was foolish to keep us here."

"No one thought the fighting would come into Assad's back yard. You're like the owl looking backward. Besides, we had nowhere to go. Did you want your son to be born in a refugee camp?"

"Of course not. What I want is to live our lives in peace. Is that too much for us to ask?"

"We can talk about leaving, but not until after our child is born," she said.

"I could be executed for what goes through my mind about the regime. The mutilation and suffering of ordinary people who have taken up arms is heart breaking. All they want is to live in freedom, out from under Assad's oppression. These are not bad people. No one should have to live like this."

"I know. I try to be a good Muslim and pray for Assad. But sometimes I pray to Allah to make him leave. The Syrian people are like a dog who can't decide to stay with the master who beats him or to leave to be homeless without any certainty for the future."

She gently rocked him back and forth. Reaching for his hand, she placed it against her belly. "Don't torment yourself." She paused, letting her request sink in. "We're going to be a family, and Allah will take care of us. We'll be alright."

Danel smiled as she used her thin maternity tunic to wipe his face. When she felt his tension ebb, she kissed his forehead and then his lips, tenderly smoothing his thick hair.

As their mood lightened, she ran hot water into the sink. Danel mechanically cleared the plates, sliding hummus and peppers into the trash before passing each plate to Ashara to wash.

"I guess we wouldn't have eaten the fish after all, even if I'd remembered it." She playfully shoved her hip into his leg. The lights began to flicker to the sound of distant shelling, and then the power gave its last gasp for the evening.

The warm night air blew softly through the open window. Ashara rested on her side facing the window, a small pillow under her unborn child and another between her bent legs. The whistles and booms from distant shelling could be heard more clearly through the night air, answering each other like cicadas on a warm summer night. Danel curled his body against her back, forming a carapace around his soft wife, who cocooned their unborn child.

The moonlight delineated the edges of Ashara's silhouette. The highlighted tips of her dark lashes flickered, signaling she wasn't asleep. Their infant hadn't settled in either. Danel watched the baby's sudden kick as a moving abdominal bulge under her sheer gown. Despite his fatigue, his own sleep remained elusive. Nuzzling his face into Ashara's thick ebony locks, he breathed in her sweet scent and reached across her to rest his hand on her belly to feel their son move.

"You should be asleep," she said as she clasped his hand on her stomach, holding it firmly as if to siphon his strength to her own fragility.

"Shhh. It feels like our son will be quite a football player, like his baba." He began to gently rub her swollen belly. Their active infant finally calmed to Danel's soft circular caresses.

"I'm ready for this birth, but I feel he's safer inside me. What happened today really scared me. Of all places, I thought the hospital was safe. What if the soldiers come when I'm giving birth? What if the baby's not healthy and we lose this one too? I'm 33 now; this is probably our last chance. If this baby doesn't survive, I will know that it is Allah's will that I not have a child. I can't go against his wishes."

Danel knew better that to offer a medicine-based counter argument when it came to matters of faith. "You're not going to lose him. I'll be there. The baby has a strong kick, and all your checkups have been good." Their anticipation of a son was tempered by the emptiness and biting disappointment of the two previous stillbirths.

"You have to promise whatever happens, you'll tell me the truth. Okay?"

"I promise only the truth, Ashara." The commitment caused him some uneasiness, though he wasn't sure why. "I stopped downstairs by Mr. Faroush's yesterday morning on the way in. He says we're the only ones left in the complex now. He sent his wife to the country to stay with their daughter and son-in-law."

"I feel better that Mrs. Faroush is in a safe place," she said.

"He told me that he's going to join her after our baby is born, so we'll have a back up to get you to the hospital."

Ashara smiled in the darkness as she heard about Mr. Faroush, the elderly neighbor with the white, bushy mustache, who befriended them when they first moved in four years ago. Mrs. Faroush treated her like a daughter, so solicitous and kind when Ashara lost the babies. The Faroushes had encouraged them to try for another child. They had had their children later, complicated by their own share of heartache when they lost their two year old to meningitis. She warmed to the blessing of such good neighbors. "He acts like this child will be his next grandson."

"I figure you should have about two more weeks before the baby comes. Let's not worry any more tonight." He sensed her body grow heavy, and his own breathing matched her rhythm as the evening's catharsis left them drained, allowing all three to fall into a deep sleep.

2

An End and a Beginning

Danel's pager beeped around 5:00 am. He groped the nightstand to silence it before it disturbed Ashara. Stirring slightly, her eyes still closed, she said, "Don't go now. We just got to sleep."

"I have to go. I'm on call. I'll be late tonight." Heading to the bathroom to relieve himself and perform wudu, the ritual washing before prayer, he yawned, rubbing the sleep from his eyes. After dressing, he stood in the living room before Allah. After bowing, he prostrated and renewed his declaration of faith.

Glory to my Sustainer, the Most High. Repeating the passage three times, he finished his recitations and stopped back into the bedroom to say goodbye.

"Take care of our son."

"Did you pray?"

"Yes, we need Allah's protection all the more these days." After kissing her on the top of her head, he left for work.

Ashara's moist forehead alerted her even at 7:00 am that this day was going to be a scorcher. Danel usually closed the front windows at night for security. Before reciting her prayers, she lumbered over to open the window to divert any cross breeze to the back of the apartment. Casually she parted the lace curtain to watch Mr. Faroush rearrange some garbage sacks in the dumpster to make way for three more that he heaved onto the top. His wife's orange and yellow striped plastic shopping bag hung on the railing ready for him to take to the market.

Despite the heat, he was wearing the same blue plaid, long-sleeved shirt and light tan flak jacket she'd come to regard as his unofficial uniform. Its pockets held a piece of wire, a nail, a screw and a tool or two needed for an impromptu repair. Before the other families evacuated the complex, candy in one of his pockets drew a following of kids, who'd earn their treat by guessing which pocket hid the candy.

Glancing up unexpectedly to catch Ashara watching him, he gestured with a confident wave. She smiled and saluted him back. Her fondness for Mr. Faroush was tinged with anxiety, since she knew that he wouldn't be close at hand for the next couple of hours. *He'd be safer if he'd gone with his wife to the country*, she thought, *instead of staying to help us.*

The shelling had started early that morning, about 6:00 am. It sounded far off then. Now, an hour later, the booms and the anticipatory whistles had moved closer. The hairs on Ashara's arm rose to attention as she waited for the next one. Moving closer to the window, she cocked her head to better gauge their location. She started to massage her belly as Mr. Faroush trundled up the street, bag under his arm, and disappeared around the corner.

By late afternoon, the temperature in the apartment was up to 33° C, when Ashara felt the first contractions start faintly in the small of her back. The tightening was slow but short lived, at six minute intervals. Initially unsure if they were labor pains, she busied herself with a perfunctory gear check. Removing her backpack out of the closet, she checked its contents: extra socks, a night gown, underwear, a lightweight robe, a toothbrush, the Koran, a light blue one-piece outfit for her son's first trip home and a soft white flannel receiving blanket. She had repeated the ritual several times during these last weeks.

Picking up the receiver to call Danel, she heard no dial tone. She impatiently clicked the receiver as if to shock it into answering her, but it was unmoved by her urgency. Biting her lip, she reached for her cell phone, but it wouldn't cooperate either. She wondered if one of the cell towers had been hit.

Mr. Faroush hadn't stopped in when he returned from the market, so Ashara walked downstairs to summon him. Ringing the bell, she waited for him to answer before banging on the door. "Mr. Faroush, it's time. The baby's coming." She pressed her face against the window to detect any movement inside.

Her angst was palpable as she trudged back upstairs to call Danel again, but both phones were still out. Pacing back and forth, she considered her options. Beads of sweat rolled down her back in the stifling heat inside the apartment. The last two contractions were closer to five minutes apart. Waiting was no longer an option.

Ashara tamed her long black mane into a demure bun, securing it with long hairpins at the nape of her neck. Covering her hair with a lavender silk hijab, she tied the laces of her white athletic shoes. Slipping her arms into the backpack, she grabbed her purse and locked the door. Nearby shelling punctuated the ordinary sounds out in the street. With only four blocks to go, she would be there in no time.

Her small steps punctuated her waddled gait as she made her way to the first corner. Previous shelling had disfigured several apartment complexes in the next block. Grotesque steel reinforcements, twisted like ribbons frozen in midair, protruded from the ghostly rubble of what had once been apartments. The street was deserted, except for a large gray cat who bounded out of a trash bin. Rubble from the bombing blocked the street so no car could pass. Scarred sycamores stood as sentinels, bearing witness to the wanton demolition.

Relieved that the shelling seemed several blocks away, she leaned heavily against a short decorative stucco wall of one residence. The vice-like grip of the next contraction commandeered her body. This one was much closer and longer than the last. Focusing on a damaged finial, defiantly perched at the far corner of the wall, she willed herself through the contraction with rhythmic, panting breaths. As its grip subsided, she breathed deeply, fighting the urge to rest before the next wave. The chasm between contractions had to be dedicated to gaining distance, with two and a half blocks yet to go.

The next street had been spared, and she caught sight of curtain movement in one house with a woman's silhouette behind the lacy fabric. Many but not all homes looked deserted. A car backed out of a driveway and sped off. Out of nowhere burst crisp tet-tet-e-tets of sniper fire, answered by a return volley somewhere from the opposite direction. This would explain why she saw no one on the street. An interlude of running boot steps preceded the next round of shots. Their exact location was elusive, behind her, above her, across from her, taunting her. Instinctively turning to face the buildings, her heart quickened as she sidled forward, crab-like, shielding her infant between her back and the wall in front of her.

The next contraction asserted itself into her forward movement. Ashara grabbed the wrought iron fence in front of her. Lowering her head against its rails, she willed her breathing into a defensive rhythm. A cobra-like squeeze radiated from her lower back across her abdomen. She didn't need her watch to time her contractions. When the contraction subsided, she edged forward.

More rifle volley sounded, this time very close, but behind her. Advancing, she glanced backward, then rounded the corner into the next street, when her foot struck something large, soft yet unyielding, tumbling her forward onto a body at her feet.

Screaming, she straddled the faceless corpse. Its sticky congealed blood now stuck to her white shoes and her hands, which had broken her fall. Broken eggs, bread and rice kernels were strewn about the man. Potatoes, which had tumbled cornucopia-like from a striped market bag, lay nearby. Ashara instantly recognized the blue plaid shirt and tan flak jacket.

"Mr. Faroush, Mr. Faroush, no, no. " Wailing, she crouched next to him, shaking his jacket back and forth to revive him. "Mr. Faroush, wake up. Please." She wiped her sleeve across her tear-soaked face, finally accepting that he was gone. She slipped off her backpack, rummaging through it for the white receiving blanket. Unfolding it, she tenderly covered the old man's face and chest, kissing her palm and pressing it onto the blanket. Kneeling beside her dear friend, she endured the next violent contraction until she could rise gingerly and walk around his body. She had one street to cross before the hospital.

Surrounding her, the snipers were now perched on the hospital roof with their opposition returning fire from the medical building across the street. Her path lay directly between them, leaving the only option to stay her course and cross Atawi Street and enter their crosshairs. Halfway into the intersection, a violent contraction crumpled her to all fours, wadding up her body like discarded paper. Her breathing was now a desperate pant-blow through the pain, when a torrent of warm fluid gushed down her legs. The protective ocean in which her baby swam abandoned the infant.

By now a crowd from the emergency room had gathered at its thick glass doors, watching a woman crawl across the expanse of the wide thoroughfare in front of the hospital. Traffic had been diverted by police barricades out of harm's way, avoiding the impromptu battlefield. A young orderly in pale green scrubs with a wheelchair bravely ventured out, but, rebuffed by a volley of tet-e-tet-tets, retreated. Sister Helen burst through the ER's inner doors and spotted the crowd of patients and staff gawking through the front windows.

"What's going on here?" her deep tenor voice bellowed, parting the onlookers like Moses at the Red Sea, allowing her meaty girth to move unobstructed to the front doors. "Someone go get Dr. Ottawa. That's his wife," she shouted.

Raised Catholic, Sister Helen had defected to the Anglican Church to punish her parents for placing her illegitimate child up for adoption. The middle-aged nun was at her best when taking charge.

The orderly made a second attempt to fetch Ashara, but rifle fire again beat him back. Sister Helen, her cherubic face flushed and determined, instantly calculated risk and reward. She swashbuckled her ample hip and buttock to shove the young orderly aside and commandeered the wheelchair.

"You can't go out there," someone said. "It's suicide."

"They wouldn't shoot a nun. Besides, I'm a Protestant on Allah's turf." Sister Helen made the sign of the cross twice, a remnant from her Catholic upbringing. Her own fear, publicly disguised, buckled her knees and quickened her breathing. But for Sister Helen, determination trumped fear as she deliberately chauffeured the wheelchair forward into no man's land toward Ashara. Rifle volley renewed its ferocity above her head, but venturing out the double doors had committed her. Continuing forward, she dared the warring factions to stop her.

"Well, this is a fine mess, my friend," she said, approaching the young mother. Sister Helen locked the chair's wheels. Then, lifting Ashara to a kneeling position, she removed her backpack. "Ashara, put your arms on my shoulders, and we'll get you up into the chair. Can you do that?"

Startled by staccato shots overhead, Sister Helen glanced up to see an insurgent in a brown bandanna peering over the roof's parapet, his rifle pointed directly at her. Abruptly his rifle fired into the air as he jerked up. Slumping over the parapet, his dead body tumbled four stories to the courtyard below.

Exhausted, Ashara smiled faintly. "You must be one of those angels Sister Helen talks about."

"Ashara, I *am* Sister Helen." She maneuvered Ashara into the wheelchair and hastily bridged the gulf toward the safety of the hospital. Their triumphant entry through the double glass doors was met with clapping, Danel's embrace and cheers of "Allah Akbar." This drowned out the whirring of government helicopters, which exterminated the remaining freedom fighters.

3

The Lie

The same young orderly who had been rebuffed by the snipers now commandeered the wheelchair to transport Ashara upstairs to maternity, as she winced at the next contraction. "Doctor, it looks like we don't have time to waste."

"Ashara, let's go have a baby." Squeezing her hand reassuringly, Danel felt a stickiness from clotted blood on his own hands and withdrew to examine them. Panicking, he hastily concluded that the blood was hers.

"Ashara, where are you bleeding? You've been shot."

The orderly pressed the brake to keep the wheelchair from rolling forward.

Danel lowered to his haunches in front of the wheelchair, groping her body for the blood's source. Although no wounds were immediately obvious, her hands, tunic, shoes and backpack were splattered with varying amounts of congealed blood. "Where are you hurt?" His hands moved with clinical precision over her ankle and then up her calf past her knee, and then repeated their probing path on the opposite side, working their way up her body. "Tell me where you've been shot."

Ashara's immediate attention focused on her current contraction less than a minute after the last one. As the contraction subsided, she finally answered. "Danel, I'm fine. I haven't been shot."

"But the blood?" His hands continued to grope for a wound.

"Danel, it's Mr. Faroush's. He was killed by snipers." Weeping, she explained how she stumbled on the old man. "His face was shot unrecognizable."

"Then how did you know it was Mr. Faroush? Maybe it was someone else."

"He was wearing the plaid shirt and flak jacket. Mrs. Faroush's orange satchel was by his body. It was Mr. Faroush." The next wave of muscular tightening from the small of her back cut her short.

"Where exactly did you find him? What route did you take to get here?"

Between pant breaths, Ashara gave him the location of Mr. Faroush's corpse. "Turn the corner. On Chajara Street. Coming back from the market. Groceries everywhere."

"We'll fetch his body back here to the hospital."

"Dr. Ottawa, do you want me to send an ambulance?" said the orderly.

"No, I am going to need you to help me get her upstairs."

When a break in the contractions occurred, she used the brief respite to fill in more details. "I placed our baby's receiving blanket over his face. You know, the white one we bought in the old city? I didn't know what else to do. I didn't want to leave him; I had to move on. If it weren't for us, he would have gone with Mrs. Faroush. He'd still be alive." The tightening in her abdomen cut her short.

"Shhh. It's alright." His eyes glassed over imaging their dear friend gunned down. "This isn't your fault, nor mine. He was a victim. His goodness kept him here." Ashara gave no response as another contraction commandeered her attention. "I'll have to call Mrs. Faroush and let her know." Searching the room for Sister Helen, he spotted her assisting another patient. "Sister Helen, can you help us?"

"Anything, Danel. What can I do?"

"Our neighbor Mr. Faroush was shot. You remember him?"

"Of course."

"Ashara found him on the street on her way here. His body's still out there. Could you arrange for an ambulance to bring the body back here?"

"Sure." Unbuttoning her cuffs, she rolled her sleeves up beyond her elbow. "Ashara, don't worry; we'll bring him in."

Danel nodded to the orderly, who had already unlatched the brake, gathering momentum as he inched the wheelchair forward over the vinyl-tiled floor toward the bumpered doors. Swinging the doors open for the wheelchair to pass through unimpeded, they proceeded down the long gray corridor. The orderly hauled a large flashlight out of his pocket and handed it to Danel.

"Here, Dr. Ottawa, we're going to need this. Both generators are out, so the elevator's not coming." He pressed the button several times, and then both men headed to the stairs. "Not only are we shorthanded, but everything is that much harder without power."

"Ashara, can you climb the stairs?" said Danel.

"I'll try." As she started to mount the first step, a contraction halted her forward movement. Danel handed the flashlight back to the orderly and slid his arm beneath her legs as they buckled. He tilted her up off the ground and carried her the rest of the way. Her arms encircled his shoulders as she concentrated on her breathing.

"I think the baby's coming now."

"Hold on, we are almost there." Danel quickened his pace as he reached the second floor. Turning sideways, he pushed through the double doors to the dimly lit corridor. The orderly grabbed a nearby gurney parked in the hall. Lowering Ashara onto the gurney, Danel wheeled her into delivery. Recounting the power problems, the nurse in charge explained they had stationed candles in the delivery room and the nursery until the power returned.

"How many staff are here tonight?"

"I'm sorry, but it is just you, me and one other doctor for the whole floor. He's in surgery right now. I only left him to get some extra supplies."

"I understand."

The orderly's pager sounded suddenly; excusing himself, he left abruptly.

"Dr. Ottawa, you're on your own," said the nurse. "The other birth is a critical caesarian with complications for mother and baby. I have to assist. You're going to have to manage."

"We'll be fine. You go and do what you have to." Danel took Ashara into a prep area and helped her undress and put on a gown. He wheeled her gurney into the candlelit delivery room. Several large mirrors were stationed behind the candles to magnify the light. Not ideal conditions, but workable. He lifted Ashara slightly to transfer her to the birthing table, and then guided her feet into the stirrups. As he prepared a syringe to anesthetize her for an episiotomy, the baby's head was already moving through the birth canal. She screamed, trying to push the baby out.

"Ashara, breathe, and wait to push until the next contraction. Can you do that?" She nodded and willed herself to focus. The next contraction was not far behind. "You're doing fine, now with this contraction, really push hard. Now push."

Ashara summoned her strength, but the infant's head had become lodged. She screamed as the contraction shoved the baby's head against unyielding bone.

"Try to relax until the next contraction. I am going to turn his head." He tried to guide the infant's head to take advantage of the opening's shape. "Now push again." This time her contraction was much stronger, but the cranium jammed unrelenting against her pelvis. She cried out for the pain to stop.

Beads of sweat formed along Danel's brow.

"I'm going use forceps to turn the baby. You must stop pushing while I do this. Alright?"

Exhausted, she nodded.

Taking a deep breath, he guided the forceps up the birth canal, maneuvering to grasp the sides of the baby's skull. Gently he eased the child's head back off the pelvic wall and then firmly edged the cranium in the pelvic foramen.

"Danel, the contraction is coming now. I can't stop."

"The baby's in position, you can push now." This time the child moved unimpeded through the canal to Danel's waiting hands. His first cries punctured the tension, altering his parents' emotional tenor like the flip of a light switch.

"Our baby boy's alive." She wept at his arrival and for all the promise that their lives together held. Danel siphoned excess fluid from the tiny month and tied off his umbilical cord as Ashara's subsequent contractions easily delivered the afterbirth. He wrapped the wailing, squirming infant in a soft cotton blanket and laid him in his mother's arms.

"My beautiful boy. Such a fuss you're making." She kissed his cheek and gazed into his eyes. "He's beautiful, isn't he Danel?"

"Indeed he is, although a bit messy."

Ashara took the corner of her sheet moist with perspiration to wipe the white vernix from his little face and mouth. "Let me get a better look at you, dear boy." A full head of thick dark brown hair framed the little red face, protesting the journey he had just made. "And where did you get all that hair?" Infatuated and consumed with love, she kissed his forehead and rocked him ever so gently. "We have been waiting for a very long time for you. You were worth the wait. You're just perfect." She unfolded the blanket to inspect him and smiled her approval. "He has your long fingers. And your forehead too, very broad." Ashara looked right into the child's eyes. "You're going to be handsome like your baba. My happiness is complete."

"Allah has blessed us today." He prepared a local anesthetic and then stitched the vaginal tears. His next concern was his young son. As he moved around to Ashara's side, he beheld the radiance in her countenance and an infant whose breaths were slightly labored.

"Danel, let's call him Hamid after Mr. Faroush." Ashara caught the flicker of concern on his face. "Danel, what is it? What's wrong?"

"Nothing. I like the name. Mr. Faroush would be honored and proud. But I have to take care of little Hamid now and make double sure he's healthy. Do you think you can bear to be parted from him for a short time?"

"I'll be fine. Take care of our son." The maternity nurse checked in as Danel was leaving with the infant.

"Nurse, any news about the power?"

"I just heard that maintenance is overwhelmed. The snipers did a lot of damage. Both backup generators need some parts to get them working. That's all I know, but from the sound of it, we're probably going to be without power most of the night."

"My wife is fine, but would you just check on her. I'm taking our son up to clean him up and examine him."

"Of course, Dr. Ottawa. Congratulations."

Danel walked briskly down the dingy corridor with his son nestled in his arms. Bursting through the nursery doors, he quickened his pace. Inside were four rows of bassinettes, each containing eight mobile units. Only half of them were occupied. The nursery had an eerie glow from the flickering candles lit throughout the room. His own child struggled as his breathing became more labored. His pallor, pinkish red at birth, was now a bluish gray. Danel felt the movement in his arms and legs slowing. Laying his infant in a carriage, he wheeled it closer to the candles. Opening the blanket, he placed a stethoscope over the tiny heart, listening to his heartbeat. At barely 75 beats a minute, it was well below normal.

The sound of fluid in Hamid's lungs gurgled over the heart's rhythm. Danel's fear commingled with the vitals he was gathering. *Wet lungs, transient tachypnea.* His diagnosis deeply pierced his heart. The skin around Hamid's ribcage retracted with each breath. He needed special monitoring and oxygen support. No power was a death sentence for the boy.

As the infant's life hung on a thread, Danel's concern for Ashara loomed. How would she cope with the loss of this child whose cry she had heard and whose warm cheek she had kissed?

Little Hamid's chances of survival were quickly slipping away as his breathing became more shallow. Danel tenderly placed his forefinger in his infant son's palm, and Hamid's long tiny fingers instinctively grasped his father's finger, holding it tightly. Stroking his thumb reassuringly across the back of the little hand, he leaned over the bassinette, resting his free arm to support his large frame on the top railing. He lowered his face closer so father and son could formally meet each other.

"I'm your baba, little one." Danel smiled and moved his head slightly up and down to confirm what he has just told the child. His voice was soft and low. "Your name is Hamid, and you're my very special little boy." The infant stared wide eyed at his father.

Powerless, Danel knew his son was dying.

Watching his baby's labored breathing, Danel's eyes filled. He freed his finger from the tiny grasp. Lifting Hamid out of his trolley, Danel nestled him into the crook of his left arm. With his free hand, he filled a shallow basin with water and gently sponged the tepid water over his body, tenderly wiping the vernix from his soft skin. Laying Hamid on a clean blanket, he swaddled the infant into a soft, comforting cocoon. As Hamid's movements within the blanket calmed, Danel began to hum a lullaby his mother used to sing about a little rabbit lost in the Syrian Steppe. He spied the nursery rocking chair, and, holding Hamid close, rocked him back and forth as he clung to his last breaths. Danel recited prayers as a final sendoff for his tiny son on his journey to meet Allah, sobbing silently as the infant gasped his last breath.

Allah, Almighty and All Knowing, keep this precious child close and safe until one day his mother and I reside with you beyond this earth.

Cradling the limp body close, he pondered their life without him. He felt heavy and emotionally drained as he prepared himself to tell Ashara about their loss. This little person, who carried the burden of her dreams of a family, had deserted her, and soon would break her heart. Little Hamid enjoined his father as an accomplice by making Danel the messenger of such cruel news.

Placing the lifeless body back into his trolley, he stood entranced observing his dead son. Weary from months of tending to others, his own heart now ached with its own tragedy. Mechanically, he reached into his pocket for his pen and began filling out Hamid's information card from the front of the trolley.

After some minutes, Danel noticed how much the infant in the adjacent cart resembled his own son. He longingly stroked the sleeping infant's soft, silky black hair. The baby, named Abdul, was born only 30 minutes before Hamid according to the ID card at the front of the trolley. It was ironic, he thought, that Abdul was the name they originally chose for their son.

Danel heard the nurse's brisk footsteps out in the hall as she approached the nursery. In a snap decision, he swapped the identification card of his dead son with that of Abdul. The nurse pushed an instrument cart through the double doors as Danel clipped the ID bracelet off the live baby and slipped it into his pocket.

"Dr. Ottawa, I need to check vitals of all the infants. Are you going to be here a few minutes longer?"

"I was just going to take my new son to his mother, but I can wait if you need me to."

"I just have to deliver these instruments up to surgery. I shouldn't be long."

"No problem. I'll wait until you return."

Danel's heart pounded erratically inside his chest. His action, which was both cowardly and foolhardy, had been born out of his desire to spare his beloved wife grief.

Any conflict of conscience shifted abruptly to not getting caught. Returning to the nurse's station, he frantically rummaged through the drawers for ID bracelets. His hands trembled as he fumbled to open two new bracelets and remove the paper inserts. Groping his pocket for Abdul's clipped bracelet, he lifted its original insert from its plastic sheath. After filling out the insert with Hamid's information, he placed both inserts into new bracelets. Suddenly the door swung open as the duty nurse returned to check on the vitals of the other infants.

"Dr. Danel, congratulations again. How's your baby?"

"He's normal, healthy and handsome like his father." His light banter a ruse, he gathered up the bracelets, quickly attaching his son's bracelet to the living baby, and Abdul's bracelet on his own dead son's wrist. The nurse was listening to heartbeats of each tiny resident in the first row of bassinettes at the far corner of the nursery, carefully making notations on each chart. As she rounded the first row of infants, she moved closer to Danel. As his heart reverberated against his chest, he feared her clinical gaze would detect it through his scrubs. Picking up the baby who was sleeping peacefully, he proudly walked over to the nurse to show off his new counterfeit son.

"Ah, he's very handsome. What are you calling him?"

"His name is Hamid, after our very dear friend and neighbor." Acting as the proud father, he masqueraded the child as his Hamid.

"I checked on your wife. She's doing fine and eager to see her son. She's been through a lot."

"She showed great courage getting here by herself. This baby means so much to her."

"Well, you should go to her. I have about ten more vitals to check and then I have to go back and assist on another birth." Danel left to take the infant to Ashara. He had one more charade to enact before the keenest critic of all, Hamid's mother.

4

The Hardest Test

Overcome by exhaustion, Ashara dozed off. Danel entered quietly and gently laid the infant in her arms. Opening her eyes, misty with affection, she pulled the cotton swaddle back so she could see him better. Danel warmed to the joy in her face.

"Welcome to the world, little Hamid, my sweet son."

"You were so brave this afternoon. May this child bring you as much joy the rest of his life as he brings you today." He stroked her hair and bent over to tenderly kiss her lips. "I could've lost you both."

"Danel, how is he?" Loosening the blanket, she counted his little fingers and then did the same with his toes.

"He's just perfect, my love, just perfect." An inner shiver gripped him.

"I thought for a second when you left that you were concerned about him."

"It was just new father jitters I suspect."

"We should give thanks to Allah for this miracle of ours. Our son's first hearing should be his parents giving thanks." Reaching her hand out to hold Danel's, they recited their prayer aloud. .

"Allahu'Akbar, Allahu'Akbar. La'ilaha Llal-Laah Allah." *God is the Greatest, God is the Greatest. There is no deity worthy of worship except God.* They then thanked God for the miracle of their child's birth and asked Him to keep Hamid safe and close.

Climbing the stairs in twos to the second floor, Sister Helen could hardly wait to see the new baby. Hearing their recitation, she remained respectfully outside Ashara's cubicle until they were finished. Ashara positioned the infant at her breast, even though her milk had not yet begun to flow. Sister Helen neared the bed to meet little Hamid, who suckled contentedly.

"Your Allah smiled on you both tonight. Another family was not so lucky."

"What do you mean?" said Danel, feeling a bitter sting as she explained.

"One of the infants in the nursery didn't make it." Resentful of her for recounting the death, his skin blanched now that his son's body had been discovered. Up until now the matter was private, but a new shame flushed over him now that others knew. He'd given no thought to the pain of the real parents.

"Yes, we're blessed." Ashara reached out to grasp Sister Helen's hand. "I owe you so much for bringing me into the hospital. If it weren't for your courage, I wouldn't be here. We both owe you our lives. I know Allah sent you to us."

"There now, it was nothing. You did the hardest part." She squeezed Ashara's hand briefly, disengaging to stroke Hamid's soft crown. "I expect to do a lot of babysitting, young man." Sister Helen loved babies and was genuinely looking forward to getting to know Hamid. "I just wanted to check and see how the three of you were doing."

When she opened the door to depart, they could hear the weeping of the real mother and father. Wincing, Danel felt small beads of sweat along his hairline, embracing that there was no backing away from this deception. The knowledge that he had breached medical ethics and committed a crime was his alone to bear. Watching Ashara so contented was his justification, he thought, wondering what punishment Allah would extract later. Her happiness, knowing no limits, rivaled his guilt in intensity.

"Danel, I'm so happy. I was so afraid this birth would be like the others." He released her bed's side railing and gently nudged Ashara and Hamid over. Tenderly slipping his arm under her neck, he lay beside her, pressing his body close to hers with Hamid nestled between them. Reaching his free arm across them, he held his family close.

His tenderness was short lived as his mind drifted back to the switch. Kissing her lips and then Hamid on the forehead, he eased out of bed. He walked to the nursery to assess the crime scene and bid farewell to the real Hamid one final time. Despite the lack of staff on duty, the infant's body had already been efficiently cleared. Sitting at the nurse's station to check for any evidence, he reached into his pocket to retrieve the clipped bracelet. Finding it missing, his eyes darted about as he searched the counter top.

Unexpectedly, the duty nurse returned, her crisp short steps sounding out of nowhere. "Dr. Ottawa, what're you doing here?"

If she were accusing him or suspected something, he could not tell. Searching her face, he found no hint. "Honestly, I needed to just sit quietly and reflect. Besides, Ashara needed to rest."

"I understand. I heard about her harrowing trip in. The whole place is talking about it. She's fortunate to be alive."

"Allah protected her and our son; that's how I see it."

"You were lucky that all the stress on her didn't harm your baby." As she leaned over the counter to collect a tray of meds, he spied the missing bracelet on the floor next to his chair. It must have fallen out of his pocket when he was preparing the new ones. Edging his foot slightly sideways, he pushed the bracelet under his chair out of view.

"I think I'm just going to sit here and complete my son's papers while I decompress. Is that alright with you?"

"Of course. It'll give you a respite and free me up to help someone else. Did you hear? We lost an infant this evening. It looks like it had something to do with transient tachypnea. The lungs were very wet. The poor thing didn't have a chance without power."

He clenched his teeth, taking no external ownership. "Sister Helen told me."

"I just came from the parents and they're devastated. It was their first. The child was breathing well one minute, and I guess got into trouble pretty quickly. They're both young, and there'll be other babies." Removing a stethoscope from around her neck, she tilted her head, reflecting. "Still I don't know how you get over this kind of loss. Dr. Danel, you don't look well. Are you alright?"

"I'm fine. It's just the toll from almost losing Ashara and our son to snipers." Shaking his pen to start the ink flowing, he began filling out Hamid's papers, averting his eyes from the nurse's gaze. "Ashara delivered two still born infants, and they haunted her. We're so grateful this turned out the way it did."

The nurse headed around the counter to Danel's side. Leaning against the row of low cabinets behind him, she rested there casting a puzzled gaze at the floor.

He quickly placed his foot over the bracelet. Sure he was about to be discovered, his heart raced.

Sliding off the cabinets, she bent down to investigate. "Oh, there's my pen. I wondered where I'd put it." Clicking the pen's top several times to make sure it still worked, she placed it securely back into her pocket.

Catching his breath in his throat, he slowly exhaled.

"I'll never know why one baby is spared and another dies. Working with neonates is so rewarding, but their vulnerability is sometimes excruciating to witness," she said. Her reflection gave her a chance to rest. Looking downward again towards Danel's shoes, she shook her head. "Well, enough of my philosophizing, I've patients to tend to." She leaned across him and collected a tray of meds that had been delivered in her absence. Setting the tray down, she checked each vial for dosage and patient name.

His foot was frozen over the bracelet.

"I'm off. See you in a while. Don't get too good with that paperwork, or you may just find that the supervisor will assign you the task permanently." He managed a smile as she picked up the tray on her way out to the corridor.

Bending over, he scooped the clipped bracelet into his pocket. Rummaging through the lower drawer, he found the birth registry forms and began filling in the infant's new identity. Name: Hamid Ottawa, followed by mother's name, father's name, religion: Muslim. As a final precaution, he double checked the area where he had been working, making sure nothing incriminating was left behind, and then headed back to Ashara.

Danel entered her room softly. She opened her eyes whose warmth helped him justify what he'd done. If Ashara knew, her counsel would be that *pure water does not spring from a foul well. How many times had he heard her say that when she caught him in a casual untruth,* he thought. *But then she would also say that there is no such thing as a casual untruth.*

"How're you feeling?" he asked.

"Exhausted, but very happy."

"Me, too. Are you up to talking about Mr. Faroush?"

"Sure, though there's not much more I can add that you don't already know. He left for the market in the morning and never came back. When the contractions started, I went looking for him. When I couldn't reach you, I was afraid to wait any longer."

"I'm so sorry I wasn't there for you. I would've come right away had I known."

"Do you remember the last thing you said to me when you left this morning? You said the baby wouldn't be here for two weeks."

"I know, but still." Pulling a chair over close to the bed, he sat down and took her hand.

"Allah and little Hamid had other plans. That's how we have to look at it," she said. "I don't know if the same snipers I encountered killed Mr. Faroush. It seemed like they were following me the whole way here."

"We'll never know."

"I laid a kiss on his chest and thanked him for his sacrifice." Tears slipped down her cheeks at the retelling. "I didn't want to leave him there, but I didn't know what else to do."

His finger softly traced the ridge of her knuckles. "Sister Helen sent an ambulance for his body. He's in the morgue now. When I go home, I'll get his daughter's phone number."

"He'd be alive now if he had gone to his daughter's farm with Mrs. Faroush. It was my selfishness that allowed him to make this sacrifice."

"Ashara, we didn't ask him for this. He wanted to do it. I asked him the morning I stopped in if he wouldn't be better off going to his wife. It was Allah's plan for him." His large hands picked up their tiny bundle. Walking to the window, he examined his new son's face in the moonlight. "Little One, I promise to guard and protect you your whole life. You've brought your mother and me unimaginable joy." Kissing the child tenderly, he was amazed at the easy transfer of his affection to the surrogate.

Danel shivered, considering the irony that the beneficiary of the switch was the person who most abhorred deception. "Do you think he looks like us?

"Why shouldn't he? He's an Ottawa born and bred." Realizing that Hamid had passed the hardest test, he relaxed. Hamid had convinced Ashara he was her son.

5

A Liar and a Thief

Her adrenalin long since ebbed, Sister Helen felt physically and emotionally spent. Only now did she process the extent of the danger she had flirted with. Her heralded bravery was foolhardy, she thought. She shivered remembering the sniper's rifle directly aimed at her. As the evening's last patient had been moved upstairs for more comprehensive care, she slumped into a metal chair in the emergency room. Her nun's wimple, normally starched and pristine, bore the telltale wrinkles of a rough day. Puss splatters from a lanced boil on an old woman's back had spewed onto her white, starched collar and ample gray bodice. Her legs, spayed outward, protested that they would carry her no further.

A kind young nurse handed her a cup of tea that she had warmed on a Bunsen burner in the lab. "Sister Helen, you look like you could use a little comfort."

Surveying her bodice, she sipped the tea, feeling its calming warmth spread. "Just look at me, I'm a walking medical chart. Almost everyone I touched today deposited biological debris on me." The young nurse smiled and then shrugged.

Stumbling upon them on his way through the lobby, Danel sat down next to Sister Helen. The nurse, still smiling, headed to the front desk to finish her notations and filing before her replacement arrived.

Danel exhaled deeply. "It's been quite a day. It looks like we both slept in our clothes for the last three shifts. Have you eaten anything today?"

"Not really." Her stomach growled.

"How about accompanying me to dinner? Perhaps we can scrounge up something from the cafeteria."

"I would be delighted, Dr. Ottawa, if you're sure your wife wouldn't mind and Allah wouldn't object to you carousing with an overweight Christian."

"Ashara would highly approve, and Allah loves all mankind, so we're safe." They took the stairs down two flights, with Sister Helen blazing their path with a penlight. The last of the kitchen staff were cleaning up, eager to get home. Danel begged for two cups of tepid soup, which the cook salvaged from the bottom of a pot already in the washing queue. Since the cashier had gone home, no one else wanted to open up the register. They settled at a small steel table in the empty cafeteria.

A thin edge of pale, greenish-grey grease edged the inside rim of their cups. Sister Helen fished out a limp sliver of meat.

"What do you suppose this is?" She proffered the specimen toward Danel, who found a similar piece in his own cup.

Chewing slowly and deliberately, he tilted his head. "My guess is fowl, perhaps chicken, but its flavor is missing in action." He stroked his chin. "Where the flavor escaped to I have no idea, but it didn't end up in the broth." Despite finding it wanting, they consumed the scrawny chicken, few black beans and noodles with gusto. His preoccupation rendered him a very poor conversationalist.

"How are Ashara and the baby doing?" Sister Helen drank the remaining broth directly from the cup.

"They're both asleep. Ashara resisted sending Hamid back to the nursery, but I thought she'd sleep better not worrying about crushing him. She finally agreed because the baby would be back to nurse in a couple of hours. She adores him already."

"Are you sleeping here at the hospital tonight?"

"I really want to, but I owe it to Mr. Faroush to let his wife know what happened. She's staying with her daughter and son-in-law in the country, and their phone number is at home."

"Can't the hospital or the police do that?"

"The only reason he stayed behind was to help Ashara get to the hospital. Mrs. Faroush shouldn't have to hear it from a stranger."

She nodded. "You're a brave man. I don't envy you that call. How will it be at your complex with him gone? Will Ashara and the baby be safe?"

"I'm very worried. When Mr. Faroush was still there, I wasn't as concerned. But now with him gone, there's no one to help her. There was shelling in the neighborhood about three weeks ago and nothing since. Well, except for today."

"But you've no idea that the shelling won't start again."

"Precisely. We're the last family left in our complex. With Mr. Faroush dead, there's no backup. Even without the bombing, that in itself is not ideal."

"Is Ashara scared?"

"She hasn't said, but she's got to be worried."

Pushing her empty cup away, she folded her arms on the table.

"What makes it worse is that she can't call me if the phones are out."

"I have an idea." Leaning forward, she shifted in her seat.

"What do you mean?" He pushed his cup to the side.

"What if I went to your flat for a couple of hours a day?"

Danel leaned his chair back on its two hind legs.

"I could take some of the paperwork I was brought here to do, so it's not as if I wouldn't be getting the hospital's work done. I could be some company for Ashara and help with the baby."

"Wouldn't the director have some objections?"

"How can he object? The hospital doesn't pay me a salary, and technically I'm here to help as necessary." Bobbing her head in a corkscrew motion, she rolled her eyes. "The hospital isn't going to send away anyone willing to help when their own staff is deserting in droves." She spread her palms outward. "I'm only really answerable to my superior at the home office. Besides, what's he going to do, fire me?" Removing the napkin tucked into her collar to wipe her mouth, she folded it and laid it beside her cup.

"You don't think that the home office would have something to say about this?"

"How would they know? As far as they're concerned I'm doing God's work as I see fit. If I get the work done that I came to do, they couldn't object, even if they found out."

"I wouldn't want to be the source of any trouble for you, but I'm warming to the idea."

"Danel, trouble is what Ashara went through today getting to the hospital. That puts trouble in perspective, doesn't it?"

"Ashara and I should talk it over, but I suspect she'll be grateful. You're too kind to us."

"You can think that, but I'm really selfish. I'm a fool over little babies, and I want to get to know Hamid."

Her proposal answered a number of concerns over Ashara and Hamid's return home, but at some level Danel sensed this solution too convenient. His pager sounded, summoning him back to emergency. Glancing at his watch, he realized there was another hour left on his shift.

"I clocked off duty an hour ago so I am going home," she said.

"Sister Helen, I don't think I thanked you for what you did today. If you hadn't brought Ashara in, they might not have made it."

"If I hadn't brought them in, you would've done it."

"Yes, but then the three of us might be dead. We owe you more than we can ever repay."

"Your friendship is thanks enough. You invited me to dinner tonight, but it was somewhat paltry. Since we're discussing repayment, you still owe me a good meal."

"Allah as my witness, you can depend on it."

Danel treated a case of severe gastroenteritis in the emergency room before finishing his rounds. Leaving the hospital at 9:00 pm, his lengthy strides made short work of the four blocks back to their apartment, on the same route that Ashara had taken hours before. From the street, he saw the lights in their apartment were on. Ashara hadn't remembered to turn them off since the power was off when she left. All that seemed so long ago, even though it was only that afternoon. He went directly to the phone where Ashara had taped Mrs. Faroush's number. Listening for a dial tone, his hand trembled.

"Mrs. Faroush, this is Danel Ottawa."

"Danel, how good to hear from you. Did Ashara have the baby?"

He clenched his teeth. "Yes, he was born late this afternoon, and he and his mother are doing just fine."

"What did you call him, Abdul?"

"No, we named him Hamid."

"Ah, my husband's name. He must be so pleased. Is he there with you? Was he able to help Ashara get to the hospital?"

Summoning his courage, he paused slightly. "Mrs. Faroush, I'm so sorry. He was killed some time this morning by sniper fire on his way back from the market." He fiddled with pencils in a tall cup near the phone.

"Danel, what're you talking about?"

He heard her gasp followed by sobs and then all other sound was sucked from his consciousness. The frequent bearer of such news to families, he felt ill prepared. Her sobs calmed momentarily so she could speak. "Danel, where is he now? I want to see my husband."

"I sent an ambulance to bring him back to the hospital morgue. I would have called earlier, but I had to come home to get your phone number."

"We talked about the danger of him staying behind. He said no one would hurt an old man."

Her voice cracked through the sobs. "He was foolish to think that the violence couldn't touch him. I'm coming to see him."

Having pieced together what had happened to her father, her daughter Fatima took the phone from her mother. "Dr. Ottawa, is this true about my father?"

"I'm so sorry." He recounted what Ashara told him. "Your mother wants to come to see him. Fatima, you can't let her do that. The wounds were devastating."

In shock, she was very quiet, absorbing the tragedy. "I'll talk with my mother and my husband, and call you tomorrow." Fatima was now crying. "Dr. Ottawa, thank you for calling us. Allah be with you, Ashara and your new son." Her weeping punctuated her message. "Let's not forget that on this dreadful day, a new soul was born to take my father's place on this earth."

The child that was born to take her father's place was dead, he thought. "Allah, be with you as well, Fatima."

Truly alone now without the onus of concealment, Danel sat erect on the faded tweed divan, knees apart, feet together. He slipped his hands into his pocket and fingered the clipped infant bracelet. Zombie-like, he moved soundlessly to the kitchen sink and lit it with a match, watching as it curled and shriveled. As the flame petered out, he finally broke down. The tears gushed from multiple springs: the grieving family whose child he stole, Mr. Faroush, his dead son, the surrogate Hamid, his protection of Ashara, and at the basest level, his own character. His swollen lids nearly occluded his dark eyes by the time he collapsed on the sofa. Once his eyes sockets dried up, he succumbed into a bottomless sleep, which morphed into a fitful one, tortured by images drenched in guilt, blame and shame.

Four hours past midnight, he started awake to the accusing glare of the lights Ashara had left on earlier. Unwilling to reface the unconscious demons lurking in sleep, Danel headed to the bathroom to wash off the menace and revive himself.

Turning on the shower full blast, he stripped, abandoning his scrubs in the heap. The gaunt face he glimpsed in the mirror returned his stare, but he looked away quickly and cast his eyes instead on his torso, his ribs clearly defined beneath the skin. *I'm a liar and a thief,* he thought, *the worst kind of man, Ashara would say.*

Stepping into the shower stall, he lowered his head to let the hot steamy water roll down his back. His nostrils inhaled the hot vapor deep into his lungs, holding it there before exhaling it slowly. Standing motionless, he waited until the hot water was depleted and turned off the spigot. He groped for the dry towel on the hook by the stall. By the time he headed into the living room to pray, he couldn't recall drying himself or even dressing. So heavy was his guilt that his hands trembled as he tripped over the frayed carpet edge. Righting himself, he dropped to his knees and prostrated himself before the All Knowing Allah.

His prayer, first acknowledging the All Powerful and All Knowing God, then focused on his weak and impoverished character. For himself he begged for forgiveness and humility to carry on. For Ashara, he asked Allah to shield her from what he had done and never let her taste the bitterness of knowing that her true son was lost. He feared her discovery of his lie and the accompanying loss of trust. He acknowledged that he could never forgive himself, and Allah gave him no sign of forgiveness either. Rising, he reached for his keys and wallet, then turned off the lights and left to see Ashara and Hamid.

Ashara was awake and nursing Hamid when Danel arrived. The infant's wide eyes beheld her, as he suckled voraciously. Softened by her blind acceptance of this infant, a sudden warmth embraced him, allowing him a sip from the cup of self-justification instead rather than from the well of self-loathing. If he'd been unable to save his son, at least he saved Ashara.

"How did you sleep, Ashara?"

"Soundly. I didn't have even the energy to dream. After several hours, the nurse brought Hamid to feed, and we fell asleep together. Such a beautiful connection." She melted, watching her baby nestled at her breast. "Has any mother ever loved her baby as much as I love Hamid?"

"I think not." He bent down to kiss her and fondle Hamid's soft crown. Feeling the vulnerability in the soft spots in Hamid's foramen, he reflected that he owed this child much, not just for what he had given Ashara, but for what he had given up.

Ashara shifted Hamid to her shoulder and gently patted his back, jarring the air bubbles out of his stomach. After several seconds, a small belch escaped. Now satiated and warm, his drowsy eyes succumbed to sleep.

"Ashara, we should discuss the situation at our apartment."

She looked up waiting.

"Sister Helen and I talked last evening about you going home now that Mr. Faroush is gone."

"I've been worried about that."

"What would you think if Sister Helen came and spent several hours a day there to help you with the baby?"

"She would do this? What about the hospital?"

"It was her idea. What are your thoughts?"

"I think it's a great idea, but I don't want her to get into any trouble. Would the hospital spare her?"

"They pay her no salary so they don't command her time. She could bring some administrative work there, so the hospital would be getting its needs met."

"But she does nursing, and the hospital would miss that. There are not many nurses left and patients would need her help."

"True, but since she is not licensed in Syria, they can't complain without incriminating themselves."

"What about her NGO, surely they'd mind?"

"She doesn't think the hospital would tell them, and she certainly wouldn't."

"Danel, if it's possible to be more grateful to her than I am now, it would be for her help and company when I return home."

"Good, then it's settled. I'll talk to her this morning."

A menace crossed Ashara's face, evidenced by a slight crease across her forehead. He was no stranger to this look.

"We risked the danger in Damascus before Hamid was born, but everything's changed now that there's three of us."

"I know." Folding his arms across his chest, he walked over to the window overlooking the vast city to the north. Three pockets of smoke rose beyond the city limits. By the time he turned to answer Ashara, a fourth explosion sent another cloud to the far left edge of his view. "The regime is against doctors leaving. We have to be careful and discuss this with no one."

6

Confess and Covet

After two more days rest, Ashara was eager to go home. Danel loaded her and the baby into a cab, along with her backpack and several home-grown floral arrangements from staff. The cab followed the same route Ashara had walked. As they drove, she marked each contraction's focal point as a station along her pilgrimage just three days earlier.

"Driver, please stop here."

The cab abruptly pulled to the curb. The pavement where Mr. Faroush had lain was still blood stained and littered with grocery remnants.

"Look over there, it's his market bag." Unbuckling her seatbelt, she lifted the door handle and had one foot out the door."

Pulling her back into the cab, he said, "Ashara, you stay put with Hamid. I'll go."

She resisted momentarily and then pulled a white flower out of a bouquet at her feet. "Place this where he lay," she said, handing it to Danel.

Retrieving the bag, he surveyed the site. Broken eggs shells, dried from the sun, and a few rotten orange peels still remained. A loaf of bread had been pecked to a few crumbs. Most jarring was the large circumference of dried blood that stained the sidewalk. Laying the white lily where the body had lain, he bowed his head in prayer before returning to the taxi. He squeezed her hand. "He's with Allah."

Squeezing back, she struggled to restrain tears. "Driver, we can go now."

Walking into the empty apartment, it seemed to Ashara eons since she had been home. Now she was a mother, so different from the woman of three days ago.

"We've no food. Will you be alright if I leave you for a while?"

"Of course, but please be careful. Snipers can come from nowhere. I'll be waiting."

The trip to the market took Danel on streets that he hadn't been to in weeks. While he went to the hospital daily, he had been blind to the destruction within the rest of the neighborhood. Pockmarked stone walls, piles of rubble in streets that were formerly well kept, balcony rails missing or leaning precariously and broken windows bore witness to the civil strife. Yet oddly some buildings remained untouched like random survivors.

The trees affected him most. Ash, sycamore and willow were seared and burnt, some dead and some showing resilient new growth at the ends of scarred branches. They stood immobile, in silent, unwilling testimony. These living things were not blessed with free will or motility, or surely they would have left by now.

At the market, his choices were limited, and his selection of perishable items had to factor in the unreliability of refrigeration. Potatoes, rice, beans, peppers, tomatoes and beets would work. The vegetable and fruit vendors in the open market had dwindled to the few who had not yet fled. He bought some chicken for chicken minon, a liter of milk and khubz arabi bread for supper. Inside the market, he stocked up on diapers, since he was unsure of coming shortages. He lingered, looking at formula, bottles and nipples. Ashara was breastfeeding, but formula was insurance that the infant would be nourished in case her milk dried, she became ill or more likely, they journeyed out of Damascus.

He returned within an hour, and she helped him put away the food. She had diapers on hand for the baby's return from the hospital but was glad to have the extra given the uncertainty of shortages. Unloading the baby formula, she looked puzzled.

"Danel, you know that I want to breastfeed Hamid."

"I was hoping that some evenings I could feed the baby and let you sleep. A father shouldn't be deprived of nurturing his son." He winked at her sheepishly. "Besides we don't know what tomorrow will bring. What if you became ill or we decide to leave here? The formula is a backup. I'll rest easier with some options if you can't breastfeed."

Ashara nodded. "Do you have to go back to the hospital today?" She loaded the last of the groceries into the cabinet.

"No, the director told me that I deserved a day off. I talked to Sister Helen, and she'll come for two hours tomorrow morning—if that works for you."

"Tomorrow morning will be just fine, and I look forward to her company."

Sister Helen biked from the hospital at ten o'clock the next morning with her satchel, crammed full of files, secured in her rear basket. She dismounted and chained her bike to a rail on the lower level, eagerly bounding up two flights and arriving out of breath. Still panting when Ashara answered the door, she said, "Am I too early?"

"Your timing's perfect. Hamid and I have been waiting for you."

Sister Helen set down her bag just inside the door, grinning at Hamid nestled in the crook of Ashara's arm.

"My, oh my," Sister Helen cooed. "Would you mind if I held him?"

"Of course you can. Would you wash your hands first?"

Sister Helen brushed past Ashara on her way to the kitchen to wash before Ashara had finished her sentence. She skipped back to mother and son, rubbing her palms together to warm them. Carefully, she slipped her large hand under Hamid's head, supporting his neck and torso on her wide forearm. She held him out in front of her to take in the full measure of this wondrous new person.

"How handsome he is." She cradled him close to her bosom, swaying slowly. Lowering her head to sniff his essence, she breathed deeply, closing her eyes. "Is there any smell sweeter than a newborn baby? I believe I'm falling in love." Kissing little Hamid on the top of his head, she rocked him back and forth. "You and Danel are truly blessed."

Holding him closer to her face, she introduced herself. "Hamid, I'm Sister Helen, and I'm here to help your mother. We're going to have a great time." Hamid's wide eyes stared as she moved her head affirmatively up and down. Her exaggerated gestures made her seem almost comical. *What a great mother Sister Helen would have made*, thought Ashara.

"Ashara, I'm here to help. What can I do?"

"I would be grateful if you could just look after Hamid while I shower and say my prayers."

"What do you say to that, Hamid? Let's give your mama some time to herself." Grinning, her head nodded like a dashboard bobble-head doll. A large gas bubble wended its way up from Hamid's stomach, suggesting a smile as it passed over his lips.

"We'll be just fine. Take your time." She waltzed Hamid over to the window that looked out onto a large jacaranda tree in the courtyard below. Its branches of pinnate leaves cast fleeting, intermittent shadows that danced across grass patches and gravel under the spell of a warm soft breeze. In the distance, a small dog barked.

"Hamid, can you hear the little dog? The dog says, 'Woof, woof, woof.' Can you say, 'Woof woof woof?' Well, maybe not yet. " Laughing at herself, she hugged him lovingly. She believed even the tiniest human took in what they were taught, and it was only a matter of time before they could access any infusion of knowledge.

Gazing out over the city, her eyes pinpointed areas of fighting by the smoky puffs which hung midair. A small nest wedged between the vee of two jacaranda branches was eye high from the second story.

"Over there, Hamid, is a mamma bird bringing food to her babies. Do you see that?" She tilted him toward the window to get a better look, knowing full well that the distance from the window to the tree was beyond a newborn's visual range.

Hamid had begun to cry. Ashara's ears perked at his plaintive "Wah-wahs," like a gazelle catching the high-pitched bark of her errant fawn on the summer evening's zephyr. Hastily, she tamed her wet locks into a braid down her back. "He's hungry again. Such an appetite."

"I'm going to turn you over to your mother, Hamid." She reluctantly placed Hamid in Ashara arms. "I envy the intimacy you have with him. If I were ever to violate my vow of celibacy, it would be to have my own child and experience what you have with Hamid. I think I was born to be a mother. Maybe that's why I'm drawn to babies."

"You do God's work, Sister Helen. I admire your sacrifice. Easing the suffering of others is a different kind of intimacy." She loosened her blouse and settled Hamid in close to feed.

"I guess I'm getting too old to blame my parents, but had it not been for their insistence that I give up my child, my life would've been very different."

"You had a child?"

"I committed the ultimate sin by conceiving a child out of wedlock. Catholics don't handle that sort of thing very well. I actually converted to Anglican just to spite them."

"Do you ever wonder about your child? Was it a boy or a girl?"

"Even now many years later I think of my boy. He resides in a melancholy part of my heart."

"The people who adopted must have been very special. It would be hard for me to love another's child as my own."

"I never met them. My baby was adopted through a Catholic organization, and I wasn't allowed to know their names. All ties were severed with the paperwork, except the tie to my heart. I don't think that will ever go away."

"But don't you find great satisfaction in the work you do?"

"Of course. Please don't think I'm unhappy. It's just that there's a missing part of me. Being here with you and Hamid reminds me of him." She watched Hamid's little mouth sucking in and out. "You say that you couldn't love another's child, but that wouldn't matter to me. To be a mother is my greatest longing." She fiddled with a loose thread on the sofa cushion. Unable to break it without creating a pull, she stretched it out, tucking it along the seam line to remain invisible until she could come back with a pair of scissors.

"I'm sorry. It never occurred to me that helping us would be hard for you." Ashara looked up from Hamid. "Danel and I considered adopting after the second stillbirth."

"Would you have done that if this child had not survived?"

"I can't say for sure. I just don't think I could love another child as much as one of our own making." Feeling her arm fall asleep, she shifted Hamid to her other side.

"I dedicated myself to serve my Creator. No one put a gun to my head. That commitment is central to my life. But I'm drawn to babies; maybe I see my own child in each small face."

"For us Muslims, there's no greater acceptance than dedication to Allah. The Koran speaks of family as an institution, like the cornerstone of society. This child's my last chance. I can't imagine now not having him—or not being a family."

"Ashara, I don't know why you're so convinced of this. These days, women are having their babies later. Didn't Sarah, the Prophet Abraham's wife, have Isaac at age ninety?"

"Yes, it's true. And Abraham was a hundred." The two women began to laugh. "Well, I suppose if you're the mother of the entire nation of Israel, Allah can afford to bend human fertility rules."

"But Sister Helen, this breast that now nurses Hamid would be a waist level, shriveled prune if I had him at ninety." Ashara's giggling dislodged Hamid's suction with a small pop, and Sister Helen's belly rippled in rhythmic cadence. Wrinkling his forehead, Hamid's mouth searched for her nipple. As she guided his tiny mouth back in place, she calmed herself to accommodate his sucking.

"What does it feel like nursing him?" The two women had formed an easy friendship months before. "I wasn't allowed to nurse my son before they took him away."

"It is a beautiful experience with a closeness that I could never have understood before this."

"Does it hurt your nipples? Is it a sexual feeling?"

"No, not at all. She caressed his soft head. "But, there's a peacefulness and calm that comes over me when I nurse him. Like I'm doing the most natural thing in the world. Does that make any sense?"

"Sounds beautiful, like you're getting a shot of endorphins to boot."

Noticing that Hamid had stopped moving his mouth, Ashara resettled him on her other breast. He latched on immediately, suckling for another five minutes before a heaviness descended on his eyelids.

"Hamid, no sleeping until you give your mama a couple of bubbles." She held him out lengthwise along her forearms with his head cupped in her two palms. Bracing her elbows against her rib cage, she gently vibrated the little bundle up and down until a juicy burp escaped, startling him.

"Nice burp. What a good boy you are. " Ashara smiled her approval and cradled him close. Soon his alertness succumbed to the warmth of her body.

At the end of three hours, Sister Helen's case of files remained untouched.

"Sister Helen, would you like to set up on the dining table and do some work on your files?"

"Did I bring some files?" They both guffawed. "I should be getting back to the hospital, but I promise to do better on my charts tomorrow. Today was an orientation to the world according to Hamid. But would you let me change him before I go?"

"Of course. But you don't have to do that if you have to get back."

"It would give me a few more minutes with him." Hamid looked even smaller when Sister Helen held him, like a giant holding a kitten.

"Ashara, if you give me a list, I can pick up any groceries you need on my way tomorrow."

"I have a list already started in the kitchen. I was going to ask Danel to stop on the way home. I'll go get it."

Sister Helen laid Hamid on a changing pad on his mattress and loosened his diaper tabs. Removing the soiled diaper, she wiped his soft bottom. She reached for a clean diaper, shaking her head at its tininess. *How adorable*, she thought, as she positioned him for an exact fit. It would be weeks before he outgrew this extra small newborn size.

When Ashara returned with the list, Sister Helen was holding Hamid against her shoulder and singing him a sweet song about someone named Mary with a lamb.

"Is the Mary in your song the same Mary who was the mother of the prophet Jesus?"

Sister Helen smiled. "No, it's just a little girl named Mary whose pet lamb followed her to school and disrupted the class. It's a very old American nursery rhyme." Sister Helen kissed the dear baby on each cheek and laid him face up in his crib. "Tomorrow, Ashara, I'll be more help to you and also do some work for the hospital. Today was all about getting to know Hamid."

"I think Allah would approve of your priorities." Following Sister Helen to the door, she handed her the leather satchel. "This is very heavy. Perhaps tomorrow you won't pack it so ambitiously."

"Perhaps not." Sister Helen tucked the grocery list into the side pocket hidden in the folds of her gray bodice. "I'll see you tomorrow, after I go to the market."

"Sister Helen, today was a good day."

"Indeed it was," she countered, smiling back over her shoulder as her cherubic face disappeared down the stairs.

7

The Baptism

Ashara had just gotten back to sleep when the alarm awakened her. Danel insisted on sterilizing bottles and preparing some formula last evening so he could feed Hamid during the night, but Ashara resisted when he had gotten up. She could hardly believe that it was morning.

"Is it already time for you to go?" She parted her thick hair, which had fallen over eyes still clouded in sleep. "What time is it?"

"Go back to sleep. I let you have your way last night on feeding Hamid, but tonight I am going to feed him. You've been through a lot and you need your rest."

"You work too hard. You shouldn't have to lose sleep at night feeding our baby."

"When Sister Helen comes today, I want you to nap. Doctor's orders."

"Yes, Dr. Ottawa." Ashara smiled warmly. "Will you be late tonight?"

"Hard to tell. These days I never know what to expect. I'll call if I am going to be late if the phones are working. Don't be upset if I can't get you."

"I won't. It's just that now there seems to be a wider chasm between us when you're there and I'm here. Normally I'd think nothing of it."

"Normal doesn't exist anymore." He headed to the living room for his morning prayers. The secular pressures of their lives challenged them to keep up their devotion. For Ashara, her Muslim faith grounded her, especially through the ordeal of the stillbirths. Sometimes she wondered if his devotion was more for her than him.

A cool morning breeze after a light rain during the night brought a welcome respite from the heat. Hamid was still quiet, so she pulled the light cotton coverlet around herself and drifted off. She woke when Danel sat down on the bed.

"Ashara, I have to go." He spoke quietly and bent down to kiss her, rearranging her hair off her face. "Yesterday I got some maps. We keep avoiding discussion about our leaving."

She started to interrupt, but he gently placed his finger on her lips.

"We have to face that it is just a question of time before the fighting comes close again. Could you face losing Hamid to a bomb?"

Ashara shuddered.

"There aren't a lot of good options for us. You can see that, can't you?"

She nodded. "After the stories I've heard, caring for an infant in a refugee camp really scares me."

"But staying here scares me more." He stroked her cheek softly with the back of his hand. "No more of this now. We'll talk tonight." He kissed her on her forehead. "Now go back to sleep while you can. Sister Helen should be here around ten. I love you."

Having gotten up twice during the night, Ashara felt new mother fatigue. The shelling had returned close enough to be heard in the distance, and she realized she could no longer avoid leaving. When the doorbell sounded, Ashara looked at the clock. It was only 8:30. Still tying the sash on her robe, she opened the door. "You're early this morning."

"Danel told me that you had gotten up with Hamid twice last night, so I thought you could use a break."

"Even though I love being with him, I'm exhausted." Ashara yawned, then covered her mouth with both hands and rubbed her cheeks wearily. She followed Sister Helen into the nursery. Hamid's little arms and legs made small motions. As Sister Helen wound up the music box that powered his mobile, the moon, sun and stars followed each other in a slow, jerky orbit.

"And good morning to you, tiny one." Sister Helen's gregarious smile diverted Hamid's attention. She lowered her face closer to him and stroked his cheek with her finger. "Have you got a smile for Sister Helen?" She picked him up and gave him a big kiss. Waltzing him over to the monkey rug on the wall, she explained which monkey was chasing and which was escaping and how the bananas figured into the whole scene.

"We've hot water this morning, so I am going to bathe while we have power. Can you handle things with Hamid?"

"We'll be just fine, won't we, Hamid?"

Ashara filled the tub and eased herself into the hot water, feeling it relax her muscles. She slid lower into the water, resting her chin right at its surface, closing her eyes. Her mind was back with Danel pressing the issue of leaving. She had read about the filth, lack of privacy and poor sanitation at the refugee camps. Her biggest worry was for Hamid's health in such an environment. Immigration hung over their lives, fueling her resentment. *We've done nothing to deserve this*, she thought. *We're good people, loyal citizens, why is this all happening?*

She submerged her face below the waterline to hide in the silence beneath the water's edge. The troubles, though, survived in the quiet deep, and she soon resurfaced to finish bathing. *We'll talk it through tonight*, she thought. *Just talking isn't a decision. It's just information.*

Ashara stepped out of the tub. Standing naked on the mat, she shook her head at her postpartum pear shape. Anticipating that Hamid would be hungry by now, she dressed quickly in a thin cotton nursing blouse and maternity slacks. Not finding Hamid in his crib, she scoured the apartment. Surprised, she found Sister Helen in the kitchen feeding Hamid a bottle.

Both arms akimbo, she said, "Sister Helen, what are you doing?"

"He was hungry. I saw the bottles, and since you were in the bath, I decided to feed him."

"It's is my job to feed my child, not yours. I'm his mother, not you."

"I was only trying to help. I figured you were using the bottle along with the breast. I meant no harm."

"Well next time, you should ask instead of just assuming."

"He's almost finished, do you want to take over?"

"I don't want to take over. My breasts are full and I wanted to breastfeed him. But you can finish."

She avoided looking at Ashara until Hamid finished the formula. Placing a towel on her shoulder, she patted his back until he burped and then transferred him to Ashara before going to the dining table to work on her charts.

Disappearing with Hamid into her bedroom, Ashara reappeared shortly to assess the damage with Sister Helen. Venturing a reconciliatory step into the icy atmosphere, she said, "I'm sorry. I have a lot on my mind. I know you were just trying to help."

"I should have asked you. It was my fault." Sister Helen sheepishly took responsibility.

"It wasn't anyone's fault. The bombs have me on edge. "

"The war's on everyone's mind. I saw that Danel had put some maps into his desk at the hospital. You have to be considering immigrating. I know I would if I were you."

Although Danel had warned Ashara to speak of leaving with no one, Sister Helen opened a window to talk. The taboo against speaking of immigration isolated Ashara. She risked exposure if her instincts about Sister Helen were wrong. Citizens of value discovered contemplating immigration were imprisoned. For Ashara, trust was visceral, a hopeful reliance rather than an intellectual decision.

"Have you heard about the conditions at the camps?" said Ashara.

"One of the orderly's sister and brother-in-law went to Lebanon. I heard the camps there are in old abandoned buildings with as many as three families to a room. Sunnis, Alawites, Jews and Christian all mixed together like a bowl of konafah noodles. It creates lots of tension."

Ashara sifted Hamid onto her shoulder.

"They went there because it was the closest, but they had to go through the mountains, and many without cars had to walk. It was not an easy journey."

"I can't imagine walking that far with an infant. We don't have a car, but we've got to go somewhere if the shelling comes back." Ashara hugged Hamid, swaying back and forth, her anxiety evidenced in her strained brow. Kissing the soft spots in Hamid's crown, she said, "We're all so vulnerable, in control of nothing."

"Have you and Danel made a decision yet?" Sister Helen probed tentatively.

"We talk about everything but this. Danel grapples with the hardship his departure will add at the hospital. We're are caught between two poor options: go or stay."

"Sometimes you have to put yourself above others. Hamid has no one else but you two. He has to be your first consideration. I would hate to see you go, and you must."

Hamid's eyes drooped, and his little mouth stretched into a perfectly round yawn. "How about I put him down for a nap?" said Sister Helen.

"No I'll take him, and then I'm going to catch up on some sleep. Call me if he wakes up hungry."

A shadow of disappointment crossed Sister Helen's face. "Of course."

As summer's last days grew shorter, Sister Helen's presence at the apartment lengthened to seven- to eight-hour stays. While Danel felt relief that Ashara was not alone, two women alternately twisted their days around opposite poles. Mutual respect and genuine caring for each other ricocheted from one pole, with vying for control of Hamid at the other, like two sisters sparring for the same boyfriend.

"I just heard Hamid stirring." Sister Helen's keen ears pricked, anticipating Hamid's little cry before any sound escaped.

"I would prefer that you not pick him up every time he cries. He should get used to amusing himself."

"Yes, but he is so adorable, I can't resist him. Once you go, I won't have him anymore." A morsel of resentment lingered each time Ashara acquiesced to Sister Helen. "Hamid hasn't had his bath yet today. You bathed him yesterday, do you mind if I do it today?" Sister Helen was keeping score.

"Alright." Ashara laid Hamid in Sister Helen's arms and left to fetch a clean diaper. Busying herself changing the crib sheet and replacing the changing pad, Ashara heard Hamid's distressed cry, rushing into the bathroom to check on him.

Hamid lay naked stretched over Sister Helen's forearm over the basin, with his head tilted downward supported in Sister Helen's wide palm. She ladled warm water with her free hand over Hamid's scalp. A few drops had splashed into his eye and startled him.

"I baptize thee in the name of the Father, and of the Son and of the Holy—"

"Sister Helen. What're you doing?" she demanded.

"I'm baptizing Hamid."

"You're what?"

"I'm baptizing Hamid."

"You're baptizing my Muslim child into the Christian faith? What in the name of Allah for?"

"A child who isn't baptized can't enter into the kingdom of heaven. Since Muslims don't believe in baptizing their infants, I felt that I should do it for him."

"He's Muslim, and his father and I decide his faith." Ashara shouted her indignation at Sister Helen's audacity.

A deep rosy pink infused Sister Helen's fair complexion as she grappled with Ashara's affront. That a child should be destined for purgatory when she could prevent it seemed incomprehensible.

"If you hadn't come in just now, you wouldn't have known about it. You'd raise a Muslim son, but being baptized, he'd enter the kingdom of God."

"You miss the point. You have no right to exercise any option over Hamid's spiritual future. You aren't his parent." Hamid's bottom lip curled out as he began to cry. "You've really overstepped your bounds this time."

"All I've done is try to help you. And this is what I get, an accusation of I don't know what?"

"I think you need to leave." Ashara grabbed a towel off the rack and reached for Hamid, but Sister Helen resisted. "Now." Ashara pulled harder. "No matter how much you wish he were yours, he's mine. Please let go of my child."

As reason took control, Sister Helen suddenly relaxed her grip, causing Hamid's head to bump into the faucet. Hamid's face turning scarlet as he wailed, and yielding him to Ashara, Sister Helen abruptly left the room.

Ashara dried Hamid and bundled him up in the towel, holding him close. "Shhh, little one." She heard the shuffle of files roughly gathered up and shoved into the satchel, brisk footsteps and the door slam.

Shaking with rage, Ashara held Hamid, pacing the apartment. Her indignation over the baptism dominated, but her role in the confrontation lay just under the surface. She mulled every detail, like scouring for bones in a piece of fried fish. One thing about which she had no doubt was that Sister Helen should not come back.

That evening, Danel returned to an upset wife. Sister Helen didn't return to the hospital, so he was ill prepared for the tempest at home. His eager anticipation of time with Ashara and Hamid and the promise in tomorrow's day off was squashed like pinching off the head of a tick. Ashara's dark mood swept broadly over her face, like the long shadows of late afternoon spreading across the courtyard below. He knew instantly that something was amiss.

"What's wrong?" He bent to kiss her cheek and fondle Hamid's soft crown. His query broke open a dam of angry energy and accusations. Danel plucked up Hamid as he listened.

Ashara rose to pace, slapping her upturned palm into the left thigh, the timbre of her voice rising at each resentment. The small bruise on Hamid's head was the final indictment.

"But we're Muslim, and we don't believe in baptism. There was no harm done."

"So now you're taking Sister Helen's side?"

With no acceptable response other than silence, he felt as though she amended her indictment to include him. Expelling Sister Helen left a dilemma with no ready remedy. His wife and infant son would be alone in the apartment all day long with no help or protection. "What would you have me do, not let her come back?"

"That's exactly what I expect."

"Do you have any idea of how vulnerable you are in a complex with no other residents?"

"I could always call you."

"You can see how well that worked when you went into labor."

They needed Sister Helen, of this he was sure.

Ashara had expected Danel's indignation, but instead his logical response disarmed her. In truth she couldn't really explain the tension with Sister Helen. They ate their meal saying very little while Hamid slept.

Finally, Danel cleared his throat. "I brought home maps so we could talk tonight about leaving."

Anxiety rose and stifled what little appetite she had. Shoving her plate aside with the food untouched, she took a long drink of water.

"This breach with Sister Helen adds urgency to our decision. Can you see that?"

"Of course. I know it's not safe being here alone. Today I could hear that the shelling is moving closer." She cleared the dishes to the sink and wiped the table clean for Danel to spread out the map.

"The way I see it, we really only have three choices: Lebanon to the west, Jordan to the south and Turkey to the north."

"You are not even considering going east to Iraq?"

"Instability there might be like jumping out of the cauldron into the fire pit. Do you disagree?"

"No, not entirely."

"Iraq has to heal its own wounds. They're not equipped to deal with a refugee population. Their own displaced citizens would have to come first."

Hamid had been chortling for the last fifteen minutes but was starting to fuss. Danel felt his mood lighten when she brought Hamid to him.

"You had quite a day with two ladies fighting over you." He held the baby while Ashara prepared to nurse him. Once Hamid had begun to feed, Danel refolded the map.

"We can talk while Hamid nurses. You don't need to put the map away."

"No, I think that Hamid's the wise one here. It's been a hard day for both of us, and a good night sleep will help us put things in perspective. I'm off tomorrow so we can take our time to work things out."

She felt her own tension drain as Hamid drank his fill.

"Tomorrow we'll play with Hamid, go to the market and plan our future."

As the ice between them melted, even though nothing had been decided, they were at least on the same side. "Tomorrow sounds like a good day."

8

Process of Elimination

The early morning sun splashed its first diagonal rays across the coverlet, spilling onto the floor and zigzagging up the wall, belying the ominous danger in the distant booms. An acrid smell, carried in on a light breeze, invaded Danel and Ashara's nostrils. But, this bright, warm September morning was filled with promise for the young family eager to cherish a day together. Danel drew Ashara close, smelling her scent and brushing his fingertips along her smooth skin. She snuggled closer, savoring the moments with Danel before Hamid woke.

"Do you think that we'll remember how to spend a normal day together?" he whispered softly into her neck. With his eyes still closed, Danel nuzzled his face into her thick, disheveled tresses.

"Spending a day together will be easy, but I am not sure I know what normal is anymore."

"Well, let's start with a kiss and see where that goes." He gently rolled her over to face him, and she responded eagerly to his soft kisses first on her lips and then her neck.

"Hmmm, this feels very normal." She felt him stiffen as she wrapped her legs around his.

Hamid's untimely whimpers diverted his mother's attention.

Sighing, she untangled herself from Danel's embrace. "Maybe this is the new normal."

"Perhaps Hamid could learn a little about delayed gratification?" He hoped rather than expected that Ashara would let Hamid cry.

"Danel, we haven't made love for a long time. I don't want to rush. Perhaps Hamid's parents could delay their gratification until there is time to enjoy each other. We have the whole day."

"Well, that's a promise I can wait for, and I aim to collect." He rose to catch her wrist as she was leaving. Drawing her closer, he kissed her long and almost too hard. She drew back slightly.

"Danel, what is it? Is it about not making love?" She searched his eyes.

"No, it's about almost losing you and Hamid, about what we've come through and all we must still tackle. Hamid just grounded me with a bit of reality. That's all."

"You're sure? You'd tell me if there was something else?"

"Of course." He kissed her softly, releasing his grasp. His eyes followed her as she disappeared to attend to Hamid. A slight crease across his forehead was the only outward manifestation of the inner burden. While his doctoring was an efficient insulator during the day, at quiet times his guilt surged, demanding validation.

His morning prayers called on Allah for courage and the protection to get his family to safety. He begged forgiveness for what he had done and to never let Ashara be wounded by his deception. Praying brought Danel some peace, since surrendering to the Higher Power relieved the sole responsibility of his burden. He knew too well the gravity of his secret.

After prayers, he found Ashara still nursing, but Hamid was losing interest as his belly filled. Watching them, he realized how much he had fallen in love with the child. It no longer mattered how he had secured him, for he knew that he could never give Hamid up, not to relieve his guilt and not to do the right thing. Once he'd switched babies, he would pay dearly to be a passenger on a train with no reverse gear.

"Ashara, how about taking Hamid to the market next?" For the last several weeks Ashara had sheltered Hamid from the public, depending on Sister Helen for groceries.

She smiled. "Do you want to go to the market, Hamid? I think your Baba wants to show you off?" Ashara secured Hamid in the cloth carrier and raised the sling up over her head to rest on her shoulder. She glimpsed a slight hesitation cross his face. "Danel, would you prefer to carry him?"

The young father eagerly lifted the sling off Ashara's shoulder and slipped his arms through the carrier. While she fastened the strap across his back, Hamid nestled snuggly against his father's chest, like a baby marsupial in his pouch.

Ashara covered her hair with a hijab. "Wait. I need my list and market bag." She hesitated. "Do you think it's alright to use Mr. Faroush's bag?"

"I think he'd be pleased."

Ashara nodded, tucking her sadness over the old man back inside her heart. "I'm glad we're doing the market first. Our heavy decisions can wait 'til later." Hand in hand they left the apartment, masquerading as an ordinary family on the way to market in any country. Soon the distant sounds of shelling reverberated, reminding them that they were in Syria.

Hamid had fallen asleep on the way home. Danel had yielded his transport role to Ashara so he could carry the groceries. On the way to market, he considerately avoided where Mr. Faroush had fallen, but lost in conversation, they took the shorter route that Mr. Faroush had traveled on the way home. Ashara gasped when she realized where they were.

"He would still be alive had it not been for us."

"There'll come a day when we'll think of his kindness with fondness not guilt. It's just going to take some time." Ashara noted how close to their block he was shot. He'd almost made it to safety.

The apartment had grown very warm while they were out. Danel set the striped market bag on the kitchen counter and started to open the windows. "You feed Hamid, and I'll put away the groceries. We can talk while he is napping." He cleared off the kitchen table and set out his maps along with some notes he had taken about the camps. Ashara returned with Hamid on her shoulder, patting his back. She sat down opposite Danel, who turned the map to face her. Picking up his notes, he tapped the disheveled pile on its end. "We have some choices, and none of them are very good. But do you agree that we're foolish if we stay here?"

She nodded. More distant shelling diverted their attention towards the window.

"Iraq is out of the question. Are you still in agreement?"

"Yes, there is too much hostility there. I had hoped we could go to Lebanon. It's so close."

"Yesterday I called Ahmed Tibi. Do you remember him?"

"Of course. He was in your class at medical school. He came here when your father passed. Tall, good looking, but very quiet and shy."

"That's the one. He spent a lot of time with our family when we were in medical school. My father and mother were very fond of him. He's now practicing in Beirut. I thought perhaps he could help us."

"Oh, that would be so wonderful."

"I don't want to build your hopes. He and his wife have taken in his sister, her husband and their two kids, plus his wife's brother and their family as well. All eleven of them are in their four-room apartment."

"I see. There would be no room for us." Sighing, she rose to change Hamid and put him down. When she returned, they listened to him chortling at the mobile over his crib.

"Ahmed said that conditions in Lebanon are very dangerous. The overcrowding has led to a lot of sectarian violence."

"How so?" She recalled her vacations in Lebanon as a young girl. Her memories were filled with a warm sun on her back, sitting on her father's shoulders and laughing as he jumped over the Mediterranean's waves. Those times seemed a millennia ago.

"There're more Syrians in Lebanon than any other country, over 150,000 Syrians there now with more coming. The Lebanese there are very resentful."

"Why would they resent the refugees? Surely their hearts can sympathize with what Syrians are going through."

"The government didn't set up camps, so the refugees have flooded the cities. There isn't enough medical treatment for the Lebanese, let alone all of the Syrians." He smoothed his hand across Lebanon on the map. "Their infrastructure, which was old and faulty to start with, is now greatly strained. Ahmed says lots of days there's no water or electricity. Riots break out often, and the people are blaming the Syrians for their woes."

"I had hoped we could go there since it's so close, but it sounds too dangerous."

He nodded. "That's exactly what I thought. Ahmed also says that their army is closing many of the crossing points between Syria and Lebanon, so there's a chance we could get there and be turned away."

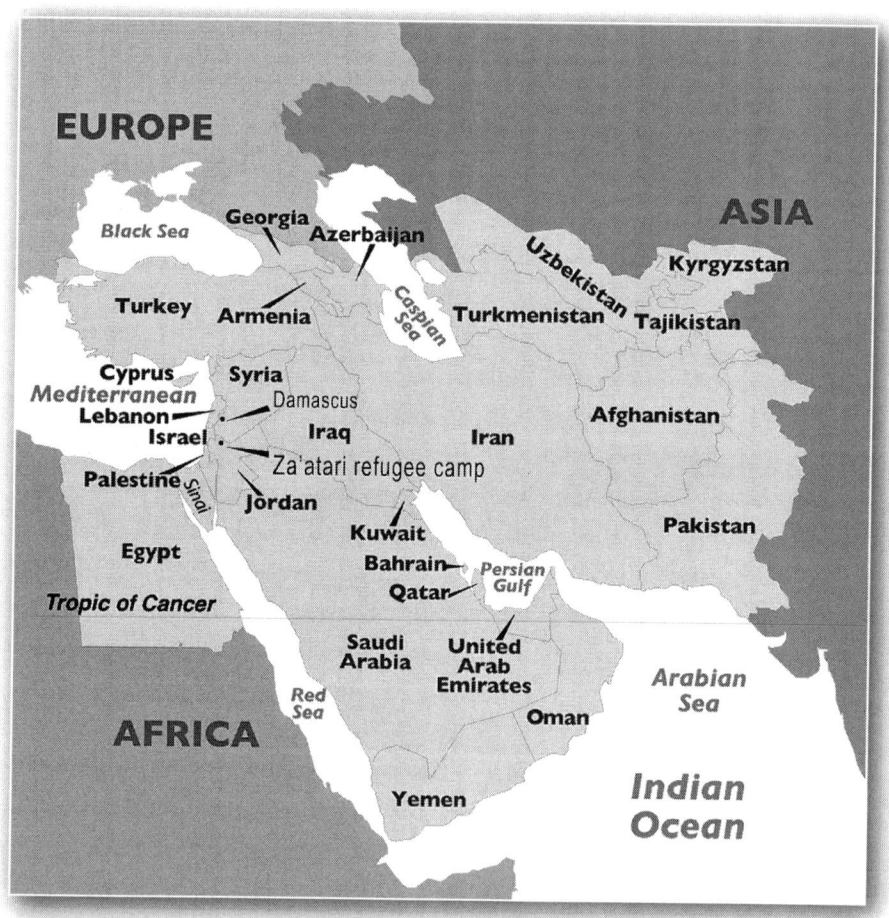

Ashara set her elbows on the map, resting her chin in her hands.

"We could go to Turkey, but that's a long journey through Homs and Aleppo, and there's still a lot of fighting there. There's a large camp, Oncupinar, in Kilis, right here." He found Kilis on the map and measured the distance from Damascus. "It looks to be about 375 kilometers."

"I suspect that the Syrians in Aleppo and Homs would naturally flee to the closest border, which is Turkey. I heard on the television that Assad's forces are attacking the refugees. That's a long way to go exposed to Assad's troops."

"I have heard that by attacking the refugees, they reduce the men that will return to fight them."

"Should we rule out Turkey?"

"I think Turkey is not a good option."

"That leaves Jordan then." Danel centered Jordan in front of her. "Jordan has a camp that hasn't been open that long, right here at Za'atari." He pointed out the camp's location he had marked with an X. "It's about 10 kilometers from the border, so that would be about 130 kilometers from us."

"That's not as far as Turkey. I guess that's a positive, yet small consolation in this whole mess. We should have left months ago."

"Let's not rehash that again. Now you're like an owl looking backwards. You were pregnant, did you want to have your baby in a tent?"

"If we left months ago, I could've had Hamid in a Lebanese hospital."

"But we didn't, so are you blaming me now?"

She abruptly pushed her chair away and looked out the window. She counted eleven pockets of smoke, marking skirmishes like pushpins on a war map. She walked over to Danel, clutching his head against her. He wrapped his arms around her. "The only one I blame for this is Bashar al Assad. I'm sorry. This is all so hard." She held back the tempest behind her eyes. "We're losing everything. How can we feel good about any of this?"

"At least we won't be losing our lives. We can rebuild. If we stay alive, at least we have a future."

"At least from Jordan we'll be able to get home quickly when this is all over."

He pulled back, regarding her. "I don't think you fully understand. It's not like we're holding up somewhere until Assad is gone and then we come back."

Puzzled, she stepped back.

"We may never be able to come back, and even if we do there'll be nothing to come back to."

"You're saying we definitely won't come back to Syria?"

"We'll be cast adrift without a rudder, and only Allah's wind will determine where we land."

"I don't see how you can be so sure."

"There's a finality to this that you seem to miss." Clenching his teeth, he thought that knowing this now would give her time to accept the reality. "In Za'atari you're only given a tent, so we can't take much. We'd take warm enough clothing for the winter, something to cook with, plates and utensils and whatever Hamid will need."

"You paint a very primitive picture."

"I just don't want you to be blindsided. But at least there are no bombs there."

"So you think we should go to Za'atari in Jordan?"

"I think it's the best of four very poor options." Danel pushed his chair back, leaning on the back legs.

"Four options?" She raised her eye brows.

"Yes, Iraq isn't even in consideration. That leaves Turkey, Lebanon, Jordan, and the fourth option is to stay here." Three successive shells sounding out much closer than earlier punctuated their decision.

"Staying here is a death wish. How are we going to get to Za'atari?"

"There are busses that go, but they're easy targets." He'd heard about helicopters strafing busloads of refugees. "I think we should try to get a car. What do you think?"

"If we get a car, we can take more provisions."

"I can check around the hospital to see if someone knows of one we could buy. We won't be able to take much with us, but with a car we could take more than we could carry. One of the orderlies at the hospital has a brother-in-law who drives a cab and has a car to sell. That's one possibility—if he hasn't sold it yet."

"I'll work on getting our papers and things together while you work on getting a car."

"You'll need to bring formula for Hamid." She started to protest, but Danel squeezed her hand. "We don't know what kind of privacy there'll be. If we don't need it, we won't use it. Alright?"

"Alright." She bristled. "When do you think we should go?"

"It's safer at night. If I can find a car, making arrangements to buy it should take two days. Then maybe another three days after that we should go. So five days in all at the outside. Do you think you can get us ready in that time?"

"I think so." Her mind was already organizing what needed to be done.

"I am going to try to gather some medical supplies from the hospital."

"That's stealing. How can you do that?"

"I won't be taking my last salary payment since I won't be here to receive it. Certainly we can't tell them we're leaving, so I regard this as my salary in supplies. The hospital will just be paying what's owed."

She abhorred bending the truth in any direction, but his logic was sound. "In the end it's all about survival, isn't it?"

"Ashara, we are but small chameleons in the desert, trying not to be the next predator's supper. We have a child to protect and that means leaving him with two parents to raise him. Is there any other way to see it?"

"I suppose not."

9

Reconciliation

Haunted by the specters of camps and the logistics of getting there, Ashara slept fitfully. In the wee hours before dawn, she whispered, "Are you still awake?" Danel stirred slightly, shifting onto his side.

"Yes. My mind is awash in an ocean of details. I worry about you and Hamid if I were detained or killed."

She shivered at the menace in his voice.

"You'll just have to be careful."

"I will, but I have to open up to someone to find us a car."

Plumping her pillow, she rolled over to face him. "I know we have to go, but I'm afraid to leave. I just wish I were at peace with it all." She shivered even though the night was warm.

He slipped his arm under her neck and held her.

"Safe." Ashara sighed deeply. "I don't even know what the word means anymore. I feel the safest with you holding me."

Danel stroked her head. "Let me be your safe haven then." He tilted her chin up to kiss her. "Tomorrow should be about preparing and not fretting. I'll focus on getting us out of here, and you get us ready to go. We each have our special tasks."

"I'll do my part, though I think you have the harder job. When my fear overpowers me, I think of Hamid."

"You're right. We're all he has," said Danel. "He's the mortar between our bricks, and you're my foundation." They kissed each other softly, savoring these last moments. "Let's pray to Allah to hold our family close and help us through our challenges." Entwining their hands, they closed their eyes, silently lifting their spirits toward their Creator, placing themselves unabashedly in his keeping.

Extricating himself, Danel got up first. She watched him dress, sensing this was one of the last times they would start a new day in this room.

"Danel, what of Sister Helen?"

"What do you mean?" He sat down of the edge of the bed to tie his shoes.

"What will you say to her?"

"I'll tell her that she overstepped her bounds when she baptized Hamid, what ever her reasons. What're your thoughts?"

"Exactly as yours. My own feelings are still a mystery. I know I reacted strongly and she didn't deserve to be expelled the way she was. Please tell her that I…" Ashara hesitated as she thought hard about an apology. "You tell her just what you have said to me. I think that's best."

Danel had loaded his satchel with enough money to buy a car the evening before. After kissing Ashara goodbye, he locked the door behind him. His lanky strides made short the trip to the hospital, his mind preoccupied with the logistics of their departure. While confident that Ashara would execute her part perfectly, his own mission was precarious. His inquiries about a car might tip off someone with an agenda or a grudge.

His first task though was to repair the damage between Sister Helen and Ashara. When he arrived, she was working the front desk. Danel first broached what was for her unspeakable.

"Good morning, Sister Helen." His neutral tone gave no hint how he leaned.

"Danel." She nodded her acknowledgement, but her affront two days later had grown larger with each replay in her mind.

"Could you spare a few minutes up in my office?"

"Of course. I'll be up as soon as I update these files."

"I'll wait for you." Although the reconciliation stage was set, the chill in Sister Helen bode an unpredictable outcome.

Twenty minutes later, she rapped lightly on his office door. "You wanted to see me?" Normally jovial, the nun's tone was flat.

"I want to talk about what happened with Ashara. I don't want us to leave things like this."

His forthrightness startled her. "Like what?"

"We both know that Ashara overreacted."

Surprised, she shifted onto more neutral ground, feeling safe to explain herself. "I meant no harm or disrespect." She waited for him to defend Ashara, but he was silent. "In my religion, baptism is a spiritual lifeline, assuring that the soul could one day enter the Kingdom of God." She gathered her words carefully to explain a ritual for which there was no equivalent in the Muslim faith. "I'm not a wealthy woman. A missionary has very little material goods. I love Hamid and wanted to give him something special."

Initially convinced that she had overreached, his open mind was compelled by her motives.

"I felt that there's no greater gift than being welcomed into God's house to live out eternal life in his presence. Catholics believe that God's children who aren't baptized are destined to live in limbo and never see the face of God."

He tilted his head, concentrating his gaze directly at her.

"Yes, but we are Muslims, and we don't believe in Baptism. For us, Allah is the Compassionate, the Merciful, the Source of Peace, the One Who Bestows and the Just. Don't you see, there can be no such concept as limbo with such a just God?" He leaned back in his chair, his hands spread in front of him.

"Then tell me how baptizing Hamid has harmed him?"

He had no answer save that it offended Ashara.

"On many occasions, Ashara and I discussed that my God and Allah are one and the same. If Allah wouldn't mind a Christian baptism, I don't see why Ashara should."

Respect for her logic trumped, as he realized that both sides carried equal weight.

"Can we get past this? At this point I see all that matters is that we owe you so much and you're our friend."

She softened. "Yes, I think we can. No good can come from harboring ill will. You have to understand that I love Hamid, and my heart is broken about losing him."

"What're you talking about, 'losing him'? You and Ashara quarreled, but that isn't an end to a friendship."

"One reason I came up here is to tell you that I'm leaving Damascus." She paused. "The situation here in Damascus has deteriorated, and I'm being recalled, along with other missionaries, to our office in Amman. We'll probably be redistributed but definitely not sent back to Syria any time soon."

Leaning forward, he laid his hands in his lap. "We will truly miss you. You have been a dear friend." His shoulders slumped as he rose to look out at the street below. "We appreciate all that you did to help Ashara. But your energy and spirit buoyed me so many times in the last months. I'll miss that too."

"You should get out now while you can."

"We talked and prayed about it these past two days and have come to the same conclusion. How soon will you go?"

"It could be as early as tomorrow or perhaps a day or so after that. A transport from Turkey is coming to get us. It started in the north, first in Aleppo, then Homs and few other cities, and is heading south to Damascus."

"Do you know where you and Ashara will go?"

"We've decided on Jordan. There is a camp called Za'atari, just ten kilometers inside the border."

"Yes, I've heard of it. But how will you get there?"

"I've got to buy a car, which is not easy these days. One of the orderlies has a brother-in-law with one to sell. That's a possibility."

"Danel, be very careful about who you trust. I hear things here because I'm neutral. The regime's rewarding informers."

"We know it's dangerous, but there's no other way. We could answer an ad but would have no way of knowing if it was a trap."

"How soon do you leave?" Regarding Danel and Ashara as good friends, she had grown attached, especially to Hamid. Her superiors had warned about forming attachments, calling them liabilities in a calling responsive to winds of conflict.

"My job's to find a car, and Ashara's working on pulling together what we'll need. My hospital connections are probably my best option to locate a car."

"I'll keep an ear out for an opportunity as well."

"Thanks. This talk of leaving hijacked what I really wanted to say to you."

"There's nothing more to say. We've put it behind us."

"I still want to tell you what Ashara sent me to do. She wanted you to know that she knows she over reacted, and that we'll go to our graves forever grateful to you."

"Tell Ashara that all's forgotten." She clasped her hands under her chin. "Tell her that I'll hold her memory close and special. We part friends, Danel." In an unprecedented gesture for a Muslim man with another woman, Danel opened his arms to hug the nun.

"Promise me that you won't leave without saying good-bye."

"I promise." She turned abruptly to cover up the storm clouds building behind her eyes.

Danel's next priority was to follow-up on his one lead, the orderly whose his brother-in-law wanted to sell a car. Booting up his computer to pull up the duty roster, he scrolled down the screen, stopping at the orderly's name, Ahmed Sultan, who was scheduled to start on the cardiac ward at ten o'clock. With two hours to wait, he draped his stethoscope around his neck and headed to the emergency room, already full of patients.

Sister Helen was working the charts at the front desk. With the air cleared, they exchanged warm glances. By 10:15 he finished with a patient and let the front desk know he was on break. Eschewing the elevator, he took the back stairs up to cardiology on the third floor. Ahmed was moving a patient from intensive care into a four-bed room.

Danel asked Ahmed to step outside when he was finished and waited in the corridor until Ahmed appeared. "Ahmed, I heard that your brother-in-law, the one who drives the cab, has a car that he wants to sell. My wife wants to see her mother in the country and we're interested in buying a car."

"Dr. Danel, you're a day late. My brother-in-law found a buyer yesterday, and he's bringing the money today. The car's sold."

Danel grimaced at the loss of the convenient solution to their transportation problem. "I see. Well, I'm sure something else will come along. I just thought I'd ask." A line of sweat formed along the crease in his forehead.

Back in the emergency room, Danel checked in for his next patient's chart.

Sister Helen raised her eyebrows, expectantly questioning his success.

"No luck. The car's sold." He kept his voice low.

"I'll keep my radar on. Maybe we'll get lucky. These days there's a shortage of cash. More and more patients are bartering. Perhaps a car will turn up."

Returning records to accounting, she overheard one of the administrators trying to figure out if it were possible to take a car in trade for services rendered.

"How am I supposed to enter a 1998 Fiat into the system?" The exasperated administrator put her question out to anyone. "You'd think someone at the front desk would check with us before accepting a car for payment."

Sister Helen edged closer to the computer screen to get the name, *Talat Saeed*, noting the address was not far from Arnous Square. *Date of treatment, yesterday.* Despite her excitement at discovering a car, Sister Helen couldn't resist engaging. "The hospital forms will have to add a barter line in accounts receivable. Choose one from the drop down: auto, chickens, goats, mothers-in-law." The tension eased as the staff carried the drop down farce even further.

"Well, figuring out what to do with the car is beyond my pay grade." The admin placed a note on the file and set it in the inbox for her supervisor to wrestle with when she came in.

Gathering the rest of her charts to file, Sister Helen set them down across the inbox while she pulled a handkerchief out of her pocket to blow her nose. When she picked them up, she included Talat Saeed's file on the bottom of her stack, and walked briskly back to the emergency room.

Standing at a filing cabinet with her back as a shield, she wrote a note to Danel. *Patient Talat Saeed has a car, 1998 Fiat, offering to the hospital for payment. I've got the file over here with me.* She nonchalantly walked over to Danel, handing him the folded paper as he was treating a patient. "Here are those dosage amounts you requested." He caught a covert wink as he took the note from her.

"Thanks for looking these up for me. I'll get them where they need to go." Dismissing Sister Helen, Danel placed the stethoscope on his patient's back.

"Now breathe deeply." He listened for congestion. "Again." He relocated the stethoscope's chest piece over to trapezius muscle on the opposite side to pinpoint the wheezing source. He barely registered the asthmatic echo, as his mind fixated on the car Sister Helen uncovered. Notating the patient's chart, he prescribed an asthma inhaler and an anti-inflammatory drug. "But you're going to have to stop smoking." He clicked his pen, returning it to his breast pocket before shaking the patient's hand. "You can get dressed now." His stomach tightened. Finding the car was one thing, but obtaining it unnoticed was another.

Walking over to Sister Helen, he handed her his last chart.

"Dr. Ottawa, I'm handling incoming patients now. You'll have to take this to Maryam down on the end." She handed the chart back to him with Talat Saeed's file underneath. Leaning forward over the counter, she pointed out the young woman in the light blue hijab two meters to her right.

Maryam looked up and beckoned Danel over to her.

"No problem." Danel took both files and moved down the counter to Maryam. "Here you go." Handing her his last chart, he slid Talat Saeed's file under his arm. He had almost made it through the double doors.

"Dr. Ottawa?" He halted, fearing she had noticed the file under his arm. "Dr. Ottawa?" Danel turned.

"You forgot to sign off on this chart."

"Sorry about that." Scribbling his signature at the bottom of the chart, he smiled at the young woman. "Good catch. If you hadn't noticed, the charge nurse would've been after me." She returned his smile with equal warmth.

He went directly to his office, closing the door quietly. Quickly he ran his finger down the form on the left of the jacket, stopping at the phone number. He starting to dial his mobile phone but thought better of it, since the cell phone would have a traceable record. A call from his office would be more difficult to trace. After two rings a woman answered.

"I'm looking for Talat Saeed."

"He's not here. Who's calling?" The woman's low raspy voice was gruff and unpleasant.

"I'm from the hospital finance office, and he offered a car in payment yesterday when he was here."

"Oh yes, he's expecting your call." Her tone softened.

"I just need a few details. When do you expect him?"

"Two hours. I can have him call you."

"There'll be no need. I'll call back." Hanging up the receiver, he looked at his watch. Already it was early afternoon, and if this didn't pan out he would lose another day. Returning to the emergency room, he would continue his rotation until he could call back. At three o'clock, a middle aged man came in complaining of a dull abdominal pain near his navel, vomiting and a high fever. As Danel palpated the abdomen, the man complained of sharp pain in the lower right abdomen. Danel excused himself to talk to the charge nurse.

"Who's up for surgical rotation right now?"

"The other two surgeons on duty are operating. You're the only one available."

"I can't take it right now. I have something I have to do." The charge nurse eyed him suspiciously.

"Dr. Ottawa, can this patient wait? Can someone here help you with something?" Since the appendix was dangerously close to rupture, he would have to operate.

"It's not that important. I'll go prep. Please have the orderly take the patient up to surgery right away." Calming himself, he rationalized that the car's urgency was his, and not the car's owner, who had already received hospital services.

As he prepped, the admin approached her supervisor about the patient who wanted to pay with his Fiat, complaining that she had no way to add a car into the system. "It's going to take some creative accounting."

"Give me the file and I'll call the patient," said her supervisor.

Sorting through the inbox files, the young woman discovered the file was missing. She searched again more thoroughly this time, checking that it hadn't gotten stuck in another file. The search then spread to all personnel in the finance office.

"Sister Helen was in here when I was working on it. Maybe she remembers what I did with it." The admin left her desk for the emergency room, running into Sister Helen in the hall.

"Sister Helen, do you remember that patient who was trying to pay his bill with his car?"

"I remember. The one where we needed a special barter category?"

"It's missing. The supervisor wants to call the patient to work things out. I could swear that I put it in the inbox. Did you see it? "

"I didn't see where you put it, but I'll go and check my files. Maybe I inadvertently picked it up." Sister Helen walked back to the emergency room.

"Do you know where Dr. Ottawa is?" The charge nurse looked up at Sister Helen.

"He just went up to do an appendectomy. What do you need him for?"

"His wife just called. That's all."

"You may catch him before he goes into surgery, but you better hurry."

She walked through the double doors, picking up her pace once she entered the hall and took the elevator up. She encountered Danel with his scrubbed hands upended on his way into the operating room.

"Danel, they're searching for the Talat Saeed file downstairs. They asked me about it. Did you reach him?"

"I called but he was out and I got stuck with this surgery before I could call back."

"Did you give your name?'

"No. The file is on my desk. Just take down the phone number so I can call him back." Sister Helen left directly and retrieved the file on her way back to the finance office.

"I found it in my stack. I guess I picked it up with my pile when I set down the files this morning." Maryam looked puzzled.

"Sister Helen, do you know who called the man?"

"How would I know that? I've been here all day and didn't even know I had the file."

"Well, someone did because he called and said a man from the hospital had contacted his wife. We don't have any men working in finance. Could anyone have had access to your stack of files?"

"That makes no sense. Who else handled the file before you got it?" Danel completed the surgery and left directly for his office. Forgetting to latch the door, he picked up the phone to dial. The same raspy voice answered.

"Is Mr. Saeed there? This is the hospital calling." Ahmed Sultan, the orderly whose brother-in-law had sold his car, rapped on the door and felt it give way. He entered uninvited, surprising Danel mid-sentence. As Danel hung up, Mr. Saeed took the phone from his wife.

"Dr. Ottawa, can I come in?"

Annoyed at the disruption, he said, "You're already in."

The orderly laughed nervously. "I guess I am. The man who was buying my brother-in-law's car couldn't come up with the money. Do you still want to buy it?"

"Yes, I do." After working out the price and details, they agreed to meet in an hour, when Ahmed got off work. "This transaction's between you and me, right?"

"Sure. No problem. I'll take you to my brother-in-law's."

Sister Helen intercepted Danel in his hall on the way back to emergency. "Danel, finance is onto something. They know a man called Mr. Saeed. He just called back to say someone from the hospital called and then hung up on him."

"I called him and hung up when Ahmed Sultan came in. The first deal fell off and his brother-in-law's car is now available. I made a deal with him."

"Good. It would be foolish to follow through with Saeed at this point. There's talk that you're looking for a car and that you're leaving."

"I told no one." He smashed his fist into the wall.

"You've got to leave now. You can't come back." He checked his watch. Ahmed would meet him in about ten minutes.

"I guess this is where we say goodbye." He hesitated, unprepared for the farewell.

"Danel, travel safely. Kiss Hamid for me. I'll keep you all in my heart, and I pray God will hold you in his hands."

"You, as well. May our paths cross again. Until then, be safe." They hurriedly embraced, smarting from the cruel realities that would swallow Danel and his family in the wave of immigrants and reassign Sister Helen to somewhere else in the world. "

Travel under Allah's protection, Sister Helen, he thought as she closed the door behind her. He shoved his cache of medical supplies into his satchel, took one more last look around his office and hurried unnoticed down the back stairs to meet Ahmed.

10

Extrication

The sun had just descended below the earth's edge, smearing the sky with orange, vermilion and carmine streaks. As Danel's key turned in the lock, Ashara met him at the door holding Hamid.

"You didn't call. I got very worried."

"I couldn't. Today was a day that defies telling. We're going to have to leave tonight."

"What are you talking about? You said we wouldn't go for several days."

He closed the door behind him and laid down his satchel with the medical supplies. The apartment was littered with cartons, bags and suitcases. "Ashara, what's all this?" His tone was incredulous, almost scolding.

"Did you get the car?"

"Yes, I got the car. But it's a Renault, not an American minivan." His quick calculation estimated that at most a third could fit in the small car. "What's in all these boxes and suitcases?"

As she reeled at the criticism, a rosy glow radiated to her cheeks.

"We're now in late summer, and unless you tell me that we'll be home in two months, we'll need winter clothes." Her pupils widened with adrenalin. "Unless you tell me you've arranged for a heated apartment at Za'atari, then we'll be in tents with no heat through the winter. We'll need blankets, pillows, winter coats." Danel raised his hands to silence her litany. Backing off, she said, "If you think you can't fit it all in, I can redo them tomorrow."

"There'll be no redoing anything tomorrow. We have to leave tonight. Right now."

"Right now? Why? What's happened?"

"It's a long story that's been all day in the making. But by now the entire hospital knows we're leaving."

"Oh no. How could that've happened?"

"The Renault was sold yesterday to someone else. Sister Helen learned of a patient who was trying to use his car to pay for medical services, and she took his file for me to call."

"But how did anyone find out?"

"The file was missing and that led to me. That's the short story. But I'll tell you these details on the way." She couldn't fully follow the story, but there was no mistaking his angst.

"Surely you wouldn't be detained for taking a file. You could explain that you didn't even know you'd picked it up."

"Yes, I could say that. But if you think that anyone is going to believe me, you have to think again. There's no room for doubt with this regime. You'd be ridiculous if you thought that. They're not going to wait around to catch me in the act of leaving."

"Don't speak to me that way."

"What way?"

"Like I'm an idiot."

Recognizing that quarreling was wasting valuable minutes, he caught himself.

"Ashara." He spoke her name loudly to halt the argument. "I'm sorry. We can go over all of this in the car when we're safely out of Damascus. But right now, we've no time to waste. They could be coming for me *right now*." Placing his hands on her shoulders, he looked into her eyes. "Can you tell me what's most important so I can start loading the car?"

"That's not how I packed. I packed by category, not order of priority. I'll have to go through everything to distill it down to the most important, but I have to feed Hamid first."

"Hamid will have to wait. You can feed him in the car."

Now sufficiently frightened, she set Hamid down in his crib.

"Ashara, did you make formula for Hamid today? "

"Yes, I did. Luckily that's done."

"Good. Now you're right, we're going to need winter clothes, but what we can take is limited. The same goes for blankets and pillows. You have to condense. What we don't take, we leave, so just stack it over there."

She set to opening up suitcases and boxes, pulling extra garments and bedding out.

"I packed cooking gear and dishes. Do you want me to reduce that as well?"

"Ashara, I didn't pack this, so I can't know how to advise you. Looking at this pile, we'll be able to take three of the large suitcases, and perhaps two to three medium boxes. Maybe we can stuff some bags in remaining small pockets. That means we have got to cut this in half. Can you do that quickly?"

"I'll try." Tears welled in her eyes.

Seeing that he had upset her, he grabbed her arm. "Ashara, this is my fault. I didn't set any limits on what you could pack. I know I told you we'd have more time. We knew this was going to be risky."

"I know. I'm not blaming you. I just never expected that we would have to flee like dogs in the night. This is all we have in the world, and we're leaving most of it behind."

"Ashara, look at me. This's all just stuff. We won't be leaving each other behind. Everything else is replaceable."

Ashara nodded.

"I've treated patients, men and women that the regime's detained. They were tortured and mutilated. Their faces hollow and empty, not daring to speak of the horrors that their bodies revealed. We can't get caught."

Gazing into her eyes, he wiped a drop that escaped the corner.

"We can redo this quickly. How soon do you want to leave?"

"Within 30 minutes. That's the maximum, if not sooner. I parked the car behind the complex. It's a longer distance down to the car, but at least it'll be hidden."

She was already assessing what was packed where, mentally sifting through their possessions. "Are there any of these that I can start taking, or should I wait?"

She was already ripping open a carton. "You can take the big suitcase and the carton at the end of the sofa. Over there." She pointed to a small box. "And this backpack has our money and our important papers. You can take that as well." Danel considered leaving the backpack and the medical supplies to last, but decided that should they be interrupted they would be better off in the car.

Inserting a knife blade into all the sealed boxes, she slit them open and pulled bedding and clothing, books and kitchenware out of boxes and redistributed only the essentials they would need to survive. Two changes of clothes would suffice for the cold and warm seasons, making one set available for washing while the other was worn. Other items stacked in the dining area were prioritized in a queue for possible inclusion on a space-available basis. When Danel returned from ferrying the first load, her progress in ordering chaos amazed him.

"What next?"

She commandeered their evacuation with military precision. "Take the contents of those two boxes and combine them. Then tape the box up, and it can go." Hardly glancing up as she barked orders, she shifted her attention to two more suitcases to combine their contents into one. A small, black velvet purse tucked into the side pocket had almost been overlooked until she spied its silk drawstring. It held a few pieces of gold jewelry that she inherited from her mother, Danel's father's gold watch and a small gold locket with her grandparent's photos. For her their sentimental value was priceless, but if necessary they could be bartered should their money run out.

Checking her watch, she grimaced that 15 of the 30 minutes had lapsed. His dire assessment was sufficient to convince her the danger was escalating. Hamid's fussing was on target, and shortly his hunger would take center stage. She turned on the mobile to distract him, knowing that this diversion would not hold for long.

"Here you go, dear boy, Mama will feed you soon." Hamid watched the mobile turn above his head and waved his arms to reach it. "That's a good boy." She stroked his soft cheeks and then focused on her next task: rations.

In the kitchen, she loaded the sterilized formula into a thermal bag. Earlier that morning she had frozen plastic bags filled with water and now packed them around the bottles to keep the formula cold. Several small loaves of flat bread fit perfectly along the sides, helping to keep the baby bottles upright. She laid some red grapes, peppers and a wedge of cheese on top of the ice for their supper, leaving just enough room for a thermos of water to fit snuggly in a cavity she had preserved in the front for easy access. She zipped it up and moved it over to the staging area where she stacked other items for Danel to take. With each reappearance, he became more agitated.

"You have five more minutes and then we must leave."

"Over there, you can take the two black suitcases and the thermal bag. Make sure the bag is accessible so we won't have to stop if we need it. How much room do you have left?"

"Not much. I think I can take one, possibly two, more small suitcases, maybe a backpack and one more small box. That should leave us room for ourselves and Hamid in the front."

"Go. Take what's over there." She gestured to the items by the door. "The next trip's your last, and we'll all leave together."

Reluctantly he agreed to one more load, almost tripping as he took the apartment stairs in twos before breaking into a full gallop to the car.

The contents of three suitcases had yet to be redistributed. She laid open all three at once, pitching discarded clothes over her shoulder to condense their contents into one.

All that remained was Hamid, whose crying was now uncontrollable. But he would have to wait a little longer. She placed a pacifier at his lips which he sucked on voraciously. It would be no time before he raged again. With dervish-like frenzy, she swept his room of diapers, baby lotions, wipes and any remaining baby clothes and packed them in the final suitcase. Keeping out three diapers, one for changing him in the car, and the other two she added to her purse along with a package of baby wipes. Danel arrived winded from his final sprint up the stairs.

"Ready?"

"Almost. I want Hamid's mobile. You go get that."

"Ashara, don't be ridiculous."

"Now, Danel. I want it. Don't argue, or I will go and do it myself, which will take longer." Taking the last backpack into their bedroom, she collected the Koran from their nightstand, and met Danel at the front door. Donning her hijab, she plucked her frantic infant from his crib, along with a small stuffed rabbit and the discarded pacifier, and wedged him into the baby carrier. The warmth from his frenzy radiated as he nestled against her. With her purse on one shoulder and the baby bag on the other, she tiptoed over the discarded piles.

"There, there, Hamid. Danel, is there any room left for small odd items?"

"Perhaps, but." He started to protest.

"Then, with your spare hand and arm, chose what you think you can carry that will fit from the front of that line against the wall. Where is the mobile?"

"I put it in the suitcase I'm holding."

"Good." Together they took a last nostalgic look around what had been their home for the last four years, now strewn with the remnants of their life. "I'm ready. Let's go." She kissed Hamid's head while Danel locked the door, and they hurried down the apartment steps for last time.

As Danel loaded the last suitcase into the car, Ashara settled into the front seat and secured her seatbelt. Hamid was already thirty minutes past his feeding time when she guided his tiny mouth to her breast. Modestly covering her breast and his tiny head with a receiving blanket, she supported herself on the arm rest as he suckled.

Danel repositioned a few items to make room for the last armful he gathered on the way out, stuffing them into various crannies between the larger possessions. He then slid into the driver's seat, buckled his seatbelt and moved the gear shift forward.

Each mentally revisited duties that their hurried departure had cut short. Were the lights turned off? Was the refrigerator door closed? Was the stove off? Two blocks away Ashara's breath caught in her throat.

"Danel, we have to go back."

"We can't go back. Whatever you've forgotten is gone."

"I think I left my mother's jewelry and your father's watch on the counter in the kitchen."

"What do you mean you think? Either you did or you didn't."

"I remember taking them out of the suitcase and laying them on the counter. I just don't remember if I put them back into another suitcase."

"What did you do with the contents of the suitcase they came out of?"

"I just don't remember. I know that I got distracted by Hamid. But after that…"

"That was less than 30 minutes ago. How can you not remember back thirty minutes?"

"Well, berating me isn't going to help."

"How could you leave them out of the suitcase? This's unbelievable." His irritation overshadowed her stellar performance repacking their belongings. Considering his own behavior this day and her distress, he felt ashamed. Her face spoke without words the deeply personal violations their immigration had wrought. "Let's not play the blame game. We'll just go back and get the jewelry. I'll go in. Where did you leave it?"

"I'm not sure. I think I set the cloth bag on the counter by the refrigerator. Maybe I should be the one to go."

"Absolutely not. You stay put with Hamid." The car veered onto their street as a military vehicle pulled in front of their complex. Two soldiers got out and stood around as if waiting for something.

Ashara gasped. "Danel, look." She pointed up ahead. "Allah, save us. What should we do?"

Stopping the car in the middle of the street, he depressed the clutch to shift into reverse. He turned around to back up out of the street, but it was too late. A second vehicle had already turned the corner and was bearing down on them. Skipping first gear to shift directly into second, the car jerked forward as he looked into the rear view mirror.

"There's a second vehicle's behind us."

She whipped her head around to see for herself.

"Turn around and don't look suspicious. Keep your eyes in front." He eased forward slowly, continuing past the apartment, like a resident returning home for the evening. A final look in his mirror as he rounded the corner revealed four soldiers with guns drawn heading into the complex. Four blocks passed by before they could speak.

Danel finally broke the silence. "We can't go back now. Perhaps we'll find it in one of the suitcases. " They imagined that by now the soldiers were breaking in their door."

"If you'd gone back into the apartment just now, you would've been there when the soldiers came. I'm so sorry"

"You couldn't have known. It's alright."

"What would've happened to you? And what would've become of me and Hamid without you?" She drew Hamid closer.

"It was very close, but Allah had other plans for us. I knew someone would report me, someone seeking favor with the regime or revenge for I know not what."

"What kind of monster would do such a thing?"

Slowly, in the safety of their car, he unraveled the events surrounding the car, how Sister Helen had found the second car, the missing file and her warning to leave immediately.

"Sister Helen still helped us, even after how I treated her?"

"We talked about what happened and she explained herself. I don't agree with what she did, but I found kindness in her motives."

"Kindness in baptizing a Muslim child?"

"She had nothing to give him but a pass into God's kingdom. I don't agree, but I understand now why she did it. It was for Hamid, who she truly loves."

"And does she hold a grudge towards me?"

"No, she told me to tell you that all's forgotten and that she wishes us a safe journey."

"I'm glad." Ashara rocked Hamid gently and kissed his forehead.

"Danel, the jewelry was sentimental and could have been used to barter for things we need. You were right when you said being together is the most important thing." Her hand rested on his thigh. Glancing over, he reciprocated by squeezing her hand. By now, he thought, the soldiers were tearing their home apart, rummaging through the remnants for clues of their whereabouts.

Book Two

11

Murder of Innocents

The city lights grew smaller in the rear view mirror. On this moonless night, darkness enveloped the Renault as it crossed the city's perimeter and turned onto M1 Highway toward Jordan. Danel took a last glimpse of Damascus before he entered the ramp, unsure if they would ever return. The highway traffic was so heavy that one of the lanes in the opposite direction had been commandeered to augment capacity going toward Jordan. As lonely as their escape journey had been until now, they were now accomplices with other Syrian strangers in similar desperation.

The cars moved at a slow pace, barely 36 km/hr. The taillights of cars ahead morphed into long red electric ribbons, like a conveyor belt moving far into the distance. Many people were walking along the highway's side and median, carrying young children and leading older children, goats and pigs. Small wagons piled high with bedding, pots and pans, chairs and other possessions joined the queue as it plodded forward over the rocky soil. Their march was steady, neither quickened by what they were escaping from nor hastened by what they were going toward.

Staring out at her countrymen, Ashara rubbed Hamid's crown as he suckled. "Danel, do you know difference between those people and us?"

"What do you mean?"

"It's what you risked to get us this car."

"It almost cost us our lives." She shivered, grateful that Allah selected horsepower over foot power for their journey to Za'atari. "But we don't know their stories, and their risks could have been as great as ours."

"Allah has been good to us."

"Yes, many times He has protected us."

The odometer marked barely a 40 km progress before the traffic began to crawl. Finally, forward progress halted, with foot traffic outpacing the vehicular conveyor belt. Impatient drivers honked their frustration. Their narrow escape left Danel no time to fill his tank. His eyes shifted frequently between the bottleneck immediately ahead and the gas gauge, whose indicator had edged below half. Turning off the engine, he tried to conserve petrol.

"Why did you turn off the car?"

"This stop and start isn't good for the fuel. We should conserve if we want to make it all the way to Za'atari."

Other drivers milled outside their vehicles in the warm night air. Opening his door, Danel stood on the chassis, stretching vertically to discern the hold up. Ashara burped Hamid and laid him in her lap to change his diaper. The driver in front talked on his cell phone, gesturing animatedly with his other hand. When he flipped it shut, Danel ducked his head back into the car.

"I'm going to see if that guy knows anything about the holdup. You wait here." He left his door open and approached the man as the woman passenger got out to join them. Suddenly agitated, Danel started to leave and then went back to ask the man something else. Shaking his head, he walked briskly back and climbed into the car.

"What did he say?"

"His cousin's in a car about a hundred vehicles ahead. Apparently there are men ahead who are stopping all traffic looking for Alawites."

"What do they want with Alawites? Who are they?"

"His cousin says they're thugs, not insurgents or Assad's men."

"Why're they stopping cars? What do they want?"

"He says they are taking Alawite infants into the woods and killing them."

Holding Hamid closer, she froze. "But why would they do that?"

"Your guess is as good as mine. Contempt towards Alawites is everywhere. Many Sunnis want revenge for what our Alawite President has done to them." Running his fingers through his hair, he rested his forehead on the steering wheel.

"But that hatred was generations in the making. Assad didn't start that. So why now?"

"I'd heard about similar atrocities on the way to Turkey, but all reports said that the road to Jordan was safe."

"You knew of such things and said nothing to me?"

Startled by her raised voice, Hamid began to whimper. She kissed his head to calm him.

"What would that have done except scare you? We'd decided that Jordan was the best alternative, and there'd been no reports of infanticide."

"What're we going to do? We can't just wait for them to get to us." Their car was hemmed in by the gridlock. Since they were hunted in Damascus, they could not return even if the highway back were clear.

"We're going to have to leave the car here and walk back," said Danel.

"Walk back to where?" She turned around. "There's nothing back there to go to."

"I don't know. I'm sure we can't stay here and wait for them." He turned on the ignition and carefully maneuvered the car inch by inch out of the lane of traffic onto the shoulder. "We'll try to find some shelter off one of the side roads or spend the night in the woods. Gather what you need for Hamid, and I'll get the backpack with our papers."

Climbing out of the car, she laid the carrier and baby on her seat. Out of the back seat, she took the formula out of the thermal bag, grabbed two lightweight receiving blankets and some spare diapers and wedged them into the baby bag. Danel slid his arms into his backpack and crossed around to the passenger side to get the bag that contained the formula and the diapers.

"We have to go now. What else do we need?" Those possessions, important enough less than two hours ago to risk packing, now paled as they faced the danger to Hamid.

"Nothing." Placing the carrier over her head, she positioned Hamid snugly against her chest.

Danel pressed the lock button down, closed the car door and put the keys in his pocket.

A frenzied flow of humans joined them trying to escape. Carrying an infant over the rocky soil made for uneven footing. As screaming behind them intensified, the stampede quickened. Floating above the chaos, Danel's ear perked as he heard his name being called.

"Danel," a man's voice in the distance bellowed. He scanned the throng in front of him but could not pinpoint the source. Baffled, he kept running as the voice grew louder. "Danel! Ashara!" The voice was coming from the driver of a white van with large black letters, a U and an N, and "Disengagement Observer Force" written in Arabic across the hood. The driver called his name again.

A large, burly man, carrying two squawking chickens, almost ran over Ashara when Danel stopped abruptly. He caught Ashara by her arm, pulling her up as she stumbled, and edged her over closer to the van. "Danel. Over here." This time the voice was a woman's coming from behind the driver of the UN van. As they got closer, he recognized Sister Helen.

"Danel, it's me. Sister Helen." Peering into the van, he saw other nuns with Sister Helen in the second row, leaning over the driver.

"Sister Helen. What're you doing here?"

"The transport came to get me about an hour after you left. We picked up several more at other hospitals and we're now heading to Jordan."

Her words, "after you left," felt to Danel like ages ago, rather than several hours.

"Why's everyone running the wrong way? Where's your car?"

"There're thugs up ahead stopping cars and pedestrians. They're hunting Alawite infants like prey, taking them into the woods to murder them."

"Lord Jesus." She gasped, making the sign of the cross. "Where're you running to?"

"We're just trying to escape them. My car's up front a ways, but in this gridlock there's no moving it, and we can't go back to Damascus."

"The soldiers came looking for you at the hospital."

He turned back, trying to determine how close the men were.

"Danel, we could take Hamid with us. They wouldn't stop a UN van."

"Wait a minute. That's out of the question," protested the driver. "My orders were to collect the nuns and a few NGOs." He turned around in his seat to face Sister Helen. "We can't take an infant with us."

"We could meet you at Za'atari." She addressed Danel and Ashara, ignoring the driver. "What do you say?"

Danel drew Ashara aside to discuss the situation. "What do you think?"

"No, Danel. I won't be separated from Hamid. It's out of the question," said Ashara.

"We have no way to defend ourselves, Ashara. These men have guns. Hamid will be more vulnerable with us."

"We're a family. We should stick together." She grabbed his shirt, pleading. "Please, I can't give him up."

Biting his lip, he rubbed his forehead. "I know how you feel. I don't like it any better than you do. But if they could offer him safe passage, shouldn't we put that first?"

They regarded each other as Ashara deliberated. Firmly convinced himself, he struck the one argument that could persuade her: putting Hamid's safety first.

She hugged Hamid closer, watching Sister Helen's face staring out the window.

"We have no time. They're coming."

Closing her eyes tightly, she bit her lips. "Alright, Sister Helen should take him." Her eyes glassed over as they walked back to the van.

"Mr. Amir, Za'atari, it's not far out of our way, is it?" asked Sister Helen.

"No, but Sister, my orders are to take you directly to Amman." The other passengers joined in support of the plan, urging the driver to do the right thing.

Sister Helen grabbed his shoulder. "Mr. Amir, we've no choice but to help these people." Turning to Danel and Ashara, she said, "What did you decide?"

Ashara hesitantly lifted the carrier off her shoulder and over her head, tears spilling over the dam of her thick lashes.

"Danel, you and Ashara go back to your car and wait until the traffic opens up. Then continue on to the camp, and we'll be following behind you."

Ashara finally found her voice. "But what if they stop you? If these thugs are bold enough to be killing like this, we can't count on them to be rational when it comes to a UN transport full of nuns."

"You're right, but I think that this is better than risking the woods. You've nothing to protect yourselves."

"Wait," said Danel. Removing his backpack, he tilted its contents toward the headlight. He rummaged through various papers before pulling some documents from the inside. Returning to the driver's side, he offered papers to Sister Helen. "These could help if you're stopped. They're Hamid's papers. You should take them just in case."

"Are you sure we shouldn't keep the papers with us?" said Ashara.

"I know how hard this is, Ashara, but Hamid is safer having the papers with him."

She knew the nuns would need them if they were accosted.

Danel took Hamid's little hand in his and bent to kiss it.

Ashara kissed her small bundle, still encased in the soft folds of his carrier. "Be safe, Hamid. Your baba and I love you, and we'll be with you very soon. Be a good boy. Sister Helen will take care of you, and Allah is watching." She kissed him one more time on each cheek as the driver opened the van door to receive the whimpering infant. He carefully passed Hamid back to Sister Helen. Danel handed the driver the bag with Hamid's necessities as Hamid was swallowed into the van's interior darkness.

"We'll meet you at Za'atari, right?" Danel reiterated.

"In a few hours, once we get through this traffic jam." The driver confirmed that he would detour to take the infant to Za'atari.

"Sister Helen," Ashara called into the van. "Hamid should be hungry in about two hours. There's formula in his bag, along with diapers." Ashara paused to recollect any other instructions that Sister Helen would need. "Once again our son's safety is in your hands."

Sister Helen, leaning over with Hamid nestled in the crook of her right arm, extended her left arm behind the driver through the open window and reached for Ashara. The two women firmly held each other's hands as the responsibility relinquished by one was accepted by the other.

Her composure shattered, Ashara cupped both hands over her mouth.

"Be safe, both of you." Sister Helen spoke what Ashara was too distraught to say.

Danel slung the backpack over his shoulder. Taking Ashara's arm, he guided her back towards the car against the flow of bodies. In her wildest imaginings, she never could have predicted that she would willingly relinquish her child. She suddenly stumbled.

Danel picked her up from the ground before someone trampled her. "Are you alright?"

"I'll be alright when we're reunited. Right now my heart is aching."

"I'm as heartsick as you."

"I have this horrible feeling we may never see him again." She shuddered.

"We can't think like that. We'll see him in a couple hours, Allah willing."

"May Allah be with all of us, and especially Hamid."
"Allah Akbar."
"Yes, Allah Akbar."

In a short while, four men armed with type 56 assault rifles surrounded the car. Judging by their unshaven, filthy faces and blood-spattered army-issue khakis, Danel thought them to be defectors. One aimed his flashlight into Danel's eyes, momentarily blinding him, before shining it on Ashara's face. Its light scanned the car's interior searching for an infant. The man nearest Ashara pointed his bayonet inside her window directly at her. When she saw fresh blood on the steel blade, she held her breath.

"Where're you going?"

Danel couldn't make out the man's features with the light shining directly at him. "We're going to Za'atari."

"Just the two of you?"

"Yes." Danel's heartbeat thumped against his chest.

"Get out of the car." The man beckoned with his flashlight, revealing his features for Danel, who resolved never to forget them.

"What are you gawking at? Move it." He pushed his rifle barrel into Danel's ribs.

Ashara stared at the dashboard, not daring to turn or make eye contact.

"What's in the trunk?"

"Our clothes, bedding, pots and pans."

"Open the trunk."

His rifle butt beckoned to Danel to get closer. "Open it."

Danel had packed the car, but he was ignorant of specific contents. He reached for a large, black suitcase easily accessible in the front. Baby clothes and diapers would expose them should Danel open up the wrong suitcase.

"Not that one. This one over here." The man gestured for Danel to open the last suitcase he loaded, the one which held Hamid's mobile.

Swallowing hard, Danel unzipped the case, exposing its contents.

The brute at Ashara's window, impatient now to resume the hunt, called back toward the trunk, distracting the man with Danel. "Hey, let's go. There's nothing to find here."

As the man looked away, Danel hastily threw a towel over the mobile, obscuring it from sight, save a small blue star that escaped by the back hinge of the suitcase.

"Be quick." The rifle nudged Danel's back as the man's left hand shined the flashlight's beam cursorily into the suitcase. Obstructed by the trunk's lid, the suitcase would only open three quarters of the way. Danel held his breath as the beam glanced over the star undetected.

"Move on then." The man motioned Danel forward with his rifle as he slammed the trunk lid closed.

Climbing into the driver's seat, his foot trembled as he depressed the clutch. Steadying his hand to start the ignition, he shifted into gear, inching forward. As the car slipped into second gear, the Renault pulled ahead to anonymity in the traffic flow.

Ashara shook uncontrollably, her hands clammy despite the dryness of the desert night.

Gradually their immediate fear subsided. Danel told Ashara what had happened when the thugs opened the trunk. Humbled by their own impotence, she offered Allah a dua aloud.

O Allah, we, on this day beseech You to accept as trusts, ourselves, our son and those who have him in their custody. O Allah, guard us with the protection of faith and surround us with Your care. O Allah, include us in Your mercy and do not divest us of Your favors.

His hand reached for hers. They would just have to wait for His answer at Za'atari.

12

Ingenuity

Capitalizing on the chaos and desperation of the refugees, the executioners worked their way through the line of vehicles, slaughtering the innocents whose parents realized too late their intentions. Driven by the taste of blood, they became impatient with the pace of the slaughter. Each car was penned in by the crush of other cars around them.

The occupants of the UN van were strangers before they had been collected hours earlier to share the journey to Jordan. Their conversation, prior to accepting Hamid, focused on exchanging names, countries of origin and casual sharing of their assignments. While each had observed unspeakable cruelty, each still retained, in varying degrees, their belief in the goodness of all mankind. Their naiveté lulled them into a sense of false security, believing themselves protected while traveling under the auspices of the UN.

Sister Helen gently rocked Hamid until he quieted. Considering feeding him early to avoid any crying, she thought better of it as he started to doze off. She hoped he would sleep through any encounter with the men.

Their wait was short lived. The same thugs who accosted Danel and Ashara now presented themselves to the van driver.

"Where are you going and what're you carrying in the van?"

"We're with the UN and our destination and the personnel in this vehicle are not subject to any interference according to international law." Mr. Amir had served with the UN for nine years, mainly relocating supplies and personnel to areas that needed them most. He spoke flawless Arabic as well as seven other languages.

"Is that so?" The man's arrogance was menacing. "You hear what the good driver says, my friends, we have no authority to interfere with this vehicle?" The others laughed.

"What's your name?"

"Amir."

"Well, Mr. Amir, in Syria we have a different rule of authority." The nuns held their breath, not daring to make sound. "You see, in this country, this rifle is the real authority, and, right now, Mr. Amir, it's a higher authority than your international law. Now kindly step out of the vehicle." He tapped his rifle barrel on the door.

"I repeat, you have no authority here."

"Well, I guess you didn't hear me, so I'll have to unblock your ears." The leader nonchalantly hoisted his rifle up over his shoulder, and thrust its butt full force into Mr. Amir's temple. Stunned, Mr. Amir's head jerked back, as an accomplice opened the driver's door and yanked him down onto the ground.

"Now I think you're in a better position to hear me. Yes?"

Mr. Amir started to rise, stumbling to his feet. His head throbbed and blood ran freely down his cheek onto his uniform.

"Now, do as you're told and there'll be no more trouble. Put your hands against the van."

Physically wobbly, the injured driver morally held his ground.

The nuns silently prayed that Mr. Amir would just acquiesce. No good could come from his resistance.

His words slurred slightly as he talked through his pain. "I repeat myself. You have no right or jurisdiction to—"

The leader interrupted him. "I can see that you are having trouble grasping what we're asking. So we are going to have to make it a little plainer." He motioned to his henchman.

"Please explain to Mr. Amir the correct behavior tonight."

The three other men obeyed, the first knocking him to the ground by slamming his rifle butt into Mr. Amir's knee, shattering his patella. Emboldened by Mr. Amir's scream, they reigned kick after kick into his torso as he curled into a fetal position. Now semi-conscious, he moaned and steeled himself to accept more blows.

Sister Helen carefully passed the sleeping infant to the nun on her right. Without turning her head, she quietly called to Sister Magdalena, a short, olive-complexioned, dark-haired nun from Trinidad. "Sister Magdalena, I saw a toolbox behind the rear seat. Open it up and tell me what you see."

"What are you thinking, Sister Helen? You can't fight these men if that is what is on your mind."

"Hurry and do as I tell you."

"There's not much light back here, but screwdrivers, a hammer, and a box cutter. Several wrenches too." Sister Helen cut her off.

"Pass up to me the heaviest wrench or the hammer if that's more substantial. Also send up the box cutter."

The nun did not move.

"*Now* Magdalena. I said now. Then pass a screwdriver or any other suitable hand tool to everyone else."

"Suitable for what?"

"Sister Magdalena, a man can't discern a gun barrel from a screwdriver when applied from behind into his back. I'm not asking you to hurt anyone. I'm asking us all to help ourselves."

Each nun accepted their weapon as it was passed forward. Sensing their reluctance, Sister Ambrose, a quiet, compliant nun, spoke up. "Sisters, remember *the salvation of the righteous is the Lord: He is their strength in the time of trouble.*"

"Well said, Sister Ambrose. *God is with us in all we do.*" Sister Helen exposed the box cutter's blade, securing the safety catch in the open position so that the blade could not retreat. Sheathing the blade with her handkerchief, she positioned it into the rosary pocket of her long skirt and the wrench in the pocket on the opposite side. The merciless beating they were witnessing sent a tsunami of adrenaline through her veins as she rolled up her sleeves.

"Sisters, be ready to assist. Christ is on our side." Instructing the nun holding Hamid to keep the infant quiet, she made the sign of the cross twice before she ventured out to the men beating Mr. Amir.

"Why don't you fight someone your own size?" At 86 kg Sister Helen clearly outweighed the leader by 9 kg.

He was at once amused and startled at the absurdity of the nun confronting him. "Sister, we don't fight women. We have other more interesting things we do with women. Perhaps you'd like to see what my men have in store for you?" His accomplices ceased pummeling Mr. Amir. "But we need everyone out of the van so they can see how much you'll enjoy this."

Two men pointed their rifles into the van and instructed the other nuns to get out. Each filed out obediently, with the last carrying Hamid who had just awakened. His small cries punctuated the tension.

"What is this? A prize in the van?" A man with a bushy mustache roughly yanked Hamid from the nun's arms, frightening him into a frenzy.

"What do you want with this child?"

"Why is a UN van of nuns traveling with an infant? Do you have his papers?"

"Of course we have them. He's an orphan we're transporting to an orphanage in Jordan." She reached out to take charge of Hamid, but the man taunted her, twisting Hamid in the opposite direction to prevent her taking him. "You're scaring him."

"Well, since he has no parents, you won't mind if we take him with us. We have a little orphanage of our own beyond the highway."

Sister Helen's venom boiled. *Mother of God, pray for us.* She refocused her attention on the leader.

"So you have something special you do to women? Well, I have something special I do for men." Sister Helen delicately pulled up her skirt above her knee, as coyly as a prostitute would lure a patron.

His member hardened at the prospect of desecrating a nun.

Swiveling her hips in a sensual gait, she moved closer. About a meter and a half in front of him, she planted her left foot firmly. "This is what we call the football maneuver." Her right leg swung back behind her, and the torque of her body delivered a kick to his genitals. "You won't be serving up much for any woman for some time."

Blind to Sister Helen's resourcefulness and with no warning, he crumbled helplessly, clutching his gonads.

Signing herself, she waited for him to rise. The remaining ten nuns outnumbered the men better than three to one. Emboldened by Sister Helen's offence, the sisters surrounded them, occluding the men's view of Sister Helen and the injured man. Utilizing the chaos to their advantage, three nuns thrust their tools into the backs of the men. "Drop your weapons or I'll pull the trigger," warned Sister Magdalena. "Lay them down in front of you." She jabbed her wrench into the back of the man in front of her. "Now."

The injured man stumbled to his feet to meet Sister Helen's fist at his left temple. She ducked as he tried to return the punch and then swung back behind him. Grabbing his arm, she twisted it backward, jerking it upward against his scapula. While her right arm held him immobile, she reached into her pocket and slid the box cutter from its sheath. Her left arm reached over his shoulder and around his neck, pressing the tip of the blade into the skin covering his jugular vein.

"Tell your man to release the child." Adding pressure to the blade against his neck, she drew a small trickle of blood. "My blade can go deeper if that's what you prefer. I said release the child." A little more pressure drew a flow of warm blood down his neck and onto his shirt.

His head beckoned his men to comply as her arm tightened against his trachea. "Give them back the child."

The man holding Hamid roughly shoved him back.

"Now tell them to drop their weapons." She stretched his arm further toward his shoulder. "Tell them now, or I'll break your arm off."

"Drop the weapons." Each in turn threw his weapon on the ground.

"Sister Magdalena, open the van and put the weapons in the back." The small wiry nun made several trips to the back of van, carrying two rifles at a time.

"Now tell your men to help our driver back into the van. If they cause him any more pain, I'll slit your throat. Tell them."

He coughed as she exerted more pressure against his trachea, then relayed her instructions, directing his men to be careful with Mr. Amir.

Supporting the beaten driver on each side they dragged him barely conscious and laid him across the second seat. A crowd of onlookers gathered, gawking at the nuns subduing four men with rifles. Those who had fled to protect their families, not daring to risk confrontation, were captivated by the resourcefulness and courage of the nuns.

"Now, you have one more task. Tell your men to take their shoes off and put their identity papers inside them." He repeated her command and the other three complied.

"Sister Magdalena, collect the shoes and put them into the van." Releasing the man, she shoved him to the ground and pulled a wrench out of her pocket.

"You too, off with the shoes. One move to escape and I'll smash your skull. Now do it."

Balancing on one foot and then another, he removed his shoes. "Now your identity papers." He took a worn, cloth wallet out of the right vest pocket of his jacket and tossed it on the ground. "I said put them in your shoes." She slapped the wrench against her palm. "Don't think for a second I won't use this."

He complied.

"Thank you, gentleman, the refugees in Jordan will make good use of your shoes. You can pick up your identity papers from the authorities."

More onlookers joined the crowd already gathered, surrounding them. Many carried flashlights which they shone directly on the men's faces. Should they not live past tonight was of no concern to Sister Helen. If they survived, the evidence against them would bring swift justice.

"Get up and move. Pray to your God that you don't drown in the blood that you've drawn tonight."

Two of his comrades supported him as he limped away. The crowd parted to allow the men to exit into the darkness. A young mother released the small child she held by the hand and started to clap. One by one others joined her to thank the nuns and for the inspiration that miracles can come from the most astonishing places.

As the nuns got back into the van, Sister Helen asked if any of them could drive. Sister Rebecca, a tall, middle-aged nun from Scranton, Pennsylvania, volunteered that she could drive, but her license was expired.

"Your expired license is the least of our troubles. Sister Ambrosina, you sit up with Sister Rebecca in case she needs help."

Hamid's cries demanded he be fed.

"Sister Magdalena, there're bottles in the baby bag. Can you feed Hamid while I tend to Mr. Amir?"

Mr. Amir was semiconscious. The gash across his temple was still bleeding. She folded her handkerchief several times along the bias. "Anyone have a handkerchief I can use?" Eight white handkerchiefs were passed forward. Folding one four times, she placed it over the wound, applying pressure to stanch the blood flow. As it slowed, she stretched her own handkerchief over the folded one covering the wound and tied it at the back of his head.

Next she unbuttoned his shirt, which exposed massive bruising around his ribs and chest. There was no way to tell how much internal bleeding his organs had sustained. Feeling down his arms and legs, she was sure that one arm was broken, and his smashed knee was now so swollen she could feel it throbbing inside the leg of his pants.

Knowing that Danel and Ashara were anxiously waiting for Hamid at Za'atari, her desire to reunite the family pulled strongly. She estimated that with the pace of the traffic it would take at least three hours to reach Za'atari. Assessing Mr. Amir's condition, her instinct told her he wouldn't survive for long without medical attention. He needed surgery in a hospital, and the nearest one was behind them back in Damascus.

"Sisters, I don't believe Mr. Amir will survive the three-hour journey to Za'atari, let alone making it all the way to Amman. He needs to get to a hospital now."

"Are you proposing that we go back to Damascus?" said Sister Rebecca, the nun who took over the driving.

"This is a decision that we all have to make. We should not take lightly going back into the lion's mouth."

"Mr. Amir stood up on our behalf. We owe him." Sister Ambrosina, the young nun from Cordoba sitting next to Sister Rebecca, vocalized what the others were thinking. "God is with us in all we do."

"We'd be risking eleven lives to save one." Sister Helen felt compelled to be sure that the decision was made with one voice, not coerced by her own strong will. The nuns, only hours ago strangers, coalesced around a scripture quote offered by Sister Magdalena, the same nun who initially resisted arming the nuns.

"*Greater love hath no man than this, that a man lay down his life for friends.*" Their deliberation swift, their only course was to save Mr. Amir and go back to Damascus.

"Sister Rebecca, do you think you can maneuver over across the median and the far lane to turn us into the opposite direction.

"Since we're just creeping along I think I can manage it." Sister Rebecca slowly began to inch the van forward, then a miniscule right turn of the wheel, then reverse, then repeat.

"Wait. Stop the van and let me get out." Sister Helen opened the back door and hurried to the back of the van, waving her arms over her head to stop the vehicle behind them in the next lane over. She created a break in the traffic sufficient for the van to move over a lane. They now had to cross the throng of walkers with their possessions in the median. She spread her arms full out, moving them like a windmill to clear a path.

"Excuse us. Medical emergency. Van coming through. Excuse." With the van now at the far edge of the median, there was just one more lane to cross. She edged into the lane, stopping traffic. Once in the far lane, the van made a U-turn into the traffic in the opposite direction. Sister Rebecca pulled onto the shoulder and waited for Sister Helen to board. Fifteen minutes after their decision was made, they were facing Damascus, heading to the closest hospital on the south side, the same one where they had picked up Sister Magdalena on their last stop before heading to Jordan.

"Well done, Sister Rebecca." They all congratulated her.

Mr. Amir had taken up the full seat behind the driver, displacing two nuns. One squeezed into the next seat back with three other nuns, and Sister Helen wedged herself on the floor in the aisle, thankful that it was only 40 km back to Damascus.

Hamid had his supper and was now sleepy and would never remember this night. His parents' angst would be great when they failed to show up, but there was no way to get word to them. The nuns had no cell phones. They searched for Mr. Amir's but, finding none, figured he had lost it during the beating. Even if they could borrow a phone, she did not have Danel's number. The ride back to the Damascus hospital would add hours to the night's journey. With luck, maybe they could reach Za'atari by morning.

On the way back to Damascus, the nuns discussed their journey. Sister Helen silently evaluated her actions in taking Hamid from his parents. Closing her eyes, she shuddered, thinking of the danger she had brought upon everyone. *There's going to be hell to pay for this back at headquarters.*

From her position on the van floor, Sister Helen looked across the bench seat at Hamid, sleeping peacefully in Sister Magdalena's arms. Despite the consequences then and now, she accepted that she would do what she had done all over again to protect him.

"Sister Magdalena, would you mind if I held the baby for a while?" The small bundle was passed to her, and she lovingly took him, kissing his cheeks. He sighed deeply, and his little eyes sealed tighter as he retreated into a deep slumber, contented and belly full.

13

The Vigil

With 90 km to Za'atari, Hamid's parents rode in silence, each holding their own counsel.

Ashara broke the spell. "Danel, can this be the same day that started with you leaving for the hospital to buy a car?"

"It's hard to believe so much has happened. This time last night we were in our bed holding each other."

"And Hamid was sleeping peacefully in his crib."

Unless they had lived through it, neither would have comprehended that a day which started so benign had separated the family, with the most vulnerable member now in harm's way. They vacillated between whether or not they had pursued the safer course by leaving Hamid behind with the nuns or if the better choice would have been risking flight into the woods as a family. They would not know the final answer until they were reunited with Hamid, and Sister Helen weighed in on the nuns' ordeal after they left.

Despite neither having eaten since breakfast, it hadn't occurred to them that they were hungry.

"Ashara, I think we should eat something."

"I'm too worried to eat."

"We have to do all we can to stay fit."

The thermal bag, packed with forethought earlier in the day, was lodged directly behind her seat. Unlatching her seatbelt, she knelt on her haunches, leaning over her seat to reach the bag, and set it down on the floor between her legs. Unzipping it, she took out one of the loaves of flatbread and slit it lengthwise, using a knife she remembered to pack at the last minute. Laying the bread back into the bag, she took out the cheese wedge and cut several slices for inside the bread. Finally she broke off two small bunches of grapes and pulled out a bottle of water for them to share. The plastic bags of ice were now melted, but the contents of the bag remained cool. Despite their empty stomachs, their anxiety had taken away their appetites.

"I won't be at peace until I'm sure they made it past those men. We should have thought to get a cell phone number. Anyway, Sister Helen has your number, doesn't she, Danel?

"I don't think I ever gave it to her. I know that she doesn't carry a cell phone."

"So you're saying she has no way to reach us?"

"Be calm. She'll make it to Za'atari soon, and that's how she'll reach us."

They were following a bus labeled Dar'a, a city in southern Syria. When it reached Za'atari, most disembarked with no possessions, with some carrying small children or helping the elderly. A few children appeared to be alone with no adults. Danel pulled out from behind the bus to follow a line of cars heading off to a cleared area a full kilometer away from the entrance. He edged the car parallel to others in a row, with a steady stream of others falling in line beside him.

"Danel, we can leave the car and come back for our things later. We have to be at the entrance when Sister Helen brings Hamid."

"Their van was many vehicles back. It'll be at least several hours before the van gets here."

"With so many people coming through, will we be able to find each other?"

"Sister Helen's very resourceful. Let's use this time before they come to find a place to sleep." His comforting words were for Ashara's benefit, but he was astounded by the massive crowd of refugees passing into the camp. A single nun with an infant would be easy to miss—a group of ten nuns not so much, assuming they all decided to enter the camp rather than wait in the van.

He reached behind his seat for the backpack which contained their identity papers, money and other essentials, including a flashlight. Ashara took her purse, the thermal bag and a blanket for them to sit on while they waited for the UN van. Even though it was night, the flow of refugees was not abating. He estimated that perhaps several hundred had arrived when they did, with no end in sight.

As they approached the camp's entrance, Ashara's pace slowed. Bright lights illuminated the entrance, clogged by the volume of refugees and their possessions. The crowd's steady crunch on the sandy ground kicked up a low dust cloud about their feet and ankles, coating their shoes and lower legs with sand-colored particles. Noticing that Ashara was no longer keeping pace, he turned to watch her scanning the crowd, looking for their son.

"Come, Ashara. There's no way they could be here yet. We've work to do, unless you want to receive Hamid here in the desert with no cover. We have to prepare a place."

"You should go do that and leave me here to watch for them.

Accepting as futile his attempts to dissuade her, he selected a location off to the side with the best vantage to scan those who came through, near where they saw busses unloading. It made sense that the van would go to such an unloading point.

"Ashara, promise me you won't wander from this spot, or we'll lose each other. We have to make sure that doesn't happen."

"I promise. I'll be here when you come back." Her gaze had left his face and was already searching the crowd.

As he left, a tall, pretty, sandy-haired woman, in her late twenties he guessed, stationed under a spotlight, was answering questions and directing people. She wore a light blue ball cap and overshirt, each bearing the UNHCR logo, helping hands shielding a human figure surrounded by olive branches, the universal symbol for peace. Approaching her, he read her name tag, Bethshari Sadat, and waited patiently for her to wind down her conversation with a man looking for the registration tent.

Her smile was warm. "Can I help you?"

"My name is Dr. Ottawa. My wife and I just arrived. We're expecting our infant to arrive in a few hours. Perhaps you could advise me about getting set up here."

"Of course, Dr. Ottawa. You're a medical doctor?"

"Yes, a surgeon actually."

"We could use your services once you and your wife get acclimated." She blushed. "Forgive me, first things first. My name is Sadat. You can call me Bethshari."

They were interrupted by someone looking for tents. Suspending her conversation with Danel, she pointed back over her left shoulder to a long line and told them to get into that queue. Then she turned back her attention. "Forgive me for approaching you about assisting us before we've even helped you."

"That's alright. I'll be glad to help once my family's settled in."

"You said you're waiting for your infant?"

"Yes, on the way here we encountered bandits. I'm not sure who they were, but they were confiscating Alawi infants. We entrusted our infant son, Hamid, to a friend, a nun actually, traveling in a UN van. We thought he'd be safer with her, since we're Alawite. We're supposed to meet her at the entrance tonight."

"You're not the first I've heard this from tonight. I can look for a nun with an infant as well. Where's your wife?"

"She refused to leave the entrance so as not to miss them."

"I see. Well, the first thing you should do is secure a tent for your family. Over there is the line for a tent assignment." She gestured over her shoulder once again. "Then tomorrow you should go over there, to the very large tent with the UNHCR letters. They'll give you an appointment for registration."

"Can't we attend to registration later?"

"You can, but it's not wise. With registration papers you'll be allowed to get food rations and a hygiene kit. "Do you have any food with you?"

"We have a little left, but it won't last past tomorrow."

"You should register first thing so you can get into the bread line. Then you can get your rations from a tent over that way." She pointed into the opposite direction. She smiled at him and then semi-shrugged. "Don't worry. It's a lot to absorb on your first night."

He glanced over at each tent, reviewing where he should go first.

"When you're settled in, we'll see about you working in the hospital."

Danel glanced back to wave to her a last time, but she was already engaged with another family. He walked back to Ashara to share what he had discovered. "Are you sure that you don't want to come with me? It'll be a long while before they come."

"No, you go, and I'll keep a vigil for our son. I'd be no good to you."

"So be it. Please don't leave this spot. I'll be back as soon as I find a place where we can stay."

Turning away, he headed for the queue waiting for tent assignments. The line appeared to be about 18 meters long. *Not too bad*, he thought. But as he went to join the end, he saw that it wound around the side of the tent and stretched four times that far along the side. His only consolation was that it appeared to be moving, albeit slowly. He had been waiting for twenty minutes when he glanced around to see that the line had grown even longer than when he had first joined it.

Soon he struck up a conversation with a man and his ten-year-old son. His family, which included a wife and five children, had come from Dar'a. They fled with nothing as the bombing started. He later learned that their neighbors were killed immediately. When they looked back down the block, they saw their house go up in an explosion. He wept as he recounted his story. Empathizing with the man, Danel felt grateful they had escaped. All that was missing was Hamid.

It was after 1:00 in the morning when Danel received his tent assignment. Situated at the end of a long row, it sat in the far right corner of the camp. He estimated it to be 4.5 to 5.5 square meters, equipped with two foam mattresses. He was grateful that they wouldn't have to share it with another family.

Sanitation was his next concern, since Ashara would be sure to ask about it when he reported back. The UN worker explained the location of the latrines relative to their tent. Located about 30 meters behind them, at the outer edge of the camp, just slightly below grade, they were not as bad as he feared. Anticipating defecation fields or latrine trench pits, he found them well lighted with latrine stalls as well as showers and separate facilities for men and women. Now with a place to sleep and basic sanitation, he could join Ashara. Perhaps by now Sister Helen and Hamid had arrived, since it had been about four or five hours since they parted.

Searching the crowd near where he had left her, he found her quite agitated. "Ashara, no sign of them yet?"

"No, something very bad must have happened. They should be here by now. We have to go look for them."

"Look where, Ashara?"

"Anywhere. I don't know, but we just can't stand here. I met a woman whose baby was taken from her. What if they found Hamid and took him?"

"If we leave here, we run the risk of them arriving and not finding us. We have to wait where we said we'd be."

Distraught, she began to weep. "I never should have left him. They could all be dead. This is my fault for agreeing to separate."

"Ashara, stop. You don't know that, and neither do I. I could name at least twenty scenarios that could have delayed them, and none of them involve harm to Hamid."

"Well, I can't. Name one, Danel, name just one." Her imaginings were having their way with her.

"They could have run out of gas or the van could've broken down."

"You're right. I've been standing here just thinking the worst."

Noticing that the blanket she had brought to sit on had not even been unfolded, he drew his handkerchief and wiped the sand dust off her face. "Ashara, you've been standing all this time?"

"I didn't want to risk missing them."

"You're exhausted, and it's time to rest."

"I can't leave here; what if they come and I'm not here."

"Then Sister Helen will find someone to ask. Just like I did. Someone will direct her to the tent that was just assigned to us." He took her arm, pulling her along until she stopped resisting. "If they don't come before the morning, we'll start inquiring after the van when we rise. But I believe that when we wake up, Hamid will be here waiting for you."

She wanted to believe what he was saying, but the harbinger of never seeing Hamid again haunted her.

In the dark, as they walked past row after row of tents; along the dusty, sand gravel, they could hear occupants inside snoring. A young child had awakened with a nightmare, and the mother was soothing her, singing the same lullaby that Danel had sung to his real son on the night he died. Its melody drew him back to that night. The winds of fate were fickle, and for all he knew Hamid might be safe this night with his real parents had it not been for his actions.

When they had reached their tent, Ashara inspected its confines, concluding it would do to set up housekeeping for their family. Next they walked together hand in hand to the latrines where they parted, he to the men's, and she to the women's. Ashara was glad the women's latrine was devoid of mirrors, as the clean water she had splashed on her face, dripped back into the basin sand colored.

Pacing back and forth, he waited for her outside. "Not as bad as we thought, right?"

She rolled her eyes but thought better of the scathing comment perched at her tongue's tip. "It could be worse. We'll make it all work." She reached for his hand as they started back to their tent.

Danel lifted the front flap back for Ashara to enter. The sides and the back each had a window flap sewn into the main sheet, which he pulled up with a lightweight rope to allow for some cross ventilation. A soft breeze had come up, bringing welcome relief to the warm night air as he moved the two mattresses next to one another. After she lay down, he drew her into his arms and kissed her softly.

"I know you want him with us—as do I. We entrusted him and the others to Allah, and we have to have faith that they're in his protection. Our job right now is to rest so that tomorrow we can apply ourselves to finding him."

She tilted her chin upwards for her lips to meet his. "I love you very much, Danel. This would be unbearable without you."

"I love you too. All will be well, you'll see."

Despite the breeze, the tent was hot, and he released her to her own mattress, holding her hand until he felt it go limp. He soon drifted off with thoughts of Hamid and Sister Helen foremost in his mind.

Allah, I beseech you to carry them safely to us.

Ashara was awake at first light. She leaned over to Danel and whispered. "Danel, are you awake? We should go look for Hamid."

"Yes, I am, but let's go first to the latrines. I'm sure Sister Helen's here by now."

When they exited their tent, they were surrounded as far as their eyes could see by a sea of white tents covered in a sandy dust that was indiscernible last night. They turned a full circle to take in the immensity of makeshift housing. No trees or shrubs dotted the landscape. They trekked first to the latrines and then to the front of the camp, looking for the nuns. Scanning the crowd, they concluded they were not there.

"We should go to the registration tent. They'll know if there've been any inquiries about us." As they walked over, Danel recognized Bethshari, still on duty, directing traffic.

"Bethshari, have you been here all night?"

"Yes, I came on about an hour before we met last night. Is this your wife?"

"Yes, pardon me, this is my wife Ashara."

Ashara nodded.

"I'm pleased to meet you. Did you find your son?"

"No, he didn't arrive last night, and we are coming to inquire about him now."

"I didn't see any nuns last night, but there's an information tent that deals with displaced persons. I would start with them." She pointed over to the far right, slightly toward the front of the camp.

"We'll head over there then. Perhaps they can suggest a course of action." Danel looked over to be sure he recognized the right tent.

"Let me know what you find out. I'll help with what I can."

The line was short, and they quickly moved to the front and entered the large tent. Inside were five lines of about twenty people, each of which queued up to a UN worker behind a metal counter. Large floor fans stationed at its four inside corners kept the warm air moving. Taking their place at the end of one of the lines, they waited patiently until finally their position had moved to the front.

"Next in line," said the clerk at the counter in front of their queue.

Danel took the lead. "We are looking for our infant son who was to arrive during the night in a UN van with about ten or twelve nuns. They would've asked for Danel or Ashara Ottawa."

The woman wore a tan hijab and the standard, light blue overshirt with the relief agency's logo. "Sir, no such party arrived during the night, at least since I've been on duty. Let me see if there's an inquiry registered in the computer." Her fingers clicked her through to the appropriate screen. "Now what is the name of the child."

"Hamid. Ottawa. O-T-T-A-W-A." Ashara responded eagerly.

"No one by that name is listed. When did you expect them?"

"Last night. They were traveling from Damascus in a UN van with about ten or twelve nuns from various NGOs."

"A UN van, you say?'

"Yes, they were traveling to Amman and were to detour to Za'atari to deliver our son."

"Why didn't your son travel with you?"

"We gave him up to the care of the nuns because gunmen were kidnapping and slaughtering Alawi babies." As Ashara became more distraught, tears threatened to brim over her lower lids.

"I'm so sorry. We've had many families last night reporting these incidents. But the UN van, there was something about that." She called over her shoulder to a short, dark-haired woman at the end of the counter. "Magda, what was that they were saying about the UN van from Damascus last night?"

"Something about the driver being beaten, but I don't recall any more than that. Mr. Cameron knew something about it, but he won't be in until noon."

"Could you phone him perhaps? We're desperate to learn about our son." Danel leaned forward, resting his forearms on the counter.

"I'm sorry. We've no way to reach him, but if you come back at noon you can speak to him yourself."

"Thank you. We'll come back then." Sensing Ashara gear up to argue, he guided Ashara out of the tent.

"Where's your spine? Surely they could have reached him if you'd persisted."

"Ashara, these people are all we have to help us. It serves no purpose to alienate them on our first day in the camp. My spine's where it always been, and I can see your mouth hasn't moved either."

"I seem to be the only one here who's concerned about Hamid." As her arrow hit its mark, a warmth bloomed across his face.

"You can't mean that. Can't you see that my heart's breaking too?" His tone matched her pitch. "Are you so self-absorbed that all you can think of is your own fear?" He paced back and forth in front of her. "Do you think that a father doesn't care as deeply for his child as the mother?"

"I didn't say that. I just meant. . . "

He cut her off. "You think when I attend to practical matters necessary for our survival that I have stopped caring about our son. One of us, Ashara, has got to keep our wits about us. If you'd had your way last night, we would've been walking back to Damascus looking for them." He then beheld his damage as she stood before him sobbing. "Is this what we do now? We accuse one another of unspeakable motives?"

"I'm so sorry. I didn't mean what I said."

"We're all we have now. We can't tear each other apart."

"I took out my frustration on you. How could I be so selfish?"

Pulling her to him, he hugged her so tightly she could hardly breathe. Her deep embrace returned his, and they swayed gently back and forth in the desert sun surrounded by strangers.

14

Without a Trace

The September desert sun had already driven the temperature to 32°C by ten o'clock. An ominous haze hung in the sky, and the air felt heavy with dust. A dry, steady breeze had come up abruptly from the north, its intensity suggesting an approaching shammal, formed as the air current passed over the Eurasian landmass. Refugees swept into the camp like waves approaching the shore from a distant horizon.

Bulldozers and heavy equipment could be heard in the distance beyond the camp's perimeter, like the din of bees about a hive. They prepared new roads and level ground for housing to accommodate the addition of upwards of a thousand refugees per day. The Ottawa's argument had been cathartic. Danel's practicality supplied a respite for his anxiety, but Ashara's longing for Hamid possessed her, refusing to be assuaged.

The two hours before Mr. Cameron would arrive could be filled acquiring their registration papers. They found their way to the tent that Bethshari had pointed out the evening before. Encountering a long line which snaked around behind the tent, they braced themselves for a long wait. The queue created two concentric circles, which moved in opposing directions, as one end was fed into the tent and the opposite end was augmented with new arrivals.

A young worker with a clipboard attempted to rearrange the queue that the refugees had self-organized. "Those of you who have received your registration appointment for the next hour should form a line over to the right. Everyone else should remain in the main line to be assigned an appointment." Moving back along the winding queue, she repeated the instructions like a carnival barker.

The refugees appeared numb, plotting small gains as they moved through the queue. Several near Danel and Ashara pulled out to reassemble in the line to the right. They exchanged looks with each other, all this just to secure a paper that would allow them to eat. Since they had already completed a full circle around the tent at about a meter a minute, he calculated they would be assigned an appointment and be on their way to see Mr. Cameron by noon. Their actual registration appointment would bring them back in four hours, just in time since the food they brought with them was almost gone.

"Please hurry. Mr. Cameron should be there in about ten minutes." Ashara widened her strides in anticipation.

"Slow down, Ashara, you'll trip if you aren't careful. I'm as eager as you are to meet with him."

She waited for Danel to catch up.

The queue outside the displacement tent had dissipated, but inside the tent were the same five lines from earlier, this time containing about ten people each.

"Ashara, let's stand in separate lines. We might get to the front faster in one than another." The administrator at the head of Danel's line recognized him immediately.

"You're right on time. Where's your wife?"

"She's over there." He beckoned to Ashara to join them.

"Mr. Cameron's here, but he had to go over to registration first. He should be right back. Have you received any word about your son yet?"

"No, nothing. We're very worried."

Ashara noted the woman's name tag, Fatima Abdulkarim. "The nuns we left him with had some formula, but not enough to last more than a day."

"You can wait over there, and I'll call you over when Mr. Cameron gets here."

Their wait was short lived, for soon a lanky, fortyish Englishman with a tousle of blond hair and a scraggly, reddish blond beard, entered the tent. His British accent was pronounced as he conversed with the woman who had assisted them. They could overhear her describe the circumstances of their inquiry as she motioned to point them out. His manner seemed affable, almost friendly. Mr. Cameron nodded his understanding and approached Danel and Ashara.

"I'm Phillip Cameron. I understand from Mrs. Abdulkarim that your son was traveling with the nuns in the UN van."

"Yes, that's correct. They were to arrive several hours after we did last evening, but they never showed up. We were told earlier today that you knew something about the UN van she was traveling in." Ashara's hope for real intelligence rested on the flimsy recollection of Magda, the woman at the far end of the counter earlier that morning.

"I only know what filtered to me when last evening's refugees came in. Dr. Ottawa, did you encounter the bandits raiding the cars traveling here?"

"Yes, that was our reason for entrusting our son to the nuns. We figured that they wouldn't be stopped. We're Alawi, and they were searching for Alawite children. We learned of their intent by accident as we waited for traffic congestion to clear."

Ashara leaned forward on tip toes. "A friend of ours, a nun, was traveling in the van and suggested that our son would be safer with them. That was the only reason we agreed to relinquish him. " She lowered her feet back to the ground. "I mean that we had no option."

"I don't know much. The bandits did stop a UN van, and reports were they beat the driver very badly. The nuns intervened and were able to disarm the men. That much I heard. There was one, described as heavy set, who took charge of the leader as the other nuns worked on the other men."

"That must've been Sister Helen." Danel knew her courage and determination too well not to recognize these actions as classic Sister Helen.

"But what of the child?" said Ashara.

"I know that at some point they tried to take the child, because one of the men was seen holding him, taunting one of the nuns who tried to take him back. But I have no knowledge of what happened after that. I could make some inquiry. Do you know where they were heading?"

Ashara gasped, visualizing little Hamid with the thugs they'd encountered.

Danel wrapped his arm around her shoulder. "They were originally traveling to Amman, although I never knew their exact destination. I assumed that since they were in a UN van that there was some kind of headquarters in Amman. But that may be an incorrect assumption, since all of the nuns were with NGOs. Za'atari seemed a short detour that would have taken them only a short distance out of the way."

"There are several UN offices in Amman. I can make some calls and see what I can uncover." Mrs. Ottawa, we'll do what we can. By the way, how old is the child?"

"Not yet five weeks" said Ashara.

"Would you describe him for me?"

"His eyes are a dark brown, and most of his birth hair is gone. His new hair is dark brown, only just growing back. His skin color is similar to ours."

"We would be very grateful." Speaking for both of them, Danel was keenly aware that in Za'atari without friends, relatives or resources, they were vulnerable and beholding to strangers like Phillip Cameron.

"Do you have any cell phone numbers for the driver or the nuns?"

"No, unfortunately, we've none."

"Do they have your number?"

"I think not. We only know the name of the nun, our friend who volunteered to help us by taking the child. Her name is Sister Helen."

"Why don't you come back in the morning about ten? I'll let you know if I've made any progress. Perhaps in the meantime they'll arrive, and you'll be reunited with your son. Then, of course, you must come back and introduce me to him." Ashara smiled at the prospect.

"We're very grateful for any help you can give us."

"Tomorrow then."

"Tomorrow."

The north wind assaulted their faces as they exited the tent, hurling small grains of sand and dust at their skin, their eyes squinting in defense. Other refugees had wrapped scarves around their faces and donned additional clothing to minimize their skin's exposure to the shammal. The wind howled, wending through the narrow footpaths between the tents, flapping against the sides, a relentless cacophony as the canvas sheets protested. The sand's vicious assault was the price paid for relief from the heat.

Ashara rearranged her hijab to cover her mouth, and rummaged through her purse for a spare, which she handed to Danel. He wrapped the cloth around his head, then covering his mouth.

"There's nothing more we can do about Hamid until tomorrow, but we've a lot to accomplish before he arrives." Danel was keen to divert her attention to more practical matters.

"I had thought we would watch for him. We can't risk missing him."

"Ashara, neither of us is going to stand around waiting in this gale. If the sand doesn't get us, our thoughts surely will. We have to find where we can access fresh water. Our food is almost gone, and we have to eat."

"It's just that he's so much on my mind."

Having no inclination to argue, he felt certain that their best course was to keep busy. "Plus, all of our things are still in the car."

"Do you remember where the car is parked?"

"I noted a utility pole when we drove in. It's almost a full kilometer from the entrance. We'll have to make several trips to get all our things." They turned right out of the main entrance past several Jordanian security officers, against the flow of incoming refugees. The cars, whose numbers had magnified exponentially from the night before, were now covered in thick layer of sand. Regardless of any car's color last night, this morning they were all the pale tan of the desert dust. Absent any organized direction when parked originally, thousands of cars were arranged in random, uneven rows on the desert floor outside the protective perimeter of the camp. Danel had mentally registered a large utility pole as a landmark the night before, but now in the daylight he realized that there were many such utility poles along the border fence.

Frustrated, they wandered through the sloppy aisles, systematically eliminating each utility pole. A sudden crash of glass, followed by the opening of a car door two aisles to their left, drew their attention to the dark blue Renault now covered in sand. Zigzagging through the cars obstructing his path, he left Ashara to tag along several meters behind him.

As he came upon the car from the front, the rear door on the driver's side stood open, blocking his access. A suitcase and its disemboweled contents were strewn on the ground, and the vandal was inside the car rummaging through another suitcase.

Danel closed the door enough to pass and yelled directly into the vehicle. "Hey, you! Get out of there!" Startled, a young man in his late teens leapt out of the car at Danel with his fist drawn. A solid right jab to Danel's lower lip and jaw threw him into the adjacent car. Ashara had come up from the back of the car, trapping the youth between them. Reacting instinctively, she pummeled him repeatedly with her purse until he shoved her aside to disappear into the maze of cars. Recovering from the punch, Danel started to pursue when Ashara caught his arm as he tried to move past her.

"Out of the question. He might have a gun." Discretion overruling his valor, he abandoned pursuit.

"Ashara, are you alright?"

"It appears I'm better than you." A large bruise covering his chin and jaw was establishing itself, and fresh blood oozed from a slit in his lip. Taking a handkerchief from her purse, she dabbed his lip. He jerked back as it pressed sand grains into the open cut.

"I better do that." He took the cloth from her hand, applying it gingerly to stanch the flow.

"Get back into the car out of this wind."

As he climbed into the driver's seat, she gathered their belongings that had been trampled in the tussle and threw them into the back seat before closing the car door and getting into the passenger seat. The grainy torrent of sand beat at the windows and filtered into the back seat through the broken window. A thin layer of sand had already coated the articles in the back seat.

"Allah is testing us. Is it not enough that Hamid is missing? Now this man breaks into our car to steal from us."

His swollen lip slurred his speech. "This is the work of man, not Allah. These're just things."

"They're not just things. It's all we have left to help us survive here."

"You know, just sitting here like this, I wish that we could just turn on the ignition and drive home."

"Yes, and I would feed Hamid and rock him, and then he'd be asleep by the time we got home."

"I'd carry him into his crib and lay him down gently so as not to wake him, and we'd stand there watching him sleep." His eyes glassed over, longing for those times, but they were enjoined to Za'atari as the reconnoiter point for Hamid. As though snapped out of hypnosis, he sighed deeply. "Let's gather our things up and put them back into the suitcases. I'll carry what I can, but you should stay with the car to guard that no more is stolen. It'll take longer with just one of us carrying, but at least we can preserve what we have left."

"What if someone tries to steal our things from the tent? Maybe I should help you carry the first load and then stay in the tent."

"You have a point, but since we had a break in here, let's at least protect what we know to be the more vulnerable place at the moment. We can't be in two places at once."

His repeated treks back to their tent, taking 20 minutes each way. On the final load, they carried the last two boxes back to the tent together, leaving them just enough time to make their 4:00 registration appointment.

Sand grains were embedded into the coagulated blood on Danel's lip. Taking a clean towel out of one of the suitcases, she poured some water from the plastic bags she had used to keep the thermal bag cold. Danel sat crossed legged on the mattress as Ashara knelt beside him, cleaning the wound.

"I have some antiseptic in the medical bag over there." He gestured at the black backpack against the back wall.

"How's your jaw? You need some ice."

"No, problem. I think there's some in the refrigerator. Oh wait, we don't have a refrigerator."

Routing through the medical bag, she found a bottle of tincture of iodine and a sterile cotton swab. "Very funny, Dr. Ottawa. Let's see if your sense of humor will carry you through the sting of this iodine."

Wincing, he pulled back as the iodine penetrated the wound her gentle scrubbing had opened.

"Your jaw already has quite a bruise. How does it feel?'

"Sore, but I don't think anything is broken."

"Do you feel up to keeping the registration appointment?"

"Of course."

Ashara extended her hand to help Danel up. Wrapping clean scarves around their heads and faces, they changed into thicker clothing that protected all exposed skin. As they left the tent, they lowered their faces to minimize the wind's assault and held each other by the arm as they headed into the wind towards the registration tent to become official residents of Za'atari.

The line for the actual appointment was more manageable. They queued up outside the tent for only twenty minutes before entering its protective shell. Once inside, they made it to the front of their feeder line in only ten minutes. The young man registering them started as he observed Danel's face.

"Next in line. Sir, are you alright? That's quite a bruise you have there."

"I'm fine. We came upon a vandal ransacking our car, and he left me this little gift."

"That's quite a gift. Were you able to return the favor?"

"Unfortunately, he fled before I could reciprocate."

"Do you have your appointment document?" Ashara pulled it out of her purse and handed it to the man.

Now with a computer screen in front of him, he typed in their names as written on the appointment form.

"Any children residing with you?"

"Just our infant son, but he hasn't yet arrived."

"Then we can't add him to your registration." Without looking up, he typed in "none" and moved to the next data line on his form.

"But he'll be with us shortly." Ashara bristled at his official exclusion of Hamid from the listing.

"I'm sorry. We use these records not only for identification but also for reporting occupation statistics in the camp. We're not permitted to count anyone until they actually arrive in the camp. Counting you as a family of three would give you extra rations."

Danel observed the storm cloud brewing in Ashara' demeanor: the stiffening in her back, the slight rise on her toes as she leaned on the counter and an escalation in her voice's pitch that would surface with the next words she spoke if he did not intervene. "Sir, will it be a problem to add our son to the registration papers once he arrives?"

"No, that will be an easy matter. In fact, as soon as he comes in, come directly to the appointment line, and we will help you right away. You shouldn't have to wait."

Ashara backed down to a flat-footed status. This formality of not counting Hamid stung like the iodine she had applied to Danel's swollen lip. For the UN worker behind the counter, the infant's absence merely rendered him an uncountable statistic. For Ashara, not counting Hamid galvanized his missing person status into her very identity: *devoted mother, childless, broken hearted.*

Danel answered the remaining questions. Soon a hum from a large, shared printer behind the counter spewed out an official registration document. A prepackaged box of relief items, a welcome gift of sorts, containing a blanket, a bucket for hauling water, plastic water bottles to store water and some cooking utensils appeared on the counter.

Now officially registered, they located the rations distribution tent and waited in yet another line to collect their initial rations of rice, beans, vegetable oil, salt and sugar, calculated to provide about 2,200 calories per person per day, enough to last the two of them for a week if they were frugal. The camp had a market where local vegetables and fruit could be purchased, and they were able to buy some peppers and onions.

An outdoor cook stove was provided with the tent, and Ashara prepared the ingredients for their evening meal in a covered skillet from one of the boxes they brought with them. Emptying two suitcases, he created a V-shaped break front around the stove, which he draped with a blanket to protect the gas flame and the skillet contents from the wind and sand.

Ashara extinguished the flame and carried the meal back into the tent. They were both very hungry, but lowered their heads to thank Allah for the sustenance and invoke his blessing on Hamid, Sister Helen and the other van occupants.

Later that evening, Bethshari stopped by their tent. The shammal followed its typical pattern of quieting to a gentle breeze in the evening, resting for the next day, which would renew the vicious wind. Ashara sat on a blanket under the entrance canopy outside the tent.

"Ashara, I've been looking for you. Did you receive any word about your son?"

"Nothing yet. Mr. Cameron's making some inquiries, but we'll have to wait until the morning to reconnect with him."

"The waiting must be very hard on you."

"Yes, it is. I miss him sorely. Not knowing where he is tortures us. One of the hardest things is knowing that I willingly gave up my child and put him in harm's way."

"You can't think that. Other parents that night who didn't have your option kept their children with them and were overcome."

Hearing the two women talking, Danel came out to join them. "You're very kind to inquire about our son, Bethshari. I'm sure you've heard your share of very sad stories here in the camp."

"Yes, I have, and many are very sad, but many are uplifting too. I've seen how resourceful and hopeful people remain, and it inspires me to work on their behalf."

"How did you come to be here?"

"My father and my mother work for the UN as interpreters. I learned Arabic from them at home in Manchester, England. They exposed me from the time I was a little girl to the political winds and the suffering of the common man caught in the cross hairs."

"Ashara often remarks that none of this is of our making," said Danel.

"That's so true. It was my father, actually, who opened the door for me to come here. My mother thought it wasn't safe, but she reluctantly supported me."

"Do you find that there are those who can cheerfully bear this situation?" Ashara wrestled with her own acceptance.

"I find that each must chose his own view of the world around him. That choice for some makes the difference between their survival in these conditions and those who'll succumb to bitterness and resentment, which eats you from the inside out. I look to the children for hope."

"How's that?" said Danel.

"I watch them play and adapt to these surroundings, insulated by the cocoon of childhood. Despite these conditions, they find a way to laugh."

"Would you care to have a cup of tea?" said Ashara.

"Another time I would like that very much. But I have to report for duty in fifteen minutes."

"You're welcome anytime."

"Forgive me, but I also had a selfish reason for coming. I thought perhaps I could come tomorrow, if your son hasn't arrived of course, and introduce you to Dr. Abu Majeed. He's from Lebanon. He's not a refugee, but came to the camp to help and now manages the incoming doctors. Za'atari is easier to bear if one can be useful."

"We hope our son will arrive tomorrow, but if not, we should be glad to meet Dr. Majeed," said Danel.

"Good." She looked at her watch. "Ashara, there are many children who have come here unaccompanied. Their parents send them ahead until they themselves can come. Sadly some parents never make it here. We could use some help with them if you're willing, and we also need teachers for the school here."

"I would consider this later, but right now my main concern is my son."

"As you wish. What is your son's name?"

"Hamid."

"Hamid. That's a good name. Its Arabic meanings of thankful and highly praised indicates that you named him well. Until tomorrow then."

"Thank you for checking on us. We'll see you tomorrow," said Danel as they watched Bethshari disappear around the corner into the next row of tents.

15

Crumbs Along the Trail

With the shammal's ferocity now calmed to a whimper, the accompanying temperature drop afforded a pleasant soft breeze that blew through the tent window. Although the wind had died, the air was still dust laden. Evening coughs and wheezing of inhabitants replaced daytime's windy howl and the steady buzz from the bulldozers. As darkness descended, Ashara and Danel retired to their mattresses, gazing through the canvas's opening at the sliver of moon beginning the new journey of its next phase. Somewhere out there were Hamid, Sister Helen and the other nuns, rendered elusive even though watched by the same celestial sentinel. Eyes wide open, they lay examining the course of the day now past.

"Ashara, are you asleep yet?" he whispered.

"Not yet. Hamid's face haunts me. He's everywhere: in my heart, my thoughts, my soul, everywhere but here."

"Do you mind if I talk?"

"No, go ahead, as tired as I am, my mind refuses to rest."

"I find myself wondering now about Sister Helen. I know you've had your doubts from the beginning, but now even I wonder if all this was a plan." Pausing at the crunch of sandy footsteps and muffled voices going past their tent, he waited for them to pass. "What if she kidnapped him? She could be out of the country by now." Ordinarily, he would resist exposing such a thought to Ashara, but its possibility smoldered and needed the air of another to either ignite or be smothered.

"The possibility occurred to me as well. She confided to me that she once had a child, before she took her vows. Her parents insisted she give up him for adoption because she was unmarried. I believe she still aches for that child and suspect that Hamid is her surrogate." Under other circumstances, the conversation of parents across pillows might discuss a child's bout with cold or which school he should attend.

"You never told me this."

"I felt it was her private affair. Maybe I should've told you so you would've understood my misgivings. Surely you saw she coveted him. That was what the baptism was all about. Wasn't it obvious to you?"

"No, it wasn't obvious. I believed her reason: that the baptism was the only gift she had to give Hamid. She loved little babies and got attached to Hamid. That's what I saw. I thought you were being paranoid."

"Paranoid? Well, where's our son, the child who has disappeared without a trace?"

"Do you blame this on Sister Helen? She couldn't have arranged for their driver to be beaten. She was the one who volunteered to put herself and the others in danger to save Hamid."

"Yes, and she was very quick to suggest it, wasn't she? A perfect ruse to get him away from us."

"Ashara, that's enough. We have no proof of this. Painting her as a villainess won't help."

"Your propensity to believe the best about others handicaps you. You've always been quick to side with her."

"Forgive me for bringing this up just as we are trying to fall asleep. I needed to get this out in the open between us."

"We've argued enough about Sister Helen. I just want our son back."

"I know that the wiser course is to wait for real intelligence about their whereabouts. Without any real clue, we would be searching for seed like a blind chicken. Yet I feel emasculated by my own powerlessness."

"What's frustrating is that those who can help us don't understand our urgency."

Though it was too dark to see, he rolled over to face her. "I'm sorry I didn't believe you about Sister Helen. Can you forgive me?"

"Of course. You felt as you did based on what you knew of her. Your reaction was appropriate, though not insightful. " Leaning across the mattress, she groped for his hand, drawing it up to her lips to brush a soft kiss across his bent knuckles. "We should pray together. We need Allah to keep us strong and get us through this."

"Are you alright if I say our invocation aloud?"

"Yes, please."

O Allah, all knowing and all seeing. Cast Your protection over our little son and those whose care surrounds him. In Your name, we surrender our acceptance to Your wishes, for You are all wise and all powerful. We pray for Hamid's safe return and the good and honorable intentions of his caregivers. O, all powerful Allah, strengthen our resolve and that of others to locate him. Shore up our characters to expect the best intentions of others, and grant us courage to rest our faith in You. This we pray, O Allah, on this night of supplication. We are nothing without You and beg for Your divine intervention.

Watching the slim curved wedge of the fingernail moon suspended in the gauzy haze of the desert sky through the canvas opening, Ashara listened to his words. "Your words are at one with those in my heart. May our pain and supplication speak eloquently for us, for I know that all-loving Allah sees our misfortune." Soon, the tension in their bodies slackened through their prayerful supplication to finally surrender to a deep sleep.

The second day, the gale started early, initially sprinkling sand grains through the window and then coating them and the mattresses with a fine layer of dust. The grit insinuated itself into Danel's dream. He was wandering in the desert alone, blinded by the sand, searching for water, when he lay down to rest. Every position his body took ground the abrasive dust into his pores. Finally he woke, brushing the sand off his face, and closed the window flap. *Even in sleep*, he thought, *the sand finds its way in.* He could hear others moving about outside, and the smell of the neighbor's breakfast wafted in.

Two children across the path squabbled over a ball, and their mother intervened by confiscating it. "When you have learned how to share, you'll get your ball back. Now take this jug and go fetch some water." The youngsters argued over who was at fault as they trudged off to the water supply.

Ashara sat up and pursed her lips, spitting "pigh pigh" into an imaginary spittoon until all of the invasive grains were gone from her tongue and lips. "Ah, the sand is all over me." As she pulled her tousled hair back from her face, sand sifted through the strands, falling onto her breasts and down her nightdress. Dressing quickly to cover her skin, she covered her hair with a pale pink hijab. The evening before, she had packed towels and toiletries into two backpacks so they could shower when they woke. It would be the first shower since the night before Danel went to purchase the car. Today she thought they should do something to keep the sand out of the car's broken window.

He watched her dress. "Today, Ashara, I'm hoping that we'll get our son back." His renewed optimism buoyed her. Donning their backpacks, they headed to the latrines.

Both waited in a line for the shower. In the women's line, a mother in front of her, perhaps five years older, held a small baby on her hip.

Ashara asked the child's age, estimating it was close to Hamid's.

"Would you mind if I held him? I have a son this age, but he hasn't yet arrived here."

Smiling, she shifted the baby to Ashara. "Where is your son?"

"We were traveling here two nights ago when the bandits were accosting families looking for infants."

"Yes, the news of that is all over the camp. Did they get your son?"

"We don't know. We entrusted him to a friend, a nun, traveling in a UN van, but the van has disappeared."

"I'm sorry. I hope that he's safe and you'll see him soon. Are you still breastfeeding?"

"Yes, and that concerns me since I can feel my own milk decreasing. I'm worried it will dry up before he gets here." The line had progressed with only two others ahead of them. "I sent only enough formula for maybe a day with the nuns." A shower opened up so the woman took back her infant, hurrying off to the stall. Midway she stopped and called back. "My name is Rachel Bakir. My tent is on the southwest side. Registration can tell you how to find me if you want to talk."

"Thanks. I'm Ashara Ottawa." A stall then became available for Ashara. Showering quickly, she did not see the woman before leaving to meet Danel.

"Disgusting. Things are not sanitary in there. Next time when we shower we should cover our feet. People are defecating in the shower." She shuddered her disgust. "There is no attendant and the women are just not cleaning up after themselves. Soap scum is thick over the faucets and the washbasins. Hair clogs the shower drains. I stood in filthy water up to my ankles, and the commodes are buzzing with flies taking refuge from the wind."

"The men's facilities are no better."

"I met a woman, Rachel Bakir, while I was waiting in line. She had a child with her about Hamid's age and she let me hold him. I closed my eyes and smelled him, imagining he was Hamid."

They walked back holding hands, Ashara savoring the brief moments holding another's child, and Danel mulling over their conversation last evening about Sister Helen.

Back in the tent, she opened a container that held the remnants of last night's meal, a mixture of rice, peppers and onions. They ate quickly out of the same container, both eager to see what Mr. Cameron learned yesterday. Winding their way through the footpaths toward the front of the camp, they found a tsunami of refugees had just entered the grounds, their bodies hunkered, slanting against the driving wind. The new arrivals milled about, gathering their bearings like ants swarming atop a mound.

Bethshari was organizing and conducting the foot traffic along with two other men with megaphones, barking out information, sorting and directing the refugees to relieve the congestion at the entrance. Her skin was entirely covered, save a small area around her eyes which she protected with a pair of sunglasses. Her hair was sequestered in a tan hijab that she had pulled up to mask her mouth and nose. Spying Danel and Ashara crossing her path, she called out over the wind's low growl. "Any word yet?"

"Not yet, but we are on our way to see Mr. Cameron."

"Good luck. I'm sending good thoughts to you." Acknowledging her with a wave, they entered the displaced persons tent.

Danel spotted Mr. Cameron right off at the steel counter. "Mr. Cameron, Phillip, did you find out anything?"

"Ah, good morning, Danel, Ashara." He extended a firm handshake to Danel and then tipped an imaginary cap to Ashara. "Come back to my office so we can talk more privately." Gesturing for them to sit down, he took his seat behind his desk. "There are several UN facilities in Amman. It took me a while to find the one that handled the collection vans."

Ashara leaned forward expectantly.

"Several drivers were sent four or five days ago to collect UN and NGO workers throughout Syria. Two of the vans are still unaccounted for, one is probably carrying your son and the nuns, but we're not sure which it is. The drivers are equipped with radios and cell phones. We can't be sure at this point if the van with the beaten driver is the one carrying your son or the other. Both vans were expected last night."

"Did they try to reach the drivers?"

"Yes, but neither are responding.

"What can we do?"

"There is not much to do until they hear from one of the drivers."

Danel and Ashara looked at each other; their thoughts swung like a pendulum between the best and the worst.

"You can come back in the morning and perhaps they will've learned more. I'm sorry I can't offer much more than that."

Danel shifted in his seat and leaned forward. "It is very hard to just wait. We want to do something, but don't know where to start."

"We've notified the Jordanian authorities, as well as the Syrian authorities."

Aghast, Ashara covered her mouth at the mention of the Syrian authorities.

Mr. Cameron noticed her concern. "I wouldn't worry too much about the Syrian authorities. They'll cooperate since we're searching for a van full of NGO workers who are nuns. Our biggest worry with them is that finding an infant or a van of nuns will not be a priority, given their hands are full dealing with the insurgency."

"For them it is such a small matter, but for us it is our whole world." Ashara's earnest gaze held his until he looked away.

"We appreciate what you are doing to help us. Would you take down our tent location in case you learn something?" said Danel.

Phillip pulled a small spiral pad out of his breast pocket and took down the general location, lane and tent number.

Disheartened, they left with more questions than before they entered.

"Danel, if they didn't go to Amman, where could they have gone? A whole van of nuns doesn't just disappear unless something bad occurred. That van driver was not happy about the detour to Za'atari."

"We can't assume that they were harmed. Perhaps they got lost."

"There is but one highway to Amman. Don't be ridiculous."

"Perhaps the detour to Za'atari threw them off."

"We took the road here ourselves. It would have been very difficult to miss it. All we had to do was follow the car in front of us."

Frustrated that he had no better answers, he stopped walking. "Would you have me join you in thinking our son is dead?"

"That's not what I meant."

"I can't let my mind go there until I have some evidence that harm has come to him. I trust Sister Helen to make sure that doesn't happen."

"You can do that, but there are many things that even Sister Helen can't control."

"We'll go insane with this waiting if we don't keep occupied. Maybe today we should meet Dr. Majeed that Bethshari mentioned. What do you think?"

"Perhaps."

They spent the rest of the day exploring the camp, including the bread line. Now in possession of their registration certificate, they stood in line for an hour waiting for one rationed loaf. They were able to buy some meat at the market along with some grapes. The tedium of long lines was a part of every endeavor, yet the lack of refrigeration meant they could only buy enough food to last through its unrefrigerated shelf life.

"I'm considering working in their hospital. What do you think? It could bring us a little money to buy what we need."

"You can if it will keep your mind off things. At least you'd be useful."

"What about you? Would you consider helping with the children who come here unaccompanied?"

"I'm not sure I could be much good to anyone with Hamid on my mind."

"What if we don't find him for months? You have to keep busy."

"A couple of months?" she halted. Extending her hands in front of her chest, she looked heavenward and then back at him. "He won't know me in a couple of months. What if I couldn't recognize him or he fell into someone's hands other than Sister Helen's?"

"We would recognize him, I'm sure."

Frowning, she considered the dramatic physical changes that occur in a baby's first months. "Well, even if we didn't recognize him, DNA tests can be used to make an identification, right?"

"I am sure that isn't going to be necessary."

"But they can do it these days, can't they?"

"Yes, it's doable, but not many places have that capability."

Ashara observed the flicker of concern cross Danel's face.

"But a couple of months is ridiculous. We'll find him long before Hamid will have changed enough that we would not recognize him."

Later that afternoon Bethshari led Dr. Abu Majeed to their tent. A thin young boy with a bowl haircut, about ten years old, accompanied her. His thick dark bangs drooped over a lovely pair of pale gray eyes framed in thick dark lashes.

"Danel. Ashara," She called above the howl into the tent.

Exiting through the flap, Danel ducked slightly, smiling when he recognized Bethshari. Ashara followed behind.

Bethshari introduced the Ottawa's to Dr. Majeed, an extraordinarily handsome man in his early forties, tall and lean with large hands and tapered fingers.

"Please call me Abu." He extended his hand to Danel.

She next introduced her young friend, Saeed.

Bowing slightly, Saeed extended his hand western style to Danel and nodded respectfully to acknowledge Ashara. "I'm pleased to meet you." Saeed shadowed Bethshari as a self-appointed aide, leading new families to registration or tent distribution. His mastery of who lived where and the shortest path to anywhere, gained while running errands for Bethshari, was an asset.

"Likewise." Danel shook the youngster's hand.

"Saeed is my shadow and unofficial aide. His mother sent him ahead to Za'atari to wait for her while she cared for her aging parents." Bethshari hoped that meeting Saeed might soften Ashara's resolve not to assist until their son arrived.

"Do you have other family here?" said Ashara.

"No, my father and brother were killed in a bomb raid. My mother and grandparents are all I have left."

"I understand from Bethshari that you're a surgeon, Dr. Ottawa." Abu Majeed's manner was comfortable, even affable. He clasped his hands expectantly in front of him, hunching his shoulders slightly up and forward, conveying a warm eagerness to know them.

"Please call me Danel. Yes, I practiced at a hospital in Damascus, but we fled several days ago with our son."

"Bethshari told me of your misfortune, but you're expecting your son very soon. Is that correct?"

"We're very hopeful that his delay will be short lived. The authorities are doing what they can to locate him."

"I was hoping that while you are waiting, we could tempt you into helping at the hospital infirmary. We're very short handed, and right now we only have one surgeon. We can pay you, not much of course, but it would make your life here in the camp easier. You could buy some necessities."

The football, confiscated earlier by their mother, suddenly escaped the neighbor children and bounded into their midst. Danel instinctively trapped the errant ball and passed it to the older boy.

"Ah, I see you play football, Danel."

He laughed. "Well, I've been seen a time or two on the pitch."

"We have a field marked off beyond the camp where some of the men play. Perhaps you would join us sometime."

"Yes, I'd like that."

"Good then. I look forward to learning if you're a better surgeon than you are a footballer."

"I can save you the wait, Abu. My surgical skills far outstrip my moves on the pitch, although I've been known to have a good day here or there."

"What position do you play?"

"I'm comfortable as a striker. But I must warn you that our lives in Damascus left very little time for honing my skills."

"Ah, so you like to score. Very good. Our infirmary is over on the east side. Bethshari or Saeed can direct you there, or ask any one of the workers or security officers. Please do stop by tomorrow and tour our facility."

"I look forward to it."

"Mrs. Ottawa, we would like you to come as well and see what we have here. Perhaps you might want to help us."

"Dr. Majeed, you are too kind."

"Nonsense. Call me Abu."

"And you can call me Ashara. I can't offer my help now because we're expecting our son, but perhaps I can accompany my husband before he arrives."

"I look forward to seeing you both."

Bethshari winked at Danel and Ashara as they left. Once out on the path, Bethshari and Saeed walked with Dr. Majeed a short distance before he made his way back to the infirmary.

"Is this the lady you told me lost her baby?" said Saeed once they left Dr. Majeed.

"Saeed, you and I are going to get her to help other children here. Don't tell a soul. That'll be our secret. Are you in?"

"I'm in, but why doesn't she want to help?"

"Her little baby is missing and that is all she thinks about. It's probably like your mother right now. She knows she can't get to you, but she thinks about you all the time. Does that make sense?"

"Yes, I think about her all the time, but when I'm helping you I don't think about her as much."

"That's exactly why we want to get Mrs. Ottawa to help the children. Then she won't think about her baby as much."

"What're we going to do now?"

"You, my young friend, are going to go to the children's tent, and I'm going home. But, I'll see you tomorrow."

A shadow of disappointment moved across his face, like a high, passing cloud over the desert floor, as he watched Bethshari pass outside the entrance and disappear into the flow of refugees.

16

Sole Focus

The news from Phillip Cameron on the third day revealed nothing further. Authorities were still searching, but with other priorities, the progress was slow. Their patience chafed at another day of waiting.

"Danel, are you so positive that we can't do better on our own?"

"I've thought this through many times, but without resources we don't have a place to start. We don't even have a base where those that are continuing to search could contact us. At least here we have that. As much as I hate the uncertainty, I think we are better off waiting for the authorities to do the work. If we go back to Damascus, my fate is uncertain, and we might hurt Hamid's chances of being discovered. Tell me if you've a better plan. I'm truly open to anything you can suggest."

"If I'd a plan, you would have heard it long ago. Our feet are planted in cement. As strange as you may find this, I actually believe that if Sister Helen has kidnapped him, he is in good hands. Despite her coveting him, I've never doubted her love for him."

His thoughts mirrored hers. They had no choice but to tread water for another day until Phillip reported the next morning. "Let's stop by the hospital and look at the facilities. That will help us take our minds off this for a short while."

Making their way to the entrance of the camp, they met Saeed playing al ghomaid with some other children. He had just tagged another boy and was removing his blindfold when he spied Danel and Ashara.

"Dr. Ottawa, it's me, Saeed. Bethshari's helper. Remember?" A wide grin spread across his face as he ran up.

"Hello there, Saeed. I see that Bethshari gives you some time off then?" said Danel.

"Well, she doesn't come until later today because she starts on a different shift. I'm waiting for her now. They make me sleep when she's working the late night duty." Saeed tossed his blindfold to his friend. As he ran over, Danel noticed a limp that he had not seen last night.

"Saeed, what happened to your leg?"

"You mean my limp? I got that when the bombs hit in our village in Dara'a. I was with my father and my brothers going to the market, but they were killed right away. I was the lucky one."

"I'm sorry. I didn't know."

"It's alright. I miss them, but I can still run and work. You really don't need a straight leg for that. It doesn't hurt." He hopped up and down like a jumping jack and then slapped his thigh for emphasis. "See? Are you looking for Bethshari?"

"No, actually we are on the way to the hospital where Dr. Majeed works. Can you tell me where it is?"

"I'll show you." Without hesitation, he grabbed Ashara's hand to lead her. The hospital, made of prefab materials, was one of the few hard-walled structures in the camp. Danel was struck by its large footprint, with a second story where all structures were single level. Patients and families moved in and out of its entrance.

With an authoritative swagger, Saeed approached the duty nurse with Danel and Ashara in tow. "This is Dr. Ottawa and his wife. They're here to see Dr. Majeed."

"Ah, I see Bethshari occasionally lends you out for concierge duties. Do they have an appointment?" No stranger to Saeed's managerial talents, she played along.

"Bethshari is not yet here today. These are my friends, and Dr. Ottawa is considering working here."

The young nurse with a French accent and a floral hijab diverted her address to the Ottawas. "Welcome. Are you newly arrived?" Her warmth was genuine, tinged with enthusiasm for a new addition to their short supply of physicians.

"Yes, we came three days ago. Bethshari's made it her business to get us connected with Dr. Majeed."

"That's just like her." She gestured toward Saeed. "And when she's not here, she leaves her henchman to work on her behalf." He beamed at the acknowledgement. Admonished by his mother to make himself useful before she sent him to the camp, he had taken her advice to heart.

"Let me see if Dr. Majeed is in his office." Eager to bear the news of her prize to Dr. Majeed, she briskly passed through a swinging door down a narrow corridor. Danel could hear three knocks on a door before the door swung back into position, quivering several times before it came to rest.

In what seemed like less than a minute, Abu Majeed burst through the doors with the duty nurse trailing. "I'm delighted to see you. How wonderful, you have brought your wife. Good morning, Ashara." He extended his hand warmly to both of them, oozing grace and ease, as though they were long-lost friends. "These are humble facilities, but we accomplish much because of the dedication of our workers. Za'atari's newly opened, and we only have this hospital and several primary care locations so far to care for our rapidly expanding population." He swept his arm across the large waiting area. "More facilities are planned, but we are very dependent on the UNHCR and their partners for funding."

A cacophony of coughs filled the room, already crowded with patients, while sick children, as well as those too young to leave unattended in their tents, played. Dr. Majeed led them back through the double doors, past a series of examining rooms, to a large open patient care area, where privacy was afforded by curtains suspended on metal rods. Every available area was occupied. On the second floor were the surgical facilities, which Danel assessed as basic yet adequate.

"We're equipped to handle not only minor emergencies, coughs and colds, but births and other surgeries such as hysterectomies, appendectomies. Some more complicated surgeries we have to send to a hospital in Amman because we don't have sufficient staff to accommodate the needs."

They listened intently as Abu showed them through.

"Particularly problematic are the respiratory ailments, often very critical in the young and the elderly, which are exacerbated by the heat and the dry dusty desert climate. We have only a limited number of surgeons at this point, so you would be a welcome addition." Dr. Majeed winked at his presumption.

"What about antisepsis? I'm sure this is a challenge, especially when the shammal is blowing?" said Danel.

"Your arrival at the start of this shammal has already exposed you to its cruelty I see."

"Yes, we've had enough of it, but it has not had enough of us yet. How long will it last?"

"That all depends on weather patterns in the far north, but they can last seven up to eleven days."

"Let's hope this one will be short lived then," said Ashara.

"Sometimes they just peter out, but other times they're doused by a great rain, which causes more hardship here."

They had come full circle and were now back on the first floor in Majeed's office. "How would you assess the health of Za'atari's inhabitants?" said Danel.

"Ah, that's a good question. Many come here injured or already sick. Last night we admitted a 38-year-old man who'd been severely burned in a bombing raid. He came from Dara'a, where medical care and facilities are greatly debilitated or almost absent. He traveled by car for about three hours, and then his friends loaded him onto a mattress and carried him across fields and desert to get here."

"It must have been hard for you to leave your practice in Lebanon to come here. You're to be commended on your dedication to helping others," said Ashara.

"Yes, it was hard for me to leave Lebanon and come to the desert. Once you have lived on the coast, all other places are found wanting." A wistful cloud passed momentarily across his face at the mention of home. "But it is nothing compared to the suffering of these people. What's your specialty, Danel? I'm a pediatrician by training, but here I am a general practitioner."

"I'm a general surgeon. Working in Damascus once the bombing began drove many of our surgical staff away. I've had to perform many different procedures, although I've had little practice with plastic surgery."

"If you join us, you'll add general practitioner to your résumé in addition to your specialty." Again he winked, almost jovially, captivating his visitors with his charm. "Such versatility is most welcome here. Some of the plastic surgeries we can send off site to Amman, although their resources are very stretched. Ashara, if we can convince Danel to join us, perhaps you would like to work here as well. What did you do in Damascus?"

"I worked for the ministry, in finance. Your offer is very enticing, and I would very much like to help. But right now I'm focused on getting our son back. I'm afraid that I wouldn't be much good to anyone until he's safe here with us."

"I see." Abu Majeed, a man unaccustomed to refusal, mentally catalogued her excuse as one he could overcome at a later time.

"But once he arrives, I would like very much to help if I could bring my son with me to work."

"Quite a number of our workers are mothers who do just that. So your son, what is his name?"

"Hamid."

"Yes, Hamid will be very welcome here."

"So then, Danel, can we expect you tomorrow?"

"I would need time when necessary to accompany Ashara to see Phillip Cameron who is handling our search. I assume that would be alright?"

"Of course." They agreed that Danel would come back in the morning for an orientation and arranging the proper papers. They shook hands. "We have a deal then."

"Indeed we do."

Saeed was waiting for them when they made their way back into the waiting room. "I can take you where you need to go. Where to next?" His energy and gregarious manner were captivating. He immediately grabbed Ashara's hand to lead them out into the wind.

"We're going to see Mr. Cameron next, but we can find our way," said Danel.

Ashara, who had said very little during the tour, found her voice. "Saeed, Bethshari told us that your mother didn't accompany you to Za'atari. Where is she?"

"When my father and my brother were killed by the bomb, our house was blown up. My mother was at my grandparents helping them at the time. They're too old to travel and both are very sick. My mother had to stay and take care of them."

"Why didn't you stay with her?"

"She wouldn't let me. I begged her. After our house was blown up, my mother was afraid for me. She's like that: afraid for me, but not for herself. She put me on the bus and told me to come here and make a home for when she is able to come. I'm the man in the family now."

"Are there many children here who came without their parents?"

"Yes, I have lots of company."

A shiver glanced across her shoulders. "I'm sure your mother is very proud of you. How long have you been here?"

"It's been about six months."

"Have you heard from your mother?"

"Oh yes, at first she wrote me several times a week. Then the letters were once a week. She was very busy with my grandparents. But I haven't heard anything for at least a month. My grandparents must be very sick."

Danel made a mental note to ask Bethshari about Saeed's mother and grandparents later. But for now preoccupation with their meeting with Phillip Cameron took precedence. "Saeed, we'll see you later I'm sure."

"Don't worry, I'll find you." Saeed called over his shoulder as he skipped off to join a circle of boys kicking a football in a passing and trapping drill.

The visit with Phillip Cameron proved once again a disappointment, replete with reassurances that the authorities were doing all that they could. Sensitive to their longing and his own inadequacy to remedy it, he expressed the customary apologies and told them to come back in the morning.

Later that afternoon Mr. Cameron received a call from the UN office that had coordinated the evacuation of all NGO personnel from Syria. Hanging up, he immediately bounded out of the tent, past milling refugees and various queues toward Danel and Ashara's tent.

"Danel, Ashara, we have some news." Phillip was out of breath and clearing his throat to recover from a dust-induced wheeze as they hurried outside to meet him.

As the sand grains peppered their faces, Ashara guided him into the tent out of the wind. "Yes, what news? Have they found Hamid?"

"Not exactly. We learned that the driver was beaten so badly that they didn't think that he would survive the journey into Jordan. So they turned around and headed back to Damascus to a hospital on the south side which was closer. One of the nuns drove the van. The UN driver was in a coma for several days, and the nuns had no idea where they were to be taken since the driver had all that information. When he came to, he was able to tell them what agency office to notify."

"So did the nuns then travel to Amman?"

"That was the plan, but headquarters does not want to accept liability for the nuns driving the van themselves, so they have sent for another driver to take them to Amman."

"Can they make a detour to deliver our son to us here in Za'atari?" Ashara shifted eagerly from foot to foot.

"That's just the thing. Your son isn't with them. A nun named Sister Helen told them that it was her responsibility to get the infant to Za'atari as soon as possible, so she decided not to wait for the driver. She was to hire a car or a taxi to take them."

"That's very dangerous. Didn't they try to stop her?" said Ashara.

"From what I understand, she would hear nothing about an alternate plan. She said his parents would be worried sick and that she'd promised to get him to them."

"But why wouldn't she try to reach us and tell us?"

"She had no way to know how to reach you. Did you give her your cell phone number?"

"No, in the hurry to escape the bandits we neglected to exchange numbers."

"Well, in any event, this Sister Helen is on her way here, and it seems that you three will be reunited very soon."

"Did they say when she left to come here?"

"Actually, they had no idea about her logistics and could offer no specifics."

"Thank you, Phillip, you have been very accommodating. We appreciate all of your kindnesses," said Ashara.

"Please let me know when he arrives." Phillip Cameron, now unburdened, was confident that he had done what he could, little that it was. He was relieved to categorize this issue as no longer of his concern.

Outside, Danel and Ashara embraced, holding each other, rocking back and forth.

"You see, I told you that Sister Helen would get him here," said Danel.

"Where do you suppose Sister Helen got the money to hire a driver? That can't be cheap, especially with the danger a driver would have to take on."

"That's a good question." Though neither doubted her resourcefulness, funding such a trip was formidable. "As least we know that he's alive and survived that night."

"The road here must still be congested, judging by the new arrivals. That should make for a very long trip, and we have no idea how long it'll take her to arrange transportation."

"Ashara, it appears that we're again in waiting mode." He draped his arm across her shoulders, affectionately drawing her sideways close to his body as she pressed her head gently against his torso.

"A skill I wish we hadn't been forced to learn, unfortunately. But we'll see Hamid soon and that is all that matters."

17

Despair and Revelation

By midmorning the shammal whimpered its last howl and disappeared abruptly, leaving the atmosphere eerily still. Large ominous clouds gathered above, throwing silent lightning bolts toward the desert floor. The first ferocious thunder burst was not long behind, cracking open the ebony edged clouds and dumping rain in torrents. Within an hour after the rain began, the storm's anger tamed, revealing a cloudless cerulean sky and air rinsed clean of the shammal's dust.

Spared now from the respiratory dust plague, Za'atari inhabitants were challenged with mud, pooling wide enough in some pathways to render navigation implausible. Since the refugees forded passage through, rather than around, the puddles, their trousers and skirts were mud laden to mid-calf, like brushes dipped in sienna paint. The children became living canvases smeared in shades of umber. For mothers, whose family water rations were limited to less than 40 liters per person a day, the deluge wrought more frustration and shorter tempers, which trickled down to husbands, children and camp personnel.

Five days after the euphoric news that Sister Helen was coming with Hamid, Danel and Ashara were still childless. Danel's waking hours were engaged with work at the hospital, which provided him a respite from the incessant longing that plagued Ashara. In the predawn hours on the sixth morning, he was awakened by Ashara's soft, muffled sobs.

"Ashara, what is it? Did you have a nightmare?"

"No. Go back to sleep."

"Then what is it?" He rolled onto her mattress, drawing her into his arms. Her pillow was drenched, and her body felt very hot. "Tell me. What's wrong?"

"My milk is all dried. I'm Hamid's mother, and I won't even be able to feed him. And where is he? Why haven't they come?" Ashara pulled her knees into her chest, curling up like a silk worm in its cocoon, mourning more than the loss of her breasts' milk.

Rocking her gently, he was surprised by how fragile her frame had become, a detail passed unnoticed by a husband consumed with his official duties. Biting his lip, he scrunched his face at how he had been so obtuse.

"Shhh. Please don't weep. He's coming soon, you'll see."

"No, Danel, I won't see, and you don't even get what's happened."

"Your milk is a loss, but we have endured too much to let that break us."

"You're wrapped up in your world at the hospital and have failed to grasp the obvious."

"What are you talking about?"

"Danel, he's not coming." Her despair escaped in sobs. "Our son has been stolen."

The stark simplicity of her pronouncement amazed him, as he had not considered its possibility. "We'll find him."

"How can you say this when the UN plus the Jordanian and Syrian authorities couldn't even accomplish this? We've no resources, and we're trapped here in this hell. They couldn't find the nuns even when they weren't trying to hide. Even you admitted that she could have left the country with him."

"Calm down. Listen to me."

Her sobs lapsed into sniffles.

"When he went missing before, before the nuns had reported in, we both felt that using official resources to locate him was our best option. We can reengage those resources and take a more active role ourselves. I'll go and talk to Phillip Cameron this morning and see if we can launch a criminal search for them as fugitives." The tension in her body ebbed as he reaffirmed his intentions to find them. "I promise you we'll find him."

"Do you mean that?"

"Yes, with all my being, and with Allah's help, we'll get our child back." He pulled the coverlet around her shoulders.

"Even if it takes a long time and she denies that he's ours, we can do the tests to prove that he's our son. Right?"

Thinking he hadn't heard her, she repeated, "Right?"

"Of course." His penchant for lying dueled with his guilt. "But I doubt that once we find him we'll have need to prove he's ours. Besides, he's on his way. I think you're planning for something that just isn't going to be necessary."

"How can you say that? Little babies and young children change rapidly in their early years. What if it takes a year? Hamid won't even know us. If Sister Helen could take him the way she has, she would have no qualms about denying he's ours."

"A year? That's absurd. Ashara, you're overreacting."

Sensing something amiss, she became more agitated. "Don't tell me I'm overreacting when my infant son is missing."

"I'm sorry. I didn't mean that your concerns weren't well founded." Sitting up, he searched for another way to explain that would not escalate into an argument.

"Well, what did you mean?"

"I only meant that.... Forget it. I'm not sure what I meant. And keep your voice down so all of Za'atari doesn't learn of our troubles."

She raised herself up on one elbow, uncannily sensing a lie. As first light intruded into the darkened tent, she could make out the contour of his face. After five years of marriage, her intuition identified the slight change of his voice's timbre and the subtle shift in his body's demeanor that accompanied a falsehood.

"I just need to know that you are willing to do everything it takes to claim him if and when the time comes. Is that too much to request?"

"How can you even ask that?"

"You interrupted me. And that means DNA testing."

"Of course I'll do everything possible."

"And the DNA testing?"

"Well, that too."

"Say it, Danel. 'I will do DNA testing.'"

"Why are you all over me for this? I don't get it. We're expecting Hamid any day and you're acting like we'll never see him again and it's my fault."

Ashara stood up. "I sense that there is something that you're not telling me, that's all. You're dodging my request. So will you or won't you do DNA testing?"

Danel fidgeted as her noose tightened. "Not exactly."

"What do you mean 'not exactly'? You would refuse to use every scientific means possible to return Hamid to his rightful parents?"

"It's not that."

"I don't understand. Danel, you're scaring me." She started to pace, venting her agitation.

"Where shall I start?"

She halted. "You start where we always agreed you would start. With the truth." Her breath caught in her throat.

Danel gulped back his hesitation. The weight of his guilt grew heavier, its burden now almost unbearable. Here at the crossroads of his secret, he wrestled with relief at unburdening and protection of Ashara from the truth. "On the night Hamid was born, he was very sick. His lungs were filled with fluid, and he desperately needed them cleared."

She settled back down on the mattress to listen. "That can't be. He was very healthy. I held him. I would have known if he weren't well."

"Please, let me finish. This is very hard to tell you." When she quieted, he resumed. "You'll remember that we had no lights and were shorthanded. I took our baby up to the nursery after delivery."

"Yes, I remember. But you said that he was fine. I saw him and he was healthy."

"That's what I thought, or wanted to believe, when I said that. After I carried him to the nursery, he was pale and his breathing very shallow. He struggled for air." Reliving his son's death, he struggled for composure. "We had no power and the generators were out. Do you remember?"

"Yes, I do." Suddenly growing cold, she shivered in the predawn air.

"I did everything I could, but without the equipment to siphon his lungs, it was futile. I tried to make him comfortable and rocked him until he passed. I asked Allah to take his soul into His keeping."

"Wait. I held him. You brought him to me. He was fine. I don't understand what you are telling me. How could he then become so well? He was fine when we took him home from the hospital?"

Grabbing her upper arms, he shook her. "Listen to me. He's not our biological son."

"I don't believe you. He looks just like us. How can that be? This baby that I nursed and loved is my son."

"No, he isn't. There was another infant born at the same time that night. I was there alone with our dead son and another who resembled him. It all happened in an instant."

"What do you mean? What happened?" She spread out her hands in an open question. "What are you saying? I don't believe you." She stepped forward inches from him. "What are you saying, Danel?"

"Look at me. I took another's healthy baby and switched him with our dead son's body. We're not his biological parents." He looked directly into her eyes, emphasizing his earnestness. "Do you understand, he's not our biological son?"

She gasped, covering her mouth as the dawning washed over her. "What're you telling me? Danel? What are you telling me?" She pounded his chest, now screaming. "You liar, you liar."

"No, this is one time I speak the absolute truth." His detached voice was cold.

"How could you? How could you do this to us? To another family? What kind of man are you?" Her hysteria unbridled, she shook violently, thrusting fist after fist at his face and torso. "Why, Danel, why?" Her sobs filled their tent, echoing off the canvas out into the universe.

Danel arrested her fists to stop the blows. "I thought of you and what this baby meant to you. I switched them to spare you the pain of another dead infant. Don't you see that?"

"But I don't understand how you even would have been able to pull off such a deception. The nurses and the other mother, they must have known."

"No one was there."

"But the ID bracelets."

"I switched them as well as the identification on the bassinettes. All changed. I was able to pass our dead son off to another family. And their son became our Hamid."

Recalling that afternoon, she frowned. "I remember. Yes, there was another family near me in the recovery area, weeping for their dead infant. I felt such joy, and they were tasting what should have been my sorrow. But why, Danel? Why this lie, this deception?" Ashara shivered uncontrollably. She felt trust dying, slipping away as her infant son had done.

He released her wrists. "I knew how much you longed for a child."

"Not someone else's child. Have you no conscience? No realization of the wrong that you have done?"

"You think I'm not affected by this lie? My guilt and shame have been unbearable."

"Not unbearable enough to stop this charade before it got out of hand."

"Don't you understand? Once I did it, there was no turning back. You believed because of the two stillbirths that losing this baby was your last chance for having a child. I just couldn't take that away from you if I had the means to prevent it."

"His death wasn't your choice; it was Allah's, for whatever reason He had."

"Yes, but I couldn't save him. I had the knowledge and even the equipment, but I was as powerless as the machine that sat idle."

"Who knows of this?"

"No one. I created his papers and ID bracelet and told no one, except you."

She sat immobile, her heart rhythmically pounding against her chest. As her sobs broke through, she crumpled back down. "If they found out, the authorities would take him away from us, and you'd be prosecuted."

"Yes. I suppose that's right."

"You suppose?" The evidence of his unburdening blotched in crimson on her tear-drenched face.

He knelt down beside her. "Can you ever forgive me?"

"Whether I forgive you or not, it is Allah that will pronounce judgment."

"But what of you?"

"How can I forgive what I can't even understand? This goes against all that I believe."

He was mute, resting on his haunches, his limp arms as powerless as his ability to read her.

"Despite your good intentions, you have wrought incredible evil on our marriage. I'm not sure which is the graver offense." He started to object, but she raised her hand to halt his defense. "Did you even think about where truth fit in with your little plan? The one thing you promised me when we married?"

"I regret that very little of what I did was thought through." He winced at hearing aloud his thin excuse.

She spoke in short bursts through her sobs. "This child, that is not mine, is a part of my heart. He is my very reason to walk on this planet. If we find him, could I ever bear to have him taken away should the truth be found out?" Her voice was eerily clear. "Could we live with that? Could I propagate your lie by keeping him away from his true parents? Could we return him without compromising you and revealing your crime?" Pulling away from him, she lay staring up at the tent seams as the morning sun's first rays crept over the horizon and pierced through the open window flap. "And I unknowingly perpetuated the farce. I'm as guilty as you."

"No one knows. We could keep him and no one would be the wiser."

"No one, Danel? Allah knows and we know."

He reached across to touch her shoulder, but she shrank back at his touch.

"You should leave me now."

"I can't leave you like this."

"I need to be alone. Get out of here. I can't stand the sight of you."

"Ashara, please. We have to work this out together."

"Work this out? This day you have taken away my son, my hope, my trust and my marriage. How, Danel, do we work that out?"

"We have always been able to work through our troubles."

"This is not a trouble. This is too horrible for description. Get out. I need to be alone." She rolled over on her side away from him. "I can't even look at you. Just go."

Danel dressed quickly and approached her, but she shriveled away from him. As he left the tent, he heard her whimpering, "Hamid, my dear little one. My dear Hamid." A cold fear wrapped its fingers around his heart. He walked briskly to the latrines and then out the back of the camp to the football pitch. Pacing back and forth, he broke forward into a full gallop around its perimeter, unleashing endorphins in a desperate run. With each lap around the field, he replayed their conversation from the early morning and the events surrounding Hamid's birth over and over, like a stuck phonograph needle, as salty tears tinged in bitter regret washed down his face.

Haunted by alternative choices long since passed, he stopped back to check on Ashara's condition, but she was gone. He considered searching for her, but respecting her request for solitude, he opted instead for the refuge of the hospital. His work had been an opiate to remove himself from the painful vigil that Ashara had chosen. Perhaps it would work this morning as well.

Even this early, the hospital reception area was already buzzing with refugees and their potpourri of afflictions. Abu Majeed was making his last notation in a file.

"You're very early this morning."

"Yes, I guess I am."

"You don't look well. Are you ill?"

Danel averted his eyes. "I just have some things on my mind."

"Did you receive some bad news about Hamid?"

"Nothing like that. I think the best thing is to get to work."

Abu flinched at Danel's brush off. "Well, there's plenty for you to dig right into." He handed Danel his first chart. "Let me know if I can help."

"Thanks, Abu. I'll let you know if there is anything you can do. I don't mean to be evasive."

Danel tended to a steady flow of patients, and by midafternoon he realized that he had not even taken a break for mid meal. Majeed approached him and asked if he would care for a breath of air and a cup of tea.

"Yes, I could use some. I just have to finish my notes on this chart."

"Good, then I'll have just enough time for a smoke. Meet me outside when you finish."

Jotting his notes, Danel instructed the man to come back in three days so he could check the wound and change the dressing. He returned the chart to the pending file and stepped to the back to scrub his hands before meeting Abu.

Just finishing his last puff, Abu chatted with Bethshari. "Ah Danel, Bethshari has just been scolding me about the poor example of a physician smoking. You're just in time to rescue me."

"Bethshari, don't let up on him. It's a very bad habit. And look at what he smokes, not even filtered."

"Danel, what was in the package from home?" said Bethshari.

"Package from home? You got me there. No one from Damascus knows we're here. What package?"

"Saeed told me that Ashara got a package from her sister that was wrapped so securely that she needed a box cutter."

"Ashara has no sister."

"That's odd. He fetched the cutter for her, but he had to get back to me before he could learn what was in the package. He was very curious about its contents."

Concern shadowed across Danel's face, like the ominous clouds that quenched the shammal the day before. They had kitchen knives and scissors in the tent, and who could possibly be sending a package to them?

"Oh, no, Allah, please no." Danel broke into a desperate sprint towards his tent, with Bethshari and Abu trailing several meters behind. As he approached, out of breath, he called out. "Ashara, Ashara, are you in there?" He yanked back the entry flap to see his wife reclining on the mattress with her back to him. Relieved that she was napping, he softly called, "Ashara, are you alright?" Carefully he knelt next to her, touching her shoulder, which felt strangely cool, to turn her toward him. "Ashara, what have you done?"

Blood from her wrists had pooled in the concave recess formed by her body's fetal curve. He rolled her over onto her back and saw that her slacks and blouse were drenched in scarlet. Rivulets ran down his cheeks. "Ashara, wake up. Please, wake up." He drew her tenderly into his arms, cradling her gently, with her head resting against his shoulder, rocking her back and forth, pleading for her to come back. Her blood, coagulated in shallow spots, was still quite moist and fluid in the deeper pools around her middle.

Abu and Bethshari burst into the tent out of breath. As their eyes adjusted to the dim light, the volume of blood drenching her body left them initially speechless.

"Oh my god," screamed Bethshari. She frantically ransacked the tent for some towels to stanch the blood. Handing them to Danel, her stomach heaved and she fled the tent to vomit just outside the entrance. Her fortune had been never before to have seen death this close. Wiping her mouth on her sleeve, she returned to help. "Danel, her wrists, we should bind them." She was now crying. "The cuts are so deep. We have to do something. Abu, can't you do something?"

Abu's was already engaged, feeling for a pulse. "I can't get a pulse. Danel, lean her back and let me look at her eyes."

Danel tilted her limp body back so Abu could part her lids and shine his penlight into her pupils for a response. Although her color was ashen, her countenance was peaceful, save for the delicate crease of a frown barely visible across the left of her forehead. As the two men's eyes met, Danel burst into deep convulsive sobs.

"No. No. No." His pleading with her was primal, pulling her even closer to him, holding her tightly to defy the finality of her death. His large hand cupped hers, closing the deep, open gash at her wrist. His other hand, sticky with her blood, brushed back a few renegade stands of hair that had fallen across her face. "Ashara, why?" He wept into her thick ebony locks now free of a confining hijab, smelling her scent for a last time. "Come back, Ashara. Please come back. Don't leave me." He rocked her back and forth. His loud sobs resonated, echoing outside the tent, unrestrained through the clear desert air.

Bethshari wet a small cloth with water from a plastic jug. Kneeling down next to Danel, she wiped the smudge of Ashara's blood deposited when he brushed back the wisps of hair from her face and took each of his hands and gently washed away the blood. Softly she crept behind Danel, still holding his wife, and knelt behind him, wrapping her arms around both of them. "Danel, I am so sorry," she said, her consolation barely piercing his raw sorrow.

Abu knelt next to Danel and touched his shoulder. "Danel, she's gone. Let me take her." Gently he shifted Ashara's corpse out of Danel's arms and laid her carefully back down on the mattress, covering up her slit wrists, upper torso and face.

"Come on, Danel. Let her go."

Still rocking slightly, Danel remained on the mattress, his chest heaving as he sobbed. Resting his clasped hands on his forehead, he moved side to side.

"Bethshari, radio the hospital to bring a stretcher," said Abu, as he helped Danel stand.

Blood had soaked deep into the mattress, and its seepage created a wide arc onto the dirt floor. The sheer volume of blood, as much as three liters Abu estimated, and the deep cuts into her wrists painted a picture of a very painful death.

Shivering uncontrollably, Danel held his upper arms.

With Ashara's body covered, Abu wrapped his arms around Danel's shoulders as a father would a small child. Danel rested his head on Abu as a new wave of sobs overtook him. When they subsided, Abu released him. "Danel, my friend, come with me. Our staff will take care of things. There's nothing you can do here. Bethshari, will you wait for the medics and see to it here?"

"Of course."

"There doesn't appear to be a note, but would you check?"

"I will. You take care of Danel."

Abu lead Danel out through a small group of neighbors gawking curiously out front. They stepped back, horrified by the blood on Danel, allowing them an unimpeded path down the narrow lane. Bethshari stood as sentinel at the tent flap, watching them depart. Her thoughts had already shifted to Saeed, the bearer of the box cutter, and how she would break the news to him.

18

Ashara's Conundrum

Danel walked along in a daze to Abu's quarters. "Where are we going?"

"You're staying with me tonight."

Offering no resistance, grateful to turn over control temporarily to someone else, Danel felt adrift. Ashara had been his mooring and now she was gone. They walked into a back entrance of the hospital and climbed stairs to the second floor.

"My quarters are humble, but they're out of the wind. You are very welcome here." He showed Danel into a small apartment with a living room kitchen combination, two barely adequate bedrooms and a bathroom. "Please sit down. Make yourself comfortable."

Abu prepared a pot of tea. Without permission, he poured some arak into Danel's cup, topping his own off with similar amount.

"I'm Muslim, and for the most part I refrain from alcohol," said Danel, accepting the cup politely. He set it down in front of himself, and after a few moments pushed it aside.

"In my country we drink a lot of arak. You may have heard that Lebanese consume more alcohol that any other Arab country."

"Yes, I'd heard that." Participating in the small talk took effort.

"Do you know why that is?"

"No. I've no idea why."

"It's because of all the tourists from other Arab countries who come there to drink."

"You're a good Muslim, Danel, but tonight I'm your physician and I'm prescribing it for medicinal purposes. You must do as your doctor orders."

Danel smiled and then shrugged as he took in his first sip, feeling its calming warmth move down into his system.

"Allah isn't opposed to us helping ourselves in times like this."

Danel felt his body relax, easing his immediate shock. They spent the next hours long into the evening talking through what happened, how the camp had affected Ashara, and that she woke up crying in the wee hours that day. He filled Abu in on their life in Damascus, Ashara's yearning for a child, Mr. Faroush's death, her trip to the hospital and Sister Helen. He had come to regard Abu as a good friend, but not good enough to share the events surrounding Hamid's birth. Such facts could be entrusted to no one. He deeply regretted sharing them with Ashara. In his myopic estimation so close to her suicide, he felt he made a very poor trade, his guilt over Hamid for his culpability in Ashara's death.

A change in subject offered Danel a small respite. "Abu, I've been curious as to why you left Lebanon. Surely there was enough suffering there to satisfy your desire to heal."

"Yes, you're right, there is much work to do there."

"I'd been thinking about the poor Syrians for some time and the lack of medical care. The aid agencies move very slowly. I knew the need here was greater and that Za'atari was opening up."

"Still you were successful in Beirut. It just seems like a lot to give up."

"Perhaps it was, but I never felt satisfied. I can't explain why. I guess what convinced me was a report on the child mortality among the Syrian refugees from innocuous maladies like colds, small infections that ballooned out of control."

"What about your family? Did they try to talk you out of it?"

"I was an only child, and all I had left was my mother. Then she had a stroke and died within three days. There was nothing left to hold me there. I figured why not."

"I guess that's my situation now. I have no family."

"You have Hamid. He's what is left of Ashara."

He shivered at the irony of Abu's statement.

"Danel, are you cold?"

"No, I just had a shiver. I have to figure out how I'll ever find Hamid."

"Yes, but that's not a task for tonight. Wherever he is, with what you have told me of Sister Helen, he's being well cared for. She's risked much to take him the way she has."

"Perhaps. I'd best be going now." He stood up. "I need to go back to our tent."

"I meant what I said about you sleeping here tonight. Alone in the dark tent with Ashara's ghost is not the best way to pass the first night."

"Perhaps you're right."

"The daylight will be your friend." Abu called for some food, and a young worker brought each a bowl of lentil soup and some flat bread. "This isn't much but it will do you some good."

Though he hadn't eaten all day, he was not tempted by the soup. "You know I haven't prayed much since we arrived here. Perhaps Allah took Ashara to get my attention."

"I think Allah would choose something more subtle to get your attention." Abu hesitated considering whether or not to say what was in his mind. "Danel, may I speak plainly?"

"Of course."

"What Ashara did, it was her choice, and neither Allah nor you drove her to it. You have to believe that."

"If only I could. I go back over and over in my mind wondering if coming here was the right choice. Then I think about our apartment and for a split second I wish we were back there. After a few moments I snap to and realize that the apartment might be blown up by now."

"And you come to the conclusion that you had no choice, right?"

"That's right. It's almost as if we were caught up in something so large that we were powerless from the start, only we didn't know it."

"I know. Others here come to the same conclusion."

"And my work here in the hospital helped me but further isolate Ashara. I just wasn't there for her."

"Again it was her choice to stay so isolated." Abu treaded lightly.

"She wanted our son back so desperately she saw nothing beyond that."

"I could see that the first time I met her." Abu recalled that first meeting when he invited her to work at the hospital. "Even then everything was on hold until after her child arrived."

"I have these moments when I just can't conceive that our lives have been so uprooted. I feel we've become victims, and at the same time I abhor thinking of us in that vein, unable to take charge of our lives."

"Yes, but you did take charge, and what you've done here in getting involved at the hospital is taking charge. It's about living your life productively no matter where you land."

"But I failed to see the crisis growing under my very nose." He felt his composure slipping as he veered into the open wound of her suicide. "By missing her despair, I failed the one person to whom I owed everything."

"It's late. We should both get some rest." Placing his hand on Danel's shoulder, he handed him a clean towel. "You'll have lots of time to process all of this; save some for tomorrow. Tonight you need to sleep." He led Danel to a room sparsely furnished with a bed, a chest and a small lamp. "I keep this room in case I ever have a visitor, but you're the first. I think you'll be comfortable."

"Abu, I'm very grateful for your kindness."

"It is nothing. Now get some rest."

Danel prepared for bed and said his prayers, asking Allah for forgiveness and to hold Ashara close. The arak had relaxed him and he quickly slipped into deep sleep lasting but a few hours. He awoke in a tearful sweat. Emerging from the fuzzy realm of the unconscious, he reached for Ashara, realizing as he awakened fully that she was gone forever.

Lying on his bed, he stared at the ceiling in the darkness. *She sorely missed Hamid, but it was my revelations that pushed her over the edge.* He felt the urge to return to their tent right then, but thought better of it in the darkness. There were so many unanswered questions. *Tomorrow I'll go to our tent and see if there was anything that she left behind to help me understand.* Another few hours passed, with Danel slipping in and out of sleep. His eye sockets ached, but eventually no tears would come. Finally, right before dawn, he descended into a deep sleep that lasted about an hour.

A first light, Danel woke as the early rays filtered in through the window. He lay there motionless just thinking, and then rose and quietly let himself out of the apartment, walking out into the pleasant morning air. Even at that hour he sensed that the day would be very hot. Heading to their tent, he half expected Ashara to be there waiting for him.

As he approached their lane, he could hear the occupants in nearby tents already stirring. Missing were the chirping of birds that filtered through his open window in their Damascus apartment. *How far away it all seems. How much was lost in so short a time.* He stopped at the tent entrance, closing his eyes momentarily to gather courage.

Gone were Ashara's body and the blood soaked mattress. Even the box cutter she used was missing. The ground was raked and the bloody soil removed. A single mattress occupied the space, a stark reminder that he was now alone. The dream of being a family had evaporated. With no note, he was left to wonder.

Searching the tent for some sign of goodbye, he replayed her last words over and over. "This day you have taken away my son, my hope, my trust and my marriage." His pace was deliberate through the tent's confines, touching her possessions: a hairbrush with tangled strands of her long dark hair, the lavender hijab she wore the night they had given up Hamid, the musical mobile that hung on his crib. Winding it up, he thought about how many times had they played it for Hamid as he drifted off to sleep or to amuse him when he was awake.

"Danel, are you in there?" A soft voice interrupted him.

Walking to the flap, he pulled it back. "Bethshari? Thank you for taking care of things yesterday. I don't know what to say."

"I was glad I could do something. I'm sorry about Ashara. Perhaps I could have done more to help her. If I could've been more of a friend to her, maybe that I could've made a difference."

"It was I who brought her here and pressed her into giving up Hamid. I abandoned her to work in the hospital. If anyone should carry blame, I'm the one."

"Yesterday, after you left, I waited for the medics to come for her. I hope you don't mind, but I looked for a note."

"I was just doing the same thing, but she left nothing."

"She did write a note."

His breath caught in his throat. "Where was it? Did you read it? Did you give it to the authorities?"

"It was in the trash. She tore it up. I felt you were the only one who should see it."

"But why was it in the trash?"

"I suspect that she rethought it; perhaps in her despair she wanted to destroy it."

"What do you mean destroy it? I thought you said you found a note."

"Well, I'm not sure it's a suicide note." She reached into her pocket and pulled out a small manila envelope and handed it to Danel.

Opening it, he peered inside the envelope, which contained torn scraps of paper.

"I just thought that you might want to piece it together, so I brought some tape."

Visibly shaken, he stammered. "How can I thank you?"

Bethshari opened her arms to console him as though he were a child waking from a bad dream. Releasing him, she brushed his bangs off his forehead out of his eyes.

"Many who come here don't make it. The life and the loss are too much. Ashara carried an extra heavy burden."

"But I didn't help her carry it."

"You can't blame yourself. In the end it was her choice. You must see that, don't you?"

"I don't know."

"I'm going to leave now so you can work on your note." She tapped the envelope. "I hope it gives you some answers and some peace."

Danel sat cross legged on the mattress, spreading the small scraps of paper out in front of him like the broken pieces of his life. Looking for common edges, he matched torn words that fit together. A light breeze wafted through the window, and he lowered the flap. The uneven creases on each piece suggested that it had been crumpled before it was torn. But the number of pieces, about twenty-four or so, confirmed that their destruction was her final decision. The ink on several was streaked as though a tear had fallen on them.

Piecing several small sections together, he winced reading them out of context. Two excerpts, "cannot be undone" and "the only parents he'd ever known," foreshadowed his learning her final thoughts. Once he located pieces with connecting edges or aligning letters, he taped them together. On some he could make out phrases that made sense spanning two pieces. After putting together four sections, he moved them in proximity to each other until he could make out a rectangular sheet of paper. He finalized their assembly into one coherent document and taped it together.

Danel took a deep breath. Holding the taped letter in hand, he stood to reopen the window flap to allow for some air and more light. He sat down again cross legged on the mattress, positioning himself to take best advantage of the light filtering through the window.

My dear Danel,

Even as I write this letter I waiver on whether to leave it for you or destroy it, because I know that if I'm truthful, it will hurt you even more than my death. But then you know me too well for me not be truthful with you. As you read this you will come to know that my death is the only possible outcome for me.

Our waiting for Hamid these past weeks has been excruciating. I blame myself for giving him up, but that's hindsight and cannot be undone. But now I know that I'd given my heart to an innocent who was not mine to keep. If or when we were to find him, I would always be listening for the knock at our door, or the moment when the deception would be discovered, and I would lose him again. As he grows older, not only might we feel the pain of giving him up, but he too would suffer from being taken from the only parents he'd ever known. That's a burden I don't wish for him or for us.

Continuing the lie on the night our son died is not a choice I can accept. As hard as giving Hamid back would be, I know that Allah would command me to return him to his rightful parents. Yet I cannot be sure if the hour came, I could do the right thing and give him up. My weakness then would condemn me to living my life against Allah's will.

In returning him to his biological parents, we would have to expose how it all came about, and that would place you and me in jeopardy. Surely we would be prosecuted, tortured and executed. I can't wish this for you, even if I could accept it for myself. If we were to escape our just punishment, what kind of marriage could we have when trust had become a casualty of the original deception?

If you pursue Hamid, may Allah guide you and keep you and him safe. I pray that Allah will have mercy on me as His humble servant caught in a moral conundrum. Please know that I love you and Hamid dearly. I know that your deception was to spare me and never intended to cause me pain. You must not blame yourself for my death, because it was my decision and mine alone. If I could, I would have spared you

the pain of finding my body. But like so many things, it was not in my power. I beg for your forgiveness.
Allah Akbar.
Ashara

He reread the letter over and over, postulating rebuttals to her reasons. In the end he could not counter the moral dilemma of doing the right thing. In the face of Allah, there were no excuses. A righteous man must do the right thing.

His breathing became labored, and a lump in his throat made swallowing difficult. Weeping, he held the last painful communication from Ashara against his chest.

After some time, he roamed the tent, like a caged tiger still trying to counter the finality of her decision. But there was no counter-argument to death. He found a large cooking pot and a packet of matches in the corner and carried them to the mattress. Reading the letter one final time, he whispered softly that he loved her. Placing the letter into the pot, he lit a match, which flashed brightly. As the orange purple flame tamed, he set it against the corner of the letter, watching it consume the paper until the last words he could recognize were *Allah Akbar* and *Ashara*. Finally it eradicated her name. The burned scent filled his nostrils. He knew this was a smell he would never forget.

"Dr. Ottawa, are you in there?" A women's voice called outside the tent.

"Yes, just a moment." Taking his handkerchief out of his pocket, he wiped his eyes and blew his nose. He opened the flap to see a short, middle-aged woman in a tan hijab holding a baby on her hip. "How can I help you?"

"I heard about your wife. I'm very sorry."

"Thank you. Did you know my wife?"

"Yes, I talked to her yesterday morning."

"You talked to her before.... " Hesitating, he resisted saying "before she killed herself."

"Yes, before it happened. She came to see me." She shifted her infant to her other hip.

"I didn't even know she knew anyone in the camp. What's your name?"

"I'm Rachel Bakir. I live several paths over that way." She gestured over her shoulder, pulling her hijab modestly closer to her face. "I met Ashara at the showers when you were newly arrived. I had my baby with me."

"Yes, she told me about you. She held your baby."

"She came to visit me several times and played with him. She missed hers so much. I think that it just helped her to be around a baby the same age."

"It did I'm sure. She missed him very much."

"But yesterday when she came she seemed very upset."

"Did she say anything to suggest that this was what was on her mind?" He gestured back into the tent.

"No, if she had, I wouldn't have let her leave. I offered her tea but she declined."

"What else did she say?"

"Not much. It was like she'd given up hope that your son would be found. She said he'd been stolen. I asked her to stay until she calmed down, but she said that she had something she had to do."

"Did she say anything else?"

"She promised to come back later, but I was going to check on her when I heard about her death from a neighbor. I should have come to find you after she left, but when she said she was coming back later it didn't occur to me she'd take her own life."

"I wish you had, but then I can say the same for me. I failed miserably to understand the depth of her despair. I missed all of the signs."

"So you didn't suspect that she was thinking of taking her life?"

"No, it was a total shock. Can you remember anything else?"

"Not really. She held the baby for a long time. She sang to him too. Very sweet." Searching for the right words, she could only say how sorry she was.

"I appreciate that you were her friend when she needed one the most."

Shifting her infant higher on her hip, she reached out to gently squeeze his arm. "Allah is with her, and he is with you as well. You are both are on separate paths now, but you have the same God guiding you. Allah Akbar."

"Allah Akbar." Touched by the kindness of this stranger, he watched as she disappeared into the alley between two rows of tents.

19

The Hawk of Qureish

The immigration from Damascus, leaving with nothing and going to nothing, paled next to Danel's hollowness. His life purpose to build a family was now in shambles. Ensconced in his thoughts was the echo of "Where do I go from here?" His work had a noble purpose, masquerading as a disguise for his shortcomings. Two days after Ashara's death, Danel showed up at the hospital and signed onto the duty roster.

The charge nurse expressed her surprise. "Dr. Danel." Fumbling with a chart, she shifted uneasily, avoiding his eyes. "We didn't expect to see you for a while. I'm very sorry." She tilted her head slightly.

He acknowledged her condolences with a nod. "I have to be of use somewhere."

"We're glad to have you back, of course. I just thought you might need some time, that's all." She handed him a chart, pointing in the direction of its accompanying patient. "Just let me know if you want to leave." When he engaged with the patient, she quietly left to report to Dr. Majeed.

"How did he seem?"

"It is hard to tell. Very distant, but he said he has to be somewhere. He's with a patient now."

Majeed frowned and returned to annotating his own charts. Chewing his bottom lip, he walked briskly to the reception area. "Nurse, where is Dr. Ottawa now?"

"He is in examining room one with a patient. Would you like me to get him for you?"

"No, I'll just stop in myself." Abu walked casually back. Tapping lightly on the door, he poked his head in. "Dr. Ottawa, can I have a word with you?"

Danel excused himself. "I shouldn't be but a minute."

Out in the hall, Abu stood with his arms crossed over his chest, his hands tucked up underneath each arm. "Danel, what're you doing here? It's too soon. We don't need you here so badly that you can't take time to grieve."

"Abu, you're very kind, but the thing I need most is to keep very busy. I'll go crazy if I don't work."

"I support you staying busy, but unresolved grief is a recurring curse. It resurfaces when you least expect it. You need to give your grieving some air."

"What's here for me but a dusty tent that wasn't even our home? Ashara regarded it as an abomination. And now her ghost resides there along with the reminder of my failings. At least here I can help someone, even if I can't help myself."

Abu had no rebuttal.

"You see, right now this is the only place I belong. I should get back to my patient." Needing no permission, he retreated.

"Alright. I'm here if you want to talk."

"Thank you, my friend." A feeble wave accompanied his thanks as he pulled the door to the examining room closed behind him.

One evening a week later, Bethshari came to his tent. They had not spoken since she brought Ashara's torn up letter.

"Danel? Are you there?" It was late and she had just gotten off of her shift.

Opening the flap, he invited her in. "Bethshari, it's good to see you. Can I offer you some tea?"

"Yes, I'd like that."

He busied himself at the camp stove. "Fixing a cup of tea was so much easier in Damascus. But here we make do, right?" He was surprised he felt uneasy with her there.

"Yes, this place makes a task of the easiest things. It's been an especially hard day for me, and I'm appreciative of your hospitality." She paused slightly. "How're you coping?"

"Coping?" He poured water out of a plastic jug into a tea kettle. "At the hospital I don't have to cope because the work leaves no time for examining what happened. But here alone without her, I find it unbearable." He looked away. "My own guilt is crushing. I think if I confront it head on I might not survive."

"You're not to blame. Ashara's decision was hers alone."

"I'm not so sure. But in time I know that I must face it, just not all of it right now."

Her words had hit a raw nerve.

Suddenly his face flushed as he passed her a cup of hot tea. "I'm sorry that I have no furniture, but you're welcome to sit here." He motioned to the mattress.

"Ah, a sofa with no back or legs. I'd be delighted." She sat cross legged at one end of the mattress, and he likewise opposite her.

"You said that you had a particularly hard day?"

"Yes, the refugees are coming steadily at a thousand a day now. Some days even more. Their stories are heartbreaking, when I have time to listen, which isn't often now that the volume's so absurd." She was hesitant.

"Go on. Is something troubling you?"

"Yes, there is something. It's why I came tonight, in addition to seeing if you were alright." She seemed to be searching for her words inside the tea cup.

"Come, Bethshari. There're no tea leaves to read in your cup. Out with it."

She looked up directly into Danel's face and bent her head slightly to one side. "Have you noticed anything different about Saeed since Ashara passed?"

"Well, no. Not really. I haven't even seen him since then. Is he unwell?"

"Yes, in a manner of speaking, he's very unwell."

He wrinkled his forehead. "What is it?"

She set her cup down and clasped her hands. "He blames himself for Ashara's death."

Confused, he shook his head as though he hadn't heard correctly.

"I know he's seen you because he's told me how sad you look," she said.

"Believe me, I haven't laid eyes on him."

"I believe that's true." She took a sip of her tea. "Do you know why that is?"

Danel set his cup into the saucer in front of him. "No, I can't guess why?"

"It's because when he sees you he hides so you won't feel disgust when you look at him."

"But why?" Until now he had admired the youngster's courage and resilience in coming ahead to Za'atari to wait for his mother.

"He's the one who brought the box cutter to Ashara. He feels that if it were not for his fetching it, she'd still be alive. He thinks that you couldn't stand to be in his presence for what he's done."

Danel, stunned, spread his hands out in front of him. "I haven't given any indication to him or anyone that's what I believe. Nothing could be further from the truth. Ashara had it in her mind to take her life. Her suicide note left no doubt of that. If he hadn't helped her get the blade, someone else would have. She would've found a way."

"That's what I told him. But he thinks that I'm only saying that because we're friends. He's not eating, and I can see he's losing weight."

She captured three strands of rebel hairs that had fallen across her face and tucked them behind her ear. "He's doing what you're doing, when the real blame lies with Ashara."

He grimaced at the comparison. "What can I do?" He ran his fingers several times through his hair. "This isn't right. Saeed is faultless. He shouldn't carry any guilt."

"I think you have to take him aside and talk to him. Are you willing to do that?"

"Naturally. But would he be agreeable?"

"I think he'll resist, but I have an idea." She leaned forward to lay out her plan.

"Tell me how I can help."

"Tomorrow, I'll make an excuse to deliver a package, a heavy one, to the hospital. I won't be able to lift it by myself and will ask him to help me. I doubt he'll refuse me."

"He adores you. I'm sure he'll help."

"Let's agree to a certain time that you wait outside for us because I don't think I could coax him into the hospital. He won't be able to run. Then you can speak with him. What do you think?"

"I think it'll work. What time do you propose?"

"I clock in at 10:00 am tomorrow. We could come to you about 10:30. Could you manage to be available then?"

"Of course. I'll be outside waiting on the bench by the employee entrance."

"Then it's settled." Bethshari lifted her cup and saucer, handing it to Danel. "Can I help you clean these up?"

"No, I can take care of this." He hesitated and smiled. "The blue in the cup…." A barely audible laugh escaped his lips as an afterthought. "Never mind."

"What about the cup?"

"It's silly."

"What?"

"I'd noticed the blue is like your eyes. They're good, kind eyes."

A warm glow rose in her cheeks.

"Your kindness tonight instructed me to look beyond my own sorrow." In the dim light, he thought he almost saw a blush across her face, as she briskly hugged him before departing.

"Tomorrow, 10:30 on the bench." She hurried out of the tent, somewhat bewildered by her own feelings.

Danel wiped the cups with a towel rather than wash them. *Ashara would have protested,* he thought, *but then she's not here.* Already 10 pm, he lay down on his mattress, gazing through the flap at the desert ceiling filled with a myriad of stars, their luminescence undimmed in the vast dark away from city lights. *How strange to find beauty in this place,* he thought. Exhaling a deep sigh, his mind went back to Saeed. *I'm the only one who should be burdened over Ashara's death. There's plenty of guilt, but I'm afraid that all of it is mine.* He fell asleep reflecting on Saeed and Bethshari, his thoughts complicated by his uneasiness about another woman when his own wife was so recently passed.

Morning dawned slightly cooler than the previous day as the earth's revolution moved Za'atari toward autumn. Staring out the tent's window, he followed an eagle high above the camp, making use of the heat to catch a lift as the thermals rose from the desert floor. Odd, he thought, that this is the first bird he had noticed since coming to Za'atari.

His thoughts lingered briefly on Bethshari and then shifted to Hamid, the infant that he had vowed to take care of and love for the rest of his life. Little Hamid was still out there without his parents. The arguments in Ashara's letter haunted him. His initial thoughts were to rebuff her, to bargain with her, even though her death was irrevocable. But now, each day he gave her arguments more credence, and the brilliance of her logic was crystalline. She had been right about the danger he placed them in. How strange that he himself never considered what Ashara saw as so obvious: that she herself would have been suspect just by the fact that she'd said nothing and accepted the infant as her own. No one would ever believe that she had not been his accomplice in engineering the switch. He had placed them both in great danger. *And what about Hamid? Where is he?* The trail had grown cold after Sister Helen removed herself from the other nuns. *Where should I start looking?*

At 10:00 he had finished with a patient. He checked his watch when the charge nurse handed him the next chart. "I need to pass on this one so I can catch up on my notes. If I get too far ahead I won't be able to make proper notations."

"No problem. Just let me know when you're ready to go back into rotation."

He moved his stack of charts to an office in the back where he could have some quiet. Thinking of Saeed, he was unsure of how he would convince the child. At 10:25, he left through the employee entrance. The bench outside was unoccupied, and his hand brushed the abrasive sand off the warm metal surface, which soon would feel like a skillet under the hot desert sun. Glancing up, he saw Bethshari and Saeed coming up the path, struggling with a large box. It was not apparent whether the weight of the box or the disparate height of its conveyors were causing the bigger problem. Saeed's limp seemed to throw each step off balance.

As they struggled forward, Bethshari spied Danel first, but it was only moment later when Saeed also caught a glimpse. She felt a distinct hesitation in Saeed's gait, almost causing her to drop her end of the load. His torment struggled between fleeing and assisting her with a package that was decidedly too cumbersome for her to manage. As they neared Danel, Saeed's eyes begged her to release him.

She ignored his unspoken plea. "Good morning, Danel."

"Good morning, Bethshari. Saeed."

Saeed searched the ground, not daring to look up. Approaching the bench, Bethshari eased her side onto the front, leaving Saeed to rest his end at the rear.

"Danel, is it alright if we just set this down here for a few moments to rest?"

"Yes, of course."

Saeed divested himself of the weight and started to take off. But Danel was too quick, and he caught the child by the wrist, taking him off balance.

"Saeed, don't leave. I want to talk to you."

Saeed's chin quivered.

"Will you sit next to me if I let you go?"

Saeed nodded, sheepishly taking the longest route around the back of the bench.

Danel patted the space adjacent to him. Bethshari backed a few meters away, far enough to give them some privacy, yet close enough to listen.

"Saeed, do you think I'm mad with you?" said Danel.

"Worse." Saeed could not bring himself to look up. His feet scuffed up the sand dust in front of him.

"What could be worse?"

"I think that you must hate me for killing your wife."

"You didn't kill my wife. She killed herself."

"But I was the one who brought her the cutter."

"True. But she asked you as a friend to help her."

"It doesn't matter."

Danel sighed deeply, challenged to persuade a ten year old of something that he couldn't convince himself. He rubbed his eyes, gathering his thoughts.

"Saeed, have you ever seen a golden hamster that lives in this desert?"

"No, I haven't seen any here."

"I thought not. Do you know why?"

"No." Saeed raised his gaze but still wouldn't look directly at Danel.

"It's because of two reasons. The first is that he's a solitary fellow who lives by himself in his burrows and tunnels. The second reason that you don't see him is because he sleeps four to ten months a year."

Saeed finally looked up at Danel. "No animal sleeps that long."

"It's true. He hibernates so he doesn't need to eat as much since there's not a lot of food for him in the desert. He wakes up for four to seven days every month, gets something to eat and goes back to sleep."

"I didn't know this."

"Well, truth to tell he's very lonely, and the sleeping helps him forget about how alone he is. I guess it's like us when we forget our troubles for a while when we sleep."

Saeed nodded.

"One day, when he was awake and feeling particularly lonely, a rock hyrax was foraging for grass near the hamster's burrow. He was very talkative. Have you ever heard a hyrax chatter?"

Saeed made a high-pitched kind of chattering noise.

"Yes, I see you're acquainted with this dumpy little fellow. Well, he wasn't so little actually, compared to the hamster. He was almost as big as a cat."

"Was the hamster afraid?"

"No, he was so anxious to talk to someone that he overcame his fear. Did you know that the rock hyrax is a distant cousin to an elephant?"

"No, I don't believe that." Saeed moved toward the edge of the bench and crossed his ankles.

"Yes, it's true. His incisor teeth are shaped and positioned like an elephant's tusks. But another reason the hamster didn't need to be afraid was the hyrax was a plant eater just like him, so he knew the hyrax wouldn't eat him."

"What happened next?"

"Well, it was the hamster that spoke first, since the hyrax was so busy calling out to his family members who were also looking for grasses and bugs nearby. 'How are you this fine morning?' the little hamster asked."

"Was the hyrax surprised that a hamster could talk?" Saeed swung his legs back and forth under the bench.

"Not particularly, since he himself was used to talking to about 80 others in his herd."

"That's a lot."

"Yes, if the hyrax were Syrian, we'd call it a tribe. Anyway, through the conversation, the hamster explained how his life was so solitary and that he sleeps much of the time. In fact, he was incredibly lonely."

"Did the hyrax feel sorry for him?" Saeed pulled both legs up onto the bench and hugged his knees.

"Not really sorry, but he was touched. He'd never before known loneliness himself, since he was a member of such a big family. So while he understood the hamster's words, he really didn't know what loneliness felt like."

Bethshari shifted her footing a little closer, drawn into the story.

"Then the hyrax had an idea," said Danel.

"Find another hamster to live with him?

"No, he asked the little hamster, 'Why don't you come with me and join my family? They've said many times that with hyraxes there is always room for one more.'"

"Did he go?"

"Not right away. He doubted the other hyraxes would accept him. But then his loneliness was so extreme, he figured why not, and followed the rock hyrax back to the family compound."

"Did the others accept him?" Saeed eagerly looked for a happy ending.

"They didn't have a chance."

"But why not?"

"On the way back to the colony, a giant, magnificent hawk of Qureish was cruising through the sky. Do you know the hawk of Qureish?"

"My father told me about him. He's the hawk on the Syrian coat of arms, right?"

"You're right. Your father must've been an educated man."

Saeed beamed at the compliment to his dead father.

"This hawk of Qureish, though, was a mother with three hungry eyasses waiting for her."

Saeed gasped. "Oh no, I don't like where this is going." He rested his head on his knees, squinting his eyes shut.

"Nor did the hamster. The mother's very sharp eyes spotted the hamster immediately, even though she was very far away up in the sky. She swooped down to grab the hamster in her talons. He squirmed and cried out, but it was no use. By the time she reached her nest, the hamster was dead from the pressure of her grip, and she fed him to her chicks." Danel waited a moment for Saeed to react and then lifted him up and settled him onto his lap. "Do you know why I told you this story?"

"Not really."

"It's because I want to see how wise you are. I want you to tell me who's really to blame for the hamster's death?"

Saeed's brow furrowed as he deliberated. His hands writhed back and forth over each other as he considered the characters.

"You seem to be thinking very hard. Let me help you a little."

"Alright. Give me a hint."

"No hints, just a question. How would you rate the intentions of all three?"

"Well, the hamster had good intentions because he was lonely and just wanted company."

"That's right. Now what about the others?" Danel shifted Saeed slightly on his lap to get more comfortable.

"The hyrax was just being friendly and wanted to help. He was very generous to invite the hamster to come home with him."

"And what of the great hawk? If the other two had good intentions, was the hawk to blame then?"

"No, she wanted to feed her hungry chicks. We can't blame her for taking care of her chicks."

"So you're a wise boy, but what's your answer to my question about who was to blame?"

"Well, I think that. I think...." He inhaled deeply, biting his bottom lip before exhaling. "I think that no one was to blame."

"And why's that? Something bad happened to the hamster. Surely someone's to blame."

Saeed considered thoughtfully and leaned forward to emphasize his conclusion, his chin resting in his hands. "Maybe there doesn't always have to be someone to blame. Maybe things just happen."

"Ah, that's right, Saeed. You're as wise as I thought."

A wide grin spread across Saeed's face and he leaned his head shyly into Danel's chest. He drew the boy close and hugged him. Bethshari imagined the guilt virtually lift off Saeed's shoulders, dissipating into the desert heat. *So simple*, she thought.

Danel carried the discussion back to his original point. "And so, Saeed, I'm not mad at you because—"

Saeed cut him off and finished his sentence. "Because no one is to blame."

"That's right. It's between Allah and Ashara now."

"Do you think Allah wanted her to die?"

"I don't pretend to know what Allah intended, but I do know that Ashara's heart was broken, and now that she's with Allah her pain has stopped." Danel lifted Saeed off his lap and settled him on the ground in front of him. "I'm not mad with you, Saeed. I never was."

Saeed hugged Danel hard.

"But now I have to go back to work before I get in trouble with Dr. Majeed and he finds blame with me." He smoothed Saeed's hair and winked at Bethshari. "You can leave the box here on the bench, and I'll send someone out to fetch it."

Bethshari walked over and squeezed Danel's arm. "I think that you're as wise as Saeed, Dr. Ottawa. I hope that you'll heed your own lesson." She wiped Saeed's bangs off his forehead, and, taking him by the hand, led him back down the path toward the center of the camp. She glanced back over her shoulder to catch Danel still watching them and smiled as she turned back to talk to Saeed.

Book Three

20

Desert Bloom

Conventional expectations of a Muslim husband in mourning did not include lingering thoughts of a beautiful young woman who Danel had known for only a short while. A seed of fondness for Bethshari and Saeed, innocently sown, sprouted into something indefinable: a vague stirring when he saw her from afar, a quickening of his pulse in her presence, a touch of melancholy as he watched her leave. Initially convinced this was just gratitude for her support, he was now not so sure. His shame that these feelings were disrespectful to Ashara competed for emotional oxygen with his grief, guilt and the search for Hamid. *Perhaps this will fade,* he thought. For now, the search was moving to center stage. *Where are you, Sister Helen, and what have you done with Hamid?*

As soon as Bethshari and Saeed passed out of sight, he reported in to the charge nurse.

"Dr. Ottawa," a woman called across the lobby.

He turned around to see Rachel Bakir with her two older children in tow. "Rachel. How are you?" He felt genuinely glad to see her.

"We're battling the desert dust, but my kids are losing. It's a curse, this constant dust."

"I think the little ones suffer the most."

"What of Hamid? Has he come yet? Have you heard anything?"

"Not yet. I'm still waiting." *That's right, Danel, all you do is wait. You're waiting for someone who's not coming,* he thought.

"I'm sorry. Perhaps he'll come soon."

His eyes met hers, suspicious of her thoughts. But she didn't have to speak what he was already thinking: *why haven't you gone after him yet?*

"Come see us when you have some time. I think Ashara would want us to be friends."

"I believe she would."

Rachel fastened a child-size surgical mask on each of her kids, a physical barrier to the sand. "We'll see how long they leave these on. They're only children."

He patted each child on the head. "Be good to you mother, and keep these masks on when you're outside." As Rachel hurried the children off, Danel's thoughts drifted back to Hamid. *What kind of a man deserts his son? Only a coward.*

The day was long and the line of patients was longer. Finally, at 8:00 pm, he finished for the day. Exhausted, he plodded along the dusty lane towards his tent and found himself turning down the path toward Rachel Bakir's. Several children were playing in the lane, and he dodged one chasing a ball on a collision course with him. He peered inside her tent and called her name.

"Ah, Dr. Ottawa. I'm glad you came." She carried her little one on her hip."

"I see he's been eating well. What's his name?"

"Amal."

"He's grown."

"Yes, he's very healthy. Allah has blessed us. Would you care to hold him?"

Danel smiled sheepishly, reaching for the infant whose little arms opened eagerly. "He reminds me so much of our son. Is he a good baby?"

"I never hear a peep out of him. Always so happy."

As Danel jiggled him playfully, the baby chortled. "That's how our Hamid is."

"Can you stay for a cup of tea?"

He started to refuse it as an imposition, but something made him not want to leave. "It would be most kind of you." He closed his eyes remembering the touch of Hamid and the joy he felt around the child.

"My husband is not here, so we'll have to have it outside. I hope you understand."

"Of course. Your husband's blessed to have so honorable a wife."

She ducked inside and carried out two oversized cushions, motioning for him to have a seat. "I already have a pot of tea prepared, so it'll just take me a moment." Quickly she returned with a tray with cups and saucers, honey and napkins. "I wasn't sure how you like your tea."

"This is just fine." He set the child inside his crossed legs, leaning against one of his knees. Amal's tiny hand had grabbed Danel's thumb to teeth on it. "It looks like he is getting ready to cut a tooth."

"He tries to bite on anything he can reach and drools quite a bit."

"Ashara told me that your husband didn't accompany you to Za'atari. What does he do for a living?"

"He was an apothecary, but now he fights with the insurgents in Homs."

"Not a job that a pharmacist would be trained for. What made him fight?"

"That's a good question. He's a skinny little man and not a fighter at all. Actually he is very gentle and kind."

"Hardly a profile of a freedom fighter."

"You're right. The regime thought that the rebels were getting some aid and medicine from a local pharmacist, but they didn't know who. So they gathered up all the area pharmacists, including my husband, and tortured them. He was there for a month. We'd no idea where they had taken him or if he was still alive. Eventually they let him go, but by then they had planted the seed of hatred in his heart. He sent me and the children here and said he'd come eventually. I was pregnant at the time. But that was over a year ago and he hasn't come here yet. He's never seen Amal."

"Have you heard from him?"

"I hear from him occasionally. He gets word to me through others who have family here. He can't tell me much without giving away where they are. But for me it is enough to know that he's still alive."

"Do you think all of this fighting is worth it?" He raised his cup and sipped, savoring the calming effect of the warm tea.

"I asked my husband that same question. What's this worth if in the end we lose you? He said, if not him, then who else would you have fight for the right to live like a free man. Do you know what I said?"

"No, what?" He picked up his empty cup, passing it to her for a refill.

"I said the last person I would send to fight the regime is a skinny pharmacist who doesn't even know how to shoot a gun."

Danel smiled, recognizing that her humor embraced the naked truth of ordinary men called upon to exhibit remarkable courage. "Your husband must be a very brave man."

"Or a very stupid one. I suppose each of us has to do what he thinks is the right thing and pay whatever the cost. I know that my children need a father, and I pray to Allah to protect him and bring him out of this alive. But I think our President Assad will not give up so easily."

"I suppose not." Danel picked up little Amal and held him up over his head. The baby laughed and waved his little arms.

"What of you, Dr. Ottawa? What about your baby?"

"Please, call me Danel. My Hamid haunts me. At first I really believed he was coming here with the nun that took him."

"This is the Sister Helen that Ashara mentioned to me? Do you think she has stolen your son?"

"I absolutely do. Ashara told me this and I wouldn't believe her. I told her she was paranoid. I'm part of what drove her to take her life."

Danel settled Amal in his arms and caressed his soft crown as he had done for Hamid many times, brushing his lips across the baby's forehead.

"I think Amal likes you. May I pour you more tea?"

"No, thank you."

"It is no crime to think the best of those you trust, as you did with Sister Helen. But now that you know, have you decided to go after him?"

Danel hesitated because his own course of action was not well formed. "I fear I'm not as brave as your husband."

"My husband would never describe himself as brave. I think it is not something that we are, like kind or strong or good. Courage comes to us only at the moment that we really need it. I don't think that any one of us has a storehouse of bravery that we can tap into. You shouldn't worry about whether or not you're brave enough. When the time comes, Allah will make sure you'll have all that you need. And then some day Hamid will tell his children about how brave his father was."

"Right now I know I have to make a plan. Enough time has passed that Sister Helen is not going to give him up easily, if I can even find them."

"But he's yours, and a father would go to the ends of the earth after his own son."

"Yes. I know that in Damascus I'm hunted, so there is much risk for me, but even greater for both of us if I find him. A man with a baby will be easy to track."

"I think you'll find that where your son is concerned you will have enough bravery for both of you. The father and son bond is made of flesh, blood and spirit, and such a bond is very strong. But stronger than that is the love between you."

Danel winced at her reference to flesh and blood, but her point about love being stronger moved him.

"I hope you're right." He handed Amal back to his mother and smiled as his chubby arms reached for her. "I must be going now." He stood up and smiled at mother and child. "Thank you for your hospitality and your kind words, Rachel. I understand why Ashara came to be with you and Amal. It's felt good to me as well."

"I'll pray to Allah that your search is successful and that soon the two of you are reunited."

"And I will pray that you and your brave pharmacist will also have a reunion soon."

It was almost dusk when Danel wound his way back to his tent. A soft warm breeze blew grains of sand against his cheeks. He couldn't explain why, but the visit with Rachel and Amal had clarified that his mission now was to find his son. He had crossed over an invisible precipice — where before was a stolen child, was now his own son. The choice now was so illuminated that he could scarcely believe it had ever been obscure. Whatever his reasons or his methods, his actions had placed the infant in his care and responsibility. No matter how ill-conceived the bond between father and son was begotten, his path was now as clear as the diamond-like stars showcased against the deep ebony of the desert sky. For the first time in many days, he had purpose.

As he approached his tent, he saw Bethshari waiting in the lane.

"Danel, you were a genius. Saeed is totally changed and back to his old self. I can't thank you enough."

"He's a very fine boy. I'm glad we could set him straight."

"What's this 'we'? It was you that found the right words."

"And it was your caring that brought him to me. See, we're a good team."

"Indeed. I just saw Abu Majeed on my way here. I told him what you did. He instructed me to fetch you to his apartment right now and the three of us will celebrate."

"But it's so late."

"It's not even 9:00. Is Abu working you so hard that you have no energy for a little diversion?"

"It's not that."

"Well, have you had your evening meal?"

"You forget that Ashara's gone and I'm not much of a cook."

"Then it's settled. We go to see Abu."

He laughed. "I guess I don't have a voice in this."

"That's right, Dr. Ottawa. When Dr. Majeed summons, we obey." She slipped her arm in his and pulled him forward as they started walking down the path toward the front of the camp.

"You know when Ashara and I first came here, we were in the last row of tents, and now there are another five rows behind us. Amazing that people are still coming, and equally amazing how Za'atari keeps growing."

"We are getting close to 1,200 a day now. Za'atari groans as its belly is engorged. I see poor peasants whose clothes are threadbare, and then I see children walking about in expensive American sneakers."

"The uprising plays no favorites. That reminds me of Saeed's mother. Has he heard anything from her lately?"

"No, nothing, and it's been almost two months now since the last letter. He was very upset when his last letter was returned."

"He's counting on his mother coming, and now doesn't know where she is. Naturally, he's distressed," said Danel.

"Yesterday I asked Phillip Cameron to see if he could look into it. He has contacts. I'm not sure what he can do, but he'll try."

"What will happen to Saeed if his mother is killed?"

"I suspect he'll be sent to an orphanage somewhere in Jordan, definitely not back to Syria. I'm very worried about him."

"He's so vulnerable. I can't even imagine myself at age ten being sent alone to a place like this."

"You know what I have been thinking?"

"What?"

"I have been thinking if that happens I would try to adopt him."

"Is that even possible? I mean, would the authorities let you do that?"

"I know that in Syria it would be very difficult, but here in Jordan, where they have too many refugees, it would be one less that they would have to find a place for. I think it would be doable."

They had turned right past a congregation of refugees milling about. A voice called out, "Dr. Danel, good evening." He recognized the portly woman he had treated the previous day for a peptic ulcer. Taking the medication he prescribed would be easy, but changing her diet in the camp would be more challenging. But he had no cure for her malady's real cause, the stress of living at Za'atari.

"Mrs. Abdulla, are you feeling any better this evening?"

"Yes, a little I believe. The medication's helping." She stood up, smoothing the wrinkles in her long-sleeved aqua tunic, striding a few steps to close the distance between them.

"Good. Just keep up the medication. Don't forget I want to see you in about two weeks then." He waved as he continued walking.

"You're getting to be a celebrity it seems." She marveled at his recall of Mrs. Abdulla by name, knowing too well the refugees accessing the health services mimicked the volume of those that entered the camp. Despite her gregarious personality, it became increasingly difficult to remember individuals or details about them.

"Nonsense. A person remembers her doctor."

"No. It's more than that. You saw her as a person when you treated her, and that's why you could recall who she was. That's special. How many doctors under more civilized circumstances could say that, recalling a person by name and their malady out of the context of the hospital?"

"Hard to say." A slight blush warmed him as he edged the conversation in a different direction. "There is so much need here. Sometimes I'm overwhelmed. It can suck you into the vortex, and you feel like you can never climb out. I have been thinking about leaving soon to find my son."

"I was wondering when you'd be ready for that." She executed an off-balance sidestep to avoid a small sand snake camouflaged among the grains, which slithered across her path before disappearing under the edge of a tent.

"Careful you don't fall." He reached to catch her, but she had righted herself.

"I'm fine." She pulled forward, consciously avoiding his grasp. "Sometimes I wonder what the desert fauna thinks about the human aliens invading their ecosystem." A sudden, unspoken barrier between them arose spontaneously, like a sand eddy spirited heavenward by an afternoon desert wind.

"I need a plan about Hamid. Perhaps we can discuss this with Abu over dinner."

"Perhaps." Her pace quickened.

"Bethshari, slow down. What's your hurry all of a sudden?"

"Abu's probably wondering where we are."

"What's up? You seem, I don't know, different. "

"It's your imagination."

"Is this about me leaving to find Hamid?"

She bit her bottom lip. "I won't pretend that I'm not sad about your leaving."

"But you know that I must find my son."

"Of course I know it. It's just that…. Never mind."

"It's just that what?"

"I said never mind. It's nothing."

He grabbed her wrist. "It's not nothing. I can see all of a sudden you're upset. Now what is it?"

She tilted her face upward to deter any spillage from her eyes that had glassed over. "Do you really not know?"

"No. What is it?"

"It's just that I have feelings for you. I'm not proud of this, since Ashara has just died. But my heart has no conscience." Waiting for Danel to respond, she could make out Abu about a hundred meters ahead, who had come outside for a last smoke before his guests arrived. "I can see I've offended you. Please forget what I said."

"No, it's not that. I don't want to forget what you said."

"Then what? You must think ill of me for not respecting Ashara."

"I too have feelings for you, but I dared not speak of them. I loved her very much, and I'm ashamed that I'm having such feelings. I don't want to dishonor her memory."

"I didn't plan to feel this way. It just happened. In war, things happen, and we don't have the luxury of waiting until the timing is more acceptable," she said.

Their disclosures would have to be tabled as they had almost reached Abu. Sniffling deeply, she turned around, pretending she had dropped something, to wipe her eyes. The dim evening light disguised the blotches in her cheeks.

"We can discuss this later," he said.

"Yes, of course."

They had reached Abu, who dragged the last few puffs. "Abu, still polluting your lungs I see, comingling tobacco smoke with desert dust. You won't live to your forty-fifth birthday if you keep this up," said Danel.

"Now you sound like Bethshari. She's constantly on me about my smokes." He reached to shake Danel's hand. "I am glad you came, my friend. I told Bethshari you wouldn't come, but she was game to try and persuade you. I see she accomplished her mission." He winked at Bethshari. Grinding his cigarette into the heel of his shoe, his hand cupped the extinguished butt between his thumb and middle finger. Foraging in his back pocket, he retrieved a pack of cigarettes, carefully wedging the half smoked bottom among the unsmoked. "Nothing gets wasted in the desert." He placed his hand against Bethshari's mid back to guide her inside, gesturing Danel to follow her.

Inside, Abu had set the table with three glasses and a bottle of red wine from Chateau Ksara.

"Abu, where ever did you find the wine?" said Bethshari, lifting the bottle to read its label. "It's from the Beqaa Valley in eastern Lebanon. Is there a black market here for fine Lebanese wine that you have been hiding from us?"

"Unfortunately it's one of my last bottles from the stash I brought with me. I haven't been able to locate a supplier here in the camp."

"Three glasses?" said Danel. "You know I don't drink."

"Yes, I know this, but I know you make exceptions for medicinal reasons."

"Attempting to corrupt a non-drinking Muslim man again, Abu?" said Danel.

"Nonsense. I'm simply doing Allah's bidding."

"In serving up a glass of temptation?"

"Not at all. I'm offering a hard-working doctor a well-deserved respite. I think Allah would approve. I know that Bethshari believes this to be true." He cast a sly glance in her direction. "Now we should have a toast to three friends who are doing their best in a very trying place." He filled each glass half way and passed the glasses.

"Well then, in the interest of friendship I won't refuse," said Danel.

"To friendship then," said Abu as the three raised their glasses.

"To friendship," echoed the other two.

Abu set down his glass and motioned for them to sit. "I have a light supper of course, but Allah, the timely arrival of the UN supply truck and my patient Mrs. Katabi have all three conspired to spare us from my cooking."

"Can I help? I'm not a great cook, but I can be useful in the kitchen." She stood up. "At least I have a leg up on Danel, who tonight confessed that Ashara was the cook in their family."

"Actually, everything's prepared, so stay where you are."

She eased back onto the sofa next to Danel. The light banter relieved the tension. She had not planned to show her feelings tonight but was caught off guard by Danel's decision to go after Hamid. Sitting on Abu's small divan, so close that their elbows and thighs lightly brushed the other, they felt the tinder from their earlier conversation smolder.

Abu returned with an appetizer platter, laden with nuts, pomegranates, grapes, hummus with pine nuts and olive oil, olives, and flat bread. "We can thank the UN supply truck for the freshness and variety, and of course, the timeliness I attribute to Allah. You both are very quiet. Let's see if some good food can liven up the evening where the wine has failed." Wrinkling his nose at their untouched glasses, he filled his empty glass and raised it for another toast.

"Uh, oh," said Bethshari, "I fear that the good Dr. Abu means to regale us with stories and more toasts. Drink up, Danel, if you want to insulate yourself. He can be very wordy." She laughed as she took a deep sip from her own glass. "This is very good, Abu. My compliments to the sommelier."

Abu made a deep bow. "We are exposed to such suffering here in Za'atari, an evening like this can go a long way to reminding us of what we once had and perhaps one day have again. Perhaps, Danel, you would care to give thanks to Allah for this occasion?"

"I would be honored."

O Allah, we thank you for Your care and this food. We also thank You for friendships, which nurture us and remind us that You are all around us and those we love and serve.

"Please, eat," said Abu. "Only Allah knows when the next supply truck will come or what will be on it." He handed each a small plate, gesturing for them to fill it from the communal platter. Once they had taken, he filled his plate as well. "I was about to ask, before Bethshari warned you about my long windedness, about your son Hamid. Have you had any news?"

"Not really. We were discussing this on our way over here." He glanced over at her briefly, as if looking for permission to speak of this. "I've accepted that he's not coming and that Sister Helen means to keep him."

"Do you know where they might be?"

"I've no idea. I know that they made it to Damascus, but the trail ran cold after that. They could be anywhere."

"Does she have support or resources there to hide?" said Bethshari.

"Not that I'm aware of. She was well liked at the hospital, but being well liked is very different from arriving with a child that isn't her own."

"Would the NGO or her own order assist her?" asked Abu.

"It wouldn't be wise of them to help her conceal or smuggle a child. Their goodwill in Syria is worth far too much to risk helping someone kidnap a child."

"Does she have financial resources?"

"None that I noticed. She lived very modestly and ate her meals at the hospital. She told me she didn't receive any salary."

"So what's her motivation for taking an infant? If she had no means or resources, how can she even care for it and support herself?" Bethshari leaned forward to add some pomegranate to her plate. "This is superb, Abu."

"She confided to Ashara that she had conceived a child out of wedlock when she was a teenager. Her parents made her give the baby up for adoption, but she had longed for a child ever since. Ashara sensed this early on. Only I was too wrapped up in hospital business to give it any credence."

"What kind of person is she?" This question was very typical of Bethshari, who always sought to understand what motivated people. Danel related the story of Ashara's trek into the hospital the day that Hamid was born.

"Courageous, generous, kind and very capable, it would seem," said Bethshari.

Abu's intuition told him Sister Helen was a very clever, resourceful person who would stop at very little to get what she wanted. "I think she's still got to be in Damascus."

Bethshari set her empty plate back on the small table. "How can you be so sure? I would think that her best course would be to get out of the country as soon as possible. Hanging around in the same city she was last seen doesn't make sense."

Abu leaned forward in his seat. "That's exactly why she would stay, because that would be the one place that everyone, especially the child's parents, would think she would flee. Danel, doesn't this seem very plausible?"

"You both make sense, but I believe like Abu that the course is to go to the city where she was last seen. But where to start looking?"

"Perhaps the best place is where it all began, at your hospital?" said Abu.

"We fled just in the nick of time. When the army got wind that we were leaving they went to our apartment to intercept us. Going back there risks being incarcerated. I'm no good to Hamid if I'm in a prison."

Rubbing his chin, Abu's brow creased. "But I thought you told me that the hospital there was very shorthanded."

"That's true. They are desperate for qualified personnel. "

"What was the relationship that you had with the director there?"

"Actually we were good professional friends, though I didn't tell him I was leaving because it would have put him in jeopardy. I never even said goodbye."

"How do you think he would regard you if you told him that now that Ashara is gone that you want to come back and help there? Would he turn you in or would he be grateful?"

"I suspect the latter, but I would want to talk to him first about it."

"What if you gave the bear a little honey to sweeten your return?"

"How would I do that? I have nothing to offer but myself."

"What if you were to offer to entice a Lebanese doctor to come and work as well?"

Danel looked perplexed. "You mean you? You'd leave here and go to Damascus?" Danel shook his head in disbelief. "But you said you wanted to be here because there was so much need."

"Are you telling me that there isn't a lot of need in Damascus with all of the doctors and nurses fleeing? It sounds like the need there might be worse than here, if what you're telling us is true?"

Danel and Bethshari sat dumbfounded.

"You both look like I just laid an egg in the middle of the floor. Surely if you don't believe me, I'll have difficulty convincing your director that I'm in earnest. But, let us have our salad and we can discuss further." He leapt up and removed the empty appetizer platter. "Keep your individual plates. Unfortunately, I only have four plates, so we'll have to repurpose them for the next course." He darted into the kitchen to rinse the platter for the next course.

"Delighted with his idea and its dramatic effect on his guests it appears," said Bethshari, confident that Abu was out of ear shot. "What're you thinking?'

"This could put him in danger, and I'm not willing to do that."

"Yes, and his accompanying you could keep you out of danger. He makes good sense that two doctors would be very appealing given the situation in Damascus. It would show loyalty if the regime questioned you."

Abu swept back with his next course, which he presented with a slight bow. "This is my mother's recipe for fattoush. Fried flat bread with vegetables, greens and her secret ingredient, sumac, which gives it a distinctive sour taste."

"You're full of surprises tonight." Danel scooped a portion onto his plate, his fingers guiding several coin-sized slices of squash onto a piece of the fried flat bread. "The sumac gives it a slight bite. Very delicious." Talking with his mouth full, he went on. "When I came tonight I thought I wasn't hungry, but you have really whet my appetite."

"Just you wait, I have saved the best for last."

"You mean there's more after this?" Bethshari took her first mouthful, chewing thoughtfully, savoring each taste. "It's decided, Abu, you're a better host than you are a doctor."

"You're both very kind." After several mouthfuls, he poured each more wine. "We can discuss my proposal as we eat."

"There is no way that I could allow you to accompany me. You would be in danger there, and I couldn't have that on my conscience."

"It wouldn't be on your conscience because it's a decision that I would be making. Before you say no, let's just discuss the logistics. There's no harm in that, is there?"

"I suppose not. But what about Za'atari? You're needed here, and with both of us leaving, it would put the hospital here at a disadvantage."

"Two other doctors joined since you arrived in the camp, and I spoke to our director this morning, and he says three more physicians will be here by month's end. So I think we have Za'atari covered."

"But where would you stay and how would you go after Sister Helen if you were both working there? You need to be practical about this," said Bethshari. As she made her point, each nodded. "What you need is feet on the ground."

"What are you talking about?" said Danel.

"She has a point. We could orchestrate a search using hospital resources, but we would need someone to go to various locations where we think she might be."

"That's where I'd come in."

The two men regarded her, simultaneously coming to the same conclusion. "Absolutely not. There is no way you are coming to Damascus with us," said Abu.

"Wait a minute, who said that there was even an 'us' going to Damascus?"

"Both of you listen to me." She set her plate down. "Danel mentioned that Sister Helen's a nurse by training. Right?"

"Yes, that's true."

"So it makes sense that she has to support herself and the baby. The only way she can do that is in a nursing position. Don't you agree?"

"Yes, but what's your point?" said Abu.

"The point is that the circle of possible employers for someone like this just got narrower. If she goes to a hospital, you can investigate this from your positions in the hospital. But what if she doesn't go to a hospital? Her other options would be clinics, emergency centers and the like. That will take someone visiting those places and asking questions, which I could do far less conspicuously than the two of you."

"I don't disagree with your reasoning. I just have to think through for myself whether I can in good conscience accept the generosity of two friends for so dangerous a mission. So the two of you can stop right now. This is something I have to sort through," said Danel.

"I tell you what. There is no commitment here on your part. What would you say about calling the hospital director tomorrow and asking him how he would feel about you coming back and bringing someone else with you? Do you think he would be honest with you about whether or not the authorities would come after you and if he would protect you?" said Abu.

"I think there's no harm in a phone call. I believe he'd protect me, but I'll reserve judgment on that until I talk to him."

"Alright then, that's a fair compromise."

"I suppose there is no harm in making the call."

"Now, are you ready for my final gastronomic offering?" said Abu.

"If it is anything like what you have served thus far, we can hardly wait," said Danel.

"Do you want us to close our eyes?" She was only teasing, but Abu took the bait.

"Yes, young lady, that would be a very good idea. No peeking now, either of you."

They closed their eyes, expectant smiles on their faces. "I can't imagine what this could be," said Bethshari.

"Abu, our eyes are closed here and we are tired of waiting."

"Then feast your eyes on this." The platter now held four torpedo shaped, deep fried kibbeh, still slightly warm. "The meat, I believe is lamb. You know this is the national dish of Lebanon."

"Did you make these?" Danel had already helped himself and broken into the croquette. Bulghur, minced onions and the ground lamb spilled out onto his plate. Using a piece of flat bread to sop up the juice, he used a second piece to scoop the contents into his hand and then his mouth.

"I wish I could say that they're my creation, but we owe them to the gratitude and culinary skill of Mrs. Katabi. Plagued by a urinary tract infection we finally got under control, she expressed her gratitude in kibbehs. So Mrs. Katabi's kibbehs are a fringe benefit of my doctoring and her antibiotic."

"Here here, to Mrs. Katabi." Danel raised his glass.

"And here's to her doctor and the miracle antibiotic." Bethshari's toast echoed Danel's, complementing the revelry of an evening with good friends.

21

Saeed Adrift

A full moon hung over the camp when the dinner party ended. The tension between Danel and Bethshari lightened under the spell of camaraderie and good food. Most of the camp had settled in for the evening. The alleys toward the rear of the camp were bathed in the subtle light of a late September moon and lulled by gentle snoring from residents deep in slumber. Lack of foot traffic allowed the dust to settle, and a cool breeze embraced them without the accompanying grit kicked up during the day. Walking side by side, they contemplated how to get back to where they had left off on the way to Abu's.

"I can't remember when I last had an evening like this one. I think perhaps it was before Hamid was born and we entertained our neighbors, the Faroushes. I long for normal times."

"I think we had one tonight."

"I agree."

"Listen, Danel, about what I said before dinner. I overstepped my bounds. I had no right to even hope that you could have feelings for me."

"I'm falling in love with you despite my reservations concerning Ashara. Is that wrong?"

"I know that I never planned to feel the way I do."

"Would Ashara think I never loved her to so quickly feel this for someone else?"

"Danel, she left you. Whatever her reasons, she decided that she was better off without you."

"Does that release me to love again? Or has she doomed me to a guilt so large that—"

Before he could find the right words, Bethshari finished it for him. "So large that you deny yourself any happiness? Yes, there's that possibility, but as bad as things got for Ashara, I can't believe that she would've wanted that for you."

"She wanted me to find Hamid." They arrived at a cross path. "Do you have to go back right now? Can we talk some more?"

"Of course, it's not that late," she said. Strolling together, they passed Danel's tent before they realized how far they had come.

"The football field is only a little farther. There is a bench where we can sit and talk. It would be a pity to waste a cool evening."

On the outer edge of the camp, away from the tents and the people, the desert offered a solitude that was elusive within Za'atari's perimeter. The press of humanity violated privacy and denied the space necessary to recharge emotionally and spiritually.

"You know I came to this bench that morning," he said.

"What morning?"

"The morning that Ashara took her life, we had a big fight. She told me to leave and I came here. I ran laps around the field, like I could run away from our problems. But the irony was that I was running in circles. Quite a metaphor for this place, isn't it?"

They reached a backless concrete bench facing across the pitch into the vastness of the desert. He bent over to brush gritty sand off the seat. Gesturing for her to sit, he picked up the night noises of the desert fauna, venturing from their burrows and rock crevices to forage and commune. "Listen, do you hear the activity out there?"

She tilted her head to listen.

"They've adapted to a life that begins when the sun goes down. We should take a lesson from them and become nocturnal," he said.

"But if we did that then half of Za'atari would be out here on the pitch with us right now invading our privacy." Turning sideways to face him, she touched his cheek. "I want to come with you and Abu to find Hamid. I want to do this for you." She paused. "No, that's not exactly true; I want to do it for us." Her eyes held his gaze momentarily, then closing them, she gently brushed her lips across his.

Savoring their sweetness, his responded slowly to her kiss, harnessing the intensity of his feelings, only barely tasting the promise behind their touch. "Are you asking for a commitment from me?" he whispered. "I'm not sure I have that to give to anyone right now or if I ever will."

"No, I couldn't ask for that right now. I'm only asking for a chance for us. That's all. If you leave now to find him and I don't go with you, it will be the end of us."

"But I would come back with him. I would find you."

"I think not. I believe that you would take him with you and keep on going and not come back here. And that's what you should do. What would be here for a doctor with an infant? You couldn't work because Hamid would need you."

He pulled her close to him, and this time he kissed her with a deep hunger and longing. As his tongue probed and explored, she responded as eagerly. He touched her breasts tenderly, almost hesitant. Reassuring him, she guided his hand inside her blouse. His thoughts drifted to Ashara, calling him back, reminding him that his secret did not pass with Ashara to her grave. His secret pulsed inside with a renewed vitality of its own life, not to be denied, demanding that it not be shoved aside. It told him, "*You don't get to forget what you did now that Ashara is gone. I'll be with you for all of your days. We are one.*"

The secret broke the spell, pulling him back and releasing her.

"Danel, what is it? What's wrong?"

"It's nothing. We can talk again tomorrow. Come, I'll walk you back."

During a restless night of soul searching, each was aware that something had been withheld. Danel's pain issued from full knowledge, and Bethshari's from the darkness of not knowing.

Clouds had rolled in by first light threatening much needed rain and along with it the misery of mud and filth. Since she was not scheduled to work until ten, Bethshari dressed quickly, hoping to catch Danel before he left his tent to go to the hospital.

Phillip Cameron emerged from the relocation center heading for the tent where UN employees checked in each day for their assignments. "Bethshari," he called.

Deep in thought, she crossed through the throng of refugees on her way to see Danel.

"Bethshari," he called again.

Her eyes scanned the crowd. "Good morning, Phillip. What's up?"

"We've had word about Saeed's mother. I'm afraid the news is not good. She and her parents were killed in a bombing over a month ago, as you suspected. She won't be coming to be with him."

She gasped. "First his brother and his father, now his mother and grandparents." She shook her head.

Phillip looked at her sheepishly, clearing his throat.

"Phillip, what is it?"

"It's just that I was hoping you would tell him. I mean since you are so close. I'm not really good at this sort of thing, and you, well, you know, I think he would take it better from you."

"Of course. But he's not going to take it well from anyone. His mother's dead." She took a deep breath. "I'm sorry. I didn't mean to bark at you. Forgive me?"

"Nothing to forgive. Bloody bad business all around."

"What will happen to him now? I mean what happens to an orphan at Za'atari?"

"We've been sending the orphans to Amman, unless they have relatives somewhere that will take them. We don't keep them here if their parents or some other relative aren't coming. They have a placement office in Amman."

"Would they send him back since he is Syrian?"

"No, that would be sending him back without patronage to a country where he would surely not last very long. They would repatriate him in Jordan no doubt."

Biting her lower lip, she chewed on it pensively. "He should still be at the children's tent right now. I'll go directly and find him."

She thought about how to break the news that he has no one left in the world. She didn't have long to wait because Saeed was already up and playing football with two boys in front of the children's tent.

"You're up early, Saeed."

"I was hoping you would need me today." Flashing a sunny smile, he hobbled over to greet her. "What're we doing this morning? Can I be your assistant today?"

"Well, I was hoping we could go for a walk, that is, if your friends can spare you." She held out her hand, which he grabbed without hesitation.

"OK, where're we going?"

"Well, let's walk to the soccer fields."

"Alright. Did you have a good party with Dr. Abu last night?"

"Ah, the good doctor told you about his plan?"

"He said it was our secret. He asked me to let him know when the UN supply truck arrived. He made me promise not to tell you."

"You're a good secret keeper, Saeed."

"Why did you want to come to the soccer fields? Is there a game going on?"

"No, I just wanted a quiet place to sit and talk."

An apprehensive gasp caught in his throat. "What did you want to talk about? Is it about my mother?"

"Yes, it's about her and your grandparents?"

"I wish you would tell me she is coming soon. But, I'm afraid that you are going to tell me…that she is not coming."

"Dr. Danel said you were very wise." They had reached the same bench where the preceding evening she and Danel had spoken of their love and the future. "Sit down next to me."

Saeed hesitated. "She's not coming is she?"

"No, Saeed. She and your grandparents were killed almost two months ago, right about the time her letters stopped. It's taken the authorities this long to verify that they were killed and file a report."

His tongue tasted the salty tears that poured freely down his cheeks.

She pulled him close and held him as he sobbed, rocking him gently.

"Did it hurt? Were they in a lot of pain like when the bomb hurt my leg?"

"No, it wasn't like that," she lied. "The bomb killed all three instantly. They never felt a thing. Allah just reached down and plucked them up directly to him. Your mother had been so brave to stay behind with your grandparents, and Allah didn't want such wonderful people to suffer."

"If Allah cared so much, why did he let them die?" Between his sobs he cried, "Allah. He could have saved them. He's all powerful. He knew Mama was all I had left, why would He take her?"

She continued to rock him. "It's not for us to understand Allah. We just have to accept that He has a plan even though we don't know all of it."

"What's his plan for me?" He pulled back slightly, and his earnestness dissolved her.

"Well, first we'll try to find your other relatives."

"I have no other relatives. They're all dead now. That's why my mother sent me here. There was no one else left to take me. Can I stay here in Za'atari until I'm grown up?"

She shuddered at the thought of Saeed's entire youth wasted in a refugee camp. "There's an agency in Amman where they help place children whose parents have died with other families."

He stood up, yelling at her. "I don't want to go to another family. I don't want to leave here. I want to stay with you."

She pulled him back down to the bench, holding him. "I'm not sure they would let you do that. They know that this is not the best place for children."

"There're lots of children here, and they're doing fine."

"What's here, Saeed, isn't fine."

He pulled away to see her face. "Don't you want me? I would be good and help you. You would never be sorry."

Hugging him tighter, she ached at the thought of leaving him. "Perhaps we can find a way. I can work on that."

His sobs gradually quieted. "Please don't leave me, Bethshari. Promise you won't leave me. Promise?"

"I promise, Saeed." *How poignant such a promise,* she thought. *How does this fit with my love for Danel and his leaving to find Hamid?*

As the boy gradually calmed, she released him.

Sitting quietly swinging his legs back and forth, his mind was back in his village. "Are you sure my mother felt no pain?"

"Yes, I'm sure. Since it happened when they were sleeping, they didn't even have time to be afraid."

"I'm glad she wasn't scared. Were my grandparents sleeping too?"

"Yes, they were asleep. One minute they were sleeping, holding hands peacefully, and the next moment they were with Allah. They were all very happy, except for one thing."

His legs stopped swinging. "What was that?"

"They knew they would have to wait for you to grow to be an old man with your own grown children before they would be with you again. But they're happy to wait because they want you to have the experience of a happy life with lots of kids and grandchildren."

Saeed smiled, carrying the picture she had just painted to the next step. "Maybe you could wait for me."

Drawing several drops parked just under his lashes to wet her handkerchief, she wiped the dirt off each cheek. "What do you mean wait for you?"

"Until I'm older. I mean so we could marry. Then we could have sons and daughters. And maybe by then the war would be over."

She hugged him and knelt down at his eye level on one knee. "Saeed, you honor me with these thoughts." Taking his hand, she continued. "But you're ten, and I'm eighteen years older than you. I think that you'd be better off with a beautiful young girl closer to your age."

"I wouldn't want anyone else. I only want to be with you."

"You're running ahead of yourself. But for now, I promise not to leave you. But you have to understand that I won't marry you either. Agreed?"

"OK, agreed. But when I am eighteen, you'll be…." He paused to calculate.

"Thirty-six. That makes me too old to keep up with an eighteen year old. Why, at thirty-six, I'll be losing some of my hair and my teeth, and looking very old." She sucked in her cheeks and hollowed her chest. "Like this, this's what you'd have to look forward to."

He started to laugh despite himself.

"Here blow your nose." She fished her handkerchief out of her back pocket. "Do you think you'll be alright for a while? I have to go see Dr. Danel and Dr. Abu. I also need to have a conversation with Mr. Cameron. Can you be brave?"

"I can't stay with you while you work?" He sniffled.

"I need for you to go play for a while, and I'll come later and get you."

"I'll wait for you."

Rummaging through her backpack, she found a second clean handkerchief. "Take this." Accepting it, he wiped his nose and the wetness off his cheeks.

"I can't stop crying."

"Saeed, someone who doesn't cry can't get past their grief. They get tangled up in it and never heal. Did you cry a lot when your baba and your brother were killed?"

"I cried all the time at first."

"Then what happened."

"Well, at first I cried a lot and thought about them all the time. Then I cried less and thought of other things. I mean, it's not that I didn't still miss them. I just didn't think of them all the time."

"That's the way this will be. You loved your mother very much, but gradually she'll have a different place in your heart. Just as special, but you'll learn to love and depend on others, and that will help you. But for now, you cry about her as much as you need to." She hugged him tightly. "Remember you're not alone. She's still with you, and I'm here too." She tenderly kissed him on the top of his head. "Will you be alright for a while?"

He nodded, wiping his eyes and nose along his sleeve.

"Use the handkerchief I gave you." She affectionately wiped his bangs out of his eye. "Let's walk back together." They followed the path to the children's tent. "I'll see you later."

"OK. Later," he said, joining several children playing out front.

"Hey, Saeed, want to play some football?" One of the boys spotted him as they approached.

She watched him trap a ball crossed to him by a tall boy about 3.5 meters away, pass it back to a chubby boy on the opposite side, and then disappear into the group of youngsters.

22

Damascus Plan

Buoyed by a new determination to find Hamid, Danel rose early and said his morning prayers. He had drifted away from the habit in the wake of Ashara's death. Not only had Ashara abandoned him, but in his depressive state he had ignored Hamid and Allah, the two that had the power to give meaning to his life. The support of his friends the previous evening had shaken him out of the malaise. For the first time in many days Danel now had a purpose. Entering the hospital, he asked the duty nurse if Dr. Abu had come in yet this morning.

"Dr. Abu's already in his office. Should I tell him you're here?"

"No, I'll just go see him."

Her eyes followed him across the reception until he passed through the double doors.

"Ah, Danel, you're here early this morning. It appears that you are none the worse for wear after your alcohol consumption last evening."

"I'm fine and have already made amends with Allah. I asked him to spare you for your reckless endangerment of those in your employ."

Abu laughed right out loud. "I like to consider myself an agent of character strengthening, especially where you're concerned. I'm just testing your faith and resolve, my friend." He motioned for Danel to sit. "Have you given any more thought about my offer last night?"

"You mean about accompanying me to Damascus?"

"Precisely. I'm more determined than ever."

"I'm still not entirely comfortable, and I can't understand why the need there would entice you any more than here."

"Let's just say it has the added benefit of assisting my friend, and a big city hospital more suits my various purposes."

Danel eyed him, unsure of his meaning. "I can't decide though until I talk to the director, Dr. Kahlil Majaresh. Until I know the climate there, I can't risk it for either of us, especially for you."

"What will you tell him about Hamid?"

"I've been debating. I'm not sure it's wise that he know my true reason for returning."

"I agree. It could cast suspicion on our activities there. You say that he's a friend?"

"He always has been. I'm not sure though until I talk to him if he carries any resentment about the way I left. But for now, I think he should believe that both Ashara and Hamid are dead."

"That's wise. You can decide later if you can trust him with that information. Until then, it's best that he see there's nothing to keep you at the camp now that you don't have a wife and a baby to keep out of harm's way."

"You can use my office for privacy when you call him."

"Thanks."

Rarely at a loss for words, Abu fidgeted with a paperweight on his desk. "What have you decided about Bethshari?"

"You mean about accompanying me?"

"Pardon me for being so intrusive, but I suspect that you're in love with her, although I'm not sure that you have allowed yourself to recognize that yet."

"So you're now a psychiatrist?"

"Any fool can see what's evident, except the fool that resists. I believe that Bethshari knows it."

Danel looked down at his feet, shuffling them uncomfortably. "Yesterday, on the way to your party, she reluctantly exposed her feelings."

"And you resisted, right?"

"I don't want to dishonor Ashara. It's so soon."

"Danel, don't be a fool. The circumstances of war allow for no hesitation. You must grab for the good things when they present themselves because they can evaporate like that." He snapped his fingers. "Surely losing Ashara taught you that."

"I hadn't seen it that way." Danel chewed his lower lip.

"Resisting a good woman that loves you to honor your dead wife is the wrong lesson."

"And what do you think is the correct lesson?"

"That love is fleeting and can be snatched away in an instant. Grab for happiness where you find it, and don't think about it too hard. To me that's the only lesson to be learned."

"My guilt gets in the way."

"Guilt's a manufactured emotion. We create it ourselves; no one gives it to us. It's for us to bury with the dead. It has no restorative value to those that have passed or to those that remain."

"So you think I should let Bethshari come with us?"

"Besides the fact that she's good for your heart and soul, I think that she'd be invaluable to our mission. She'll be able to ferret out places that we couldn't hone in on. And she'll be helpful once the baby's discovered."

"Perhaps you're right. But I have some things to discuss with her before I can agree. I wasn't totally honest with Ashara. I can't make that mistake twice."

"There you go with the guilt again. Bury it, Danel."

"I can't, not yet."

Abu shook his head. "Suit yourself. It seems that you're a stubborn man."

Danel looked at his watch, eager to deflect the conversation away from the unfinished business with Bethshari. "It's too early yet to reach Kahlil. I'll let you know what he says. No decisions until we see if it's safe to return."

Bethshari wound her way back to Phillip Cameron, who was assisting a newly arrived husband whose wife was missing.

"Phillip, could I have a word with you?"

"Of course." He motioned for another worker to take his place and beckoned Bethshari behind the counter into his office. "Did you talk to Saeed?"

"Yes. I told him what happened."

"How do you think he took it?"

She scowled. "Not very well."

"I was afraid of that."

"He has no one else. All of his family's been killed. Did you expect that he would take the news well?"

"Of course not. It's just that he must have been thinking something's wrong when his letter to her was returned. Surely this news didn't come as a surprise."

"Honestly, Phillip, he's ten years old." *Ah the British stiff upper lip*, she thought. "There's a big difference between worrying that the worst might have happened and having hope that there is some other explanation. What's the procedure here for orphans with no immediate family?"

"Normally arrangements are made to send them to the host country's orphaned children agency. In this case, we would send him to Amman."

"How soon would all that happen?"

"Several weeks at most. We think it best not to let them get any more entrenched. Always best to get them placed with a foster or adoptive parents as soon as possible."

"But Jordan is a poor country. Tell me honestly, what's the likelihood of finding a home for a ten year old?"

Phillip shrugged his shoulders. "I have to be honest; the chances aren't very good. Parents want infants, not children who have suffered enough to be damaged goods."

"If he can't be adopted, then what would become of him?"

"He would remain a ward of the country and remain with the agency either in a state-run facility or some other foster arrangement until he would be old enough to support himself."

"You mean they'd keep him in an orphanage. Not the best way to live out your childhood, now is it?" Her sense of injustice fueled her agitation.

"You act as though I'm responsible for this situation. I'm just telling you what I know."

"What if I were to adopt him? What's the likelihood that he could be placed with me?"

"I would have to look into that. But he would have to be sent to the agency so that the arrangements and paperwork could be properly filled out. It could take months for all that to be accomplished." She removed her backpack, which suddenly felt too heavy.

"Couldn't he remain here while all that was being done?"

"Not likely. They would need to check that he truly was alone with no relatives, and they're not going to do that for a child that has not even been placed with them. No, that's just not likely. Have you spoken to Saeed regarding this?"

"I'm just looking for information. Do you think it'll take you long to get it?"

"Perhaps a few days, but I'm not committing to a timetable you know."

"Phillip, if you'd rather not, just tell me." She shifted her weight to the other foot. *How could anything be more important than assisting this child with finding a home*, she thought. She calmed herself, aware that alienating him would not help her cause. While Phillip was a reluctant advocate, he was very savvy about getting information and working his way around the UN system.

"No, no. I can do this." He smoothed the short, wiry curls along the hairline at the nape of his neck, but they too resisted his preference for order. "It's just going to take some time, what with my other responsibilities."

"Thanks, my friend. I'll check back with you." She gratefully squeezed his arm.

The routine chaos at the hospital enveloped Danel until mid-morning. Updating the chart of his last patient, an elderly man with acute gout, he sent him away with a large dosage of vitamin C and a set of dietary instructions that he hoped the man would follow. As the charge nurse handed him the chart of the next patient, he signaled that he would be taking a break.

Abu, working in the curtained examining room next door, observed Danel's shoes and pant legs of his tan scrubs exit along the lower edge of the privacy curtain and then turn down toward his office.

Closing the door softly behind him, he sat at Abu's desk. His limp hands rested passively in his lap before picking up the phone to dial his hospital in Damascus. Despite the desert heat, a chill shimmied across his shoulders.

"I'm calling for Dr. Majaresh, is he in?"

A female voice devoid of warmth or recognition answered. "Who's calling please?"

Danel identified himself and waited.

"Danel, is that you?"

"Yes, it is, Kahlil. It took so long for the operator to get you I feared you were no longer there."

"There aren't many left that were here when you were. Unfortunately, I decided to stick it out. There're many days when I wish I hadn't. But enough about me, how is Ashara and the baby? Hamid, right?"

Ashara's mention caught him off guard. He flinched as if the whole affair at Za'atari were just a bad dream. "I'm sorry to tell you that Ashara's dead." He swallowed hard. "Of her own hand, when the baby took sick and died." His inner counsel warned him against too much fabrication lest he get tripped up later on details.

"I'm so sorry to hear that. I know how much she longed for a child. Such a cruel outcome for someone so desperate to be a mother. How're you doing with this tragedy?"

"With Allah's help I continue to cope. Some days are better than others. I miss her dearly."

"I remember how she suffered when she lost the first two. This one held so much promise. So where are you, and why are you calling me today?"

"We fled to Za'atari, and I have been practicing at the hospital there. But there's no reason for me to stay. I left to protect Ashara and our baby from the violence in Damascus, but now there's no need to stay."

"I see. Are you proposing to come back here to work?"

"I was wondering if you would have me. How much danger from the authorities would I face if I returned?"

"I doubt you would encounter any interference. Their menace was targeted at those who were fleeing. Assad desperately wants to staunch the flow of professional talent leaving his kingdom. There's no point in harming those that return, though very few do once they get out."

"Would you have me back after I deserted?"

"Danel, you're one of the best surgeons we ever had. I'd be a fool not to come and carry you back myself. I'd welcome you with open arms."

"Well, you won't have to carry me, but there is one other thing. I work here in Za'atari with another physician, a pediatrician actually. He volunteered to accompany me and work there if you'd be willing."

"We're desperate here for medical personnel. It was bad when you left, what was it, six, eight weeks ago? It's dire now. You realize that you're coming back to worse conditions than when you left."

"The conditions in Za'atari are very poor. Here in the desert there is no relief from the heat and the sand, and there're so many sick or injured. We too are shorthanded. But Syria's my home, and I'm lost here without Ashara."

"Then know that you and your friend are very welcome. What's his name?"

"Majeed. Abu Majeed. He's Lebanese and has been a great friend to me since Ashara passed."

"Then tell him you're both welcome. How soon would you come?"

"We have to make some arrangements, but I would expect that it could be anywhere from several days to perhaps as long as several weeks. Abu's the director in charge of new medical hires here, and we are expecting several new physicians to join the medical corps. We'll come together as soon as he can disengage."

"Very well. May Allah keep you safe, Danel. I pray for your speedy and safe return."

"Allah willing, we both will see you soon."

Abu and Bethshari had entered his office as Danel spoke to Kahlil, shutting the door quietly behind them. Sitting in two leather side chairs, they waited for him to finish the call. The grave look on their faces warned of more crisis.

"I've just spoken to the director in Damascus, and he feels that it's safe to return. He's very eager to get two doctors, as you suspected."

"That's good news," said Abu. "Did you give him any estimated time of arrival?"

"No, I kept it vague and told him that we would have to make arrangements."

"What did you tell him about Hamid?"

"I told him that the baby didn't survive, and because of that Ashara took her own life.'

"Good. The fewer people who know we're hunting for Sister Helen the better off we are."

"Danel, I have some bad news," said Bethshari.

"I knew something was wrong when you both came in."

"It's Saeed's mother. She was killed just as we suspected. That's why her letters stopped."

"Have you told him yet?"

"I told him this morning. He's brave, but this is a crushing blow for him. He has no one else in the world. All his family members are dead."

"What are his options?" said Danel.

"I have Phillip Cameron looking into things." She felt her cell phone vibrate and decided to answer it later. "What did you find out about the hospital in Damascus?"

"They are eager to get us both. The director said that the authorities aren't going after those who return." Feeling self-conscious sitting in Abu's seat, he started to get up. "Abu, do you want your chair back?"

"No, you can stay there. It's not going to be my chair for much longer anyway."

"I'm coming with you and neither of you can talk me out of it," said Bethshari. She crossed her arms on her chest and planted her feet resolutely, bristling that their discussion that had not included her.

"I have some things to discuss before we make that decision. Could we meet later this afternoon when we both get off of work?"

"I get off at 4:00. I'll come over to the hospital when I am free."

"In the meantime, Abu and I can work on some logistics. I have a car but I have no idea if it still runs. It was broken into the first day we arrived so it may be full of sand and who knows what has been stolen from it."

"And I have to figure out how to pass my responsibilities over to my replacement."

Danel's insistence on a meeting worried Bethshari. *Whatever it is*, she thought, *it's troubling to him.*

23

Danel's Conflict

Danel saw three more patients, all the while preoccupied with the car and his discussion with Bethshari later that day. He hadn't been back to the car since he and Ashara removed their possessions. He remembered sitting cross legged while she gently scrubbed his jaw and applied iodine, then wrapping their faces in scarves to protect against the shammal's gritty wind before venturing out for news about Hamid. If it weren't for her death, she would be accompanying him back to Damascus to find their son.

He reported to the nurse that he would be leaving for the day before going out to the Renault. The parking lot was now a vast sea of cars. The utility pole that was his landmark was now indistinguishable; he would just have to eliminate them one by one. Within ten minutes he found the vehicle, whose windshield was so laden with sand he couldn't make out the condition of the inside by looking through the window.

Grit clogged the key slot in the driver's door, so he gingerly reached into the back through the broken window to unlatch the back door. So much sand had filtered through the broken window, he thought he might need a shovel to clear it. A much larger sedan next to it had served as a buffer, keeping the sand to eight centimeters deep on the seat and floor in the back and about half of that in the front.

Carefully, he maneuvered himself over the back seat and into the front. Inserting the key into the ignition, he noticed blood oozing from a gash on his forearm. He turned the key in the ignition and heard a dull grinding sound. After several tries, the only response was a hollow clicking sound. Checking his watch, he saw the time to meet Bethshari approached. The car would have to wait.

Smarting from his encounter with Bethshari, Phillip Cameron mumbled to himself, bristling over one more person in the UN system failing to recognize his skills. His superiors mislabeled his reluctance to take on new responsibilities as a sort of professional laziness. Those at his level or below who needed his help were frustrated with his initial resistance. Yet the irony of Phillip Cameron was that once he decided to get involved, his results were quite remarkable.

Undeterred, Bethshari called on him to check on progress. With Danel and Abu's departure for Damascus imminent, her feelings for Danel and the fate of Saeed complicated her plans. "Phillip, hope you don't mind, but I was crossing by, so I thought I'd pop in and check on progress." Her smile belied the tension, but her hands coyly tucked behind her back fidgeted.

"It's not like I have nothing else to do, thank you very much, but I have had some success."

"Really what's the news?"

"I uncovered what agency handles adoptions out of Za'atari. Saeed will have to be under their care for any formal adoption papers to be processed."

"I was afraid of that. He'll be lost there not knowing anyone. At least here he has friends and knows how to fend for himself." She sighed. "He'll be in completely unknown territory there."

"Well, he's no stranger to coping in unchartered waters then, is he? After all, he did come here without his parents and has managed quite nicely it would seem."

"This relocation is a lot different, and we mustn't forget that this is a ten year old we are talking about." She bit her lip.

"A lot different, really? It doesn't seem much different to me."

"When he came to the camp, his mother loaded him on a bus with instructions on what to do, how to behave and most importantly, to wait for her. His whole life here was predicated on preparing a home for his mother when she could join him."

"Well, when you put it that way." He rearranged a pile of papers on his desk.

"But there's more to it. Up until two months ago, she kept up with him through several weekly letters. He never felt abandoned or alone because she reaffirmed that she was coming."

"Yes, quite, I see there is some difference." He avoided eye contact.

"When he gets shipped to the agency, he'll be sailing blind in a bureaucratic sea without a rudder or a compass. Surely you see that?"

"I already said I got it. You don't have to hit me over the head with it." He reshuffled the same pile of papers in front of him, tapping it to align the papers perfectly.

"Phillip, I love that little boy. Please forgive me if I get overbearing about his welfare." Swallowing hard, she said, "I mean no harm, and I am eternally grateful for anything you can do for us. You're my only hope of getting through this. Please tell me you understand."

His shoulders slumped and he tilted his head. "I do understand. I'm not the bad sort that you make me out to be."

"I never meant you to feel that way. Please say you forgive me."

"There's nothing to forgive." Walking her to the door, he reached for the knob.

She hugged him gratefully. "Thank you, Phillip."

He felt a blush warm his cheek.

"Now if you'll get out of here I'll continue working on what you have asked me to do."

Releasing him quickly, she squeezed his arm gently before leaving.

Despite the oppressive sun, the air outside felt refreshing after her confrontation. Her hand shielded her eyes as she scanned a group of children for Saeed. While she didn't have all of the information she needed, she had enough to know that Saeed would have to be exiled from his current surroundings in order to move forward into a more permanent arrangement. Perhaps she should start preparing him now to give him time to adjust to the idea of leaving the camp. Head down, she walked down a path where she often found Saeed among other children, only this time he was not engaged. Withdrawn from the other children, he sat against the side of the children's tent, knees pulled up against this chest, drawing circles and letters in the sand with a small twig. Watching him unnoticed for several moments, she sat down beside him.

"What're you drawing, Saeed?"

"Not much."

"You're normally out here playing."

"I don't feel like playing."

"How come? Did you have a quarrel with the others kids?"

"No. Just don't feel like it. That's all. Did you need me to help you today?"

"Not today, but I did want to talk to you about some things."

"What things?" He continued to draw in the sand, avoiding her gaze.

"How about we go for a walk together?"

"Sure. Where to?"

"Well, let's head to the pitch."

Saeed popped up and extended his hand to help her up.

"You're such a gentleman, Saeed. Thanks." She brushed his bangs out of his eyes as he returned her smile.

"Is it about what is going to happen to me? I mean, is that what you want to talk about?"

"Yes, we should discuss some possibilities, don't you think?"

"I guess. I just want to stay here."

Gulping back the lump in her throat, she tensed slightly, placing her arm around his shoulder. "I don't think that is a long-term solution for you, and the camp authorities believe that you should be in a more permanent situation."

"But I don't want to leave. I will be good. I could help and work for the UN."

"Yes, they've already noticed what a good worker you are. But a boy needs a family until he grows up. You deserve a good family."

Shrugging her arm off his shoulder, he raised his voice. "I don't want to live with strangers. Why can't I stay here with you?"

"You lived with strangers when you first came here and you made a lot of friends."

"That was different. My mother was coming then. She's not coming now." Dirty rivulets ran down his cheeks dropping onto his shirt.

"I know. That was a lot different. You have some options now. One would be to have a real family in Jordan adopt you as their own son."

"But what if I didn't like them or they were mean to me?"

"Well, we would find a good family where that didn't happen." She knew very little about the amount of screening that the authorities went through in placing orphaned children, but at least in this discussion her hope for the best placement would have to suffice.

"Could I leave if they were mean or didn't love me?"

"Well, that's a question we would have to ask. I don't know how that would work, but we could find out. There is another option, but I am not sure if it will work." Still conflicted, she hesitated even telling him at this point.

"What's that?" He perked up slightly at another option, as if anything would be better than going to strangers.

"I hesitate to bring it up since I am not sure if the authorities will allow it. I don't want to disappoint you if it can't happen."

"I promise not to be disappointed. Tell me." He pulled on her sleeve. "Tell me."

"Alright, but if it can't happen, I'm going to remind you of your promise."

He placed his hand over his heart. "I swear to Allah that I won't be disappointed. I promise."

"How would you feel if I were to adopt you as my son?"

He stopped walking, not believing what he had heard. "You mean that you would be my mother, and we would live together as a family?"

"Yes, that's what I am suggesting. But you might be better off with a complete family, I mean with a mother and a father. If I adopted you, it would only be the two of us, and I'm not sure if the authorities would allow this. That's what we would have to find out."

Saeed hopped from foot to foot, skipping ahead three paces and skipping back. "Yes, yes, yes! That's what I want. I want to stay with you. We would be a family and I would take care of you and you would take care of me."

"Hold on a minute. We don't know if that is possible yet. We can't count on it until we know if they will let it happen. I am a single woman and that is not a typical family. They may resist this."

"I'm going to pray to Allah and ask Him to help us. Will you do that too? If He hears from both of us He might pay more attention."

"There is something else though that you're not going to like, but you'll have to accept it if we want to make this happen."

"What's that?" He frowned so deeply his eyebrows almost connected.

"The UN won't help unless you're registered with them and living at the agency in Amman."

"How long would I have to be there?"

"That I don't know. I've asked Mr. Cameron to find out all the details, and he's working on that now. Do you think you could be brave enough to go there and wait for all of this to go through?"

"I could be brave, but I'm not going to like it. Can you come and stay with me?

"No, it's only for…kids." She had started to say orphans, but somehow the label seemed too cruel.

"Would you come and see me?"

"Of course. And we could write letters."

"Like I did with my mother."

"That's right, only I'll keep writing back. You won't have to worry about me being killed. Alright?"

"How soon would I have to go?"

"Soon, but I am not sure when. I'll let you know when I know more details."

"When will you know more?"

"I'm working on it. But I promise as soon as I know, I'll tell you. OK?"

"OK. You promise?"

"I promise. Let's walk back now." They instinctively reached for the other's hand.

"I think I'm scared that it won't happen."

"We both have to have faith that Allah will help us then. Whatever happens will be the right thing. You'll see."

As they parted with a hug, a small group of Saeed's friends approached them and Bethshari called several by name. "My young friends, you look like you could use a treat."

A slight skinny girl with skinned knees, no older than five, raced up and grabbed Bethshari's leg. "What have you brought us?"

"Let's see now. How many are there of you?" One of the older boys proffered the correct answer immediately. "But I asked little Fatima, so no treats unless I hear her count out the number."

Proudly, she pointed out each child as she counted to seven.

"That's correct. You should have the first pick then." Out of her backpack she pulled out seven pieces of hard candy, each a different color. Fatima grabbed the red one.

"That's my favorite color too," said Bethshari.

Each child in turn chose a color. Scattering, they called thank yous over their shoulders as they ran off. She watched until they were gone, and then walked to the employee tent to clock out for the day. Her time with Saeed had taken longer than she had anticipated and it was already past five o'clock.

Danel had been waiting for some time by the same bench where he had talked to Saeed. He paced as dueling interests battled inside him. *Abu is right. When you're fortunate to find love a second time, you shouldn't risk losing it by talking about the past. What is done, remains done. What would revealing the secret to Bethshari accomplish?*

But if we marry and Hamid becomes her son, am I not exposing her to the same torment that Ashara bore? But what if I tell her, and I lose her? I lost Ashara over my honesty, why would this be any different? Again more pacing before he sat down on the bench, bending over with his head in his hands.

"Danel, you look so serious." Bethshari had come upon him quietly, startling him. "Are you alright?"

Raising his head, he regarded her, so lovely, so kind, so intelligent, dispelling any doubt about his love for her. "Yes, I'm fine. I was thinking about us and how quickly we have found love. There's a part of me that doesn't want to believe it and another that wants to finalize whatever is necessary so that we don't lose it."

Sitting down next to him, she took his palm, holding it gently in her cupped hand. She traced the outline of each fine, long finger with her fingertips. "It may have come on suddenly for you, but I believe that there was a chemistry between us from the first night that you and Ashara entered the camp and I gave you directions. You probably don't remember."

"Yes, I do. I remember watching you when you turned away from us to help the other refugees. I knew you were special."

"I felt that about you as well. But I also felt it about Ashara. I didn't covet her husband, but I knew that we would be friends. Some people touch you in such ways." She drew his hand to her lips and placed a soft kiss in his palm.

Taking both her hands, he lightly kissed her fingertips. "I love you."

"I love you as well. I've had more time than you to think about it. I have no doubts about our feelings, yours or mine."

"Do you think that you feel strong enough that we could make a life together?"

Raising her eyebrows, a slight smile brushed across her lips. "Dr. Ottawa, are you proposing marriage to me?"

"I am, but at this point with so much uncertainty I'm not sure that it would be wise for you to accept."

"What do you mean about uncertainty?"

"Well, to start with we know so little about each other." They paused, waiting for two nurses passing by to move out of ear shot.

"That has occurred to me as well. But we would have a lifetime to find out, wouldn't we?"

"And then there is Hamid."

"And don't forget Saeed's is another life that this affects."

"Yes, the search for Hamid, our concerns about Saeed, the danger in Damascus, the fact that I'm a refugee without a home or a country. It's all so much." He extended his hands in supplication. "What woman would walk openly into such a tangle? What kind of a home can I offer you?"

She lowered his hands and placed them in her lap. "Danel, I believe that we have the most important ingredient, and that's love. If our love is strong, then the pieces in this puzzle will eventually fit. If we're in Allah's hands, then all will be well. All the rest are details that we can work through."

"But what I learned with Ashara is that love isn't enough. It wasn't enough to keep her alive."

"It was Ashara's despair over Hamid that took her, not love."

"But there was more to it than that."

Bethshari's love offered him a way to close the door on his secret. Bending down, he kissed her at first sweetly, savoring the softness and warmth of her lips, and then deeply, their tongues probing tentatively at first, then urgently, arousing and unbridling feelings. Danel broke free, reining in their passion. "Is this any way for a Muslim man and woman to behave in public?"

"Maybe not in public, but definitely appropriate for two deeply in love."

He stood and straightened himself, taking her arm to guide her up off the bench. "We can fix the public part, and the appropriate behavior of a Muslin man in love with a Muslim woman we can indulge as well. Come with me."

As Danel led her back to the tent, a light sprinkle began to fall, sending inhabitants back under cover as loud rumbles thundered amidst a lightening-filled sky. They quickened their pace to a full sprint, but by the time they reached the tent, they were both drenched. Darting inside, he hurriedly rummaged for towels, draping one across his neck and shoulders, and with another gently wiping the rain from her face and squeezing the excess water from her hair. Drying her arms, he placed the towel across her shoulders. Carefully, he removed the hair pins that held her long plait up off her neck. As she shook her head, the plait fell loosely onto her shoulders.

"Now let's get you out of these wet clothes," he said. Slowly, he unbuttoned her blouse and slipped it off each shoulder. She started to undress him, but he stopped her, holding her wrists. "No, not yet. I want to see all of you and savor each moment." She acquiesced, not wanting to deprive him of anything. He moved carefully, helping her out of each wet article, until she stood before him naked and lovely. "You're so beautiful."

Running the back of his hand softly against the outer curve of each breast, he cupped each tenderly before running his hand along her sides, then across the small of her back and her buttocks. Drawing her close, he kissed her. "Come lie down." He helped her settle, positioning a pillow under her head.

Her arms raised above her head rested in a gesture of surrender across the back of the pillow. Unconsciously, she slightly parted her thighs, watching Danel remove his clothes. His body was lean and toned, and his arousal, while controlled, was firm and ready. He knelt down alongside her, taking all of her in. Stretching out along her body, he pressed in close, kissing her tenderly until her response matched his in intensity.

The torrential rain through the thunder drowned out the sound of their coupling but could not quench its heat. Their measured pace was inevitably hastened until their mutual satisfaction ended the wild ride and deposited them into each other's arms onto the deep, peaceful waters of sleep.

24

The Lie Revisited

Danel tried not to wake Bethshari as he gingerly extricated his arm, which had deadened under her weight. The rain was still falling, but the heavy torrent had abated when the thunder and lightning ceased. A steady downpour slapped noisily off the roof into puddles along the periphery of the tent. Rain in Za'atari was both a curse and a blessing. Though still dark, Danel sensed that water had seeped inside. The mattress was positioned in the middle, away from the walls, so he counted on it being spared from the mud.

Lying still with his eyes open, he savored the physical and emotional fulfillment, but the internal battle of should he or shouldn't he still raged. So many times while Ashara was alive, he buried his guilt, only to have it rekindle like a smoldering fire, desperate for air. Bethshari stirred slightly and whispered, "Danel, are you awake?"

"Shhh, my love. Go back to sleep."

"Danel, that was beautiful. I'll never forget the first time we made love. I've never felt so loved."

As she snuggled closer, he felt her body grow heavy as she drifted off to sleep again. He wished he could do the same. The promise extracted by Ashara the night that he came home and lied about the fish flashed across his mind. "No matter what happens, promise you will always tell me the truth," she had asked. He agreed then, but shortly, when the real test came, he failed. In the end it had cost her life. *Can*

I afford to repeat the past, he thought. What would be harder to bear, losing Bethshari now, or later when we have built a life together?

Daybreak was only a few hours away. Bethshari opened her eyes and reached for Danel's hand. "You're still here?"

"Yes, what could entice me away?" Hoisting herself up on her elbow, she tried to make out his face in the dark, but in the predawn light she saw only his outline, leaving his features in shadow.

He lifted her hair away from her face and laid it behind her shoulder. "I want to share some things with you, about Ashara and Hamid, and I am afraid that I'll lose you over what I'm about to tell you."

"You could never lose me. I'm not going anywhere." She squeezed his hand.

"I'm not so sure that you'll be able to keep that promise."

"Ashara is the past, and Hamid is our future. What more is there to anything but that?"

"I want to tell you about Ashara's suicide note."

She tensed, feeling uneasy despite her commitment.

"You don't have to do this. You don't owe me an explanation."

"Yes, I do. If I'm going to share my life with you, you must know who I am. Hamid's at the epicenter—not through his doing but through mine."

"Now you are scaring me." She lay back down to listen.

Danel stared at the ceiling, fearing her recoil. Repulsion and a bitter argument was Ashara's reaction. His conundrum, to reveal or not, had come full circle, and he accepted that this chalice of regret would not pass from him. Now Bethshari would drink from it as well. How ironic, he thought, Ashara's legacy was to make him a truthful man.

"I am not quite sure where to begin."

"You start at the beginning."

"That's something Ashara would have said."

"And she would have been right."

His voice became quiet and calm. "Ashara had wanted a child more than anything in this world. Before Hamid, she had two stillbirths, which devastated her. When she became pregnant with Hamid, she was joyous but very afraid that she would lose him as well."

"I can understand that. It must have been a huge worry for her."

"On the day she delivered, circumstances forced her to get herself to the hospital through sniper fire. She was almost killed, but when she got there the hospital, generators were out, and the hospital was in darkness. There was a lot of chaos."

She lay very still, her arms crossed over her chest.

"Are you still listening?"

"Of course. Go on."

"We had very little staff that night, so I delivered the child. Ashara wept, she was so elated he was alive. This child held such promise." His voice quivered. "But I could see, even in the dim light, that something wasn't right. His breathing was slightly labored and shallow. After assuring her he was fine, I took him back to the nursery to examine him." He took several deep breaths and gathered his voice.

"Are you alright?" she asked.

"I was never alright after that night. It became obvious that the child was in grave danger. His lungs were filled with fluid, and he desperately needed a respirator, but there was no power. There was no way to save him. So I swaddled him and held him in my arms until he slipped away."

"But I don't understand. You and Ashara were waiting for him to arrive. So you must have been able to save him."

"I couldn't save him. He was doomed. The war robbed him of any chance. Had it not been for the generators being out, he would be alive. I knew what to do, and I couldn't save him." He wept silently, staring directly ahead. When Bethshari reached over to comfort him, he pulled away. "I don't deserve your touch. I deserve to swallow the bitter pill of his loss and the pain I now feel."

She drew back rebuffed. The rain was still falling steadily, no longer in sheets, as if the skies too hushed to listen.

He got up to retrieve a handkerchief and blow his nose.

"I'm afraid you lost me. If your son was dead then who is child that you're going after?"

He settled back down onto the mattress cross legged, facing forward into the dark. "When our son passed, I laid him back in his trolley. There was another child in the adjacent bassinet, a boy, born shortly before my son. I looked at him, coveting his life for my son's life."

First light filtered through the window flap, just as the truth was working its way out of the shadows.

"It happened quickly. I didn't think it through. I just knew that if I could spare Ashara the pain of losing her child, I had to try." He swallowed deeply, fortifying his courage. "I switched babies, and another family's son assumed the identity of our dead infant."

A gasp escaped her mouth, which she covered with both hands. The sun, now close enough to the horizon, sent its rays over the earth's curve, so their faces were in plain sight. He stared directly at her, waiting for her reaction.

At first speechless, she recovered her voice. "But Ashara, how could you have fooled her? Surely she would have known her own child." She gnawed on her knuckle, filtering what he had told her to find a flaw in his story.

"She had only seen the baby for a few minutes before I took him away. The light was dim, and she was exhausted. But more than that, she wanted with all her being to believe that she finally had a son. Her joy blinded her. And this child really did resemble our son."

"But the hospital staff.... How could you cover up such deceit? The babies' identity papers, the bracelets?"

"The situation, as I said, was chaotic. I created the papers and made the adjustments. The hospital was short staffed since so many had defected, so all the normal checks and balances were gone. The war that took my son's life also gave me the opportunity to give Ashara what she really wanted."

"But Danel, how could you? Did you not realize the implications if you'd been discovered?"

"To be honest, it happened fast. My main focus was to protect Ashara from another loss. I didn't think through the ramifications. I just reacted."

"Did Ashara ever find out?"

"Not until the day she took her life."

"Why did you tell her? Didn't you know that this would destroy her?"

He sighed deeply before answering. "You remember how obsessed she'd become waiting for Hamid?"

"Yes, Hamid was her sole focus."

"She was worried that it might be a long while before he would come. She kept asking if it took months, could we use DNA testing to prove he was ours. Naturally, I dodged the issue because I knew that DNA would show he wasn't ours. But she wouldn't relent. We had a big fight, and I felt cornered. She kept pressing the DNA issue and wouldn't get off it. That's when I told her what I did."

"How did she take it?"

"You saw how she took it. She killed herself."

She flinched, undeterred. "I mean then. When you argued, how did she react?"

"At first, she didn't believe me. Hamid was her son, and she refused to believe otherwise. He even looked like us." He shifted his cramped legs and pulled his knees up under his chin. "She cried, mourning not just the loss of her son, but the trust that my deception had slaughtered."

"I can't even imagine her despair. Poor Ashara." She rolled onto her side, drawing her knees up into a fetal position.

"Then she articulated with such clarity the ramifications, which had eluded me at the time of the switch: that she was implicated in the deception, that I could be jailed and probably hung if ever it were discovered. But there was something even worse."

"What could be worse?"

"That the child would be taken away from her. That she would lose him again.

"What happened next?"

"She sent me away so she could be alone and think. That was the last I saw her alive. You know the rest."

She sat up. Several times she started to speak but had caught herself. Not sure what to say, she finally opened her mouth. "Danel, what am I to do with this knowledge? Why did you tell me this—to get it off your chest?"

Unsure whether he was hoping for sympathy or relief, he shook his head. "It's not that simple." His heart thumped against his chest. "I didn't unburden myself at your expense, if that's what you're thinking."

"Then why? The only other person who knew is now dead. You could have gone to your grave with this, and no one would have been the wiser."

"That's just the point. I know and Allah knows. If we're to make a life together, it can't be based on a lie."

"So now the truth is so important, whereas you threw it away so easily before."

He remembered Ashara's calling it his casual relationship with the truth. For his act, he lost his wife, and the conversation was leaning toward losing Bethshari as well.

"I've paid a bitter and well-deserved price for my deception. To build a life with you with a child that is not truly my own, without your knowledge and consent, would be unthinkable." Standing up, he paced around the tent, speaking as much to her as he was to himself. "Could I let Ashara's sacrifice not change me? I know the risk I have taken with you, but losing you would not be as horrific as deceiving you."

"Noble sentiments, but Danel, don't you realize that by telling me you've made me an accomplice? The child isn't yours, and it wouldn't be ours. We would always live with the threat of losing him should someone find out. And there are ways to find out that someone's genetic footprint is not of his parent's lineage."

"You think I haven't thought of this? But with my actions I destroyed his connection with his real parents. He's my responsibility if not of my blood. Don't you see that?"

"I do, but what you're asking of me is to put my heart on the line and know for the rest of our days that he could be taken away. All three of us would be vulnerable."

"In her suicide note, Ashara spoke of losing him in such a way. She accepted his death on the night he was born, but she didn't have the courage to face losing him again after she'd raised him. And I haven't the courage to return him and face the consequences. I don't even know if his parents are alive."

"This is a disaster." Too agitated to sit any longer, she jumped up.

"I know that I need him and he needs me. I have to find him." He stood there facing her, his hands clasped. "I pray to Allah that you'll be a part of finding him and loving us for the rest of our days."

"You ask too much too fast. This is a crime that you are enticing me into. I need time. This is a lot to absorb and a commitment far greater than marrying you. Do you understand?"

"I do and I respect the gravity that surrounds your decision. Whatever you decide, know that I love you and want you with us." He held her gently in front of him by her arms. "I'll accept whatever your conscience dictates."

Feeling cornered, she started to pace. "I can't pretend to leave you with hope. Right now, I just don't know. Last night I felt such ecstasy and now such despair. I have to go now." Dressing quickly, she averted her eyes. She lifted the tent's flap and peered outside. The rain was now a light drizzle. Ducking out of the canvas into the mist, she didn't look back.

25

Darkness

The similarities to his last encounter with Ashara were not lost on Danel. Lying back down on his mattress, he stared at the canvas roof. Bethshari's revulsion and urgent need to be rid of his presence stung. A sadness enveloped him. What kind of fool would have expected any other outcome?

The smells of breakfast and sounds of Za'atari waking for the day filtered into his tent. Outside, he could hear several children laughing as they splashed through puddles, and an already cross mother scolding them to stay out of the mud. Today would not be a good day for the mothers of Za'atari.

He rummaged through a box in the corner for something to eat. Rain had seeped under the edge of the tent, leaving the box's bottom soggy. He found an apple that he had salvaged from a patient's discarded tray at the hospital two days previously and several pieces of stale flat bread. This day would be about getting the car to run, so he rejected his normal scrubs for Levis and a gray tee shirt.

Last night's storm served as more than a small irritant to refugee patience. Day after day, residents survived in the heat and overcrowding, exposed to the indignity of water rationing, poor sanitation and lack of privacy, but rain and mud were taking a bigger toll. A small crowd had gathered to gape at a fist fight between two neighbors. Two others had joined in to help. Fights had become more frequent, as violence became the antidote for frustration. Danel circumnavigated the melee as armed guards rushed up the lane to squelch the unrest.

Abu was stationed at his smoking post as Danel approached. "How did it go last night with Bethshari? Did you bare your soul and scare her off?" He tossed his comment to Danel like a roasted chestnut, expecting a clever comeback.

"Yes, I shared what was on my mind. I predict the worst outcome."

"What were you thinking of?"

"Actually, last night was the first time in a long time that I actually did some thinking."

"What did you say to her?"

"It doesn't matter. I had to do what I did, knowing I could pay a dear price. And it looks like that's what happened."

"Did she say she wasn't coming with us to Damascus?"

"She told me that I should not dare to hope, not just for Damascus but for a future together."

"Danel, you must tell me what it's about. Perhaps I could talk to her."

"No. This's between the two of us, and in the end, what happens is her sole decision. The decision has to be totally hers without any persuasion from me or from you. I need your word that you won't approach her on this."

"But I'm sure I could make a difference."

"Not this time. Do I have your promise?"

Abu resisted such a promise, sure he could make things right.

"Abu, do you promise?"

"Yes, reluctantly I give you my word." He took a long drag, releasing the smoke slowly after some moments.

"Thank you, my friend. Now I have come to you for a different kind of advice."

"What's that?"

"Yesterday, I went to my vehicle that was already filled with a sand dune courtesy of the shammal. After last night, it is probably water logged as well. I'm perfectly capable of cleaning that out, but mechanically we have some problems."

"Did it start?"

"No, at first I got a rumble, but on second try I got a click-click, and then nothing. Since the car was purchased second hand, I'm ignorant of the car's condition when I bought it, let alone what is wrong with it now."

Abu frowned. "I thought you were supposed to be good with cars?"

Nodding at two patients coming towards them along the path, Danel did a double take, but Abu was already grinning. "No, unfortunately, auto mechanics was one elective I declined in med school. I took general surgery instead, which I can see now was a grave error," said Danel.

"Yes, well, I understand why you'd say that, since neither one of us can do surgery on a car. But I have an idea." He ground out the butt of his cigarette with his heel.

"I'm all out of ideas so let's hear it."

"One of my patients, Adam Forester, was an auto mechanic in Homs. He works on the UN trucks and heavy equipment here in the camp. Perhaps I could ask him to help us."

"That's not a Syrian name. Is he English?"

"Actually I believe his father was, and his mother is Sunni. I could approach him."

"That would be great. Meanwhile I could make some headway with the interior, and we could meet back here later."

"That works, but I have some things to do first about my disengagement here."

"Have you told anyone yet that you're leaving?" said Danel.

"I told the director. He wasn't thrilled to be losing two of us, but I made it clear that I'll help him orient the new doctors coming on board. When he heard that, he was somewhat relieved. He said that if I get homesick for the good life here in Za'atari, he'll find a way to take me back."

"Decent chap, but I don't think you'll long for Za'atari."

A football shot across his path as he left Abu. He trapped it, juggling it on his toe, before passing it back into the middle of a group of children playing in the lane.

Saeed darted forward, lighting up when he saw Danel. "Have you seen Bethshari? She hasn't come into work, and I was going to be her assistant today."

"No, I haven't seen her, but I could use an assistant. Do you only work for Bethshari?"

"I prefer Bethshari, but I'll help you since we're friends. What're we going to do?" Saeed passed the ball back behind him to his friends.

"When Ashara and I came to the camp, someone broke into our car the first day. Since then a lot of sand has blown in, and after last night a lot of water as well. So we need to get rid of the sand and then we need a way to keep more from getting it."

"You're going to go find your baby, aren't you?"

"I'm going to try."

"Is anyone going with you?"

"Dr. Abu is going to help me find him. Why do you ask?"

"No one else?"

"No one else."

"Not Bethshari?"

"Why, did she say something about going?"

Saeed's foot found a small stone and shot it up the path. "No, I just thought maybe she was going to break her promise like my mother."

"What promise is that?"

"That she wouldn't leave me." Eager to change the subject, he added, "So we need scoopers, right?"

"Yes, two of them."

"Maybe we could use some of the plastic for covering the window."

"That's a great idea since we could see through the plastic. But I am fresh out of plastic or tape to hold it in place."

"They use plastic to cover the food that comes in on the UN trucks. I know where we can get some tape too."

"Alright, Saeed, let's get our supplies. I'll follow you." He shook his head, amazed at Saeed's resourcefulness. Even at this age, the challenges of camp life strengthened rather than hardened him, he thought. Ashara would say that the eagle that flies into the wind becomes stronger.

In the process of gathering some disposable plastic cups for scoops, utility tape and plastic sheeting, Saeed managed to talk one of the supply workers out of a loaf of bread and two oranges. "See, Dr. Danel, I got us some lunch as well."

"You're a good man to have around, Saeed."

As they looked into the car, Saeed clenched his teeth. "What a mess. Maybe I should have looked at the job first before I agreed to help."

The sandy mud covered both the front and the back seats, replacing the dry sand from the day before. Embedded in the mud on the floor and seat were shards and beads of tempered glass from the break in.

"Be careful. I cut myself when I was here to try out the engine." By midafternoon, they cleaned out the mud and opened all four doors to dry it out. In the shadow of a nearby van, they stopped to have lunch.

Danel broke off hunk of bread and handed it to Saeed. "You do good work, Saeed. My thanks to you for your hard work and a fine lunch."

"How soon will you and Dr. Abu leave? I know you have to find your baby, but I don't want you to leave."

"Maybe a couple of days. Right now the car won't start, and I am not sure how long it will take to fix it."

"Did Bethshari tell you that she's going to try to adopt me?"

"Yes, she did. When she mentioned it, she didn't know about all of the details. How do you feel about that?" Chewing slowly, he brushed some bread crumbs off his pants.

"I pray to Allah in the morning and the night that this can come true. I would take care of her, and she would take care of me. And...." Saeed hesitated not sure if he was safe to say any more.

"Is there something else you want to say?"

"You won't be mad at me if I ask you something?"

"Of course not. Ask away."

"Are you going to marry her?"

Danel choked on a piece of bread. "Why do you ask that? Did Bethshari say something to you?"

"No. But I can tell she really likes you. You like her back, don't you?"

"Yes, I do, but I am not sure if we'll marry. Right now she's very angry with me and she may be too mad to marry me. How would you feel about that if we did?"

"That depends."

He drank some water to stop the coughing. "Depends on what?"

"If you married her, would she still want to adopt me? Would you want me for your son? I mean you already have a son so maybe you wouldn't want someone like me."

He passed the water bottle over to Saeed. "I could think of no finer son than you. You would be a protective big brother to Hamid. But I have to tell you that we don't have plans to marry, so you shouldn't get your hopes up."

"I won't. But isn't hope a good thing? Thinking that things are going to get better sometimes make them happen."

"Yes, I suppose it is. It's just that when we hope and we don't get what we want, we're very disappointed and that hurts."

Saeed tore a piece of bread off and popped it into his mouth. "When I first came to the camp, I thought everyday about how good it would be when my mother came. But now that she's dead, I really miss hoping for her to come."

Danel wiped the sweat off his face with his shirt. "But you didn't answer my question, how would you feel if Bethshari and I married?"

"I'd like that but…."

"But what?"

He pulled his knees up under his chin. "It's just that I wouldn't want to lose her if she married you. I'm afraid you would take her away." He crossed his gimp leg at the ankle behind his good one. "I loved my mother, father and brother, you know, being a family. We had wonderful times when we were all together. I want very much to have that back again."

"We're alike. I miss having a family too. But right now, I just can't say what the future holds."

"I won't get my hopes up, but there's nothing wrong about praying to Allah about it, right?"

"No, there's nothing wrong with that, as long as you accept Allah's will if it ends up being different from what you prayed for." He started to roll the bread back up in its wrapper. "Do you want any more?"

Saeed shook his head no.

"Then what about those oranges. I was thinking an orange would taste mighty good right now." He winked at the boy, who proffered both oranges for Danel to select his favorite. "Which do you think is the bigger one, Saeed?"

The boy scrutinized the oranges, turning each over in his palm before deciding that the one on the right was slightly larger. "I think this one is a little bigger." He offered the larger one to Danel, who reached for the smaller one.

"You take the larger one. You earned it."

After their lunch, they worked together to stretch the plastic sheeting over the broken window, securing it with tape to stop any more sand from filtering in.

"Nice work, Saeed. I think we can even drive with it like this."

When they parted, Danel headed out to find Abu and see how far he had gotten with Adam Forester.

"Adam wasn't at the garage today, but I found out where his tent is and we can go there together. How did you make out with the car?"

"I ran into Saeed, and the two of us cleaned it out and patched up the window with plastic sheathing. I see why Bethshari is so fond of him. I guess you know she wants to adopt him."

Abu nodded.

"I worry that he'll get his hopes up, and the authorities will resist a single woman adopting."

"Careful, you may just need to marry her to make that happen for Saeed."

"My wanting to marry her is not the problem, her accepting me is."

"Have you seen her today?"

"No. Saeed was looking for her as well, but she didn't come into work today."

"Well, perhaps tomorrow."

"Perhaps. Shall we go see Adam?"

Twenty minutes later they'd arranged to meet Adam the next morning to diagnose what was wrong.

"I have to be honest with you, Doctors," said Adam. "The problem may not be fixing the car, but rather getting the parts. There are some parts here for the UN vehicles and heavy machinery, but car parts are a different story. We can't get them from Syria anymore and there are shortages in Jordan."

"How long does it take to get parts?" said Danel.

"If parts are available, maybe one day or two. But if they aren't available, we would have to find a supplier somewhere, in another country perhaps, and then see if they would be willing to ship. If that's the case, it could take some time."

"This doesn't sound good," said Abu.

"Not necessarily. I think we're worrying before we have to, since we don't even know what is wrong with the car."

-"Good point. Where should we meet tomorrow?"

"How about 9:00 am at the relocation tent? Then you can lead me to your car."

"Tomorrow then," said Danel as they shook hands.

Danel and Abu walked back to the hospital, calculating a prudent departure plan.

"There is nothing I can do now until we know about the car, so I'll try to make myself useful at the hospital for the rest of the afternoon," said Danel.

"I have to visit with the director about transitioning out of here. I spoke to him this morning. Apparently the timetable for the new doctors has been moved up, and he expected them this afternoon. We haven't even set up a proper orientation plan, but I guess we'll just dive right in."

"Now that I have made the decision to go after Sister Helen and Hamid, I'm very eager to get started. Even waiting until tomorrow for Adam to check the car is torture."

"I'm surprised you haven't heard anything yet from Bethshari."

"I'm not expecting to hear right way."

"Are you going to reach out to her?"

"No. If I don't hear from her, then that is her answer."

"You should contact her. Being passive is not going to get the job done."

"And you have a lot of experience in this area?"

"I'm just saying that in matters of the heart—"

"You can stop right there. When I saw her last, she said that she could not leave me with much hope. I have to respect that."

"Have you changed your feelings toward her?"

"I haven't changed. In fact I am at peace now that I accepted that I do love her. But if Ashara taught me nothing else, it's that love is not enough. This is just one more bitter pill I will have to swallow."

"I hope you know what you are doing."

"For the first time in a long time, I really do."

"What could you have said that so turned her away?"

"Abu, it is deeply private. You're just going to have to leave it at that."

The rest of the day passed quickly, with both doctors working well into the evening, Danel treating patients and Abu orienting three new physicians. Abu checked out for the evening, promising to meet his charges very early the next morning. Danel worked an hour beyond Abu's departure to finish up with three patients that had come in right before he was about to leave for the evening.

When he left, winding along the lanes to his tent, exhaustion overtook him. He fell asleep on his mattress still in his clothes. He awoke right before first light and listened to the wind rolling across the desert floor. Hearing footsteps, his breath caught in his throat, anticipating that Bethshari had a change of heart. He quieted, half expecting that she would be coming through the flap, but the footsteps kept going. *You promised yourself not to hope, and there you are thinking that the footsteps were hers.* He untied his shoelaces and slipped his feet out of his shoes. Lying back down, he pulled a coverlet over himself and rolled over on his side, holding his pillow to his chest and praying.

> *O Allah, the Almighty. I trust that Ashara is in Your keeping and that the demons that drove her from me have been quieted and that she is resting safely with You in peace. Grant me a righteous purpose in the search for this child, who through my own weaknesses has become my charge. O Allah, the Just, the Righteous, the All Caring, I pray that this be a just quest, and that You will wrap us in Your care. If it is in Your plan for me not to survive, I accept Your will. I pray that You will watch over this special child that became mine unjustly. Allah, You are great, and I remain Your humblest of servants.*

A second wave of fatigue descended, pulling him into a deep sleep. He dreamt of Bethshari in a white gown crossing a vast expanse of the desert far away from Za'atari. He had been wandering there for some time without food or water. At first she didn't recognize him, but after a while she called him Dr. Ottawa and offered him some water.

"What are you doing out here by yourself?" he said.

"I am looking for a burial place for Hamid."

"Hamid? Did you find him? Is he dead?"

"He was in the desert all this time, but Sister Helen had abandoned him."

"How was he?"

"He was crying for his mother. And he was very thirsty. I was able to give him some water, but he was too dehydrated. You waited too long to go after him. He had been in the desert for many days, and he died in my arms."

He bolted upright, breathing heavily, screaming, "Hamid, no. Hamid, I am so sorry." Drenched in sweat, he slowly calmed. It was now daylight. Shuddering, he tried to shake off the thoughts that crossed the threshold from the dream world. Looking at his watch face, it showed 8:40 am. He had slept over ten hours. There was just enough time to meet Adam Forester at 9:00.

26

Unwilling Complicity

Saeed woke early after a restless night, eager to find out if Bethshari had learned anything more about the potential adoption. After breakfast, he checked to see if she had clocked in, but no one had heard from her. Disappointed, he roamed the common area between the relocation tent, commissar and hospital, searching the crowd. This was the second day that she had not shown up to work. He saw Danel long before Danel saw him.

"Dr. Danel, over here." Saeed started toward Danel, waving his arms.

Scanning the refugees milling about, Danel's sights soon connected the boy and the voice. "Saeed, good morning. Where are you off to?"

"I'm looking for Bethshari. Have you seen her?"

"No, I haven't heard from her. I'm sorry."

"She's still mad with you then?"

"Probably."

"Then she must be angry with me too. She has never stayed away like this." He kicked a freckled stone at his foot, raising a cloud of dust, which rose and settled back onto his shoes.

"Her absence has nothing to do with you. It all falls on my shoulders. She'll be back soon. Don't worry." But he was not so sure. Adam Forester stood in front of the relocation tent scanning the crowd. "Saeed, I must be off, but if I see her, I'll let her know that you are looking for her."

"Thanks, Dr. Danel, and if I see her first, I'll tell her not to be mad at you anymore."

Danel patted the child on his back and headed over to Adam. He called across the open expanse, although a clear view of Adam was obstructed by refugees. "Good morning, Adam."

"Ah, Dr. Danel. There you are." The two men shook hands.

"Thank you for your assistance this morning. This way to the car." Danel gestured for them to move forward out the front of the camp.

"Have you been in the camp long?"

"I came with my wife and four children about six months ago. The bombing in Homs had been bad for some time. At first the fighting was localized, but then the devastation became more widespread. What finally pushed us over the edge were shells that went off by the children's school one morning. Several were killed while walking to school. I said to my wife that it was time to go. We left that afternoon. What about you?"

"We're from Damascus. My wife was pregnant and walked to the hospital to have our baby through sniper fire. We had to wait, since we had a newborn, but we didn't wait very long. Down this way." He pointed to the third row of cars parallel to the fence line, counting the utility poles to determine how far back the car was parked. "How has your family adjusted to living here?"

"For the children it was a new adventure. But for my wife, it's very hard managing a household out of a one-room tent. The washing, cooking, trying to keep the children clean, no privacy—it's just a lot. At first when we came there was no school here, but having them in school for several hours each day has given her a break."

"I think that the women have it harder here. I spend my days at the hospital, so my work allows me to see the whole picture. Many never expected to be here as long as they have been."

"Sooner or later something has to give. The insurgents seem resilient, but Assad keeps holding on. I hear talk that the US might send some aid, but it is probably just talk. Other leaders in the Arab Spring acquiesced to the will of the people. But Assad seems determined, so his people suffer."

"What will you do when this is all over?" said Danel. They reached the car and he pulled his keys out of his pocket.

"When this is over…that's an optimistic thought. But to answer your question, I don't know. My family lived in Homs for generations. We later learned our home was razed to the ground, so we don't know where we will go. Homs was devastated, so it may not be an option to go back there."

Danel released the hood, and Adam bent over to survey the engine. "Try to start it."

Danel turned the key in the ignition, which returned a click-click-click. "Last time I tried it, it at least made an effort to turn over."

"Sounds like you have a dead battery. We could try to jump it after I get another vehicle. There may also be a problem with the alternator. A new battery I can get easily, but an alternator may be a problem."

Danel banged his hands against the steering wheel. "Great. Will this nightmare never end?"

"This isn't a nightmare, just a mere inconvenience. If you don't believe me, there are enough nightmares at Za'atari for you to compare."

Rebuffed, he calmed down. "You're right. I'm just short of patience."

"You wait here. I am going to go back and get one of the UN trucks and we will try to jump it."

Danel climbed out of the musty car. He sat down on the compressed sand in the shadow of the adjacent car. His thoughts drifted to Bethshari. The hours before their departure were waning, and with them, any hope she would have a change of heart.

This noose of self-examination retied itself many times over the two hours that Adam was gone. He had just about decided to go look for him when he saw a UN van making its way along the aisle towards the Renault.

"Where have you been?' said Danel, making a poor attempt to cover his frustration.

"I'm sorry I took so long. I thought that going back and forth to the garage as I diagnosed each problem made no sense. I took the liberty of bringing my tools, a new battery, an alternator, and the truck in case I have to tow your car in."

"I thought you said that getting an alternator would be problematic?"

"Ah, problematic for a *new* alternator. I had my own car over there, and it needs some transmission parts that will take some time finding. It has a perfectly good alternator that will do me no good without a working transmission. So I removed my alternator in case there's a problem with yours."

"Adam, you've been sent straight from Allah."

What might have taken perhaps an hour to diagnose and repair during a normal visit to a neighborhood mechanic had chewed up the greater part of a day. By late afternoon, with a new battery, a used but serviceable alternator, and enough gas to make it to a service station, the car was ready for the journey.

Bethshari knew that her absence would hurt the two peoples about whom she cared deeply. She felt more guilt over leaving Saeed in the dark than she did Danel. The gravity of her decisions weighed heavily on her. After she left Danel in the wee hours post confession, she headed back to her apartment and showered until she had exhausted all of the hot water. More than washing away the physical remains of their love-making, she desperately needed to cleanse her involvement in Danel's disclosure. Knowing and not taking action made her an unwilling accomplice.

Stepping out of the shower, she dried herself and lay down naked on her bed, free of the clothes, which felt heavy on her skin. Emotionally drained, she dozed off for several minutes. Her eyes snapped open. Wearily she got up and fished a cotton dressing gown off a peg on the back of the bathroom door.

The English influence from being raised in London led her to the kitchen to prepare tea. Nothing could be decided without a cup of tea.

Filling a teapot with water and setting it on the burner, she grabbed a clean mug out of the cabinet and set a sieve across its brim. Spooning tea leaves into the strainer, she thought back to the many times she and her mother had prepared tea to talk over what her mother called the "bumps of life." She knew that before this was over she would have to call her parents and talk all this through, but that would have to wait until she herself had some clarity.

The tea pot whistled, breaking her reverie. Shuffling to the stove, she turned off the burner and grabbed the handle. "Ouch. Damn it." The hot metal handle seared her skin, and she instinctively sucked her finger. Hurrying to the bathroom for some petroleum jelly, she blew on it to cool it. *Not a good start,* she thought, as the finger throbbed.

Returning to the tea kettle, this time she donned a mitt. Pouring hot water though the sieve, she watched the water turn golden to tan to mocha, until she was sure that it had steeped sufficiently to unleash its medicinal charms. Her mum always said that a cup of tea was better than a doctor or a priest in times of trouble. She sipped the hot liquid, feeling its familiar soothing as it passed over her palette and eventually dissipated its warmth through her body. Even on a day too hot for a warm drink, a cup of tea was antidotal.

Her exasperation escaped as a sigh as she pushed her chair away from the small table that served as her place of eating, reading, writing and studying. But for thinking, her best posture was on the move, pacing rhythmically back and forth from end to end of the galley-shaped apartment.

The way she saw it, the Saeed issue was tied to Danel. Her adoption of Saeed had a much better chance with a husband. A single woman adopting a ten-year-old boy would meet resistance based on the flawed family unit and her religious feet planted in two worlds, Islam and Christianity. Rearing a boy without any male influence, her nationality and the adoption being granted by Jordan for a Syrian child further complicated matters.

Danel and Hamid posed the more convoluted of the two problems. Articulating the obstacles to Saeed's adoption were straightforward and logical with no emotional complications, but Danel and Hamid—not so much. *How sure am I that I love this man? I was ready to marry him on first proposal less than twelve hours ago. And now I am questioning those feelings.*

She sat down heavily on the auburn and olive divan set against the wall. When she first wrote her parents about her living quarters at Za'atari, she described the apartment as a tunnel-shaped living space. Hoisting her legs up onto the seat cushion, she tucked her knees up under her chin. Facing Danel before she knew her own heart was not to be attempted.

Hamid presented even deeper complications. The child was not Danel's, and no proof could be offered that would justify their parentage or leave them free of suspicion. No one would ever believe that she had not been a party to covering up and keeping the charade going. She watched a trail of ants carry off some bread crumbs beneath the low table in front of the divan.

The emotional risk to her and Danel paled against the damage to the baby if he ever were to be removed from them. *Could I survive such wrenching of my heart? Could our love sustain the loss of the child?*

More questions came, with very few answers. *What kind of a man would enter into such a lie? Was it a great love that had placed him in such jeopardy just to protect his wife?* She unbraided and then re-braided her hair to capture a few wisps tickling the back of her neck. *Or was it just emotional cowardice that drove him to do it, so he didn't have to face presenting her with such a colossal disappointment?*

Still, it would be easy for Danel at this point to abandon the quest. The child has been stolen, yes, but by someone who obviously loves him. Hamid would grow up loved and protected by Sister Helen, never having known either his biological or surrogate parents. If Danel were to walk away now, he would be safe from any prosecution. *Yet, he's driven to get the child back. It is as though his responsibility for the child has been galvanized by his love for him. Is this not an admirable quality?*

And where do I stand? In abandoning Danel now, am I set free, unharmed and uncommitted? No crime would be committed if I did this. But am I no better than Ashara, who abandoned the baby and Danel through suicide? I would be walking away from a man I truly love at a time when he needs me. What would my life be like if I abandoned that love now when it was put through its first test?

As she pondered, late into the evening, the answers eluded her. Having eaten nothing all day, she still wasn't hungry. Lying down on her bed, she drew her pillow up into the inner curve of her body. As drowsiness descended on her, she hoped a solution would emerge while she slept.

Eleven hours later, she woke rested in the same position as when she first lay down. Morning light in full bloom cascaded through her window, latticing its rays down the bedroom wall through the blind's slats. Work was out of the question with so much still undecided. She needed to call home.

Slipping off her cotton robe, she donned a pair of jeans and an old button-down shirt that had been her fathers. Owing to its faded color and frayed cuffs, her mother relegated it to the rag pile. She liked its roominess and the softness of the high fiber count. Her father was not extravagant, but had an appreciation for quality, especially when it came to his shirts. Inheriting a similar appreciation from her father, she tucked the shirt into her suitcase right before she left for Syria.

Her finger was still sore and crimson but no longer throbbing. After brewing a cup of tea, she searched the refrigerator for anything that could pass for breakfast. A small wedge of cheese and an apple presented themselves. They would have to do since she had no intention of leaving the premises until she had made up her mind.

She checked her watch, now 9:45 am, which would be 8:45 in London. Her parents would be getting ready to leave for work. Better to catch them both together than have to tell the same saga twice.

Besides, their best advice always came when they bounced opposing views off each other. Her backpack lay in a heap just inside the door where she deposited it when she came home. She opened the main compartment and rummaged through for her cell phone, which she hoped still had enough charge on it to make the call. Dialing, she sat at the small table with her tea, cheese and apple. "Hello, Mum, it's Beth, how are you doing?"

"Ah, cherie, how sweet to hear from you. Is everything alright, Beth?"

"Yes, I'm fine, if not overworked, but you know I like what I'm doing here."

"I only ask because we hear a great deal in the news about Za'atari, so you're constantly on our mind. Your dad's still here, shall I ask him to get on the line?"

"Of course, please call him. I need some advice."

Her mother pressed the phone against her body. "Emil, Beth is on the phone, can you pick up on the upstairs phone? She wants to talk to both of us."

"Beth, dear girl, so good of you to call."

"Thanks, Dad. I'm wearing one of your old shirts to help me think,"

"Well, I'm glad that it helps you think, but my shirts don't have the same effect on me."

"Mum, Dad, I'm hoping you are more clearheaded than I."

"What is it, dear?" asked Anouk.

"It's serious business—very complicated."

"Go on, we're listening."

Bethshari tackled the Saeed subject first, telling them about Saeed and how she had come to be so attached. What she really wanted was their blessing on her adopting him.

Emil cleared his throat. "That is a big commitment. I know you're twenty-eight, but do you foresee a lifetime with him? That means educating him, going through the teen years, helping him acclimate to a new life? Are you up for that?"

"Dad, to be honest, I can't imagine my life without him. He's a fine boy. In the face of all that has been thrown at him, he rises to the occasion. He is quite remarkable."

"But Beth, you are unmarried. Wouldn't he be better off being adopted by a traditional family with a mother and father in a country where the culture is closer to his own?"

"Mum, you make a great point. If he were just a statistic, a boy that I didn't know, I would say yes. But there is a lot of unknown surrounding a family who would adopt him."

"Do you know anything about the procedures for placing a child in Jordan? I am assuming that they would not send him back to Syria given the situation there," said Emil.

"Actually I know very little. He would have to be transferred to an orphanage in Amman first where he knows no one. The prospects for adopting a child this old are not great. Even if they could find a family, I suspect there would be very little vetting of the new parents. Jordan is very poor, and their resources are stretched very thin."

"Do you love this child, Beth?"

"Yes, Mum, I do, and he loves me."

"Then you're a grown women with your eyes wide open. Make no mistake, it is harder as a single parent, but doable. And you know that your father and I will always be there to support you. What do you say, Emil? At this stage of your life could you take on a grandson?"

"Anouk, you have given her our answer. Beth, if this is what you want to do we are 100% behind you."

"Thanks. It means a lot that you have my back." Clutching the phone, she pressed it to her chest, taking a deep breath. "Now I have a problem that is not so easy to solve. I want to tell you about it, but I can't tell you everything now. Can you work with me knowing that I can't be totally honest?"

"Sounds very ominous," said Emil. "Go on."

"I met a man here, a Syrian doctor. When he and his wife first came to the camp a little over two months ago, they had an infant who was not with them when they arrived. The infant had been kidnapped by a nun, who was also his caregiver. I've fallen in love with this man."

Both Anouk and Emil remained silent. Finally Emil broke the spell. "I hope you aren't asking our blessing on your involvement with a married man?"

"No, that's not it at all. His wife was devastated by the kidnapping and took her own life. It was very tragic and complicated by some custodial issues surrounding their infant that I can't go into now."

"Do these custodial issues involve breaking the law?" Her father had a way of cutting through the red tape. His clarity, though, could also be problematic.

"Yes, that's precisely my dilemma. I love him very much and he loves me. Neither of us expected to feel this way so soon after his wife passed, but it happened. I have never felt like this before about any man."

"You have no doubts about your love?"

"No, Mum, this is real. He is leaving the camp in the next day or so to search for the child. And I was supposed to go with him, at least until I learned of the custodial problem. I suspect if he finds the child, he'll leave the country and I'll never see him again."

It was Emil's turn to probe. "I respect your request not to tell us all the circumstances. But let me ask you this: would you be implicated in those issues if you married this man and left the country with the child?"

"Yes. I think that the authorities would see me as an accomplice, even though I had nothing to do with any of it."

"That's quite a commitment this doctor, who professes to love you, is asking you to make."

"I know that, Dad, but he didn't have to tell me any of it. He felt that he couldn't ask me to share his life without full disclosure. He never told his wife until the morning she took her own life. He vowed not to make the same mistake twice."

"Beth, like your father, I don't know all the circumstances, but a man that knowingly puts his wife in danger is thinking more of himself than you. That's not what we want for you. Do you agree, Emil?"

"Yes, I do. You'll have to make your own decision, Beth, but know that we're not solidly behind a union that has at its core some kind of deception. Anything that puts you in harm's way is anathema to us."

"I'm not asking for your blessing. I just wanted was your insight before I make my decision."

"Be very careful. If you commit a crime in that part of the world, the consequences will be grave, and we won't be able to exert the influence that we could here."

"I know, Dad."

"Just be very cautious," said Anouk.

"You and Dad are my rocks, and you raised me to think for myself. I can never thank you enough for that. I'll keep you posted. I love you both."

"And we love you as well."

Teetering on the abyss, she weighed both alternatives: on one side, back away from Danel and the complications of Hamid and try to adopt Saeed by herself; on the other, plunge into a relationship with the man she loves but with danger forever hanging over her head. Her decision weighted in favor of Danel before the call with her parents, now leaned in favor of caution. With Danel's departure imminent, she would have to decide soon.

She was suddenly very hungry. Her refrigerator's contents were meager: half an onion, one egg and a stale slice of flat bread. Her cupboard was equally sparse: a can of garbanzo beans and some sesame paste. Opening the beans, she drained some of the liquid into a skillet. Next she chopped the onion, careful to remove the green mold on the outer layer. Her stomach growled at the smell of the onions. Adding half of the beans, she seasoned them with salt, pepper and some sesame paste. Once the mixture was heated, she added the egg, scrambling the white with the yolk and folding it into the beans and onion. Taking a plate from the cupboard, she layered the concoction over the flat bread, allowing the steam to warm and soften it.

Not bad, she thought, chewing the first bite. Carrying the plate to the small table, she pulled the chair out with her foot and ate hurriedly. *Actually quite good.* She laughed out loud. Picking up her plate, she licked off the last morsels. Rejuvenated, she had come to her decision.

Her tiny apartment was very bare, as she had never seen it as a home but merely a place to sleep. It came furnished, and very little in it was actually hers. Rummaging through the drawers in the kitchen, she found some paper but nothing to write with. Scouring further, she located a short pencil in the small drawer in the table in front of the divan.

She hesitated. *Perhaps the best start is to just to begin. There will never be a gentle way to do this.*

My dearest Danel,

These last days away from you have been very hard, but necessary for us both to know that whatever was decided was the correct choice. Be assured that I have not come to this lightly. I love you very much, and on that I have never had any doubt. It's so easy for me to slip into imaginings of you as my soul mate and the beautiful life that we could build. It is the fear that these imagining would never come to full bloom that haunts me most.

I want very much to help you search for Hamid and be a part of restoring that part of your heart. I also have no doubt that I would come to love Hamid as my own and that to be his mother would be a great privilege. In time, we could give him siblings, the security of a home steeped in love and a happy childhood.

I have come to know myself better through all of this and confronted my own cowardice. In accepting your proposal, I would take a role in the deception that you created the night that Hamid was born. If I know and am silent, I am as guilty as if I had fabricated the original lie. To set that deception right would place you, me and Hamid in grave danger, which is something that I could never do.

There is no path to righteousness open to us. I cannot make it right, and I cannot live with it wrong. And it is the suspension between these two extremes in which I am trapped.

Please know that it would have been my greatest joy to be your wife and Hamid's mother, but it is an offer that I can't accept. I will always love you and want only happiness for you and Hamid.
Yours,
Bethshari

She reread the letter several times. Satisfied that it captured her meaning, she folded it three times and set aside to gel overnight. She would deliver it in the morning.

27

Protocol and Desperation

Phillip Cameron's irritation spiraled at the fifth refugee that had come for relocation assistance that morning. For an orderly man, refugees needing specialized relocation assistance were problematic. Often they were trying to rejoin a missing relative, which he regarded as tedious business. It mattered little that he was quite accomplished, because each situation was unique. Since he had been doing it so long, his network of contacts was impressive, reaching beyond the UN into other agencies that specialized in locating missing persons. And since he craved order, he rarely gave up.

"Mr. Cameron, you have a phone call in the office." A young man in a blue UN pinny stood too close to Phillip's elbow.

"Tell them I am occupied and get a number so I can call them back."

The temporary worker, assigned to relocation for the day, disappeared briefly and returned. "He says you can't call him back and it's about some orphans he is supposed to transport to Amman today. You have to talk to him now."

Phillip slammed his pen down on the counter, sucking loud tsks through his teeth. "Honestly, this is just too much. Everything comes at once." He voiced this to no one in particular.

The temp shrugged at the refugee across the counter as Phillip excused himself to answer the phone.

"Really? Today? Why can't you people get your act together? I was supposed to be given three days' notice to get him ready." The caller obviously gave his own version of pushback because Phillip's next response backed off a bit. "I know that you're just the driver. I don't mean to take it out on you, but we've chaos going on here, and I haven't had time to get the boy ready or prepare his transfer papers. What time are you supposed to leave?" Phillip shook his head at the incompetence of every department that had touched Saeed's transfer since he set it in motion. "One o'clock doesn't give me much time, but we'll get it done. Right." Muttering, he slammed his phone shut and dropped it in his breast pocket. He returned to the refugee he was helping. "Sorry you had to wait. Now where were we?"

Phillip had received some information about adoption procedures and Saeed's transfer to the agency in Amman late yesterday. Seeking out Bethshari, he learned that no one had seen her for the past two days, nor could anyone give him any idea when she would return. His first task was to find her because he'd be damned if he was going to tell the boy. That kind of messy emotional business was Bethshari's domain. Checking in with her superior, he learned that unexplained absence was atypical of Bethshari, but for Phillip, she was another not playing according to the rules. Now that the driver was leaving at one o'clock, he would have to engage Saeed himself. "No excuse for this," he muttered on his way out.

His route took him first to the children's tent, where only a handful of children remained inside. The caretaker, a volunteer parent, mentioned that some of the boys headed to the pitch to play football. She couldn't remember if Saeed was among them, but she suggested that if he weren't there, the other boys would know where to find him.

Phillip thanked her, the first helpful person he encountered so that day, and then quickened his pace toward the rear of the camp and the football field. Under his breath, he cursed the collusion of inconvenience that the driver, his mush-for-brains superiors and

Bethshari were putting him through. All this and the paperwork had to be completed.

Upon reaching the pitch, he scanned the children for Saeed. *Why is it that most refugee kids look alike?* he thought. But then, there it was, that unmistakable limp as a ball had been passed to a gimp child, making his way on the outside down the field toward the goal. He was about to be overtaken by a much larger boy when Saeed stopped short. As the older boy reached in his leg for the ball, Saeed did a step over and continued to the goal with a solid kick, sending the ball unobstructed into goal's upper far corner. His teammates went wild, jumping up and down, slapping him on the back. Then, like a herd of gazelles, all players headed back to the mid center line to restart play.

Phillip waved his arms wildly. "Saeed. Saeed." His arms fully extended like a giant windmill beckoned Saeed to come over. The other boys pointed to Phillip, yelling at Saeed to go over. "Saeed, I need to talk to you. Over here." When he saw that Saeed was walking his direction, Phillip stopped waving and waited."

"Hi, Mr. Cameron. Did you need me?" Saeed was out of breath.

"Yes, well, yes I do."

"What do you need?"

"I received word that the transport to take you to Amman leaves at one o'clock today. You have to be on the van at that time. That's in a couple of hours."

"Did you speak to Bethshari? Does she know about this?'

"Well, no. You see that Bethshari has disappeared. Actually no one knows where she is. So you are just going to have to get on with things without her."

"No, I have to see her. I can't leave without talking to her. Where is she?" Saeed was hysterical.

Unprepared for how much this upset Saeed, he scratched his head.

"Saeed, you have to go. Bethshari isn't your parent, and you now are the ward of the camp."

"Don't say that. She's going to be my mother. I have to find her." He sprinted off as the other boys called for him to finish the game.

Even Phillip conceded that he had handled the whole bloody business badly. *Where the hell are you, Bethshari? This whole messy business is just not in my job description.* "Saeed, one o'clock." Phillip called after him. "You be there at the relocation tent. Be there, you hear me."

Saeed, not turning back, waved his arm above his head more to indicate that he had heard.

Now to the paperwork, thought Phillip, who had slowed his pace now that the messy part was behind him.

After checking in where Bethshari normally reported to work, Saeed went straight to the hospital to find Danel and Abu. The receptionist told him he was too late that Dr. Danel and Dr. Abu had left for Damascus.

"Was Bethshari with them?"

"No, she wasn't. I haven't seen her in several days now that you mention it. What's wrong, son? Can I help you?"

He hadn't heard her last question, as he was already outside, frantically trying to figure out his next move.

Danel and Abu stopped by administration to makes sure all of their discharge papers were in order. Prior to meeting up with Abu, Danel took very little from his tent: some clothes, a scarf Ashara wore that last day that they had gone to the market together, her wedding ring and Hamid's mobile. He stopped to see Rachel Bakir to say goodbye. She was standing outside watching her kids eat a watermelon she had bought at the commissary.

"Rachel, how are you?"

"Danel, so good to see you. We're all fine. And you?"

"I'm leaving today to find my son. I just wanted to say good-bye, and thank you for your encouragement."

"I hope you find him and that it's the start of a better road for you."

"I'm hopeful if nothing else. I took very little from my tent, a few remembrances, but our things are still there. It would please me very much if you could find some use for them."

"You're very kind. I'd be honored to have them."

"You should take them today because someone else will be assigned the tent."

"Yes, of course. I'll get the children to help me."

"Well, then, I'll be off. I hope your pharmacist husband comes back soon. I'll pray to Allah for your family to be reunited."

"Like you, I'm hopeful. May Allah be with you on your quest and then keep you both safe once you find each other."

After sleeping on her decision, Bethshari remained firm, confident that her letter to Danel captured her true sentiments. She made her way across the camp to the hospital to deliver her letter. The receptionist was assigning a chart to a new doctor when Bethshari approached her.

"Have you seen Dr. Ottawa?"

"You just missed him and Dr. Abu. They are on their way to Damascus."

"How long ago?"

"They left 15 or 20 minutes ago. Maybe you can catch them. They talked about Dr. Danel having a car."

"Thanks."

"By the way, young Saeed was here looking for you. He seemed very upset."

"Did he say why?"

"No, he left in a hurry—I think to find you." Bethshari's heart quickened, fearing that she had waited too long to deal with Danel and at the same time left Saeed in the dark. *He must be panicking.* Breaking into a run, she headed out the entrance and toward the parking area. She could deal with Saeed later but had to reach Danel to give him the letter. About twenty meters ahead, she thought she saw Abu lowering himself into the passenger seat and Danel closing the trunk lid and walking around to the driver's side.

"Danel," she yelled wildly.

He heard his name and saw her running toward him. His angst palpable, he stood immobile.

"I was afraid I wouldn't see you before I left." She panted to catch her breath, her cheeks flushed. Droplets of sweat wound down her cheeks as she waved briefly to acknowledge Abu, who was already buckled in his seat.

"I'm sorry. It just took me time to sort it all through. I had to be sure before I gave you my answer." Her fingers clutched the letter in her pocket. The clarity so carefully spelled out in the letter now seemed inappropriate. "It's just that I tried to...I mean...I don't know what I mean." She blushed at her stumbling though something about which she had been absolutely sure. But the words, "Danel, I can't marry you," just wouldn't come.

"Bethshari, I love you very much."

"That's just my problem. I love you very much too. It would all be so easy if I didn't love you."

"Then we'll make it all work. I just want to be with you for the rest of my life." He drew her close and looked deep into her misted eyes. Resisting the gap that he had narrowed, she feared for her resolve in such closeness.

"I want to be with you too, for the rest of my life. I never doubted that."

Go on say it, she thought. *I can't marry you. Just say it.*

He pulled her to him, enveloping her in his arms, and kissed her deeply. She responded willingly, holding him tightly as though she had almost lost something precious. Her resistance dissolved as an early morning fog hovering over a mountain brook burns off in the sunlight.

Abu unbuckled his seatbelt and stood outside the car, shaking his head. "Let's get going, you two, we've got a baby to find. It took you long enough, Bethshari."

Danel and Bethshari smiled at each other and then at Abu. "We're coming," said Danel. He drew his handkerchief out of his pocket, dabbing the tears that had leaked out of the corner of her eyes. "We're together now. That's all that matters. Are you sure?"

"Very sure, although it may not be wise. But I am sure."

Her head rested against his shoulder as they walked back to the car.

"Good." He squeezed her hand to reassure, and she reciprocated.

Abu was already rearranging seats. "I'll just move to the back seat so you two can sit together."

"No need. I'll just sit in the back," she said.

"No you won't. I want you sitting right next to me so I can touch you to make sure I'm not dreaming."

As she settled into the front seat, her hand fished the folded letter out of her pocket. She crumpled it, its importance overcome by events.

"What's that?" said Danel.

"Nothing. Just something I'd been working on, but it doesn't matter now." Tearing it into pieces, she shoved them back into her pocket. "I won't be needing it anymore."

Danel slipped the gear shift into reverse to back out of the parking spot, thrust it into first, and then second, inching forward at first and then gathering speed. "Hamid, we're coming." The Renault taxied out of the parking area and turned right to get onto the main road.

"You're clear this direction," said Abu, checking to verify there were no oncoming cars.

Careful to navigate around the refugees milling around, Danel picked up speed to ease into the traffic.

Abu turned around to look out the back window. "We've got a problem. Look in your rear view mirror."

Danel glanced up and saw Saeed running behind the car, calling, waving his arms. "Oh no, it's Saeed. What should I do?"

Bethshari jerked around to see for herself. "Stop the car."

"Are you sure?" said Abu.

"There's no way we're driving off leaving him hysterical in the road chasing us. We're not monsters. Stop the car. Now."

Danel pulled over onto the shoulder, and Bethshari jumped out before he had come to a stop, loping full gallop to close the distance between her and Saeed.

Saeed was hysterical. "Where're you going? Are you leaving me? They're taking me to Amman today. Please don't leave me." He grabbed her arm, pulling her down closer to him. "Please don't leave me."

She wrapped her arms around him, holding him close, comforting him. "Saeed, don't cry. It's alright." She felt him calming. "Look at me."

"You were leaving me. I saw you going. You told me we would talk before I had to go. You were going to adopt me."

She felt ashamed. "Saeed, calm down. Look at me."

He quieted and sniffled, wiping his eyes on the front of his polo shirt.

"I only just now decided to go to Damascus, but I was coming back for you."

"But you said." His protests came from a childish naiveté that believed in promises made by trusted adults. For all the disappointment that he had endured, he trusted her word.

She cut him short. "But nothing. When I said that, I thought that it would be some days before you would have to go. I would have been back by then."

"But they're sending me today. Mr. Cameron said I have to be there at one o'clock."

"Saeed, I won't leave you. Not ever." She knelt down on one knee with her hands on his upper arms, squaring him to her.

"You promise? You promise before Allah?"

"Yes, I promise before Allah." She took her handkerchief out of her pocket and wiped his face. "Now blow." He sniffed a final time, and she affectionately wiped the tip of his nose. His hand in hers, she walked him to the car where the men with their arms crossed leaned against the hood. "There'll be another passenger going to Damascus. Saeed, you wait here. I want to talk privately to Dr. Danel and Dr. Abu." Followed by both men, she walked ahead of the car several meters.

Saeed stood observing, straining to hear. Shifting from foot to foot, his hands first gripped and then kneaded his upper arms. He bit his lower lip as they deliberated.

"Bethshari, what are you thinking? You can't just walk off with him without clearing it," said Abu. "He has no papers and you have no authority to remove him from here. They have laws about such things."

"What do you think's going to happen? The Syrian and Jordanian authorities couldn't find Hamid, even with a conspicuous nun caretaker and his own parents advocating for him. I doubt seriously there's the political will to look for this child for even a day." She folded her arms across her chest for emphasis.

"What about Phillip Cameron? He's one bureaucrat that will follow through."

"I've been missing for two days. Phillip knows that, and he also knows that Saeed didn't know my whereabouts. For all they know he could have wandered off or is staying in one of the tents with a friend. No one knows where he is and they have no proof that any of us took him."

"Except if they catch him with us," said Abu. He threw his arms heavenward and walked several meters away before walking back.

"This makes us kidnappers," said Danel.

Bethshari glared at the irony in his objection. "No, this makes us advocates of a boy who has no one in his corner. He needs us, and we need him. The rest is just details. I say he comes with us."

"But Damascus is dangerous. He'll just slow us down, and we'll have to be extra careful with a child along." They turned to watch Saeed kicking a rock down the lane in the opposite direction.

"Tell me a place in Syria or Jordan that isn't dangerous. I'm not going anywhere without him."

Finding no holes in her reasoning, neither objected. Although against their better judgment, between them there was not enough will to buck her. After some moments, Danel broke the strained silence. "Alright."

Abu followed suit. "Alright then. This must be Allah's will. He better know what He is doing because we sure don't."

Bethshari looped an arm through the extended crook of each physician's elbow and escorted them back to the car. "Saeed, you're now officially part of the Hamid Ottawa Search Team—that is if you want to be."

"I do. I want to help find the little fellow. He's needing a big brother."

Abu and Danel laughed right out loud. "What a salesman, he's going to fit right in," said Abu.

"Welcome aboard, Saeed," said Danel, extending his hand to shake Saeed's.

Bethshari hugged Saeed. "I told you I wouldn't leave you." Her hand rested on his shoulder and then she pulled him into her side. "How about you sit in the back with Dr. Abu?"

Grinning widely, Saeed climbed into the back seat. "I'm in."

"Now buckle up," she said, and she pushed down the door lock and closed the back door.

28

Discovery Strategy

Sister Helen reveled at the end of her work day when she retrieved Hamid from his caretaker. A neighbor, Mrs. Khadkodian, kept several children, newborn to age five, during the day to supplement her income. Sister Helen rapped softly on the door.

"Is Hamid ready, Mrs. Khadkodian?"

"Yes, he's been fed, but hasn't had his bath yet."

"That's alright. We both look forward to him splashing. Actually it's a special time for us."

"He's the lucky one with a mother like you, although you work too hard, Mrs. McCormick."

"You can call me Helen. With my husband gone, we need the money." Hamid's small arms reached for her, his legs thrashing eagerly. Hoisting him easily onto her hip, she felt the muscles in his legs and arm cling to her, chimp-like.

"Did you have you had a good day today, Hamid?"

He gurgled, bouncing on her hip.

Mrs. Khadkodian gathered up his clothes, bottles and stuffed animals, cramming them back into the diaper bag before laying it in the infant carrier. "Helen, we're out of formula, so you'll have to bring some more tomorrow."

"I will. You have a good evening now." Carrying Hamid across her hip with the infant carrier and paraphernalia in her other hand, she walked down a flight of stairs and over four apartments to the end unit before inserting her key in the door. She flipped on the lights, carefully noting that nothing was disturbed since she left twelve hours earlier.

"I'm going to set you right here and run your bath, Hamid." She eased him into his infant carrier and handed him a purple teething ring.

A lock of hair had escaped her hijab, tickling her cheek. Used to the confines of her habit, she was unaccustomed to wearing a head scarf. Gazing at her reflection in the mirror, she unfastened her hijab and shook her head, freeing her unruly hair. The closet door was open, and she looked at her old habit hanging, a remnant of another life. She thought back to her decision to stop wearing it.

"What's a Christian nun doing with a baby?" The owner of the first boarding house was curious, rather than suspicious.

"We were on the way to deliver the child to his parents when our driver was attacked. He's in the hospital now and we're not sure he'll survive." This was enough information to satisfy the old woman. "I'll be taking him to Za'atari once I know the driver will make it." At the time it hadn't occurred to Sister Helen to keep Hamid, but as the days turned into a week, parting with him became more difficult.

I would need a job to support us, but not at this hospital. Too risky. The next morning she and Hamid left the boarding house and took several buses to a hospital on the opposite side of Damascus.

"I'm a nurse and am looking for employment. Are there any openings?"

The nurse at the reception desk explained that they were very short-staffed and could use her assistance. "I'm also looking for daycare for the child. He's my nephew, and his parents were killed in a recent bombing. He has no other family."

"The poor child. There's a daycare adjacent to the hospital where many hospital employees leave their children."

"Have there been any complaints about the care? You can't be too careful, you know." Swaying with Hamid, she warmed to having Hamid in a nursery close to her work.

"I've not heard any. In fact, several mothers have spoken well of the staff there."

"Then I'll stop over and enroll him and come back later to complete your paperwork."

"I should be here all morning, and in the meantime I'll let personnel know you are coming."

While not surprised at their eagerness to hire, she was incredulous that there was no mention of checking her credentials. Fearful of remaining anywhere too long, she was at her third hospital. Any onset of questions alerted her to move on. Now she was simply Mrs. Helen McCormick, with new clothes, a hijab and a new life. She abruptly closed the closet door, shutting out her nun garb and the old life. *This life is now about me and Hamid.*

Hamid splashed happily in his bath, teething on a small yellow duck she found at a bazaar stall. He tossed it into the water, splashing soapy water into his eyes. Rubbing them only making matters worse, he started to cry.

"There, there. Let's see if we can't fix those eyes, shall we?" Lifting him dripping out of the tub, she swaddled him loosely in a towel, wiping his eyes and tickling him gently until soon he was laughing again. The warm water had so relaxed him that, once dry and in his pajamas, he drifted off quickly with her rubbing his back and humming a lullaby that her mother had sung to her forty years ago.

She stood watching a peaceful slumber envelope him. Nothing about him was too insignificant for her notice: his soft breathing, his dark eyelashes as the gateway to his innocence, the bottom of his little toes or his little hand that grasped her finger placed inside his palm. He had captivated her—as surely as she had stolen him.

The Renault was making good time back to Damascus. What had taken almost five hours when they first made the trek to Za'atari would take less than three hours going back. While the traffic leading to Za'atari was slow and unrelenting, the flow in their direction was very light. Were it not for Hamid, Danel mused that no sane person would head back into the lion's mouth.

Saeed had carefully removed the tape and the plastic sheathing. He stared out the window, retracing his bus journey to prepare a home for his mother, but soon he dozed off, leaning heavily into Abu.

"We should discuss a plan once we get there." Abu repositioned Saeed so his head would not keep jerking upward.

"What do you mean a plan?" Danel glanced into the rear view mirror to better read Abu.

"Well, for one thing, you left Damascus with a wife, and now you arrive with another woman. The rumor mill will be humming with details of how young Dr. Ottawa is now linked up with a lovely woman who is crazy enough to get involved with the likes of you. He winked at Bethshari as she turned around to give him a look.

"Actually, he's right Danel. We're not married, and this is soon after Ashara passed."

"Well, I aim to change your marital status as soon as possible. I don't want to risk you changing your mind."

"Seriously, Danel. People will think that you and I were involved prior to her death, maybe even that we were the cause of her demise."

"Well, that's absurd."

"Even so, we really don't need any spotlight on us. Shouldn't Saeed and I at least remain underneath the radar?"

"Well, when you put it that way." He glanced back at Abu and back to the road. "I was hoping that we could take advantage of the housing options right in the hospital, but maybe we should look for something else."

"That's wise," said Abu. "Is there separate housing near the hospital that we could check out?"

"Yes, of course, we should be able to get something quite reasonable."

"Then let's take care of that first off. We can leave Bethshari and Saeed there while we check in at the hospital."

"Alright then. We can figure out how we find Sister Helen later."

With an hour left in their journey, a warm breeze circulating through the unairconditioned coach made the occupants drowsy. In the rear view mirror, Danel watched Abu and Saeed's heads move like bobble head dolls to the rhythm of the road. Bethshari's head leaned against the door, her long hair whipping her face and the headrest. After several futile attempts to remain alert, she succumbed. Danel honed in on the daunting task ahead: finding a nun with an infant in a city of over six million people.

Silently, his thoughts rose to Allah, pleading for the strength to follow through and the cunning to outthink the clever nun. No one knew better than he how resourceful she was. He had no doubt that if she were still in Damascus, it was only because she had not yet made suitable arrangements for money, papers and passage out of the country.

As he neared the outskirts of the city, he roused his passengers.

"Wake up everyone. We are almost there."

Gradually everyone came to, rubbing eyes, stretching stiff limbs and yawning.

"Dr. Danel, it was good you were driving because you were the only one who stayed awake."

"Thanks, Saeed. I had to do it because I didn't think that Dr. Abu could have gotten us there safely."

"Thanks a lot," said Abu.

"Before we arrive at the hospital, I would like to drive past our old apartment. Just to see if it is still there."

"It is only natural that you would want to see your old home," said Bethshari.

Twenty minutes later Danel pulled up in front of what was left. All that remained was one outer wall about 20 meters from where their apartment had stood. All else was rubble. Even the jacaranda tree in the courtyard, now devoid of leaves, had been split in two, its remaining bark charred and pockmarked.

"That's where we lived. Over there on what would have been the second floor, not far from the wall."

"That's what our house looked like after we were bombed," said Saeed.

"It's pretty scary, isn't it, Saeed," said Abu.

The boy just nodded.

"Any doubts that I had about getting Ashara and Hamid away from here are certainly vindicated."

"Did you think that had you not left, Ashara would still be alive and Hamid would not be lost?"

Shrugging, he looked at Bethshari sheepishly. "It had occurred to me."

"Danel, drive on," said Abu. "All that's happened to all of us was Allah's plan. Had you not left, she and Hamid, and maybe even you, would have been blown to bits."

Starting the ignition, he shifted the transmission into first. "I just had to see for myself."

Finding a suitable apartment was easy. The landlord could not have been more accommodating, as eighty percent of the building was unoccupied. They rented two flats side by side, furnished with the former occupants' possessions. Fearing that any dickering would lead them to a competitive property, the landlord negotiated easily. Abu took a one-bedroom close to the stairs, and Danel, Bethshari and Saeed had two bedrooms next door.

"Dr. Abu, will you be lonely by yourself?"

"No, Saeed. I think I am going to enjoy the quiet. But I expect that we'll be so busy that the only time we'll spend in the apartment will be sleeping time."

"We're going to need some food. Is there a market nearby?" said Bethshari.

"Yes, not far, but I am not happy about you and Saeed being on the streets."

"Get over that. We'll be careful, and whatever happens will be Allah's will. In the meantime, he expects us not to die of starvation because we are afraid to go out of doors."

"I'm sure you can understand where I'm coming from."

"Danel, remember that Saeed and I are the wing men, and we expect to crawl all over this city looking for Sister Helen and Hamid. Look at Saeed, he's not afraid."

"Don't worry, Dr. Danel. I'll take care of her." His head bobbed up and down to reassure.

Danel exhaled a defeated sigh. "The market is two streets down and two streets to the left. Just go to the right out of the complex. Do you need some money?"

"I don't have any Syrian money."

"Here take this." He reached into his backpack and pulled out some Syrian pounds. "I have some Jordanian dinar that we can exchange at the bank. Why don't you take some of that as well and get it changed if you can."

"Good to know we're not destitute. Saeed will need some things to wear, and I brought nothing with me, so I'll need at least a change of clothes."

"Get what you need for all of us. You're the wing men. That's logistics, right?"

"Correct."

"Abu and I are going to check in at the hospital. We'll meet back here later."

Danel and Abu entered the hospital via the emergency room, over the same threshold where Sister Helen triumphantly wheeled Ashara over three months earlier. For a moment, the Za'atari episodes felt like they had never happened.

Most of the staff were strangers to him, save the charge nurse that was directing the work flow to the various physicians or nurses. "Dr. Danel, I heard you were coming back. I am so sorry about your wife and son."

"Word still travels fast at the hospital I see. Once they were gone, there was nothing to hold me there."

"We sure can use the help."

"Forgive me." He gestured toward Abu. "This is Dr. Abu Majeed. He accompanied me from Za'atari and will be working here as well."

"Welcome. It's a windfall day to have two physicians join us. What's your specialty, Dr. Majeed?"

"I'm a pediatrician by training, but at Za'atari I did everything from general surgery to delivering babies. War makes us versatile."

"Indeed it does." Admiring Abu's handsome face, she blushed slightly. "Was Dr. Majaresh expecting you today?"

"I don't believe so. We didn't know ourselves when we'd be able to come. Could you let him know we are here?"

"But of course."

An ambulance arrived with two burn victims. With no attending physicians available, the men waited on gurneys groaning and writhing in pain while the ambulance staff took off for another call."

Danel looked at Abu. "Let's make ourselves useful." Shortly the two were barking orders at orderlies and nurses, as Dr. Majaresh spotted them from acorss the emergency room.

"Danel, welcome back," called Dr. Majaresh.

"Kahlil, yes, we thought we'd lend a hand while waiting for you. Let me introduce my colleague, Dr. Abu Majeed."

Both men extended their hands. "We're very pleased to have you with us, Dr. Majeed."

"I look forward to being of service." Abu bowed slightly.

"Our attending physician can take over now that you have stabilized these men. Let's go to my office." Kahlil gestured for the doctors to follow him.

Three and a half hours later, appropriate paperwork had been completed, offices assigned, an orientation to their greatest needs delivered and a complete tour of the facility executed. "I am sorry to throw you to the wolves so soon, but as you can see, we are extremely short handed. We'll count on you first thing in the morning then?"

"Yes, we'll use the rest of today to settle in. We have a small flat very near here."

"Your old place, Danel, what's become of it?"

"Unfortunately, it became a total casualty. We drove by earlier."

"I'm sorry to hear that. Well, perhaps it would have been too difficult to stay there after Ashara passed."

"Yes, I thought that myself."

Abu diverted the discussion. "We're looking forward to helping. It is obvious there is great need here."

Abu's charm flows as thick as wild honey, thought Danel.

"I believe that Allah is answering my prayers. Now if He would only end the violence, we'd all sleep better at night. Until tomorrow then." Majaresh extended his hand.

"Tomorrow." Abu and Danel echoed.

Returning to their flats, the men found that Bethshari and Saeed had been to the market and prepared a modest cold supper. They were all famished and eager to relay the accomplishments of the day. After supper, Danel drew up a list of the major hospitals in Damascus and assigned half to Abu. "With the shortage of staff, the director was able to assign each of us an office, so when we get a break, both of us will be able to call and make inquiries. If we uncover any information, Bethshari and Saeed can follow up in person."

"Tomorrow, you two should secure some maps and get acclimated to the city, but stay away from areas where there is shelling."

"We're way ahead of you, Dr. Danel. We bought some maps at the market. We've already been studying it."

"You know how to read a map, Saeed?"

"Yes, my father showed me. He had a grocery business and sometimes I would go with him to make deliveries."

"Didn't I tell you that Saeed would be a great help," said Bethshari. Saeed grinned at the compliment.

"The hospital used to have several copies of a directory of emergency care facilities in Damascus. We referred to it to send patients to other facilities when we were overloaded."

"You're right to check other facilities. We have to cast a wide net to capture such a slippery fish," said Abu.

"Tomorrow I'll find a copy. We can't assume that Sister Helen will only seek employment in a hospital."

The night grew late, and the newly formed family bid Abu good night so they all could retire.

Bethshari tucked Saeed in. "Did you say your prayers?"

"Yes, and I thanked Him for letting me come and asked Him to help us find Sister Helen and Hamid."

"You know this is a dangerous place we are in. We'll have to be very careful."

He snuggled against his pillow. "I know. We will be."

"Good night, Saeed."

His breathing had slowed by the time she reached the threshold, signaling he has already drifted off. Closing the door quietly, she went to the adjacent bedroom to slip into Danel's arms. They kissed tenderly, holding each other.

"Danel, you know what you said today?" Her voice was barely audible.

"About what?"

"About marrying before I change my mind."

"Yes, I remember."

"I won't change my mind."

"I'm not really worried."

"It's just that."

"It's just that what?"

"I want to be married as soon as possible so we can be a real family."

"Is this urgency just because of Saeed?"

"I don't deny that being married will make adoption easier, but it's more than that. I want to be your wife and I want Saeed to have something more solid that just a mother."

"I agree. And Hamid needs a mother as well. Can you look into arrangements while I am at work?"

"There's something else."

He turned to face her.

"I don't know how any of this will end. But married to me, you would have entry rights into the UK. I think we should be prepared to leave Syria."

"Of course. I've thought of that many times. It is going to get more dangerous for Alawites."

"I love you very much."

He kissed her forehead and then her lips. "I love you too. Allah has sent us to each other, and I think he has special plans for us."

Bethshari did not reply as sleep has already claimed her.

Book Four

29

Snake in the Shadows

Sister Helen had had no contact with her parents, save a yearly Christmas card, for five years. It had been her way to let them know where she was and that she was alive. There were times when she missed them, and in several weak moments she almost called. While she cared about them, she always backed away. Unfinished business surrounded their coercing her to give up her child. But her retaliatory decision to join an order outside the Catholic faith created an abyss too wide to cross. For Irish Catholics, defection to the Anglicans was a personal schism.

Her present circumstances required their assistance, and were there anyone else to whom she could turn, she would. She needed money not only for passage but to arrange for adoption and exit documents for Hamid. These she would have to purchase for a dear price on the black market. If she could get them to pay for their passage, she could manage to save enough money for the illegal documents.

A bottle of brandy purchased to shore up her courage stood open on her nightstand. She poured herself two shots and downed them straight away. She had never carried a cell phone before, but the daycare required a way to contact her. Sitting on the edge of her bed, she dialed the country code first and then the area code for Edina, Minnesota, but a panic attack caused her to hang up. She belted down another shot and redialed.

"Mom, is that you?"

"Helen. Oh my, Frank. Frank." Margaret McCormick delivered the second "Frank" several decibels higher. "It's Helen. Go get the phone upstairs." Helen knew her mother well enough to know that by now she was crying.

"Are you alright. Are you safe?"

"Yes, Mom, I'm fine."

"I'm on the line now. Helen, where are you?"

"I'm in Damascus, Dad, Damascus, Syria."

"You scared us. You never call. I thought that," said Margaret.

"Mom, it's alright. Nothing's wrong."

"How are you and Dad?"

"We're fine, just a little older and stiffer. What made you finally call?"

"Well, I wanted to share some very special news and I also need some help."

"What is it, dear?"

Helen heard her mother sniffle, then blow softly into a tissue. "I know I hurt you when I became an Anglican. I'm sorry for that. I wanted you to know that I have left the order and want to come back to the Church."

"I knew eventually you'd come back someday," said her dad.

"That's wonderful news, Helen."

"Can you forgive me?"

"We forgave you a long time ago, but since you never called you couldn't have known." Helen winced at the dig.

"There's something else."

"What is it?"

The second belt of brandy was definitely a wise move.

"My order has, well, kicked me out."

"What do you mean that they kicked you out?"

"I'm adopting an infant, an orphan, a little boy three months old, whose parents were killed. They want to put him up for adoption, but this time I said no. This baby needs me."

"Sounds like you haven't changed much. You were always bringing home a stray cat or dog," said her mother.

"Could you find it in your hearts to accept me back with a child?"

"Helen, that unfortunate business was a long time ago," said Frank. "We thought that we lost you for good when you were sent overseas. And then when we never heard from you, well you can imagine what we thought."

Another dig, thought Helen. *Some things don't change.*

"But you coming back to us and the Church, and bringing a grandbaby to boot. Margaret, what do you think?"

"I think it'll be a joyous occasion when you get here. You can have your old room. I'll get a crib set up. I think we have the one we used when you were a baby still in the attic. A little boy you say?"

"Yes, a boy."

"Well, we'll have to switch the room to blue."

"Mom, it would just be until I get on my feet and can afford a place of my own. Please don't make a fuss over it."

"We can talk about all that when you get here. How soon would you come?"

"The adoption papers are being drawn up. But I have one more problem."

"Yes."

"Since the order has disowned me, I don't have money to get home. Could you and mom help me? I would pay you back once I get established."

"Father, we have those CD's that are coming due. What do you think?"

"Helen, how much do you need?"

Helen swallowed hard. Never in her life had she asked her parents for a dime. "I need $5,000."

"Oh my, that's quite a lot. Well, I guess Damascus is very far away. Mother, how much is coming due?"

"Seven thousand. But we'll send you six thousand."

"Six thousand? She only asked for five, Margaret."

"Frank, she may need some extra on the way. We're not going to leave her in the lurch, like the Anglicans have, without a spare penny in her pocket."

"But—"

"Frank, we can discuss this later. How soon do you need the money, Helen?"

"As soon as possible."

Her mother had pulled rank on her father. Acquiescing during the many years they had been together had taken the fight out of him. "Do you have a bank account we could wire it to?"

"Mom, nuns don't have bank accounts. We can use Western Union, but you may have to send it in several wires since they limit the amount that can be sent at one time. I can call you again after I check into how to do it."

When Helen requested $5,000, she had already investigated that the plane tickets to Minneapolis would comfortably come in under $3,000 for the two of them, which included a seat for Hamid on the plane rather than just carrying him on her lap. That gave her a $2,000 cushion. Her mom's additional $1,000 "just in case" got her close to having enough to pay for Hamid's forged exit documents and adoption papers.

Concerned about discovery at the third hospital, she had left without notice the week before, taking jobs at two separate emergency clinics. It meant less time with Hamid, but she could save faster by working more hours. With the extra $1,000, she could leave within a week, as soon as the wired funds arrived and she collected the next paycheck from each employer. Tomorrow she would go to Western Union and find out about how to wire the money. Trusting her parents to work through the process without her assistance was not an option.

Lately, she had taken to daydreaming of a new life with her son in America. Once there, she would be out of reach, and now that she was so close, her stomach was jittery. Her father would say, "Twas many a slip twixt the cup and the lip." The phrase always annoyed her as tantamount to a jinx; anticipating that the worst could happen usually meant that it would.

Her usual retort was, "Dad, you're such a pessimist."

"Helen, it's the pessimists of this world that are never taken by surprise. You're too much of an optimist. One day you'll see I am right."

"Yes, but optimists can move mountains." As a little girl, she had wondered if she were adopted. Perhaps she was the unwanted offspring of born-again missionaries who considered converting heathens to Christianity as a blessed opportunity. Her parents just came to view her as contrary, someone they would have to parent harder. Sadly, she accepted that she would always be a disappointment to them.

But now, the phrase was more apt than she ever imagined, the "one day" that her father foretold was now here. That Danel and Ashara had not come after her the first week astounded her, knowing how desperately Ashara had waited for this child. Constantly looking over her shoulder, she expected them to be close on her heels. Now the potential for the "slip twixt the cup and the lip" presented itself with every knock on the door and each stranger who stared a little too long or asked a curious question. One week, one week at most, and she and Hamid would be safe.

In the evening, the Hamid search team revisited their assignments for the next day.

"We have six large hospitals to cover, three for each of you. Danel, Abu, have you decided who calls which one?"

"We are all set. I just hope we can get time away from patients," said Abu.

"Do the best that you can without being conspicuous. We've waited this long; protecting your cover is very important. If you get any kind of a lead, call us and we'll investigate. In the meantime, Saeed and I will nose around clinics in the area. I wish we had a picture of Sister Helen."

"Unfortunately, we don't have one," said Danel. "She's portly, big bosoms, fair complexion and she blushes easily, especially when she laughs. The best way to describe her is a large personality with a low-pitched, booming voice." His forehead wrinkled as he considered his description. "Her habit is gray, and of course the wimple is white and stiff. Her veil is short, just below her shoulders and pulled back at the ears."

"I'm not concerned about the habit. We'll be on guard for any nun with an infant. What I'm more concerned about is if she shed her habit for civilian clothes. If that's the case we are looking for any heavy woman with a baby. That's half of Damascus."

Danel and Abu reported to work at 7:30 am the next morning to an emergency room full of patients.

"I guess our orientation is over, my friend," said Abu, taking in the scene in front of him.

"Ah, so it is. There is more than enough work for both of us."

They worked without a break until 10:00 am, when Abu excused himself to make a phone call. The first place on his list was St. Louis Hospital, a government hospital on Rue Kassaa. Wending his way through the maze of various extensions and operators, he landed on hold in the human resources department 20 minutes later.

"I am looking for a nun who works there who also is caring for an infant. Her names is Sister Helen."

"Hold on, please."

"No, please don't put me on hold again." But his request was too late. *How hard can it be to answer a simple question: does a Sister Helen work there?* Five minutes later, he had his answer.

"I'm sorry, Sir, but we have no one here by that name."

Abu looked at his watch. Thirty minutes had passed and it was now time to relieve Danel. He entered through the ER's double doors, honing in on Danel talking to a man who Abu knew well. He was tall, heavy set, and slightly balding with a ruddy complexion, a severely pockmarked face from teen acne, and a large push broom mustache. His name was Issam Kattani, but he went by the name of Sami.

"Ah, Sami, good to see you. I see you have met Dr. Ottawa."

"Yes, I've had the pleasure, Abu."

"Excellent, why don't you come with me? I believe that Dr. Ottawa was on his way to make a phone call."

"Yes, of course," said Danel, "unless you were able to get through."

"No. The party wasn't there."

"Then I'll leave you to it. Nice to meet you, Mr. Kattani."

Abu shepherded Sami to an examining room without checking in with the duty nurse.

That's odd, thought Danel, but dismissed his curiosity, since calling about Sister Helen was more pressing.

No sooner was Danel out of ear shot when Abu berated Sami.

"What're you doing here? I told you not to come—that I would be in touch."

"I wanted to see this place for myself. Nice set up. Does Dr. Ottawa know he's the one?"

"You leave the details to me. You do your job and I'll do mine. Do you understand?"

"No need to get steamed about it, Abu. We're old friends, and a visit from an old friend is very understandable. Just no slip ups this time."

"Get out of here. I'll be in touch."

"You do that."

Danel returned shortly. "Abu, I hit one. Sister Helen worked at the Italian Hospital of Damascus on Saliha Street about five weeks ago, but she didn't stay long. They said that she lived in a boarding house nearby, but they had no forwarding address. I'm going to call Bethshari and get her over there. Perhaps she can ferret out the boarding house and see if they know where she went. By the way, who was that guy you were with?"

"Just an old acquaintance who heard I'd come to Damascus. No one important."

Danel was already dialing Bethshari. "News sure travels fast. We've only been here two days."

She picked up on the second ring. "Bethshari, Sister Helen worked for a short time at the Italian Hospital of Damascus."

"Are you sure?"

"Yes, but I don't know much about where she went from there. You'll have to sort that out when you go there." He relayed what little information he had. "Be careful."

"Are you and Abu going to make more calls today? I mean, should I wait to see what else you turn up?"

"Things are worse here now than before I left. I doubt either of us can do any more calling today. You should go with what we've got so far."

Bethshari and Saeed located the Italian Hospital easily. Personnel were initially reluctant to give out any information, but Bethshari explained that the baby was Saeed's brother, that their parents had been killed and she was trying to reunite them.

"I'm sorry, but she left no forwarding address. Her original employment application though gave an address near here. Perhaps they'll have more information."

"Thank you for your kindness. I suspect that Sister Helen is looking for us as well."

The owner of the boarding house could offer little more other than the fact that Sister Helen told her that she had located a better paying job at another hospital some distance from them.

"She didn't give you the name of the hospital, did she?"

"No, but she did seem rather in a hurry to leave. Maybe she thought that the position would be filled if she didn't get there quickly. Seemed odd to me, you know, a nun with a baby. As soon as I started asking, she closed up. Strange woman."

That evening, Abu and Danel had very little else to report.

"I do have a little surprise for you," said Abu.

"You're always full of surprises. What do you have for us?' said Saeed.

Abu pulled a photo out of his back pocket. "Danel, do you recognize her?"

"It's Sister Helen. Where did you get this?"

"Out of her personnel file at the hospital."

"How did you get in her personnel file?"

"I made friends with a lovely young lady in human resources."

"You actually told someone what we are up to?"

"Of course not. I stopped in to ask a question about how we are paid, and seeing an opportunity, I asked her to lunch, in the cafeteria of course. I told her I would meet her there and then waited to see her leave. Once I saw she was gone, I treated myself to a look through her files before I met her there."

"And there was no one else there to stop you?"

"Danel, have you looked around the place? They are so shorthanded you could probably walk out of here with an x-ray machine and no one would stop you."

"Let me take a look at the photo," said Bethshari. "She's not really what I expected. She seems, well, kind."

"What did you expect, horns and a forked tongue?" said Abu.

"I'm not sure. I guess I expected that someone who could steal another's child wouldn't look so normal."

"That absence of evil is what was so disarming. She was very well liked here." Danel sat down with Saeed to examine the photo.

"You know what I think when I look at her?"

"What do you see, Saeed?"

"I see someone who probably loves the baby as much has his mother did."

"Perhaps you're right. But she caused a lot of hurt and drove Ashara to take her own life." Danel grew quiet. "But thanks to Abu, you now know who you're looking for. If Bethshari's right that she traded her habit for civilian clothes, this photo will help us."

30

Discarded Habit

Helen's eyes opened at dawn, but she had been lying in the dark for some time going over all that had to be accomplished in the few days left in Damascus. *I'm so close,* she thought. First off, there was formula to be made to send with Hamid to daycare. Yesterday she researched wiring funds to Western Union. Their restrictions limited the amount of funds wired to $3,000 per transaction, or about 400,000 Syrian pounds, she estimated. That meant her parents would have to send the money in two installments, at least 24 hours apart. Western Union locations in the US were not a problem, because even supermarkets were set up to wire funds. The difficulty would be in Damascus, since the closest Western Union office was 10 kilometers away. She would have to miss work and take two busses to collect her money, adding at least another day's delay.

She dialed her parents to relay instructions for two separate wires. "Don't worry, there will be someone there who can walk you through it." By the time the call was over, her mother had detailed plans for redecoration of what she was now calling the nursery. Even more vexing were her plans to take care of Hamid in the day while Helen went to work at a job that her father had already arranged at an emergency clinic nearby.

"Mom, you know I'm going to get my own place."

"We can work out all of the details when you get here."

Helen bristled. "It sounds as though you already have it all arranged."

"Well, would you rather that your father and I not do what we can for you?" *The hurt mother routine,* she thought, but she needed the money more than she needed a fight at this point. "I have to go, Mom. Will you send the first amount today?"

"No, Helen, it's almost 4:00 pm here, but we'll go to the bank in the morning, and we'll wire the money right after we withdraw the cash."

"Don't forget to wait 24 hours before sending the second amount. It is a long distance for me to go pick up the money so I'll wait until you send the second amount to make the trip."

"OK, dear."

"Mom? Thank you. This means a lot to me."

"We're glad to do it."

Festering just under the surface, Helen's resentment was like kindling, needing only a puff more oxygen to flare into a full blaze. Forced to give away her own child because she was unmarried, she was a victim of their shame. Since she was only sixteen at the time, she had no rights. Her independence would not blossom until she was eighteen, old enough to make her own decision to leave home—old enough to abandon Catholicism and join the Anglicans.

Now, she thought, *I am coming home after twenty-plus years with an ill-gotten child, and they wave their figurative palms like the welcoming of Christ when he rode into Jerusalem on an ass.*

Timing was critical. She would go to both jobs today and to her morning job tomorrow. In the afternoon she would call in sick and take the bus to Bagdad Street to pick up the money from the Western Union office. With the funds in hand, she'd book their passage and pay for the tickets the following morning.

Hamid's papers were completed; all that was missing was the final payment which she would make after she booked their flights. There were two more paychecks coming, which she could collect on the Friday. By Friday or at the latest Saturday, she would be on her way to Amman and then America. She and Hamid would be mother and son.

By Wednesday, the hospital calls had led the Hamid Search Team to a second hospital and then a third. Information from the second hospital had not been promising. Sister Helen had been there for a brief time, but at that point the trail had gone cold. They moved on to the third.

"We're looking for a nun with a baby that possibly might be working here, or maybe worked here recently." Bethshari offered the photo to jog their memory.

"She looks familiar, but I really couldn't say. You should talk to the personnel office. We're not permitted to give out information on employees. Down that hall, take the lift to the second floor, on the right. They should be able to tell you." She gestured to the double doors off the main lobby.

"Thanks for your help." Bethshari and Saeed got off the elevator on the second floor.

"She said turn right, not left," said Saeed, redirecting Bethshari the other direction. The word "Personnel" was written in Arabic on the translucent glass on the upper half of the door. Inside, a line consisted of three employees in green scrubs, waiting for assistance. Bethshari and Saeed took their place at the end of the queue.

"Excuse me, we're looking for a nun with an infant, who we think might be working here."

"What's the nature of your inquiry? We're not accustomed to giving out information on our employees."

"The infant is this boy's brother. Their parents were killed in a recent bombing, and the nun, her name is Sister Helen, rescued the infant, not knowing that his brother had survived. I believe that both Sister Helen and I are trying to reunite them, but I haven't been able to locate her. I got word that she might be here."

The woman eyed Bethshari and Saeed warily. She directed her response to Saeed. "Is this true? This is your brother you're looking for?"

Not expecting that Saeed would be drawn into her ruse, Bethshari had not bothered to coach him.

Saeed looked at the woman directly. His eyes had misted over, and he managed to squeeze out several tears, which trickled unobstructed down his cheeks. "He's my little brother. The last thing my mother said was to take care of him. His name is Hamid. We thought he'd been killed, but then we heard about a nun, a very kind person, who found him unhurt."

Bethshari handed him a handkerchief. "Please excuse us. This has been very hard on him."

"I'm so sorry. I'm just not aware of a nun working with us. Do you have a photo?"

"Yes, we do. Here you go."

The woman scrutinized it for some seconds. "Actually, she looks a lot like a nurse that we hired recently, but she didn't stay with us very long. And she wasn't a nun, and she didn't have an infant with her."

"Do you remember her name?"

"Let me see. I can't remember off the top of my head. Wait a minute. We're in the process of filing some payroll records. Hers could be in the batch we are working on now because it was not very long ago. She was very adamant about being paid for the hours that she worked." The woman left for a filing cabinet in the rear. Thumbing through the records yet to be filed, she paused briefly over a file. "I think this might be who you're looking for. Her name is Helen McCormick, and she left us about two weeks ago."

"Did she say where she was going? Any forwarding address?"

"I'm sorry, there's nothing here. Once she left, we lost track of her."

Saeed and Bethshari exchanged glances. "That's alright." She patted Saeed with a comforting gesture. "Thanks for your help. We'll keep looking."

They left somewhat dejected because this was the last hospital on the list. If Sister Helen was still working in the health care system, she would be employed in any one of the hundred plus clinics throughout Damascus.

"Saeed, looks like we really have our work cut out for us."

"Don't worry, we have Allah on our side."

"I wish I had your faith. This time I'm very worried. Time is running out, and we don't have a clue where to start. We might as well be looking for a single sardine in the sea. And by the way, nice job convincing her that you were missing your little brother."

"Thanks. I thought you might like the tears. I did them especially for Hamid."

"You're a con man, Saeed. An adorable con man." She playfully punched his arm, ducking back as he returned the jab.

They had summoned the lift and pressed the first floor button. As the doors were closing, a young man inserted his foot and the doors automatically opened.

"Excuse me. I couldn't help but overhear your discussion upstairs in personnel."

"Yes, we're very discouraged right now."

"I know this woman, this Helen McCormick."

"You do?"

"Well, not very well. She worked in the cardiac unit, and I heard her on her cell phone right before she left."

"Are you sure it's the same woman?" She handed him the photograph.

"Yes, this is the same person. I know she had an infant because I heard her talking on the phone about him to a caregiver. I remember she was concerned because he had some fever that morning."

"Do you know where she went?"

"She's working, I believe, at a clinic on the south side on Rue Champs Elysee. At least that is the street that I overheard." He looked at the photo again. "The face is the same, but she was not dressed like a nun."

"We're trying so hard to reunite the brothers. I'm not sure she even knows that Saeed survived. You've been so helpful, I don't know how to thank you."

"Don't mention it. I'm glad I happened to be there. I hope you can accomplish your mission. Too many families are torn apart. Allah Akbar."

"Allah Akbar."

It had already grown late, so they headed back to the apartment to discuss their next moves with the men. A dead end had miraculously shown promise. The next morning, Bethshari and Saeed would go to the clinic to identify Sister Helen. Danel was adamant that they should not approach her on their own.

"I don't understand why you're asking us to hold back?" said Bethshari.

"Let's not make the same mistake that I made last time."

"What mistake was that?"

"Underestimating how resourceful she can be."

"What could she possibly do once we catch her red handed?"

"You're naive if you think that someone who risked everything to steal this child would stop short of anything to keep him. Besides, we know that she can't take Hamid to work, so approaching her there would not necessarily lead her to give up his whereabouts. What we need to do is follow her to where she lives."

"Danel's right," said Abu. "What we want is Hamid and not Sister Helen."

"Bethshari, tomorrow you and Saeed go to the clinic and see what you can find out. You shouldn't give yourselves away. If you find her, call me. You may have to camp out and watch for the day."

"You're sure you don't want us to confront her?"

"No, absolutely not. That will be my job."

Over supper, Bethshari relayed Saeed's performance over his lost brother. "I say he's an adorable con man, what do you think, Danel?"

"A very convincing one it seems. Nice work, Saeed."

"Aren't you glad you brought me? I told you I would be useful."

After dinner, they pulled out a map to locate where they were headed the next morning, which was about six kilometers away. They agreed to set out after 10:00 am to give Sister Helen enough time to get to work should she have a later shift. They tucked Saeed into bed after he said his prayers and retired to their room.

"Danel, what's wrong? You seem very distant."

"Let's get ready for bed, and then there is something that I want to show you."

"Very mysterious tonight, aren't you?" Changing into her nightgown, she brushed out the long braid that hung down her back and climbed into bed. A soft light on the nightstand gave the room an intimate glow.

"I want you to read this." He handed her a white envelope with the words "READ THIS" meticulously printed on the front. She noticed it bore the hospital's name and address.

"What's this?"

"Just read it, and then we'll talk."

She slipped a plain, triple-folded white sheet out of the envelope."

"This was on the chair in my office when I returned from lunch."

She read it slowly, concentrating on each word and looked up.

"I don't understand, what does this mean? What's it about?"

He read it in a whisper so that Saeed couldn't hear. Its contents were written in uniform lettering, revealing little about the handwriting of its author. "DR OTTAWA, I KNOW WHAT YOU DID. I KNOW ABOUT YOUR SON."

"Danel, who wrote this?"

"I have no idea."

She focused again on the letter, still confused. "I thought you told me that no one knew."

"That's what I thought. Someone would have to go looking to discover that anything out of the ordinary transpired the night Hamid was born."

"So it must be someone who was here at the time—someone who would have been suspicious."

"Perhaps, but not necessarily."

"What's its intent? If the author wants something, why doesn't he or she not come out and say so? Maybe the letter is just meant to scare us."

"It accomplished that. But I believe this is just the beginning of something very bad."

"What're you going to do?"

"Nothing."

"Nothing? You can't just do nothing." Her agitation getting the better of her, she raised her voice.

"Shhh. You'll wake Saeed. Two of us are worried right now; we don't need a third."

"Did you show this to Abu?"

"No, and I don't intend to."

"Why not? He's our friend, and he is also very resourceful. Perhaps he could help."

"I said no, and I'm dead serious about it. The more people that know, the more easily something could slip out. The rumor mill at this hospital is fierce. When Ashara and I were trying to leave, word spread about me looking for a car. We were almost arrested at our apartment while we were leaving."

"How do you know this?" She pulled several wisps of hair behind her ear.

"We forgot something: a precious purse with Ashara's jewelry and some other items important to me. After we left, we remembered them and went back five minutes after we left. Two government vehicles were at our apartment, so we kept going."

"But they could've been there for someone else at the apartment. How can you be so sure?"

"Because we were the last residents. No one else lived there. There was no doubt, Bethshari, they were there to apprehend us. The authorities had orders to stop professionals leaving the country."

"So what happens now? We just sit and wait for the next letter?" She threw her hands up.

"It's not too late if you want out of this mess."

"It is too late, Danel. I'm in."

"Why do you say that? You and Saeed could head back to Za'atari, and you could orchestrate his adoption from there."

"And what about us, Danel? It's too late to dismantle the 'us.' As far as I am concerned, there's no turning back."

He tenderly brushed back a lock that had fallen across her cheek.

"We belong together. There are now two children that are counting on us. Do you have any plans besides 'do nothing' about the letter?"

"I'm not sure."

"It occurs to me that there are some things that we can do, not necessarily about the letter, but to prepare ourselves for other eventualities."

"Like what?" he said.

"We can't stay in Syria. If the revolution wasn't convincing enough, this threat, whatever it is, means we can't live here safely."

"I hadn't thought that far, but you're right."

"And that in itself adds a whole new dimension."

"What do you mean?"

"We took Saeed with no documents. Plus, there are no adoption papers giving us legal authority to take him with us. You have no exit documents. We haven't found Hamid yet. Perhaps we're close, but we don't have him. And on top of all this, we're still unwed. We can use my citizenship to get you into the United Kingdom as a spouse, but unmarried, you and Hamid are going nowhere. And without proper papers for Saeed, you and I have become kidnappers."

He grimaced. Before this day started, his considerations did not reach beyond finding Hamid.

"What's even more challenging is that I suspect we don't have much time. Whoever this is has a plan, and I doubt the writer will conveniently wait while we line up all of our travel and exit documents," she said.

"We'll learn soon enough what they want. If it is money, they have bet wrong."

"You're not going to like what I am about to say, but I want to call my parents for help." She waited for his reaction.

"You're right. I'm not anxious for them to know the danger I've placed you in. Again, the more people that know, the greater the danger. Do they know anything about me or Hamid?"

"A little. I called and discussed things with them while I was trying to make up my mind. I told them that I had fallen in love with a Syrian doctor who has some custody issues with his child. That's all they know. But I trust them, and they have connections—not just in London but all over the Mideast. That's how I was able to skip over several posts and land in Za'atari. They pulled strings for me at the UN."

"The UN is one thing, but arranging for exit documents, bypassing the normal channels and waiting periods, that's entirely different. Do you think they could do that?"

"I won't know until I ask, but I do know that their contacts are our best hope right now. Normal waiting periods for things like marriage certificates, adoption papers and exit documents, which would have to come from the Minister of the Interior, could take weeks, maybe months."

"I have to rely on your judgment, since I don't know them. Perhaps we could've waited for the normal channels to grind had it not been for this letter. But now the urgency goes beyond finding Hamid before Sister Helen leaves the country." He ran his fingers nervously through his hair.

"Tomorrow before Saeed and I go to the clinic, I'll call my parents and discuss what we should do. I'm going to have to tell them the truth: all of it. I can't embroil them without their full knowledge. If they think it too risky to intervene, then we're on our own. Do you agree?"

"Agreed." He sat very still, with his head resting in his hand. Sighing, he dropped his shoulders. "It's very late, and we will need our wits about us tomorrow." He kissed her softly, and as she retreated to her pillow yawning, he reached over and turned off the light.

31

Scolopendra

It was 6:00 am on a drizzly London morning when Bethshari called her parents. Her last contact with them ended with her dad advising against getting involved. While she had always leaned on her parents for guidance, she was not looking forward to asking for their help when she had taken an entirely opposite tack.

"Mum, it's Beth."

"Beth, we were hoping to hear from you about your Syrian doctor. Should I get your father?"

"Yes, that's a good idea so I don't have to repeat everything." Although Saeed was still sleeping, she placed the call from her bedroom with the door shut, pacing until both parents were on the line.

"Hi, Dad. How are you both?"

"We're fine, but very eager to hear about your situation."

"Can you hear me?" Her tone was hushed. "Saeed is still sleeping and I don't want to wake him.

"We can hear you. What's up?'

"I'm getting married. I thought about all of your advice, but in the end I am deeply in love and I have to see all this through."

"What's his name?" said Emil.

"You never mentioned his name on the last call," said Anouk.

"It's Danel. Danel Ottawa."

"You're sure he's right for you? You have no doubts?"

"None whatsoever. But there are some issues that we need to deal with."

"Issues. Yes, you alluded to them last time we talked. Can you tell us about them now?" said Emile.

"I need your help, and I want you to know everything before you decide."

Fifteen minutes later, she had painted the entire picture for them, from Hamid's switched identity to Ashara's death and Hamid's kidnapping—even the mysterious letter that Danel received. "I want you to accept him, and I'm afraid knowing what you know now, you won't. Still, I can't allow your involvement if you are not fully informed."

Anouk spoke up. "I'm speaking for both of us when I say that if this is your choice, then it is ours as well."

"Thanks, Mum. Dad, what about you?"

"Naturally your mother and I are of the same opinion. My big concern is your documents. Not only is obtaining the documents a problem, but I am their administrative process will be arduous. You need documents now, not in two months."

"I'm thinking that once Danel and I are married, bringing him to the UK with Hamid is doable. But a separate marriage certificate is required to travel once you have the original marriage document. And Danel will need a visa to enter the UK." She took a deep breath before continuing. "Adoption papers for Saeed are even more problematic. His accompaniment when we left the camp was spontaneous, and we had no time to collect his papers. So we would be starting from scratch with him, and we can't leave him behind. He has no family left."

"How quickly could you marry?"

"Mum, I'm not sure, but I would think that we could do it in a civil court early next week."

"What about Saeed's identity papers? Could you acquire them?" asked Emil.

"I know someone who might help."

Emile tapped his finger against the phone. "I have a friend named Jamal Amer in Damascus, at our embassy there. His son got into trouble here some years ago and I was able to extricate him. He owes me some favors." He became quiet, processing what to do. "I can approach him. In the meantime, you should make arrangements for the civil ceremony and work on getting Saeed's papers. We'll need a way to contact you."

"You can use this number. I keep the phone with me."

"Then in a few days we should talk to see where we are and what can be done," said Emil.

"Beth, be very careful. This situation could easily blow up in your face."

"I will. Love to both of you." Bethshari flipped the cell phone shut. She clutched it in both hands, resting them under her chin for a few moments. *Phillip Cameron will have to be drawn in, and he's not going to be very happy.* There was time enough to call Phillip Cameron before she and Saeed would go on their Sister Helen mission. Since Saeed still had not stirred, she took a deep breath and dialed.

"Phillip Cameron, please."

"He's occupied right now. Could he call you back?" It was not a voice that she recognized.

"Do you know how long he will be?"

"I can ask him. Who's calling?"

"Just tell him 'Bethshari.'" Perched on the edge of her bed, legs crossed at the knees, her foot jerked nervously up and down.

His voice exploded as he took the call. "What in the hell do you think you're doing?"

So much for pleasantries, she thought. "Hello, Phillip. How are you?"

"Don't act like you've done nothing."

"Phillip, what do you think I've done?"

"You kidnapped the boy and put me through hell, that's what you did."

"What makes you think I kidnapped Saeed?"

"Well, you disappeared, and he disappeared, and two and two makes four, now doesn't it? I was given less than four hours to get him ready along with all of his paperwork. I went through hoops and then he didn't show up."

"What did you think after the way you treated him. He was hysterical."

"So it's all my fault now, is it? That's how you see it?"

"That's not what I meant. None of this is anyone's fault. And if you would stop yelling at me, I can explain what happened."

His foot tapped out his annoyance. "This better be good."

"The day I left with Abu Majeed and Danel Ottawa for Damascus to find Danel's son, it was my intent to come back and handle the Saeed situation. You told me it could take days, maybe two weeks before he would go to Amman once the process was initiated. You were just going to find out information. I had no idea you actually started the process of getting him there. I thought I had time."

"Well, I never promised."

"I know you didn't promise, but I relied on your estimate. I knew that no one knows the system better than you."

"That's true, I do. But the case handler in Amman set it up without any thought to the details and paperwork I had to assemble. I had to act fast."

"I understand, but in the process of getting your precious paperwork, Saeed became a casualty."

"But how was I."

"Wait. Let me finish."

"Alright." His tongue smacked against the back of his front teeth.

"As we were pulling onto the highway, we saw Saeed in the rear view mirror. He was hysterical, chasing the car on the highway. What did you expect me to do, Phillip, send him back to you to be comforted? That wasn't going to happen."

"I would have helped him."

"No, Phillip, you wouldn't have been able to help him. He needed to feel safe. And he needed to know that the last adult in his world was not going to abandon him like all the others had."

"But he wasn't abandoned. They were all killed."

"When you're ten years old, does that make a damn bit of difference?"

"Don't use that kind of language with me."

"I'm sorry. I am just trying to make the point that I had no choice. I knew I could come back with him later, and right then and there, he needed me. Can you see that?"

Some moments passed while Phillip processed it all for his comeback. "When you put it that way, I can see how it happened. But I caught hell for it when the van pulled out of here without him."

"I am sorry for that, but you have to believe I had no idea what I had put you through. Did you tell anyone that he had been kidnapped?"

"No, of course not. At that time I didn't know where either of you were. No one had seen you or Saeed for several days, so I couldn't make the case for kidnapping. But in my mind, I knew you had him."

"Your intuition was right, but not the motivation behind it."

"So are you bringing him back?"

"Not exactly."

"What do you mean 'not exactly'?"

"I've been to the Ministry here about the procedures for adoption. I believe they will work with me." Biting her lip, she scrunched her face at the lie.

"They're going to let a foreign single woman adopt a Syrian orphan? Come on, Bethshari, what kind of fool do you think I am? We both know that your best chance to get this through was in Jordan."

"That's just it. I am not going to be a single woman. Danel and I are getting married, and we'll be adopting."

"Well, isn't that tidy. Congratulations I guess. So why are you calling me?"

"Because I need your help."

"After what you put me through, you need my help now? How convenient."

"Phillip, don't be that way. I explained what happened."

"You have never respected what I do."

"That's not true. Why else would I have asked for your help with adoption if I didn't believe that you were the one person that could work the system? You're legendary for that. I am not just saying that; I mean it. Did you think it was easy to call you now, knowing how mad you probably were?"

"I guess not. Well, okay, what do you need?"

"The way Saeed left, we have no identity papers and we need them to start the adoption process."

"You are asking me to send you the papers? Do you have any idea the hot water that could get me in?"

"Do you have them?"

"Well, yes, I have them. They were in the package to accompany him to Amman, but I retrieved them at the last minute, thank God."

"Does anyone know that you retrieved them?"

"I'm not sure. The packet was already in the van when I fished them out. I don't know if the driver saw me or not."

"Then as far as anyone knows, his ID papers could have been sent to Amman with the driver, right?"

"Well, yes, right, I guess. But what you are asking is against the rules. This would be grounds for dismissal if anyone found out."

"I know I am asking for a lot. But Saeed doesn't have a chance without them."

"But you could send him back here so I could arrange for him to go to the authorities in Amman and we do it by the books."

She was shaking her head. "Don't call them the authorities. We both know it's an orphanage and that there will be no one advocating for him there. You know he has the best chance with what I am proposing."

"I see that but—"

"Phillip, I know you always follow procedure, but I'm begging you to compare saving his life versus breaking a rule. No one could prove you did it."

"Saving his life? Come on, isn't that a bit dramatic? You really mean giving you what you want, don't you?"

"We have no idea of the conditions he would be subjected to. With all the authorities have to deal with, the nurturing of one ten year old in the vast sea of displaced children wouldn't get much attention. So yes, I believe, saving him is important."

"I'm not the heartless bureaucrat that you make me out to be."

"I never felt that about you." She held her breath, having led him to the precipice, she hoped he would make the leap. Some more moments passed. "Phillip? What do you say?"

"Alright. You better never tell a soul."

Exhaling, she worked out the details of how to get the documents from Za'atari to Damascus. If he sent them through a UN diplomatic courier, they would reach Danel at the hospital within a day, but Phillip could be in jeopardy if it were discovered that he had sent them. The other alternative would be to send them via regular post, but Phillip had heard from some of the refugees that their mail was intercepted and read before being sent on. In that case, the papers could be confiscated, and retrieving them would be very problematic. In the end, Phillip opted for the greater risk to himself. For him, lost papers were abhorrent, something out of order. But he would take his chances.

"Phillip, I don't know how I will ever repay you."

"Don't worry, I'll think of something. Are we done here?"

"Not quite."

"There's more?"

"Not much. I just wanted to say thank you. This comes from me, Danel and Saeed. Especially Saeed."

"You're welcome. And I wish all of you good luck on this."

"Thank you. That means a lot to me." When she hung up, she flopped back onto the bed, her arms and legs spread out in an X, relieved the call was behind her. Blowing wisps of hair off her forehead, she took a deep breath.

Saeed was stirring in the outer room. Rubbing the sleep out of his eyes, he slowly trundled to her bedroom door to rap softly.

"Bethshari, are you in there? I heard you on the phone."

She opened the door to see Saeed still in his sleeping clothes. "You slept in this morning. You must have been tired."

He yawned again and stretched his spindly arms up over his head and then out to the side, making a giant arc. "I'm hungry. Who were you talking to?"

"Phillip Cameron."

"Is he mad at me?"

"Let's just say he wasn't very happy with me for taking you. But he's over it now. Let's get you something to eat."

He followed her to the kitchen.

"How about you go get dressed and I'll make us some breakfast?" She opened the refrigerator and pulled out eggs, a tomato, pepper and onion for an ojji. Cracking the eggs into a bowl, she whipped them to a yellow, homogenous consistency, her mind focused on all that had to be accomplished for today. While finding Sister Helen was central, she thought that going to the courthouse first to find out about getting married might make more sense. The office might have restricted hours or there might be obligatory waiting days, so the sooner she started the process the better.

Saeed dressed and returned to the kitchen. Opening the cabinet, he took down plates to set the table. In the refrigerator he found some flat bread, which he put on a plate, and poured them both a glass of milk.

"Did you use to help your mother in the kitchen?"

"My mother said in a family everyone had to help. Even my father helped clear the table after a meal."

"I think I would have liked your mother."

"She was the best mother." Saeed slid into his seat without moving the chair out.

Bethshari divided the ojji between the two of them and set the skillet in the sink, running water into it. "We should say a prayer for our food. Do you want to say it?"

Saeed lowered his head. "*Allah, thank You for this ojji and bread. We are nothing without You and humbly accept this food from You.*"

"That's a good prayer. Now eat up, we're going to need this breakfast for energy."

"What are we going to do today?"

"We are going to find out about Danel and me getting married, and hopefully we'll find Sister Helen." Her mobile on the counter was jiggling, and she stretched over to grab it without getting up. Flipping it open, she recognized her parents' number. "Keep eating," she said, gesturing to Saeed, who had paused to find out who was on the phone. "Hello, Mum, Dad, I didn't think I would hear from you so soon."

"Your father has been busy. Have you made any progress with Saeed's papers or getting married?"

"I talked to Phillip Cameron in Za'atari, and he'll send Saeed's documents over with a courier. We should have them by tomorrow."

"That's very good. What about getting married?"

"After I hang up from you we're going over to the court to see what needs to be done. If possible, we will try to do it Saturday, the day after tomorrow." She idly moved bits of ojji on her plate as she spoke.

"Emile, tell her what you found out."

"I was just getting to that. Beth, my friend, Jamal Amer, at the Ministry can help."

"That's great, Dad. How do I contact him?"

"You don't. We have to be very careful not to implicate him. There is a man called Scolopendra who will contact you."

"Scolopendra? Like the poisonous centipede?"

"That's right."

"Does he have a first name?"

"No, he just goes by Scolopendra. He can turn documents around in 24 hours. I made arrangements for adoption papers for Saeed, a marriage travel certificate for you and Danel, visas for all four of you, and plane tickets out of the country on Tuesday."

"Dad, that's only five days from now. All this can be done in that time?"

"For a price, most anything can be done. Jamal will pay him and I will get the money to Jamal by then."

"I'm sure this will cost a fortune."

"Yes, that's true, but it is a small price if we can get you all out. What about the infant, Hamid? Have you found him yet?"

"We've found where Sister Helen works, and Saeed and I are going there today to see if we can follow her home."

"You are not going to confront her by yourselves, are you?"

"No, Danel has forbidden us to do that. Once we see where she lives, we'll call him and he'll confront her."

"Thank goodness for that. I fear you're no match for that one," said Emile.

"I resisted, but in the end I agreed."

"And well you should have, Beth. Don't go acting so independent. You have two children that will need a mother, and you can't be too careful."

"OK, Dad, I get it."

"Now, if you get Saeed's papers tomorrow and get married the next day, you should have what you need by late on Saturday to be safe. Am I understanding this correctly?"

"Yes, Danel won't go to the hospital on Saturday, so we can get married."

"You are to take all of your identity documents—that's yours, Danel's, Saeed's, the marriage form—and put them into an envelope. Since you don't have the infant's papers, we will need Danel to write down some of the information about the child: name, date of birth, hospital where he was born, name of mother and father, and anything else he can remember about the documents. He should recall since he filled them out in the first place. We will need that information for the child's visa. Are you sure that Sister Helen has Hamid's original documents?"

"Yes, Danel gave them to her the night the nuns took him in the UN van. We feel confident she still has them."

"Good. Have all this together by Saturday evening. Someone will pick up the envelope. The papers will all be ready by Sunday night. Can you do all of this?"

"I gave you our address. You still have that Dad?"

"Yes, I've already given it to Jamal. He'll get it to Scolopendra."

"I'm worried that we are giving all of our papers to someone we don't even know."

"That's how things like this work. You got yourself into a bit of a mess and getting out of it is going to involve some risk. If it weren't for the trouble with the blackmail letter, perhaps things would be different. But this is the situation that we have to deal with. You are going to have to have some faith."

"Thank you both."

"Be very careful. Promise?" said Anouk.

"I promise."

32

Beirut Inquiry

Hamid woke up cranky very early on Thursday morning. His first cries, initially coughed out in spurts, blossomed into a full-blown wail. Normally, Sister Helen would lie watching him play by himself for some time. This morning was different. It was his fussy cry, so uncharacteristic, that woke her.

"Good morning, sweet Hamid." The morning's first rays filtered through the gauzy curtains.

He responded with a whimper and then continued his wail.

"What's this fuss on such a pretty morning?" She sat up and hoisted him onto her shoulder, patting his back. Kissing his cheek, she felt a warm glow. "How are you feeling, Sweetheart?" She noticed him tugging at his ear, but she could see no redness. "Let's get you some dry diapers and then some breakfast."

Swinging her legs over the edge of the bed, she laid him down and unfastened the tabs on his diaper. Once he was changed, she laid him in his infant seat, wiping a lone tear that had taken up residence on his cheek. She placed a teething ring in his fingers, which satisfied him until she replaced it with a warm bottle of formula.

Hamid drank eagerly, his cheeks rhythmically sucking in and out as he concentrated on holding his bottle.

While he drank, Sister Helen prepared some cereal and warmed a jar of plum puree in a shallow pan of hot water. Lifting him out of the carrier with him still drinking, she positioned him in the crook of her left arm. The nipple made a small pop when she removed his bottle. She spooned a small amount of fruit in his mouth, which he turned back out onto the spoon.

"Come on, Hamid. How about some cereal?" He pushed the spoon away, splattering pabulum onto his bib and wiping it on his face. "Not feeling too well, little guy?" Wiping his face, she gave him back the bottle, grateful he would at least drink formula. "What a good boy you are." He started to cry when she took it way to burp him. "Give me a bubble and you can have it back."

There was something special about this early morning time with him. It felt so intimate, just the two of them in the early morning light. His eyes, so trusting and innocent, gazed directly into hers. "Soon we're going to America. You're going to ride on an airplane. And you are going to meet your grandparents." His mouth opened and closed for his bottle, like a little baby bird waiting for its mother to feed him.

Brushing her cheek against his, it felt slightly cooler, so she continued getting ready for work and packing his bag for the sitter. *The last thing we need is a sick infant*, she thought. With Hamid in his carrier and his bag over her shoulder, she reviewed the flat to freeze its arrangement in her mind before closing the locked door.

She walked up the stairs to the caretaker on the floor aboveelow where several other parents were there dropping off infants. "He woke up a little fussy this morning, Mrs. Khadkodian. You can call me if you see he is not alright." She kissed him on the cheek and then handed him over.

"He'll be just fine. Don't worry, Helen; I'll call you if I need to."

Sister Helen kissed him once more time, reminding him to be a good boy. Her large strides covered the short distance to the clinic in a mere ten minutes. Passing intermittent blown out windows and rubble from bombed buildings in this residential neighborhood, she reminded herself that the sooner she got out of Syria the better. An unharmed building drew her attention. *What luck dooms one to survive and another to remain unscathed?* she wondered. She shivered, then shrugged off the thought.

But these last days, she was just marking time at work. Her wish for them to pass quickly collided with their tedious passage. When her mobile rang midmorning, she instinctively knew the call concerned Hamid.

"Helen, this is Mrs. Khadkodian."

"Yes, is there something wrong with Hamid?"

"I'm afraid that he has a fever, and he keeps pulling on his ear. I'm no doctor, but I think he may have an ear infection. You should come and take him."

"I'll be right there."

Explaining to her supervisor that she would have to leave because her infant was sick, she thought that things had just been going too smoothly.

Finding an irritable Hamid, she took him upstairs to their flat to assess his condition. He felt very warm. Even without a thermometer, she knew he had a fever. She would have to take him to a doctor and get some antibiotics. To leave him un-medicated was risky since he had to be well for their journey.

While the easier path would be to take him to either of the clinics where she worked, it seemed imprudent to draw attention to herself. A third clinic, conveniently located near the sitter, was her first thought. Unfortunately, there was no way she would be going to work that afternoon either. Her afternoon supervisor was not pleased to lose a nurse that day, but she too had no choice. "I hope to be in on Friday." Sister Helen flinched, knowing that on Friday afternoon she would be riding a bus to the Western Union office.

Anticipating a second letter, Danel covered the distance to the hospital quickly. Finding none, he exhaled and settled in at his desk to focus on potential senders. He jotted down Kahlil Majaresh's name first, then added the names present the night that Hamid was born who still worked there. That was another five names. He knew no one in records to add to the list, although someone in that department could have discovered the switch. Altogether there were six names. One by one he considered their opportunity, means and motive.

It made no sense at all that Kahlil would be implicated. He wouldn't have let him come back to the hospital if he knew all along what Danel had done. Ruling out Kahlil, he felt none of the other names held promise either. Something gnawed at him, so frightening he couldn't allow himself to give it air.

Pulling out his wallet, he looked for a small piece of paper placed there several months earlier, when he and Ashara were working through their relocation options. Wedged under a small leather flap at the back of the wallet, the name and number on a small piece of paper were now faded, almost unreadable. Ahmed Tibi, his old friend from medical school who worked at a hospital in Beirut would be his next call.

"One moment, Sir. Let me check if Dr. Tibi is on duty this morning. Will you please hold?"

"Yes, of course." Danel drummed his fingers against his desk blotter. Crossing his legs, resting on his elbow, he hung his head down over the desk waiting for an answer.

"May I tell Dr. Tibi who is calling?"

"Please tell him it is Danel Ottawa."

In a few minutes Ahmed answered. "Danel, old man, where are you? How is Ashara?"

Danel inquired after Ahmed's wife and family. Taking a deep breath, he detailed what had happened since they last spoke, when he sought refuge with Ahmed's family in Lebanon. Choking up toward the end, he recovered his composure. "It's been a very hard time, Ahmed."

"I am so sorry to hear of your troubles. I so hope you can find your son soon. Is there anything I can do?"

"Well, that's why I am calling. I wonder if you could do a little research for me."

"Anything, Danel. We are old friends."

"There is a doctor from Lebanon. His name is Abu Majeed. I met him at Za'atari, and he has been a trusted friend, so I don't make this request lightly."

"What is it, Danel?"

"I need you to check into him. He practiced in Beirut before coming to Za'atari. There have been things about him that just don't add up. They were so inconsequential I barely noticed them. He accompanied me back to Damascus to practice here. Of course they were very eager to take him on what with the shortage of doctors."

"Naturally, I can understand why."

"There has been some trouble here; I won't go into details, but I thought it prudent to check into his background. With you being there in Beirut I thought you could help"

"Sure, Danel. The name sounds familiar, but I just can't place why. Can you give me a couple of days?"

"Yes, but this is very important, so the sooner I learn anything the better."

"It is that serious?"

"Yes, I am afraid it is."

"Then I'll make it a priority. I'll get back to you by Saturday at the latest. If I find anything out in the meantime, I'll call you."

Danel gave Ahmed his mobile number. "As always I thank you for your friendship. I will be looking forward to your call. Perhaps this is all about nothing."

Bethshari and Saeed left the apartment soon after Emil and Anouk called about Scolopendra. Their agenda included arranging for their marriage and ferreting out Sister Helen and Hamid. Danel was on alert in case they found Sister Helen. Not knowing what kind of wait they might have at the courthouse or if there was an obligatory number of days to wait required after filing, Bethshari decided to make that their first stop.

"Saeed, you're the navigator." Spreading the map on the front seat, she showed Saeed where they were and where they had to go. "Our first stop is the courthouse right here."

"I can get us there. You just drive." He buckled his seatbelt and folded the map to display the portion of the city where they were going.

As the car pulled out from the curb, Saeed directed her to turn left in two blocks, which put them on the main thoroughfare. Traffic was light, but shortly came to a standstill.

"Why are we stopping?" asked Saeed.

"I'm not sure." Cars ahead careened down side streets, others turned around in the opposite direction.

"Look, there's smoke up ahead." Saeed rolled his window down to the sound of muffled booms, as screaming pedestrians ran past them in the opposite direction.

"That's shelling. We've got to get out of here." They both coughed as an acrid air filled the car.

Spotting a break in the traffic, he nudged her arm. "Over there, you can fit in and turn down that street." Cars honked as she abruptly jerked the steering wheel. As she maneuvered the Renault, a shell exploded behind them, shaking the car. She sped up and continued for several kilometers until the shelling subsided.

Her hands shaking, she pulled over to park near an intersection. "Are you alright?"

Saeed's hand tightly gripped the door. "Yes. That's how it was when the shelling hit us in our village. I was really scared."

"Let's sit for a minute, I need to calm down. Can you figure out from the map where the shelling was? We can't go back, but maybe there is a different route we can take."

"We had gotten to here." He pointed out where they were when they turned around. "We tuned left down this street." His finger followed the road until he located the cross street where she had parked. Together they decided on a route that would take them way out of the way to approach the courthouse from the opposite direction. Twenty-five minutes later they were circling for a parking place. Several times they passed the same bronze statue of Hafez Al Assad, the President's father, dressed in western garb with his arm extended as though directing tourists.

Taxis jockeyed for position, sometimes four vehicles deep. The architectural olio of the city center included old buildings with Roman arches and ionic columns, some with steeples and others with Turkish domes, and modern buildings with no more charm or imagination than stacked boxes. All conspired to illustrate Damascus's checkered past of occupiers.

Once inside the courthouse, they experienced long lines and redirection to another queue and finally to a different municipal building, where marriage services had been relocated two months ago. By the time they finally landed in the right place, the official left for a late lunch. An official backed the line out to wait in the hall and hung a "Gone to lunch" sign on the knob before locking the door. According to the sign, they would wait an hour until he returned. Others in the queue grumbled.

"We could go look for Sister Helen while we wait?" said Saeed.

Reluctant to relinquish the parking place they finally landed when they arrived, she looked at her watch. "No, we've come this far, we should just wait it out."

A resigned quiet, punctuated by the occasional cough or foot shuffle, enveloped the queue of strangers. They were at the head of the line, which had grown and snaked around to the adjacent hall. "Bethshari, are you glad I am going to be your son?"

"Why do you even ask such a question? Wasn't it my idea to adopt you?"

"It's just that." He shifted from foot to foot.

"What?"

He looked down at this shoes as if the answer to her question were written on them. "Well, I overheard you on the phone this morning talking to Mr. Cameron and then to your parents."

"I thought you were still asleep."

"I was very quiet so I could hear."

"I'll have to remember that."

His brow scrunched over his pale gray eyes.

"And why should that make you question that I want you?"

"It's a lot of trouble that I bring on you. Especially now that you are hunting for Hamid."

"Saeed, the fact that we go to some lengths to have you be our son should convince you that we really want you. Some things in this world are worth it; you are one of them."

His expression lightened.

She affectionately draped her arm around his shoulders, pulling him close. "We're a family, and all this trouble, it is just details."

"I want to be your son very much." He returned her hug. "I think I must be the luckiest boy in the world."

"If that's true, then Danel and I are the luckiest parents."

Their wait for the official to return from lunch squandered an hour and a half. *Must have been quite a lunch,* she thought. After filling out a series of forms, which he stamped loudly with official finality, they were to report for a civil ceremony late Saturday morning. She marveled at a system that convoluted securing a marriage license into several hours with three lines, two buildings and an hour and a half lunch for the only official that could help them. *What a system,* she thought. *No wonder this country is in such disarray.*

"It's four o'clock. We still have time to find Sister Helen's work," she said. "Let's hope she hasn't left for the day." They hurried the four blocks to the car to find a notice and a fine for parking in an unauthorized zone. She wadded it up and threw it into the back seat. "We'll deal with this later."

Again, with the map spread out, she pointed out their current location and the clinic on Rue Champs Elysee. "Can you can get us there?" She scanned the morass of autos around them.

"Go straight ahead for, let me count it, one, two, three, four, five blocks and then go left."

The press of commuters congested the roads, honking and jostling with taxis for position. She hunched forward over the steering wheel as though shortening the distance to their destination. The trip should have taken twenty minutes but had more than doubled by the time they pulled up in front of the clinic.

She turned off the ignition. "Saeed, Danel said that we shouldn't let her know we are looking for her, but I have been thinking about how we do that. What would you think if you went in alone? She wouldn't be very concerned if a child asked for her."

"What reason would I give for asking for her?"

"Tell her your mother is sick again, and that she is waiting in the car. You could say that your mother sent you in ahead to do the waiting for her. When your turn comes up, ask her if it is alright if you go and get your mother.

"What if she asks my mother's name?"

"You say 'Fatima' and then come and get me."

Reluctant, his brow wrinkled.

"You don't have to do this if it makes you uncomfortable." She touched his forearm.

"I can do this. I'll be right back."

"Remember, ask for Helen McCormick, and not Sister Helen."

Within several minutes, he returned with the news that Sister Helen wasn't there because her baby is sick. "She won't be back until tomorrow."

"Did she say what was wrong with the baby? I hope it's not serious."

"No, I didn't ask."

"You did the right thing. We'll just have to wait." Frustrated, she frowned, worried about Hamid. Biting her lip, she thought this would cost another day. "We'll come back first thing tomorrow."

33

Suspicions

On the way back to their flat, Bethshari and Saeed stopped at the market for ingredients to prepare supper.

"Saeed, what was your favorite dish your mother prepared?"

"Definitely kawag. It smelled so good when I used to come home from school."

"That's a kind of stew, isn't it?"

"Yes, and hers was so good." He smacked his lips, licking the corners of his mouth.

"Did you ever see her make it?"

"Many times. It was my father's favorite too."

"We should try to make it for dinner tonight. I don't have a recipe, but if you tell me what you remember was in it, we could make something close."

"Well, there was meat. I think she used beef or lamb, but I always like lamb best."

"Then lamb it is. What else?"

"I remember carrots, onion, squash, eggplant and tomatoes. And then she always added a layer of sliced potatoes onto the top."

"Did she cook it in a big soup pot?"

"No, she had a shallow pan with a lid that she baked in the oven."

"We should be able to find all of those vegetables this time of year."

That evening, Danel hurried home, eager for news of Sister Helen and Hamid. As his key turned in the door, the aroma of kawag had taken over the flat.

"What's that smell?" Crossing the threshold, Danel savored the aroma, Abu close behind. "Abu, smell that." *How long has it been since I came home to the aroma of a home cooked meal,* he thought.

Abu inhaled, closing his eyes. "You are inviting me for dinner, aren't you? You wouldn't be so cruel as to send me next door."

"Of course not, Abu. You're always welcome," said Bethshari. "Although this is Saeed's recipe so we'll have to ask him."

"You can stay, Dr. Abu. We made a lot of kawag, like my mother used to make it."

Over dinner, Bethshari recounted the shelling on the way to get the marriage license.

"This is just what I worried about bringing you here. You and Hamid gallivanting all over Damascus is not safe.

"It is a risk that we all agreed to take, Danel. We have no choice. Hamid is counting on us."

Arguing with her seemed pointless.

She nudged Saeed as both men filled their plates a second time.

"Well, at least we have a date and a time, and soon we will be married. I don't want to risk you slipping through my fingers. I arranged to have Saturday off just in case you were able to make this happen," said Danel.

Abu dropped his hand heavily on the table. "Wait, I'll be on duty this Saturday. I wanted to come."

"I appreciate that, my friend, but we'll all celebrate together that evening."

"You act as if I have a say in the matter. I'll be with you in spirit though. After all I recognized before you did that you were in love with this woman. That should count for something."

"Abu, please have some more kawag." She passed him the serving dish, which had cooled enough to touch. "One of the best discoveries of the day was that Saeed is an expert navigator. Very impressive."

Saeed blushed at the compliment. "I'm the official navigator. Right, Bethshari?"

"Yes, I thought that Danel was good with a map, until I saw you in action." After Abu helped himself to more kawag, she passed the dish to Danel for thirds.

"Now tell us about Sister Helen," said Danel.

"There is not much to tell at this point. Saeed went in to ask for her, telling the attendant that his sick mother was in the car and wanted Helen McCormick to see his mother. That's when he learned Hamid was sick but that she would return the next day."

"What about Hamid? Did you find out what's wrong?"

"Saeed felt it not right to ask, and I agreed."

He nodded, but Hamid's condition worried him. "Of course. Did they act suspicious when you asked for her?"

"Not really. They asked my mother's name, and I said 'Fatima' and that we'd come back."

Picking up his glass, Danel downed it contents. "Clever ruse, you two. So the plan now is for you to go back in the morning and ask for her again?"

She picked up his tumbler and filled it with tap water. "Yes, I'll send Saeed in again, and if she's there, we'll just wait in the car until we see her leave and then follow her home."

"I'll keep my mobile on me."

"Be very careful, you two," said Abu. "A mama bear with a cub can be vicious if you rile her." He swiped a piece of flat bread through the last drops of kawag on his plate.

"Abu, you are still hungry? How about a little more? We have enough."

"Woman, don't tempt me because I have already had three plates. The Koran specifically cautions good Muslims against gluttony." He pushed his seat back from the table. Although he prided himself on a slim physique, the three helpings rounded out his normally flat abdomen. "And I'm exhausted, so I'm afraid I must say good night."

Standing, he bowed toward Saeed and Bethshari. "My compliments to the chefs and to Allah who is the source of all great meals." He shook Danel's hand. "You don't mind if I call it a night, do you?"

"Of course not. Perhaps tomorrow night Hamid will be with us."

"I will pray to Allah that He grant your wish."

"Good night, Bethshari. Saeed." By the time Danel let him out and turned the lock, Saeed and Bethshari had already cleared the table and started washing the dishes.

"What do you say if we leave these until tomorrow? I'm exhausted too," said Danel.

"You won't get any complaints from us. Saeed, get ready for bed first and say your prayers. Then we'll be in to say good night."

When he left the room, Bethshari and Danel exchanged glances. "Did you get another letter today?"

"Shhh. I would rather not speak of it until we're sure Saeed's asleep."

"Alright. Funny you should mention this. I learned today that he heard me talking to Phillip Cameron and my parents while I thought he was still asleep this morning."

"Do you think he knows about the letter?"

"I don't think so, but he heard enough to convince me that we need to be very cautious."

They got ready for bed and then knocked on Saeed's door.

"Did you say your prayers?"

"Yes. Do you know what I prayed for?"

"What was that?" said Danel, pulling the coverlet back and tucking the lighter weight sheet in. "It's too warm tonight for the full covers."

"I asked that tomorrow we find Hamid and that I'll have a new brother."

"We'll ask for the same thing tonight. Maybe if Allah hears all of us, He'll be more inclined to grant our request. Good night, Saeed." She bent down and kissed him on the forehead.

He reached out to hug her around the neck. "Good night, Bethshari. Good night, Dr. Danel."

"Saeed, let's start thinking about a better name to call me than Dr. Danel. What do you say?"

"OK, I will think about it." He yawned, snuggling into his pillow as they turned off the night light and closed the door. They waited at the door until they heard his breathing grow heavy.

Padding softly to their own room, they crawled into bed exhausted, though much about the day still needed to be shared.

"Was there another letter today?" Her voice was barely above a whisper.

"So far there's just the one. I spent some time thinking about who sent the first one. Honestly, I came up with six names and none make any sense. I did something today I'm not very proud of. But it was gnawing at me. "

She frowned. "What is it?"

"When I was in medical school, a classmate of mine, Ahmed Tibi, and I were very close. My parents knew him and he used to come to our home for dinner. He practices in Beirut."

"What does this have to do with the letter?" She lifted up onto her elbow to see his face better, as moonlight filtered through the sheer curtain.

"I asked him to find out what he could about Abu."

"Are you saying that Abu is behind all of this?"

"Shhh. Not so loud. I'm just saying that when you have an itch, it's sometimes prudent to scratch."

"But how could Abu know anything about the swap? He wasn't there, and you told no one but Ashara."

"That's true. But you saw how handily he raided Sister Helen's personnel file and then bragged about how easy it was."

"Yes, but the retrieval of a photo doesn't mean he sent the letter."

"But it got me to thinking how easily he could have delved into Hamid's birth record."

"Still that doesn't prove anything."

"But it's enough to make me want to rule him out. I don't know his motive, but I know he has the means. There were other things about him that never lay right for me."

"Like what? He always seemed to me a kind and caring physician."

"For me as well, but I never really bought his reasons for coming to Za'atari when I know there was just as much suffering in Lebanon. When I asked him about coming to Damascus, he said this hospital would suit his purpose. What did that mean?"

"Danel, you're seeing ghosts in the wind. This isn't right to suspect our friend."

"Maybe so, but I need to be sure before I rule him out. Right now he's the most likely candidate. But there's something else very troubling." Rolling over to face her, he too raised himself up on his elbow.

"What's that?"

His voice grew animated as he made his case. "The first day we were on duty at the hospital, a character came to see Abu."

"A character? Isn't that a bit melodramatic?"

"This man was big and burly, with a ruddy, pockmarked complexion and a mustache like a push broom. He was like a caricature. His name was Issam Kattani, and Abu called him 'Sami.' Abu whisked him away to an examining room to talk without going through the charge nurse. Why was that?"

She lay back down. "I have no idea."

"Because he wanted him to get away from me. It was clear that Abu didn't like me talking to him."

"Did you ask Abu who he was?"

"He said he was an old acquaintance who heard he was in Damascus. This was our first day, so I doubt if anyone just heard about Abu. I suspect that Abu let this guy know he was here."

"None of this makes sense."

"You're right. It didn't make sense to me either, that's why I called Ahmed and asked him to check."

"Did you tell Ahmed about the letter?"

"No, of course not. But I did tell him that some things didn't add up, and that this was very serious."

"When did he say he would get back to you?"

"He said no later than Saturday."

"This is very disturbing. Abu's our friend and this is no way to treat him, especially after the way he supported you when Ashara died." She sat up, pulling her hair back off her face, twisting it to lay back off her shoulders.

"Don't you think it's better to rule it out than let suspicion spoil a friendship?"

"Yes, of course, when you put it that way. The sooner we put it to rest the better." She froze as if she heard something. "I am going to just go check on Saeed to make sure he's asleep." Tiptoeing to the next room, she turned the knob, releasing it quietly. As she neared his bed, his slumber was deep and rhythmic, so she turned quietly and exited.

"He's in a deep sleep. Now I want to tell you about my call to Phillip Cameron and my parents. Phillip was very angry about the trouble we put him through and that we had kidnapped Saeed."

"We didn't kidnap him."

"I know that, but that's the way it looked to Phillip. I disappeared and then Saeed was nowhere to be found, all at the same time. I won't tire you with the details of our conversation. Suffice it to say that it was very unpleasant. But at the end, he agreed to send Saeed's papers to you at the hospital via a UN courier. They should arrive tomorrow morning, so you should be watching for them. We have to have them to get adoption papers."

"Good work. Now tell me about your parents. I am very eager to hear how things went. I'm actually nervous that they might oppose our marriage."

"I told them everything. I spared nothing."

He winced, thrusting his jaw forward.

"We agreed that we can't involve them unless they know it all."

"I just wanted to make a good impression on them, and this isn't a good start."

"They were dears about it. They called back after I talked to Phillip, and my dad was all over it."

"That's a relief." He leaned back on the pillow, arms behind his head, and stared intently at her.

"He has a friend, Jamal Amer, at the embassy here, who owes him a favor having to do with some trouble his son got into in London that my dad made go away. He's arranged for someone to create false papers for us. We have to provide him all of our identification documents: yours, Saeed's and mine. We don't have Hamid's, but you're to write down the details that you remember from the form. Someone will come to collect them on Saturday evening, along with the marriage license."

"Who's going to forge the papers? What do we know about him? How smart is it to turn over our documents to a stranger?"

"That's exactly what I said, but he says the letter you received means we're going to have to take some risk."

"What's this going to cost?"

"I've no idea, but my parents are going to front the money. We'll figure how to repay them later."

He nodded. "What is the forger's name?"

"Scolopendra."

"Scolopendra what?"

"Just Scolopendra."

"You mean like the poisonous—"

She finished his thought. "Centipede."

"This is starting to sound like a spy novel."

"Scolopendra will collect our documents Saturday. Sunday night he'll return our original documents along with visas for all four of us to the UK, adoption papers for Saeed, a marriage travel certificate and plane tickets out of here on Tuesday."

"That's only twenty-four hours to create all those documents. How is that even doable?"

"My father says it is, so we need to have faith. Unless you've a better plan, I vote we follow through with what's been set up for us."

He shrugged, spreading his hands. "I've no plan. The lone wolf mesmerized by the passing headlights has a better plan than I have." Shaking his head, he said, "So what's the agenda for tomorrow?"

"We have to find Hamid. If Tuesday comes, no matter what has fallen into place, without Hamid we aren't going anywhere."

He shuddered. "He's the centerpiece of this caper, isn't he?"

"We're all at the center because we can't leave any one of us behind."

"Now what else for tomorrow?"

"We have to get Saeed's papers. Hopefully Phillip followed through. Tall orders for the day, aren't they?"

"Indeed." He sighed deeply. "So many things have to fall exactly in place. Tuesday is only four days away. "We better get some sleep." Danel kissed her, running his hand gently against her cheek. "Someday, we will look back on all of this and wonder how we survived."

"I look forward to that day."

"I was very concerned to hear he's sick."

"I hope it's not serious and that he'll be well enough to travel."

"When I would come home at night, I could hardly wait to spend time with him. I just adored him."

"We'll get him back."

"I hope his illness is minor. I can't even imagine our lives without him."

After turning out the light, she kissed him gently and held his hand as they drifted off to sleep.

34

Documents

The sun's first rays crept over the roof of the apartment building visible out her window. Sister Helen checked for fever by laying the back of her hand against Hamid's cheek. He rested peacefully through the night, sleeping in the same position as when she put him to bed. His skin felt almost cool to the touch. *The antibiotics are working,* she thought. His tiny fists, thumbs tucked protectively under his curled fingers, rested palms up at shoulder height. The gentle rise and fall of his chest mesmerized her, his innocence contrasting sharply with the potent events that swirled around him. "I do love you, Little One," she whispered so as not to wake him.

Her hypnosis broken by a glance at her watch, she eased out of bed to dress quickly and ready his formula and pabulum. Forty-five minutes later she was dropping him and his antibiotics off at Mrs. Khadkodian's. Taking Hamid in her arms, Mrs. Khadkodian pressed her own cheek against his to gauge his warmth.

Preempting Mrs. Khadkodian's diagnosis, Sister Helen volunteered, "His fever was down this morning, but you can reach me on my mobile if it spikes up again. These bugs can be ornery."

Mrs. Khadkodian hugged Hamid, placing a big kiss generously on his cheek. "It is so out of character for this cheerful little fellow to be fussy."

As Sister Helen bid goodbye, he eagerly reached his arms to her, leaning out towards her to be taken back.

"Not now Hamid. Mama has to go earn some money today. I'll be back to get you later." Her giant hand affectionately enveloped his, and she left quickly. She wondered if the separation anxiety of leaving an infant ever goes away.

Saeed and Bethshari wasted no time getting on the road to the clinic on Rue Champs Elysee. "We are finally going to corner the fox this morning, Saeed."

Saeed was still munching on an apple he grabbed as Bethshari hustled him out of the flat. "Is Dr. Danel going to come?"

"No, he's going to delay until we track Sister Helen back to where she lives. Our task today will be about waiting and watching."

"You mean like a detective on television?"

"Exactly. Do you know what we call them at home?"

He examined his apple, choosing his next bite of the sweet flesh. "Private eyes."

Saeed looked at her suspiciously. "Really?"

"Really."

He shrugged his shoulders. "That makes no sense."

As they drew up to the clinic, no parking spaces in front presented themselves, so they circled twice. "Must be a rush on the infirmed this morning, let's hope we get lucky with a space."

"My father used to double park all the time."

"I'd prefer a legal spot so we don't draw attention."

"Over there, across the street." Saeed spotted a car-length opening that had suddenly appeared between two delivery trucks. "Hurry, that other car is trying to get it."

"Good eyes, Saeed." She maneuvered in front of the other driver and slid the Renault neatly into place, two blocks down and one block over from the clinic.

"Do you want me to go in like I did yesterday?" He took his last bite of apple.

She reached for his core and placed it into the pullout ashtray. "Do you feel comfortable asking for her again?"

"Yes, I'm fine with it. Helen McCormick, right?"

"Right."

"I'll be right back."

Ten minutes later he ran back to the car, pulling the door handle down and hopping into the passenger seat.

"Well, was she there?"

"No, she doesn't work here in the morning. She works somewhere else. She doesn't come in until the afternoon."

"Great. She has two jobs then. I didn't see that coming. They didn't tell you where she works in the morning, did they?'

"I asked but they didn't know where it was, but they did said it's a clinic. They said my mother can come in and see someone else though."

"What did you tell them?"

"I told them that Helen McCormick was the only nurse that my mother trusts." He was grinning now.

"Clever boy." She bit her lip, mulling their next move. "I don't think it makes sense to wait. Besides, from this spot we can't even see the front door. We'll have to come back later."

By mid-morning, Sister Helen checked in with Mrs. Khadkodian.

"His ear is still bothering him because he keeps fiddling with it. He feels a little warm, so I suspect that his temperature is elevated again."

"Should I come and get him?"

"Let's give him another hour before we decide."

"I'll call back in an hour." She flipped her phone shut. A sick baby on the long trip to the United States worried her. The cabin pressure on his inner ear, especially taking off and landing, could be very painful. She clenched her fists. *I've got to get him well*, she thought. Her next call was to the clinic on Rue Champs Elysee to let them know that she wouldn't be in that afternoon. She didn't mention she would be going to Western Union to pick up her funds.

Her supervisor took the news a little better than the day before. "Oh, Helen, a young boy has been here looking for you."

"That's odd."

"Yes, he says his mother was sick, so she waited in the car and sent him in to see if you're here."

"Strange. Did he give his mother's name?"

"He said it was Fatima."

Perhaps the most common name in Syria, she thought. "Well, I've helped a lot of Fatimas. Couldn't anyone else help her?"

"We offered to have someone else see her, but he said that you were the only nurse his mother trusted."

"How old was he?" She rubbed her hand back and forth across her forehead.

"About nine or ten I guess. He had a limp."

Scratching her head, she tried hard to recall a crippled boy about that age. "I can't place him or his mother. I'm not on the schedule this weekend, but I'll be in on Monday. Hamid should be over whatever he has by then." Her mind fixated on the boy. *Could they have found me? Perhaps, but who is the boy, and what could he possibly have to do with Danel and Ashara?*

Within thirty minutes, Mrs. Khadkodian preempted Sister Helen's call, requesting that she come back to pick up Hamid. With no alternate time to collect the funds from Western Union, she knew that Hamid would now have to accompany her. Jostling around Damascus on a bus was not going to be good for him.

With time to spare before returning to Rue Champs Elysee, Bethshari dialed Danel's mobile to check on Saeed's papers due by courier early that morning.

The ring startled him. "Did you find Hamid?"

"No, apparently she has a different job in the morning so won't be in at the clinic until this afternoon."

He dropped the file he had been notating. "That doesn't surprise me. You're going back later I suppose."

"Yes, that's our plan. Did Saeed's papers arrive?"

"Not yet. I was just there to check and they haven't come."

"Phillip promised them first thing this morning. Perhaps I'll give him a ring. We have to turn them over to Scolopendra tomorrow."

"Bethshari, there's something else."

"What is it? Did you hear from Ahmed Tibi?"

"No, I won't hear from him until tomorrow. I got another letter."

Her breath caught in her throat.

"Are you still there?" he said.

"Yes, I'm listening.

"It was waiting for me when I got here this morning, just like the last one."

"What does it say?"

"I don't want to say over the phone, but whoever sent it knows. I'll let you read it tonight."

"Alright. We'll talk tonight then, but in the meantime I'll call Phillip."

"Are you alright?"

She paused, framing her answer.

"Maybe I shouldn't have mentioned the letter."

"To answer your question, how can I be alright with this hanging over us?"

He wished he could hold her. "We'll get through this."

"I know, it's just that these letters really scare me, and my mind is running wild with the possibilities."

"Listen, today you focus on finding Sister Helen and our wedding tomorrow."

"You're right. Tomorrow is very special, and we shouldn't let our marriage pale in importance. I love you."

Bethshari closed her phone and sank onto the divan to collect her thoughts. She'd forgotten that Saeed was there.

"Is something wrong?"

"No, but your papers haven't arrived, so I'll have to call Mr. Cameron to find out what happened."

"I heard you talking about a letter and something about Dr. Abu."

"Oh, that was just a letter that was supposed to be with the papers. I'll get it straightened out with Mr. Cameron." She winced at her carelessness. *Children have no filters,* she thought, *and anything overheard by Saeed could easily be relayed to Abu.*

Checking up on Phillip was not something she was looking forward to. "Saeed, I wish you could make the call to Mr. Cameron. We always seem to get off on the wrong foot."

"I'll do it."

She found his eagerness endearing. "I know you would." She gently brushed her finger tips against his chin. "But this task is for me. I think there are some washed grapes in the refrigerator. Why don't you help yourself?"

As he went in search of the grapes, she dialed Phillip to learn that he was not expected in until after lunch.

"I really need to talk to him. Do you have his mobile number?"

"We're not allowed to give that number out."

"It's really important that I talk to him." Her voice struggled to strike the right balance between urgency and annoyance that he had not delivered as he promised.

"I'm sorry. I hope you can understand…the rules, you know. You can leave a message and a number where he can reach you."

"Alright, tell him that Bethshari—"

The staff person cut her short. "Why didn't you say so? Mr. Cameron told me you'd be calling. He gave me permission to give you his number."

Shaking her head, Bethshari took down the number. If he expected her call, it was because he didn't send the papers. Tapping her foot and drumming her fingers against her knee, she considered how to handle him. Without Saeed's papers to give to Scolopendra, taking

Saeed with them was problematic. Gritting her teeth, she exhaled deeply before dialing.

"Phillip, this is Bethshari. I hope you don't mind my call. The girl in your office said it was alright."

"Yes, quite right. I suppose you're calling about Saeed's papers?"

"Yes, I have an appointment tomorrow with an adoption official."

"I would have called you, but you didn't leave me your mobile number. But I knew you would call when the papers didn't arrive this morning."

"Is there a problem?" She held her breath.

"Well, yes and no."

"Come on, Phillip, no riddles."

"My, my, a little sarcastic, aren't we this morning?"

"Sorry. What do you mean by yes and no?"

"Well, the courier that I have at my disposal was commandeered yesterday by someone else, so I don't have a courier to send."

She gasped. No courier meant no papers.

"But, I have another idea."

"I hope this involves a different courier."

"Well, yes, in a way it does." He was toying with her.

"Well, you're the man that makes things happen, so I'm all ears."

"I'm going to bring them myself in the morning."

"You're bringing them?"

"I have other business in Damascus, and I thought I could drop them by the hospital. Would that work for you?"

"Phillip, you're an angel sent from heaven. Danel's not on duty tomorrow, but he'll drop in to get them. When should I send him to fetch them?"

"I should definitely have them there by ten, if not sooner."

She scrunched up her face, knowing that ten left them very little time to make it to the ministry to get married. "That will be great, Phillip. Now don't be late, promise?"

"Do you have something more important to do?"

"Since you ask, yes. We're getting married tomorrow at eleven, so having the papers by ten gives us just enough time. Are you sure that doesn't rush you?"

"Now, I'd say that is a dandy excuse. Congratulations. I'll make sure I'm there by ten o'clock. Yes, right so, ten o'clock."

"Thanks, Phillip, it means a great deal to all of us."

"Yes, I'm sure it does."

"Let me give you my mobile in case anything comes up."

"If you insist. If I say I'll be there, you can count on it."

"Phillip, I can set my watch by your reliability, it's the rest of the world I don't trust." *Why's it that talking to him always exhausts me,* she thought.

Hamid dozed, nestled snuggly against Sister Helen's ample bosom while they waited for their first bus to Western Union. His newborn hair, which had fallen out in the first weeks, was replaced by a thicker crop of fuzzy dark hair, too short to lay flat against his scalp. She gently removed his thumb from his mouth before boarding. The small pop from the broken suction startled him, but his mouth continued sucking. A warm puff of exhaust fumes assaulted them as she took her seat by the window.

Already after 1:00, Hamid was due his medicine and a bottle. Sister Helen groped the interior of the baby bag for the amoxicillin. Filling the syringe to a line marked by the pharmacist, she slid the tip into his mouth, lightly pressing the plunger as he sucked down the sweet concoction. "Take your medicine. That's a good boy." She followed with a bottle of formula that she had warmed before leaving the flat.

The bus traveled north, stopping every two blocks to pick up and leave off passengers, but had not moved for the past five minutes. Several commuters approached the driver about the stall and subsequently disembarked.

A young, bearded man about twenty-five sat across the aisle. He was among those who questioned the driver, but he retook his seat when the others got off.

"What's the holdup?" she asked.

"The driver says there was a sticky bomb and some shooting going on a couple of blocks ahead and the police stopped all traffic until it is cleared."

"A sticky bomb?"

"A bomb taped under a car."

Memory of the sniper fire the day she brought Ashara into the hospital replayed, prompting her to get off the bus. She packed up Hamid and pulled the overhead cord, signaling the driver to release the rear door. *She should have taken a taxi to the Western Union office,* she thought.

The clinic on Rue Champs Elysee bustled. In the waiting room, coughs and sneezing by disparate patients echoed. The supervisor herself was taking on patients, annoyed at the additional burden caused by Sister Helen's absence. *Helen needs to be more reliable and secure a backup sitter,* she thought, *or look for another position.*

Bethshari and Saeed wolfed down some flat bread, cheese and grapes, before heading to the car. They had been so close to finding Sister Helen yesterday, but close wasn't good enough.

"We have to park closer this time so we can see Sister Helen leave at the end of the day. We have to track her back to where she's keeping Hamid."

"We can't let the fish flip out of our net, right?"

"You got it. Hopefully, today we'll nab her."

"Shall I go in again?"

"Our little ruse is getting tired, but you're least likely to draw suspicion. We can try it one more time."

Cruising the block for a suitable perch to watch the comings and goings of the clinic, they found nothing. They circled again. "Sooner or later, one of those cars is going to pull out," she said. Four more turns around the block yielded a spot across the street from the main entrance.

"Bethshari, look, over there." Unbuckling his seatbelt, Saeed leaned forward, one hand on the dashboard and the other pointing directly at the space.

Jerking the wheel to the left, she cut off a taxi, whose horn barked out the driver's annoyance.

"Get over it." Unintimidated, she eased into the spot. "OK, Saeed, go check if she's there."

Despite his limp, he bounded up the clinic stairs and headed directly to the receptionist signing in patients.

She looked up, recognizing him. "You're the boy who's looking for Helen McCormick."

"Yes, Ma'am. Well, not for me, but for my mother. I'll go and get my mother if Helen can see her. Is she here now?" He shifted nervously from foot to foot as she came around the counter to talk directly to him.

"No, she called in and said that her child is sick. She won't be back until Monday."

"She won't be in tomorrow or the next day either?"

"No, she has off this weekend. She'll be here Monday for sure because it's payday." She winked at Saeed. "But let me go and talk to your mother. You say she's in the car?"

"Yes, but she only wants to see Helen McCormick."

"Is your mother very sick?"

"Yes, very sick."

"What's wrong? If she's very sick she shouldn't wait until Monday."

"I can go and talk to her." He inched his way closer to the door.

"That's a good idea. We have a doctor that can see her right away." Placing her arm on his shoulder, she walked him to the door and opened it. "Do you want me to come with you?"

"No, my mother wouldn't like that. I'll be right back." He hopped down the stairs and stopped at the bottom, looking back. Raising his pointer finger, he indicated she should wait one minute and then darted across the street. He pulled up the door lock and got into the front seat.

"She's not here. You need to leave right now."

"What's wrong?"

"See that woman at the door." The woman slowly moved down the steps.

"She wants to talk to you."

"What does she want?"

"She wants someone to treat you."

The woman was almost to the foot of the steps. "Look. She is coming."

Bethshari turned the key in the ignition and swung the car into the lane of traffic, hardly looking to see who was in her way. She looked back in the rear view mirror to see a hefty woman in green scrubs and hijab craning to view them. "So I guess our ruse isn't going to work again."

"We'll have to think of something else."

"You said Sister Helen wasn't there?"

"No, Hamid is still sick. She won't be back until Monday."

"That's not the answer I was hoping for." They pulled up to a stop light, and she lowered her forehead to the steering wheel, banging it lightly up and down.

"But she really will be there on Monday."

"What makes you so sure? Our near encounters so far haven't panned out."

"The woman said that Monday was payday."

She sighed. "We were so close."

"Don't worry, the fish is still in the net."

Horns honking behind her as the light changed refocused her attention. "You're the eternal optimist, Saeed. I don't know how you manage it, but I should try to be more like you."

As Bethshari and Saeed returned home empty handed, Sister Helen was wending her way on foot back over the same streets the bus had covered, searching for a taxi. As the gunfire moved closer, the commotion behind them stampeded the pedestrians, carrying her and Hamid along with them. She would have to move over several blocks if she were going to locate a taxi. Her bulk, augmented by a baby and paraphernalia, retarded her progress, making for a bumpy ride for Hamid. He coughed slightly before his vomit spewed, sending a warm wet sensation down her chest.

With no place to sit and attend to Hamid's mess, she sidled forward crablike, scanning for taxis coming from behind. A taxi cruising for a fare approached from behind. Both her arms waved wildly above her head, one holding her purse and the other the cumbersome baby bag, while Hamid's face bobbed against her. Two businessmen with briefcases, boarded it as it slowed to a stop three meters from her.

Hamid started to whimper as another cab came up fast in the middle lane. Determined not to lose it, she wobbled out into traffic, crossing toward the middle lane, her arms jerked heavenward. Screeching brakes sounded as several cars stopped short to avoid hitting her. Two cars crashed to her left as she made it to the middle lane and climbed into the taxi.

A driver in the outside lane cruised past her cab. "Lady, are you crazy? You almost got killed. Allah don't protect crazies."

As she settled into her seat, she muttered to herself. "Perhaps I am, but I needed the taxi." She set her purse and the bag down on the floor and tilted Hamid's cloth carrier away from her torso to survey the damage.

"Where to?"

"Bagdad Street near Seven Pools Square."

Twenty minutes later, with Hamid cleaned up as best as she could and the front of her blouse wet and sour smelling, the cab pulled up in front of the Western Union office.

"Can you wait here for me?"

"I can but the meter will be running. You can pay me now for the ride so far."

"That's alright." Checking the amount on the meter, she paid the driver, holding back the gratuity for the return trip. "I shouldn't be long." She considered leaving the baby bag behind in the cab but thought better of being separated from it. "Just wait for me here."

Inside, several other customers were occupying the attention of the three staff on duty, each with their next customer already waiting in line. Progressing to second in line, she glanced out the window at her cab. Three men in business suits approached the driver. After an animated conversation, one of the men took out his wallet, thrusting a wad of cash at the driver, who reset his meter. All three then jumped into the cab, which veered off into an opening in the traffic barely large enough to swallow the vehicle. *Great*, she thought, *thank God I kept the baby bag with me.*

"My name is Helen McCormick and I'm here to pick up funds. Actually, they were wired here in two batches, one yesterday and the other the day before."

"Do you have any identification?"

"Of course." She set the baby bag on the floor and rummaged through her purse.

Arching his back, Hamid struggled in the carrier.

"Your baby looks sick."

"I think he has a fever. He threw up coming over here." She slid her identification papers across the counter.

The woman looked at the photo and then at Sister Helen, then at the photo again. "It says here that you're a nun?"

"Well, I was when I first came here, but I've since left the order."

"Is this your child?"

"Yes, it is."

"Your order lets their nuns have babies?"

Bristling at the interrogation, she resisted the urge to tell her to mind her own business. "Actually he's my sister's child. She had to work and needed someone to watch him."

She eyed the photo again, trying to jog her memory. "Let me see if your funds have arrived." Disappearing into the back, she held onto the document.

Bolting at the first sign of a question had been Sister Helen's modus operandi over the last two months. Any other time she would have left, but the money to fund her escape was critical. A thin band of sweat glistened along her upper lip.

The woman returned with several five-part yellow forms. I need to you fill out the information at all of the Xs." Scribbling a black ballpoint on a scratch pad to start the ink flowing, she handed the pen to Sister Helen. "You'll have to press hard because there are four copies below the top sheet on each form." Studying the photo, she passed the papers to Sister Helen.

After quickly filling in the required information, she signed her name as Helen McCormick, peeling back the layers to confirm that her signature on the last page was readable.

The woman took the forms and began entering the information into her computer.

Sister Helen reached for her documents. "May I put these away now?"

"You can. I have everything I need. I'll be right back with your funds." She disappeared into the back through a security door, returning with the funds, accompanied by a coworker.

"Your baby doesn't look well," said the coworker.

"He has an ear infection and the sitter wouldn't keep him with a fever."

"He should be at home."

"That's where we're going now." She drew out a wallet on a strap around her neck that had been tucked into her bosom. After counting the bills, she secured them in the wallet and replaced it against her chest.

"Do you live around here?" The woman seemed too curious for Sister Helen's taste.

"No, I live some distance, but this was the closest Western Union to me." She had had enough interrogation, so after thanking them, she left as quickly. It occurred to her to ask them to call her a cab, but that would have made her destination traceable. Disappearing around the nearest corner, she was anxious to put as much distance between them as she could. Her luck was holding as she hailed a cab only two blocks from the office.

"There was something about that woman and her baby that struck me. I just couldn't place her from the photo." The woman mused more to herself than to the coworker.

"You know I had the same feeling, like something wasn't right."

"Her passport titled her as Sister. She said she left the order after coming to Syria."

"What's a nun doing with a baby?'

"That's what I thought."

"We got a circular about a nun who'd stolen a baby about a month or so ago. I think it's posted on the bulletin board in the break room."

Naturally it was missing a photo, because at the time Phillip Cameron filed the notification of missing persons, Danel couldn't provide a photo. The description of a large woman, about 81 kg, 177 cm fit the woman who collected the money. The name on the poster was Sister Helen, although there was no last name.

"Do you think we should notify the police?"

"Can't hurt. Maybe there's a reward."

Within minutes, the woman who waited on Sister Helen was calling the police with information, including Sister Helen's address, a description of her and the baby and her personal contact information in case it led to a reward. Unfortunately, the address that Sister Helen listed was the boarding house where she lived when she first came back to Damascus. By the end of the day, two policemen were interrogating the boarding house owner concerning Sister Helen's whereabouts.

35

Anonymity Unraveling

It was already dark when Danel's footsteps sounded on the landing. Although exhausted, he was edgy with too many pieces of their jigsaw unconnected. Saeed jumped up to greet him, taking his satchel. Danel put his arm around the boy and headed to the kitchen to find Bethshari working on supper. Kissing her cheek, he lifted the lid on a pot on the stove.

"You look very tired," said Bethshari.

"I saw forty patients today. I think that's a record."

Saeed went on about how they had almost found Sister Helen and the woman at the clinic wanted to talk to Bethshari.

"She's a slippery one. I hope that payday's enough to lure her or we're back where we started," said Danel.

"Don't even think that way," said Bethshari. "Tomorrow we're getting married and that's where we should focus."

"What's that you're making?"

"It's mehshi, but it's not for tonight. We'll serve it tomorrow night when Abu comes over," she said.

"What about Saeed's papers? Did you talk to Phillip Cameron?"

"Apparently the courier he had at his disposal was deployed elsewhere, so he's going to bring them tomorrow to the hospital himself. Somewhere around 10:00 am."

"But we're getting married at 11:00."

Chopping an onion, her eyes watered and she wiped her eyes on her sleeve. "He knows that and he promised to be there by ten. Whether or not he'll make it is a whole different matter."

"Nothing's easy, is it?" said Danel.

She handed Saeed three plates to set on the table. "It appears not." She gestured for them to sit. "Saeed, why don't you say dua?"

"At home we prayed after we ate. I could say the out loud part now."

"That's a good idea, Saeed."

"*Al humdu lil Allahil lazi at'amanaa wasaqaana waja'alana minal muslimeen.*" The prayer thanked Allah for feeding them and making them Muslims.

"Perfect," she said, passing the flatbread first to Danel. "I hope neither of you has any objection to kawag leftovers tonight."

Danel winked at Saeed. "That's what I was hoping for."

The evening passed uneventfully. The discussion about the second letter would have to wait until after Saeed went to bed. Bethshari flipped on the small television left behind by the former occupants. Static footage of fighting in Homs and Aleppo revealed rebels attacking government forces and bombs blowing up buildings. Women and children were being helped by the Red Cross.

"Do we have to have that on? It's bad enough we're living through this, let alone revisiting it on television."

As she reached to turn it off, Saeed said, "Look there's Za'atari."

Danel and Bethshari moved closer. The story focused on the flow of refugees from Dara'a, Allaja, Dael, Busr Al-Hareer and several other cities. The wounded, aged and children in the video were poignant, the vacant look on their faces too familiar. Danel clicked it off. "We don't need the box to show us the misery there. I'm just glad we're out of it. Right, Saeed?"

"It wasn't so bad when I was there." He sat cross legged on the floor. "I wanted to stay before I found out I could come with you."

"We've got a big day tomorrow. We should all turn in."

Slipping her nightgown over her head, Bethshari sat down on the edge of the bed. "Let me see it."

Danel took the envelope off the nightstand and handed it to her. It was addressed as before in crisp perfect lettering: "READ THIS."

Her heart raced as she opened the envelope.

DR OTTAWA, I KNOW THE SON YOU CLAIM IS NOT YOUR OWN. I KNOW WHAT YOU DID.

WAIT FOR INSTRUCTIONS."

The letter fell to her lap. "Wait for instructions?"

"Whoever it is is playing the cat toying with a mouse. The first letter put us on alert. The second letter is to scare us."

"The first letter managed both."

"The third letter will probably let us know what I must do to keep the secret."

"But we're not wealthy. We have no money."

Picking up the letter to reread the words, he walked to the window. "I doubt that it's money they're after."

"What could it possibly be?"

"I don't know, but we'll find out soon."

"But why not just come out and ask in the first letter? It doesn't make sense."

"Whatever they want, I suspect they'll have more leverage once we have Hamid." He climbed into bed, lifting the covers for her to lie beside him before he switched off the light.

"We must leave before the next letter, that's all. Tuesday can't come fast enough for me." Her voice was soft and low.

"I don't know whether I wish it to come fast or slow. A lot has to fall into place before then. We need time. One thing is for sure: we're not leaving without Hamid." He felt for her hand and brought it to his lips. Brushing a soft kiss across her fingertips, his voice choked up. "I fear for his safety. Ashara worried he would have changed so much we wouldn't recognize him. I told her not to overreact. How cruel I was."

She leaned over to kiss him. "We need to sleep now. Dwelling on the past is pointless."

The next morning was overcast, threatening rain. Sister Helen felt Hamid's cheek, which was cool. Waking up cheerful, Hamid's fever was gone. Gunfire in the distance sounded like muffled firecrackers, and she shivered, eager to be shed of Damascus.

Today she would make the final payment on Hamid's adoption papers and visa, which was a prerequisite for booking the flight. Her urgency to leave had precluded going through normal channels. She opted instead for a less-than-reputable vendor she had overheard some of her coworkers discussing.

Boarding a bus three blocks from the flat, she regretted the need to take Hamid into the seedier part of the city. Since Mrs. Khadkodian only kept children during the week when her husband worked, she had no choice. Thirty minutes later she entered a small alterations shop where two thin girls, about thirteen years old, sat at sewing machines, forcing garments under the needles, which whirred up and down.

"Mr. Karam, please."

One of the girls left the machine, passing silently through a dull green calico curtain that covered the doorway. A small wiry man with a cigarette dangling from his mouth pulled the edge of the curtain aside to see who was asking for him.

"You have the documents?" said Sister Helen.

"Yes, but there has been a small problem with the adoption papers, so I am afraid the price has gone up." He unbuttoned his cuffs, pushing his sleeves up his forearms.

"We agreed another 64,859 Syrian pounds as the final payment." That was roughly $500 American dollars, no small amount for her.

"You see, I had extra expenses." The cigarette bobbed as he talked. "If you want the documents, you'll have to pay double."

"What extra expenses?"

"A certain woman of the cloth came to my attention. This holy woman has a child who is not hers that the authorities are looking for. So you can see how preparing these documents places us, say, in a compromising position."

Sister Helen flushed. On her own she could easily have grabbed his shirt, head butted him and taken the papers, but with Hamid she didn't dare. A second burly man, wearing a sleeveless undershirt with sweat-stained underarms, stood by the curtain.

"Is there a problem here?" His overdeveloped forearm brandished a full-color tattoo sleeve, complete with a voluptuous mermaid in a starfish bra and exotic koi, their mouths exaggerated and eyes distorted.

"No problem at all, right Mrs. McCormick? Or should I say Sister McCormick."

"Mr. Karam, you're a thief."

His rotten teeth grinned back at her. "Well, if you're no longer interested in the documents." Sliding them off the counter, he pocketed them.

"First let me look at your work." She perused the documents, which to her untrained eye appeared official enough. Peeling the bills out of her wallet, she slid the money across the counter. "How do I know that you won't notify the authorities once I leave?"

"Now that wouldn't be too good for business once the police were onto my little enterprise." He turned to his accomplice. "Isn't that right?" He directed a puff of smoke upwards out of the side of his mouth.

Picking a blemish on his arm, the other man barely looked up. "Yeah, that's right."

"So you see, Mrs. McCormick, your secret is safe with me." She stuffed the papers into her bosom, slamming the door as she exited. *Son of a bitch*, she thought. *How in the hell did he find out?*

Her heart pounded as she made her way to the bus stop. The distance between her and the two vermin at the alteration shop could not lengthen fast enough. She looked down at Hamid, his fists clasped within each other as he joggled against her. "You're worth all of this, Little One, I swear you are."

Hearing her voice, Hamid's legs leveraged several bounces off her abdomen.

"Two more busses to get our plane tickets, Hamid. You're going to like America."

An hour and a half later she had two coach-class tickets for late Monday on a journey that would take them across three continents. The ticket agent told her the rebels had tried to take the airport, but Assad's men beat them back. "I suspect that the rebels will try again, so count yourself lucky to get out now. In a week you would not be so fortunate. It'll be very unlucky for my business once I can no longer book passage out of Damascus. I should go with you. Would I like Minneapolis?"

"Well, the winters are very cold, but we don't have any bombing there."

"That part I would like. You and your son have a safe trip, Mrs. McCormick."

A deep, dreamless sleep allowed Danel and Bethshari to wake up rested. Saeed had risen, fixed his own breakfast and was watching an American cartoon dubbed in Arabic when they emerged from their bedroom.

"What time did you say Cameron would bring Saeed's papers?"

"He promised no later than 10 o'clock."

"Perhaps I should go in to wait. I could work for a while until he gets there."

"I don't think so. I know what will happen. You'll get tied up, and I'll be playing the jilted bride while we wait for you. No, you should pick up the papers close to ten, and that's all."

His mobile interrupted him as he was about to offer a counter argument. "Danel, this is Ahmed. Do you have time to talk?"

"Of course." He gestured to Bethshari that he would take the call in their bedroom and then closed the door behind him.

"What did you learn? I hope it's nothing," said Danel

"Unfortunately, it's far from nothing. It's very bad."

"Tell me everything."

He sat down on the bed with his back towards the door. "Dr. Majeed is wanted by the authorities as an alleged leader of a baby smuggling ring. A year ago, as they were about to arrest him and an accomplice named Issam Kattani, the trail went cold," said Ahmed.

"Are you sure?"

"Quite definitely. The ring was very widespread, involving other doctors in multiple hospitals."

"But how did they know Majeed was the mastermind?"

"They tortured several physicians to turn witness in exchange for lighter sentences."

"How did it work?" said Danel.

"Kattani secured unwanted infants from the prostitute trade or from poor families who couldn't afford another child. Majeed arranged for legitimate documents for each child, assisted by physicians in other hospitals. By spreading the operation out over several hospitals, it was less likely to be detected. Once they had the infant and the document, the babies were put out for bid. Very lucrative."

"Kattani showed up here the first day. I talked to him, but Abu was not happy about it."

"Did you ever ask Majeed who he was?" said Ahmed.

"I did, but he danced around the topic."

"I'm sure I don't need to tell you to stay away from him. They're very resourceful and dangerous men."

"You can believe I will."

"Danel, there is also one other thing. These other physicians all had something in common."

"What was that?"

"They all had something to hide, which Majeed used to coerce them."

"Has he approached you?"

"No, he's got nothing on me." He flinched at the lie.

"Do you want me to notify the authorities here in Beirut?"

"I'd like your help with that, but it's important that you wait until Monday afternoon. I'll call you and let you know when to notify."

"It's as you request, old friend."

Bethshari slipped quietly into the bedroom just as Danel was hanging up. "Was that Ahmed Tibi?" She latched the door behind her.

He stared at the phone, shaking his head.

"Well?" She sat down alongside him.

"It's Abu who's sending the letters. And it's even worse than I thought."

"Tell me."

"Yes, but I have to leave for the hospital to get Saeed's papers. We'll have to talk later."

"You're scaring me."

"I scare myself, but we'll have to play out the charade a little longer until we can leave. Right now I have to go." He kissed her on her forehead and left the bedroom.

It was a little after 9:30 when Danel asked the front desk receptionist if a man had delivered any papers for him.

"Yes, he just left, and Dr. Abu took the papers. He's up in his office now."

Danel bounded the stairs and met Abu coming down. "Abu, do you have some papers that were delivered for me?"

"Ah, the happy groom on his wedding day. Are you nervous?"

"Not really because I know this is the right thing for all three of us."

"You won't need the papers today, since you're getting married. How about I bring them around when I come home tonight?" Abu's brotherly embrace across Danel's shoulder turned him around so the two could walk back down the stairs together.

Danel broke free and stopped. "Abu, I really do need them now."

"What's so important about right now?"

"Are you kidding? The papers were supposed to be delivered yesterday, and Bethshari had a fit when they didn't arrive. Read Phillip Cameron the riot act."

"That's a dressing down of that officious prick I would have liked to hear."

"There're ghosts around every corner for her where Saeed's concerned. I'm not coming back empty handed." He was perspiring.

"I see your point."

"I argued with her that you could bring them tonight, but she wasn't going for it." His outstretched hands, open palmed, shielded his chest. "Abu, I need to take them back with me or else."

"Well then old man, you're already kowtowing like the rooster to the mother hen, so let's go get Saeed's papers." He crowed a rooster's er-er-er-da-errrrrr.

Danel examined them briefly and then confirmed that Abu would be joining them later.

"Wouldn't miss celebrating with my favorite couple. I'll see if I can't sneak away at a reasonable hour."

"Good. The celebration won't be complete without you." Danel exhaled at the close call as he left the building.

Bethshari was waiting in a white peasant dress with a flower Saeed picked behind her ear. Danel had never seen her in a dress.

"You don't have to stare. It was the best that Saeed and I could find for a wedding dress."

"It's just perfect." He kissed her tenderly, bushing a wisp of hair off her forehead.

"Did you get the papers?"

"Yes, Abu had them and reluctantly let me have them."

Rearranging the flower behind her ear, she watched Danel in the mirror. "How did you get them away?"

"I insisted that you'd kill me if I didn't return with them."

"Good answer. Have you written down yet what we need to provide for Hamid's visa?"

"It's right here." He drew the document out of his satchel, placing it in the folder with Saeed's papers. "I wrote down everything I could think of. Hopefully it'll be all that's necessary. Now all we're missing for Scolopendra is the marriage document."

"Shhh. Saeed will hear you."

"I'll hear what?"

"Are your ears electronically wired for sound, Saeed?" She shook his shoulders in exasperation. "Actually we were talking about asking you to be my wali."

"Sure. What do I have to do?"

Danel sat down on the sofa and pulled the boy onto his lap. "A wali represents the bride in the marriage negotiations. He's also her protector."

"I would be a good protector." The boy clenched his fists in a mock fight.

"In this marriage though, I'll be the one that needs protection. You can see how easily she bosses me around."

Bethshari lunged at them. "Gentleman, will the groom and the wali get serious and accompany me?" They each took her by the arm and escorted her out into the sunlight.

At the government hall, other couples waited. Bethshari approached the official, letting him know that they were there for their 11 o'clock ceremony.

"We're a bit backed up so just take a seat." He spread his hands apologetically.

"How far off schedule are you?"

"Two hours."

Shaking her head, she sat down with Saeed and Danel and explained the delay.

"Just like when we came before," said Saeed. "Maybe someone went to lunch early."

A rejuvenated wind breathed a spark into the authorities' hunt for Sister Helen when the staffers from the Western Union office grew suspicious. A whiff of a reward overcame their natural inertia against assisting the police. With a concrete lead, backed by considerable resources, the police needed only to follow Sister Helen's tracks since returning to Damascus.

Bethshari and Saeed's inquiries, lacking official stature, had progressed at a circumspect pace. Any scent of the hounds on her tail risked driving the nun even further into the shadows. With each delay, they sensed the likelihood of her leading them to Hamid slipping away.

The owner of the boarding house where Sister Helen lived for a brief time after her arrival in Damascus was eager to share her opinions with the police. "There was something not right about a nun with an infant."

By Saturday night, the police had located Sister Helen's second hospital and were bearing down like scent hounds on a red fox. Her caginess in sharing addresses had not thrown them off the trail.

The marriage of Danel Ottawa to Bethshari Sadat took place with little fanfare before a magistrate of the court, three hours after it had been scheduled. "And to think we were worried about making it here by 11:00," said Bethshari.

"Be still, my wife," said Danel, his formality more bluff than bite. "Nothing you can say can mar my happiness. We're one giant step closer to being a true family."

"What does your wali have to say about that?" Danel winked at Saeed.

"The wali is thanking Allah for answering one of his prayers."

Danel raised an eyebrow. "One of his prayers? Does the wali ask Allah for more than one thing?"

"Dr. Danel, the wali also wants to be your son and Hamid's brother."

Danel's right hand reached for Bethshari's and his left for Saeed's. "I suspect, Saeed, you may just get everything you asked for." Smiling at his bride, he shook his head, incredulous that out of so much sorrow something so sweet could germinate. "Let's go home. We should try to arrive before Dr. Abu."

A shadow flickered across Bethshari's face. Knowing that Abu was blackmailing them would make for a night of play acting. "What time will the good doctor grace us?"

"He'll try to free up early if he can. We'll make this a very pleasant evening, right?"

"How could it be anything but joyous?"

Like the Greeks who left a Trojan horse as a parting gift for the city of Troy, Abu also bore gifts. His arms were laden with tokens of friendship for the newlyweds when Saeed answered the door. "Look, Dr. Abu is here and he has presents."

Danel's glare implored her to remain calm, as the expectation of a third letter hung in the air.

"Abu, what's all of this? Has someone forgotten to tell you there's a war on?" said Bethshari.

"It's the least I can do for my two best friends." He kissed her on both cheeks and clapped Danel across the shoulder as they hugged. "May you always be as happy as you are tonight." Releasing Danel, he continued. "Now this is for all of us to share. Perhaps we can even spare a mouthful for Saeed." He handed a chilled bottle of champagne from the Bequaa Valley to Danel. "No excuses tonight, Danel, we have to toast the bride." Next he placed a box wrapped in gold brocade and secured with white satin ribbon in Bethshari's hands.

"What a beautiful box. It is almost too pretty to open."

"What's inside is much better than the wrapping, I promise."

She carefully untied the ribbon, peeling back the brocade. Inside the box were two champagne glasses. Delicate silver alligators adorned the bowls on either side, as though they were climbing up to have a taste. The stems were long and slender, ending at the foot, spreading out into a scalloped pattern. Etched into the bowl was the Hawk of Qureish.

"Abu, these are exquisite." She lifted one out of the box, holding it up into the light. "They must've cost a fortune. You're too generous."

"With no family, I spend my money on good friends."

"Our first wedding gift. They're so lovely. Let's open the champagne and break them in."

As Abu removed the foil collar from the bottle's neck, she thought she would never use them again knowing their source. After they toasted, with Abu and Saeed using two plain tumblers, Abu took her glass and set it aside.

"Now, I have one more gift for the bride."

"Really, Abu, you've given us too much already."

He pulled a small, worn velvet bag, secured with a drawstring, from his pocket. "These belonged to my mother. I have no wife and no prospects. I want you to have them."

She inserted her fingers into the bag, loosening the neck, and tilted its contents into her palm. A pair of gold earrings tumbled out. Two grape leaves formed the base for her lobe. Below the base were three tiers of tiny amethysts, each stone secured by a delicate golden claw. Each tier, smaller than the one above it, dangled loosely, giving the appearance of a bunch of grapes. She gasped. "Abu, I don't know what to say. I can't accept these. They should go to your wife someday."

"You don't have to say anything. Just put them on."

She glanced at Danel, who nodded. Removing the backing, she inserted the gold posts into her lobes. So full of contempt for Abu's extortion, she imagined she felt them sear her lobes. Camouflaging her feelings, she tossed her head to and fro, showing them off. *These too*, she thought, *will never be worn again*. Leaning forward to kiss his cheeks, she whispered in Abu's ear, "I'll wear them with pride knowing that they were your mother's."

Danel offered his hand. "Thank you, my friend."

"Saeed, is there anything to eat at this party?" Abu grabbed the boy's head, affectionately rubbing his knuckles back and forth over Saeed's crown.

"Yes, Dr. Abu, we have some meze, hummus, and mehshi. I helped Bethshari make our feast."

"It sure sounds like a feast. But...." He scratched his chin, thinking hard.

"But what?"

"I didn't hear you mention any sweets?"

"Of course, we have ka'ak and baklava."

"What's your favorite?"

Without hesitating, Saeed chimed, "Ka'ak. Definitely ka'ak. We made them like my mother, with chopped dates and butter added to the ring part of the cookie. We also bought some jibbneh mashallale cheese to go with it. I like to unwind the cheese."

"I used to do that myself as a kid."

The wedding party revealed no external strain from the underlying tension. As the evening wore on, the immediate problem lay in how to end the party. Scolopendra was expected at any moment, and explaining him to Abu would have been problematic. By ten, Abu yawned and made his excuses. "Danel has to work tomorrow, and I'm going to sleep in all day."

"Abu, I'm glad you were with us tonight," said Danel. "It wouldn't have been the same without you." Shaking Abu's hand, he opened the door.

Bethshari followed them outside. "Abu, thank you for my earrings and the other gifts. You're a good friend."

Abu thanked them for a great meal and bid all three goodnight.

"Saeed, you should get ready for bed, and Bethshari and I will clean up. We'll be in to say good night."

When he heard Saeed running water in the bathroom, he pulled her to him and kissed her deeply. "You've made me a very happy man today."

Her head rested against his chest. "I look forward to a long and happy life together."

"You performed your part beautifully tonight. I don't think that Abu suspected we've figured it all out."

"I will never use his gifts."

"I know, they're poisoned by the giver."

"I worried that Scolopendra would show up while he was here."

"It's now so late, I worry that he'll come at all."

Saeed called that he was in bed, so they went to tuck him in. Bethshari sat on the edge of the bed, rearranging his covers. "You were an excellent wali. Did you have a good time tonight?"

"Yes and no."

His answer surprised them. "What do you mean?" she said.

"Well, the party was fun and that was the good part."

"Was there a bad part?" said Danel.

"Not exactly bad. I know you're my family now. But tonight I really missed my mother. We baked her ka'ak and I wished she were with us to taste them."

"She was with us, Saeed." She laid her palm over his heart. "She's right here. Can't you feel her?"

"Sometimes I can, like I know she's watching."

"She'll always be watching, and she's happy now that you have a family around you."

Now say your prayers."

He closed his eyes and joined his open hands together.

O Allah, thank you for my new family. Please tell my mother not to worry about me and that I will be so good that my new family will want to keep me. And Allah, please help us find Hamid because I think he needs a big brother. You are the source of all that is good and right.

"That's a good prayer," said Danel. "I want you to be good, but now that you are a part of this family, nothing could ever make us not want you."

"Good night." Bethshari kissed his head and he turned onto his side, watching them close the door behind them.

Danel resumed clearing plates as Bethshari filled the sink with hot water and detergent. "I know you're eager to hear about my conversation with Ahmed Tibi, but we should give Saeed some time to fall asleep before we talk."

"Right now I'm more concerned about Scolopendra. What if he doesn't show up tonight?"

"We shouldn't worry about something that hasn't happened."

Wiping the last dish she rinsed, he set it on the stack of dishes in the cabinet. He bent over to kiss the top of her head. "I think that Saeed should be asleep by now. He draped the wet towel over the edge of the counter. "We should check, just to be sure."

He walked softly into the boy's room, tiptoeing close to the bed. Breathing deeply, Saeed rolled over to his side, facing the wall. Danel froze lest he make a sound. Soon the heavy breathing resumed and Danel backed out quietly. "He's sound asleep."

"Good, now tell me everything you know about Abu." She turned off the light in the kitchen as he led her back into the living area, settling her next to him. After listening raptly without interrupting, she asked, "How could we have so misjudged him?"

"I think a better question is how could he have so deceived us? There's one part I haven't told you."

Crossing her hands over her chest, she hugged her shoulders. "Don't frighten me any more than I am now."

"I don't mean to. He used the same tactic to lure in all of the doctors. He found out something about them that they couldn't afford to be known and leveraged that to pressure them. There was financial payoff for them, but they were blackmailed."

"Despicable. How do you reconcile his behavior tonight?"

"I'm not sure, but I know he's a complicated man. It would be easy to just characterize him as evil, but I think he's more complex than that. On one level I think his friendship is genuine."

"I hate him and will never forgive him." She looked at her watch; it was already close to 11:30. "It looks like Scolopendra isn't going to show tonight."

"Do you have a phone number?"

"No, it was all handled by my father. He didn't want us to know much for our own good."

Danel's ears perked. "What's that noise?"

She quieted to listen. "Sounds like someone is scratching at our door."

Danel approached the door, pressing his ear against it. Abruptly he threw it open to catch whoever was there. A small waif of a girl, perhaps fourteen or fifteen, dressed in a black turtleneck and yoga pants stood before him.

"Who are you?"

"May I come in?" Not needing his permission, she entered, closing the door behind her.

"I've come from someone who needs your documents."

"Are you Scolopendra?" said Danel.

"No one says his name. He wouldn't like that. I work for him."

"What's your name?"

"I wouldn't like it if you knew it." Tucking her hands into the back of her waistband, she looked around the flat.

"We thought you were coming earlier," said Bethshari.

"I was here earlier, but you had company. I waited for the man who lives next door to leave."

"He's been gone for almost two hours. Why did you wait so late?"

"Then he had company. I had to wait for his guest to leave."

"You've been down there in the dark, watching this place all that time?"

She nodded.

"The guest next door, what did he look like?" said Danel.

"Very tall. Fat. Bushy mustache like this." She drooped her finger over her upper lip. "Do you have the package?"

Danel and Bethshari exchanged glances.

"Yes, I have it. Let me go get it."

As he disappeared into their room, Bethshari said, "You'll bring them back with the new documents tomorrow night?"

"I don't know what arrangements you made with my boss. That's between you and him. I do know that he does what he says."

He handed her a manila envelope, which she stuffed into the back of her pants. She opened the door a crack, looking side to side to make sure no one was around, and then disappeared, pulling the door behind her.

Bethshari's gaze met Danel's. "I hope—"

He didn't give her time to complete her thought. "I do too."

36

The Snare

Sister Helen propped up Hamid on a pillow, positioning his bottle so he could hold it himself. Sitting next to him on the edge of their bed, she watched him drink as she dialed her parents.

"Mom, it's me, Helen."

"Helen, we've been worried sick, are you alright?"

"Yes, I'm fine."

"And little Hamid?"

"He's fine. He had an ear infection but he's OK now."

"Thank goodness. When we didn't hear that you got the money, well we didn't know what to think."

"I got it fine. Thanks." She owed them thanks, but being grateful to her parents always had strings. Her father must have entered the kitchen because her mother sent him upstairs to get on the line.

"Helen, where are you?"

"I'm in Damascus, Dad."

"Did the adoption go through?"

"Yes, I got the papers. He's mine now."

"So when're you coming home?" said Frank.

She bit her tongue, readying to lob a grenade. "My plane leaves tomorrow afternoon late. I should get to Minneapolis the next day." After giving them the details of their arrival, she added, "Mom, Dad, there's one more thing." Taking a deep breath, she swallowed. "We're not going to be living with you very long."

"But your mother has the nursery all ready."

"Is this how you repay us, Helen?"

"I'll pay the money back. It's just that I'm a grown woman now, and I have to stand on my own two feet. Coming back home will be like being a little girl again living in your house."

"Was that really so bad?" Her mother moved quickly to the wounded ground.

"I lost my baby under your roof. I don't want to lose this one."

"That was different. He was…."

"He was what? A bastard?"

"That's your word not ours, Helen." Her dad quickly moved to the defensive.

"He was my son. His conception had nothing to do with him."

"Isn't it about time you stopped blaming your parents for everything that's gone wrong in your life?" said Margaret.

"This is exactly what living there would be like. I don't want to go back to a life where we're fighting all the time. I just needed to get this out before I got there." She scrunched her eyes shut.

"What are you saying? That you don't want us in your life now? You take our money but don't want us in your life?"

"No, Mom, I'm not saying that. I need you to pick us up. I just want to be upfront that I won't be staying there for long."

"How long then?"

"I'll figure that out after I get there. Will you pick us up?"

"What kind of monsters do you think we are? We'll be there."

That didn't go well, Helen thought as she hung up. *Why is everything with them like slogging through snow in concrete boots?*

Danel went into work early the next morning envious that Abu was sleeping in that day. On his mind was when to give the go ahead to Ahmed Tibi to pull the trigger and expose Abu's whereabouts. Central to his consideration was that they still didn't have Hamid. For spite or revenge and with nothing to lose, Abu could reveal Danel's secret and

Hamid would be lost forever. If Sister Helen returned to work Monday afternoon, it was likely they could take custody of Hamid. But if she didn't return to work, then a Tuesday departure was out of the question. If Abu knew that Danel was considering leaving, he would try to stop him. *A lot of ifs*, he thought.

He paced back and forth in his office, piecing together each scenario. *I underestimated Abu from the start, and I won't make that mistake again.* Assuming they would make their flight on Tuesday, if Ahmed informed the authorities in Beirut of Abu's whereabouts, they would need at least 24 hours to work out which jurisdiction would have the authority to apprehend him. *But what if I don't get Hamid tomorrow?* Folding his arms over his chest, he decided he would just have to take that chance.

Calling the hospital in Beirut, he discovered that Ahmed would not be in until Tuesday. He scrolled the contacts on his phone, scanning for Ahmed's home number. As much as he didn't like to bother him at home, waiting until Tuesday was risky. Once Abu knew that Danel fled, he would slip away again. He had to be stopped.

"Badr, this is Danel Ottawa."

"Ah Danel, it's been too long since we've heard from you."

"You're right. Way too long. I suppose Ahmed told you about Ashara."

"Yes, he did. I send my particular condolences. I was always fond of her."

"Thank you. I know she felt the same about you. How are the children?"

"They're fine, but growing so. You wouldn't recognize them."

"Is Ahmed there now?"

"No, he's taken the children to the park. I expect him back in a couple of hours. Would you like him to call you?"

"Yes, please have him call when he gets in. I'm sorry I have to bother him on his day off."

"Nonsense. He always likes to hear from you."

Flipping the phone shut, he deposited it in his breast pocket and headed back to the emergency room. Not five minutes after hanging up with Badr Tibi, Bethshari rang.

"Danel, he's here, next door. That man."

"Calm down, what man?"

"Saeed and I ran into him on the way back from the market. Kattani. He's next door in Abu's apartment."

"I'm not surprised. They need somewhere to meet since they can't meet here at the hospital."

"He called me by name. He called me Mrs. Ottawa."

"He didn't threaten you, did he?"

"No, but he made my blood run cold."

Stepping outside into the corridor, he lowered his voice. "Listen, you and Saeed stay in now. Keep the door locked. Can you do that?"

"Yes, but I'm scared."

"I know, but you can't let Saeed sense your fear. I'll be home in a couple of hours."

"Was there another letter today?"

"No, but given that the author is off today, I wasn't expecting one. With Kattani and Abu cozying up, I'm sure letter number three is not far off. You just stay calm."

"Okay."

"Bethshari, don't forget how much I love you."

Running into Kattani frightened her. Not having spoken to her parents since her dad called about Scolopendra, she dialed home.

"Dad, it's Bethshari."

"Is everything alright?"

"It's going as planned. We turned our papers over to Scolopendra's courier, and we should get all of the documents tonight."

"That's good news. What about the baby? Have you found him yet?"

"No, but we're close. We know where Sister Helen works, but the baby's been sick and she hasn't been going into work. We're hoping she'll show tomorrow."

"You think she'll just hand over the child?"

"No, we expect not, so we're going to follow her home and take the child from her there. It's the best scheme we've got at this point."

"Have you thought about what you will do if that doesn't work?"

She shuddered. "Please don't even go there."

"You have to think through other possibilities, Beth."

"One thing is for sure, if we don't get him tomorrow, we won't leave on Tuesday without him."

"Then let's hope it goes as planned. Because I suspect that Dr. Majeed isn't going to be deterred."

"Dad, I'm scared, and there's nothing I can do about it."

"I know you are. This is a lot to handle, but you can do this. I know you can."

"I guess I just needed to hear you say that. Is Mom there?"

"No, she's next door, but I'll let her know you called. Do you want her to call you?"

"No, just tell her I love her. I love you too, Dad."

Late afternoon, Ahmed Tibi returned Danel's call. "Danel, Ahmed here."

"Good to hear your voice. I thought we should set up something definite about notifying the authorities."

"That's a good idea."

"I was wondering if you will make an anonymous call or give your name. Would you prefer that it not be traced back to you?"

"I would prefer to stay hidden."

"Danel, have you been sucked into this?"

"It's as it was in Beirut, I received two blackmail letters, but nothing yet that has outlined what I must do."

"I was afraid of that. You must try to avoid getting implicated."

"I'm trying very hard. We're leaving the country on Tuesday. I tell you that in the strictest of confidences."

"You know you can trust me."

"You're one of a very few that I can trust."

"Will you let me know where you are?"

"After I get there. Eventually."

"Well, we don't want to unleash the dogs on him too early in case it might thwart your departure. I assume you have your son now."

"No, not exactly. We've located where the woman that took him works. Tomorrow we plan to tail her from work back to her home."

"I don't envy you, my friend. You are dealing with some grave matters."

"I was thinking if you make an anonymous call on Monday afternoon, it would take some time to contact the Syrian authorities, and I suspect that by Tuesday AM they would be arresting Majeed. By then I'd be long gone."

"I think that's reasonable. I'll call from the hospital to make it harder to track down who actually made the call."

"Ahmed, I can't thank you enough."

"It's the least I can do. I hope tomorrow you find your son. Inshallah."

"I'll be in touch."

Danel's key sounded in the door well after seven Sunday night. The day's tension washed over him, his shoulders sloping and his hair disheveled.

"You've had a long day, haven't you?" said Bethshari.

"You have no idea." He kissed her lips. "Where is Abu with a bottle of wine when we need him?"

"We don't need anything from Abu, thank you very much."

"Only jesting. Relax."

"I'm just glad you're home. Are you hungry?"

"Not really. Where's Saeed?"

"He's in the bathtub. I thought we should have him go to bed early since tomorrow is a very big day."

"You think he'll do that."

"Well, I can try. I also didn't want him up when our documents come."

"Come here." He wrapped his arms around her. "You know I haven't spent enough time just holding you."

She returned his embrace. "If we can get out of here, I plan to make sure you make it up to me."

"The truth of it is, when I hold you, it feels as though everything will work out."

"Look, if you think about all that we have done since coming back here, what still remains to be accomplished is small. Just three more pieces to the puzzle: our documents, Hamid and a safe getaway."

"When you say it like that, I see how far we've come. But three very important things remain."

"We're all playing out the hands we've been dealt."

Saeed let the water out of the tub and emerged with wet hair buttoning up his pajama shirt. "Dr. Danel, you're home."

"Yes I am, big guy." He picked Saeed up and hoisted him up over his head and around his shoulders before setting him down. "Ready for a big day tomorrow?"

"Yes, we're going eel fishing. And this time we are not coming up empty handed."

"Got to love his confidence, Bethshari."

"I tell him all the time I want to be just like him."

"Saeed, come over here; I want to talk about something serious." Danel led him to the sofa and lifted him up into his lap."

"Am I in trouble?"

"Not exactly. What did you call your father?"

"I called him Baba."

"You loved him, didn't you?"

"Yes, he was the best father."

"I know I could never take his place. I'll be a different father to you. Does that make sense?"

He draped his arm around Danel's neck. "Yes, you'll be a good different father."

"Well, that's what I want to talk about. You still call me Dr. Danel. That's what my patients call me. But I want your name for me to be special. Remember I asked you to give that some thought?"

"I remember." He nibbled on his fingers.

"What does Hamid call you?"

"That's the problem. When Sister Helen took him, he was too little to talk. But he should be talking soon, and he's going to need a name for me too." He shifted Saeed on his lap. Since you're the big brother, he'll use what you choose. So you would be the one to decide the father's name for the family."

Frowning, he resettled himself off Danel's lap.

"I don't want Hamid to call me Dr. Danel."

Saeed scooted to the edge on the sofa. "I wouldn't want to call you Baba because that was my father's name. What about Papa?"

"I could live with that. You can try it out when you're ready. Dr. Danel will work until you feel comfortable."

"I'll try it out, but I want to think about it first."

"You're going to be my son for the rest of your life, so we have some time." He smoothed Saeed's hair and patted his shoulder. "Now what have you got to eat around here?"

"We have a lot of food left from our wedding feast," said Bethshari.

"What do you say to some mehshi tonight, Saeed?"

"I can always eat mehshi, Dr. Danel—I mean Papa."

Saeed was packed off to bed after they ate, clean and with prayers said by nine. The wait for the documents seemed interminable.

"Bethshari, this suspense is killing me. Without the documents I don't know what we'll do." The dishes were done, and the drama that would enfold over the next two days could not be hurried.

"We have to trust that it will go as planned."

"Have you told your parents when we're coming?"

"Only that we plan to leave on Tuesday. I can call once we get the documents."

"I'm sorry for all this." Lifting a pillow off the sofa, she hugged it to her chest.

"What are you talking about?"

"I never wanted our life to start with all this intrigue."

"Well, it really wasn't your call, was it? We can thank Abu for that."

"Maybe that part, but the drama around Saeed is all my doing."

"And the drama around Hamid is mine. So we're even."

Somewhere around 10:30 came a soft rapping sounded at the door. He opened it to a tall African man holding a package wrapped in newspaper and tied with a string. "I believe you are waiting for a package?"

"Please come in. Are you Scolopendra?"

"No." Handing Danel the package, his eyes scoured the apartment.

"I suppose you won't tell me your name either?"

"I would prefer it that way." Smiling, his large white teeth illuminated his black face.

"Would you mind if I took a look before you leave?"

"Of course not."

Gesturing for the man to be seated, Danel untied the string.

"I prefer to stand."

"Suit yourself." First verifying that the original documents had been returned, Danel examined Saeed's adoption papers and the travel marriage certificate, which appeared in order. His, Hamid's and Saeed's visa were likewise acceptable. Next he opened the plane tickets. "These tickets are out of Amman, not Damascus. That's not what we agreed."

"Scolopendra said to tell you that the Damascus airport could very well be closed by Tuesday. The rebels are planning another assault."

"But how does he know that? Never mind. It doesn't matter."

"Is there a problem with Amman?"

"It's just that it's a very long way from here, along the road to Za'atari."

"And you are going a long way to London. A minor inconvenience then."

Danel shrugged. "Yes, I suppose you're right."

"Then I'll be going."

"Please give Scolopendra our thanks."

The man turned off the light right by the door, minimizing his visibility in the low light. Then, as the young girl the evening before, he looked both directions and disappeared into the night.

37

The Noose Tightens

In the predawn moments pregnant with the promise of a new day, Danel stared wide eyed into the dark abyss. Bethshari's slight stirring tipped him off that she wasn't sleeping either.

"Are you awake?" he whispered.

"Yes."

"What're you thinking?"

"I'm thinking that on this day our lives are balancing on the head of a pin. Today the wind will blow, and we'll learn what only Allah now knows: which way the pin will fall."

"My thoughts complement yours. I feel that Allah is testing us."

"Let's hope then we pass." She edged closer, slipping her head under his arm to rest it on his shoulder.

"I hope Sister Helen goes to work and that she hasn't left Damascus."

"What's hardest for me is the wait. Each minute is made of lead."

"Should we review our plans for the day?" He shifted slightly to face her.

"We've been over and over it."

"Are you going to send Saeed in ahead again?"

"No, we exhausted that ruse. We'll have to go early to catch her going in."

"What if there is some kind of back entrance for employees?"

"There could be, but when I was waiting for Saeed, a number of people in scrubs came and went out the front door."

"Let's hope you are right."

"You have to be ready to come immediately when I call you."

"I'll have my cell phone on me." He reached for her hand as the sun's edge slipped over the horizon.

"What if you're tending a patient? This won't keep while you finish whatever you're doing."

"If that happens I'll get the nurse and let someone else finish up. Don't worry, I'll be ready."

"You'll have to take a taxi because Saeed and I will have the car."

"Taxis wait outside the main entrance, so I should be able to get one easily." He grew quiet, searching for any detail that might have been missed. "What about Saeed? Does he know we're going to leave Damascus?"

"No, I was afraid to share any of our plans, lest he tell Abu."

"Good. Do you think he'll resist leaving Syria?"

"Perhaps on some level, when he thinks of leaving his homeland, but he's so desperate for a family that we could take him to the moon and he'd go."

"We'll have to coach him some in case he's questioned at the airport."

"Good idea." As the room grew lighter, she rolled over to face him. "Danel, he must never know that the papers are false."

"I agree."

"Could we hold each other for a short time before we have to get up?"

Danel answered by sliding his arm underneath her neck and pulling her close. She wrapped her arms around him, entwining her legs with his, and held on tightly.

"Your courage inspires me," he said.

"And yours is feeding mine."

"Would you pray with me?" Her head nodded slightly against his chest.

O Allah, All Powerful, All Knowing, give us the strength and the wisdom to navigate this day. We humbly ask You to make Sister Helen available to us and allow her to lead us to Hamid. We are but Your humble servants and are nothing without Your guidance and love. Grant us, O Loving Allah, to mirror the love You have for us, and nurture this family as we watch our children grow up to adults. Allah Akbar.
"Allah Akbar."

He kissed her forehead. "Are you ready?"

Weighted down by the day's gravity, she sighed heavily. "Yes, but I wish you weren't going into the hospital today."

"I must or Abu will become suspicious. I think everything should appear as normal. If we're able to secure Hamid, I expect he'll be over tonight to meet him."

"Such a charlatan. You can't imagine how I loathe him."

"Yes, I can, but you'll have to mask it one more night."

They dressed in silence. As she buttoned her last button, she considered waking Saeed but thought better of it until Danel left. "Can I make you some breakfast?"

"Honestly, I'm too tense to eat. I'll get something in the cafeteria when I get hungry."

"Allah's on our side. We have to have faith." She followed him to the door and handed him his satchel. "I honestly don't know why you bring this home at night. You never open it."

"It's because I want the neighbors to think I'm important."

She guffawed, pushing him out the door.

He kissed the top of her head and held her hand as he walked out onto the walkway.

Leaning against the railing, she watched him going down the stairs and cross in front of their building. Sensing her eyes following him, he turned and waved as he left the complex.

Sister Helen's emotions were on high alert. Today she would collect paychecks from both employers, and by late this afternoon she would be on a plane bound for America. She warmed Hamid's bottle, along with some pabulum and peach puree, and settled him on her lap for breakfast. "Today, Hamid, you and Mama are going on a long trip all the way to America." Although she smiled, her gut was so tense she could hardly breathe.

Rhythmically sucking the warm liquid, he was content watching her, until she broke the suction, sending a flood of bubbles back into the bottle. Before he could fuss, she guided a spoon half full with pabulum and peach into his rosebud mouth.

"Three more mouthfuls and you can have your bottle back."

When he had emptied his bottle, she draped a cloth over her shoulder to burp him. Soon a loud belch, followed by two smaller ones, escaped.

"Good boy." Settling him into his carrier, she grabbed the bag loaded with his necessities and headed for Mrs. Khadkodian's.

"Good morning, Mrs. Khadkodian."

"Ah, I see Hamid is all ready for his day." Sister Helen lifted him out of his carrier. "I may be home a little early today."

"That's fine, Helen; we aren't going anywhere."

Sister Helen kissed Hamid on his cheek. "You be a good boy for Mama." Then she left quickly before he could cry.

By Monday afternoon, the police uncovered that Sister Helen transferred to the third hospital, shed her habit, and was passing herself off as Helen McCormick. What had taken Bethshari and Saeed two weeks of tracking, they'd accomplished in a matter of days.

The officers assigned to her case worked their way through hospital protocol, ending up in personnel. "We'll need to see Helen McCormick's employee record."

The reluctant staffer eschewed giving any information to the police. "I'll have to get permission from my supervisor."

"This is an impending investigation, so get that permission immediately." His hand rested ominously on his revolver.

"What's she done?"

"Kidnapping."

The staffer disappeared and returned with a short woman whose ratio of girth to height was one to one. "Can I help you, please?"

"We're investigating a kidnapping and we need to see the personnel records for Helen McCormick. "

"I could get in trouble. Those records are confidential."

"You're going to get in trouble if you don't."

She moved to the computer screen and typed "Helen McCormick" at the flashing cursor. "What is it you'd like to know?"

"No forwarding address but there is a photo." She clicked, and the printer drive whirred, spitting out a sheet with her name, photo and other employment details.

"Is there any information about where she went after she left this hospital?"

"No, nothing. It says the reason for leaving was 'too far from home.' Did she really kidnap a child?"

"Looks that way." He grabbed a pad off the counter and scribbled his name and number. "If you hear anything, contact me here."

Despite no forwarding address, with a little more investigation, several hours later their next stop was Sister Helen's flat.

"This woman has been all over the city."

"When you're on the run, you don't stay in any one place very long."

"She's an American, so this is going to get messy."

"All we got to do is find her. Dealing with the Americans will be someone else's problem."

They walked softly up the steps to her floor. "What's the flat number?"

"3F, probably down there on the end."

One of the officers stepped to the side out of sight, while the other knocked on the door. When his knock went unanswered, he banged again louder. A chain rattled on the apartment next door, and an older woman's voice called out through the space restricted by the chain. "She's not home; she's at work."

"Where's that?"

"Don't know."

"Do you know when she'll be back?"

"Usually after 6:00." The door slammed shut.

"What do you want to do now?"

"Let's come back later. We can use the photo to put out a wanted bulletin. Now that we've found out where she lives, she's as good as caught."

After Danel left for the hospital, Bethshari woke Saeed.

He opened his eyes and yawned. "We're going fishing today, right?"

"Yes, we are. We're going to arrive early before the fish even comes into the net."

"Will I go in again like last time?"

"No, what I want to do is get there in the morning and wait for her. That way we'll know she's there without having to go in. Then we wait for her to leave. We'll have to get a good place to watch for her."

"What if she doesn't come?"

"Don't worry, she will." Her confidence was for Saeed's benefit, but she wasn't so sure. They knew that Sister Helen's afternoon job started at 1:00, so by noon they were parked in front of the clinic. She packed some grapes, cheese and flat bread in case they got hungry.

"This waiting will be the hard part," she said.

"It doesn't seem so hard to me."

"If we take our eye off of the door, even for a minute, she could come and go and we'd never know it. So the hard part will be not getting bored or lazy."

"We can be a watch dog for each other, in case one of us isn't paying attention. You watch me and I'll watch you." He slumped lower in his seat so not to be seen.

"But one of us needs to be looking for Sister Helen."

"Bethshari, is it OK to ask you a question?"

"Sure it is."

"Do you think I should call Dr. Danel 'Papa'?"

"I know he'd like you to, but it's really your decision. It has to feel right."

"Well, I know my Baba is probably watching. I don't want him to think he's not my father anymore."

"Do you think that your Baba worries about you, especially now that your mother's no longer here?"

"I'm sure he does." He picked a small piece of dried skin from his cuticle.

"Do you think he'd feel slighted if you called another man by a fatherly name?"

He concentrated, biting his lip as she has seen him do many times before. "I think he would want me to feel like I had a real father if he couldn't be with me."

"I bet you're right. But I never knew him, so I can't say for sure."

Something caught his attention. "Bethshari, look over there. Do you think that's Sister Helen?" A large-bosomed woman in green scrubs and a tan hijab hurried toward the clinic on their side of the street.

Bethshari picked up the photo to compare it to the woman. "It's got to be, the height and the weight look about right. No nun's habit, but the face is round and chubby. OK, the eel is in the net. Now we wait and watch. I'm calling Danel."

The mobile rang only twice when he picked up. "Any news?"

"She just walked into the clinic. She's in civilian clothes, but she's exactly as you described."

"Good. I have my phone right here and I'll leave as soon as I get your call."

Sister Helen had no plans for completing her shift once she got paid. Her plane was leaving at 5:00, so she had no time to waste. By 1:30 she had picked up her money and told her supervisor she'd not be coming back. Now she just had to gather Hamid and get to the airport.

"Saeed, look. She's leaving." Bethshari started the ignition and slowly pulled out into the traffic, hanging back to avoid detection. They followed her three blocks before she turned right. "It's a one way. I can't turn down there. We're going to lose her. We need to park this and follow on foot."

"Over there, someone is pulling out. Can you take it?" Before she could cross over, a small compact car slid in.

"I'll double park if I have to."

"Bethshari, there's another one."

This time there was no hesitation as she maneuvered in. "Keep your eye on her while I park."

Sister Helen was moving briskly down the street. Towering slightly above others on the crowded street, she gave Saeed easy visibility, even though she gained the advantage of distance while they parked.

Bethshari grabbed her keys and cell phone, locking the car behind her. "Do you see her?"

"Yes, she's about five buildings ahead of us."

They closed the distance to approximately twenty meters when she turned left into a complex. Afraid of losing her, they started to run, and headed into the complex in time to watch her reach the fourth floor and knock on a door.

"Why is she knocking?" said Saeed.

"That's probably where Hamid is. I'm calling Danel."

This time it only rang once before he picked up. "What's up?"

"We got her. You should come now. Wait, she coming out of an apartment. She's got Hamid with her." She gave Danel the address and told him she would leave Saeed out by the street to show him where they were. "Please hurry."

"I don't want you approaching her. She could level you with one swipe, she's that strong."

"I won't. Just get here quickly."

Twenty minutes later a taxi pulled up. Stuffing some pounds into the driver's hand, Danel jumped out when he saw Saeed waving his arms.

"She and Hamid are in that flat on the end."

The three crept quietly up the stairs. Danel motioned for Bethshari and Saeed to stand back to the side out of sight. He knocked softly and stepped aside so he couldn't be seen through the peep hole.

Startled, Sister Helen peered out. "Who's there?"

Danel placed a finger over his lips and then gestured for Saeed to come over and stand in front of the door.

Feeling no threat from the small boy, she opened the door.

Danel thrust his foot inside, pushing Saeed safely to the side, and forced his way in.

Her eyes as large as a new moon, she was at first startled. "What are you doing here?" She tried to push him back out the door, but he moved forward, as Bethshari and Saeed followed and closed the door behind them. Dressed in slacks and a plaid over shirt, she carried Hamid in the cloth baby carrier. Her backpack and the baby carrier lay by the door, ready for the journey.

"I'm here for my son."

The small face, much older that the tiny one Danel has kissed goodbye on the road to Za'atari, watched the stranger who was his father.

Overwhelmed, Danel reached out to touch him as Sister Helen twisted sideways to move Hamid out of Danel's reach.

"Who's this woman?" She eyed Bethshari. "Where's Ashara?"

"She's dead." He waited for her to react.

"Dead? That can't be."

"She took her own life after she gave up hope of getting her son back."

She gasped. "Oh my God. Danel, I didn't mean to." She searched for the right word.

His mind raced ahead of hers, cutting her off. "Didn't mean to kidnap our son?"

"I never meant to harm you. I was going to bring him back, but I fell in love and just couldn't give him up." She wrapped both arms around Hamid, pulling him closer.

"You're giving him back now." He took two steps toward her, blocking any escape.

"No, please don't take him away." She clutched the baby even tighter. Her cheeks awash, she pleaded. "Don't take him, please Danel. He's all I have." Her voice's sudden escalation startled Hamid, and he began to cry.

"Did you think I would just let you keep him? I'm not leaving without my son."

"You're scaring him."

"No, you're the one scaring him. If you care about him, give him back. He needs to be with me, and you know that."

"Shhh, shhh, there there, Hamid, it's alright. Mama's here."

"You're not his mother. Ashara was right about you all along. Only I couldn't see it."

She hugged the child, rocking back and forth to comfort him.

"Now take him out of the carrier. Do the right thing." He held out his hands.

Carefully, she disengaged from the carrier. She held Hamid close, hugging him, and then kissed each little hand, then his cheeks. Closing her eyes, she embraced him one last time before handing him to Danel.

For the first time in months, he held his son and kissed him.

"Hamid," he said, rocking slightly, emotions choking his words. Regaining control, he gently passed him to Bethshari.

As she cradled him in her arms, she swayed back and forth before kneeling down to present him to Saeed.

"Hey, little brother." Saeed offered his finger, which Hamid grasped, moving it to his mouth to suck.

"Where are his papers?" said Danel.

Sister Helen stood in shock, as though she hadn't heard him.

"The papers? *Now.*" His raised voice snapped her back to attention.

"They're in my backpack." She gestured to it by the door.

Rummaging through it, he found their visas, along with Hamid's birth papers. "What's this? Adoption papers too? Very clever passing him off as your son." He opened the plane tickets, noting the 5:00 departure. "Do you have any idea the damage you have caused?"

She said nothing.

He shredded the adoption papers and Hamid's visa. "You won't be needing these." He handed her back the plane tickets and put Hamid's birth document in his back pocket.

"What are you going to do?" Searching her pockets for a handkerchief, her hands trembled.

"Nothing right now. But I suggest that you get on that plane at 5:00, or I swear I'll turn the authorities onto you." He noticed Hamid's baby bag and carrier on the floor next to her. "Are those Hamid's things?"

"Yes." She blew her nose and wiped her eyes.

"I'll be taking them with me then."

Saeed took possession of the carrier, moving it back with him and Bethshari.

"Can I at least say goodbye to him?" Her voice cracked.

"You've already said your goodbyes."

Bethshari intervened. "Danel, let her say goodbye."

He sighed. "Alright, but quickly."

As Bethshari laid him into her arms, he immediately calmed down.

"Hamid, my dear boy. I'll always love you." Her chest heaved but no more words would come, as her tears gushed unimpeded. She kissed him on both cheeks. Caressing his crown, she gave him a final hug.

"That's enough. You can give him back now."

After passing him gently to Bethshari, she crossed both hands over her mouth, stifling her sobs.

"I meant what I said. Be on that plane or you can rot in a Syrian prison for the rest of your life."

Latching the lock behind them, she leaned her head against the door and sobbed. Crumpling to her knees, she wept, "Hamid, Hamid."

As they reached the stairs, Bethshari slowed to a stop. "Danel, you should carry your son."

Tenderly, he lifted the child into his arms. Holding Hamid close, he said, "I told your mother I'd get you back. You don't remember me, but I'm your baba."

Saeed pulled on Danel's sleeve. "Tell him you're his papa. That's what he should call you."

Trembling, he shifted Hamid to one arm and knelt down to gather Saeed in close to him. "My two sons. Look at you both. I'm your Papa, Hamid."

"And we're a family." Bethshari knelt down and encircled her arms around them.

"Where's the car?" said Danel.

"We had to leave it and follow her on foot," said Saeed. "It's not far. Follow me."

Sister Helen walked about the apartment dazed. She had no doubt that Danel meant what he said about the authorities. The plane tickets lay on the counter where he left them. Placing them in the backpack's zippered compartment, she fumbled each arm into the straps. For the first time since moving in, she didn't check the apartment to freeze its arrangement in her mind. Closing the door behind her, she knew she wouldn't be back.

Out on the street, she looked for a taxi, but seeing none she started to walk. She was half way up the block when a police car passed her.

She glanced back to see the car stop at her building. Two policemen got out and entered her complex. At the next corner, she hailed a cab. "Damascus International Airport."

38

Desperate Grief

Hamid had calmed by the time they reached the car. *We're strangers to him,* Bethshari thought. *As far as he's concerned, his real mother is back at the apartment they just left.*

"Who parked this car?" said Danel. The Renault was catawampus, almost a full meter from the curb with the back fender protruding half a meter into the lane of traffic. Oncoming cars detoured around it to the left. "Saeed, did you park this car?"

"No, my father taught me how to park better than this."

"We were in a hurry," said Bethshari. She shrugged, glad that no one had hit it.

"The slippery eel turned down a one way street so we had to chase after her on foot," said Saeed.

Danel handed Hamid to Bethshari, but she passed him back. "I'll drive and you hold your son. You've waited a long time for him. Sit in the back with Saeed so you have more room."

Saeed slid over as Danel climbed in, holding the infant. Saeed grabbed his brother's fist, lowering his head to the baby's eye level. "Hey, Hamid, I'm your brother Saeed." Hamid responded with a smile and pulled Saeed's hand to his mouth to chew on it. "It looks like he's hungry. He's trying to eat my hand." As Hamid munched, Saeed felt the crest of a tiny tooth barely poking out of the lower gum. "He's getting a tooth. Papa, can you feel it?"

Danel rubbed his finger over the gum. "You're right, Saeed." *One of many firsts we'll experience,* thought Danel. "That was a close call. If you two hadn't tracked her on foot, she'd have been on her way out of the country by now."

"Did you notice her destination?" said Bethshari, turning right into the next block.

"Minneapolis, Minnesota."

"We would never have been able to retrieve him from there."

"She had adoption papers, so we couldn't have proven he was ours. Allah heard our prayers."

"I told you he would," said Saeed.

Abu came calling shortly after he got off his shift. "When you left so abruptly, I assumed that you had found Hamid."

"I'd like to introduce you to my son."

"Do you mind if I hold him?" Abu's large hands reached out to receive him.

Although revolted by the thought of Abu touching Hamid, they couldn't risk any hostility toward Abu.

His face contorted, Hamid started to cry, clinging to Danel. His face turned into Danel's shoulder, pushing Abu away with his arm.

"I guess he has had enough of new faces today," said Danel.

Abu backed off. "Well, Hamid, you've been the subject of quite a manhunt. You're where you belong now." He brushed his finger across Hamid's cheek. "You all must be quite relieved."

"It's been torture. This is truly a joyous day," said Danel.

"You'll want to spend some time getting acquainted, so I'll say goodbye. I'll see you at work tomorrow then?"

"Yes, I'll see you tomorrow." Danel let Abu out and locked the door behind him, exchanging looks with Bethshari.

"I think it's my turn to hold him. Danel, bring him over here so I can get a good look at my new son."

Danel sat down beside her, laying Hamid in her lap, with Saeed kneeling in front. "I think he looks like you, Danel." This time he didn't wince, instead accepting it as a compliment.

"Let's take a look in that baby bag and see if there is anything we need to buy right away." Danel and Saeed counted a day's rations of formula, a box of dry pabulum and several jars of baby food, plus eight diapers.

"That's not going to be enough to last us. Danel, you take Hamid back, and Saeed and I will go to the market to get the other things we need," she said.

Tired of waiting for Sister Helen to arrive home from work, the officers applied to the building manager to let them into her flat. Very little of her belongings remained, save a small pile of torn papers on the counter that looked like a visa and perhaps some adoption papers. "This bird has flown the coop. I wonder who tipped her off." One of the officers scooped the scraps into a plastic bag.

"I don't know, but maybe we're not the only ones looking for her. We can circulate her photo on the television. I'll call in and get that started."

At the airport, Sister Helen bought a bottle of water and some snacks for the journey. As she walked to her gate, she noticed her photo on a TV monitor. The caption read *Helen McCormick, suspected of kidnapping*, and a phone number to call. She froze, lowering her face and looking away as two security guards walked past her. A women's rest room, immediately to her right, offered immediate asylum before she had to board, but she still had to get to the gate. Inside she adjusted her hijab, pulling it down over her forehead and close at the sides to conceal more of her face. As she waited inside a stall, her hands trembled as she heard the last call for boarding her flight.

Swallowing deeply, head bent low, she hurried to the plane. Her heart was thumping wildly as she handed her boarding pass to the attendant.

"Have a safe flight," said the attendant, looking directly at her.

Sister Helen nodded with a faint smile, and turned sideways to fiddle with the strap on the backpack on the opposite side. Most of the passengers had already boarded as she hurried down the jet bridge. She glanced at her boarding pass. Seat 34C was a window. Moving down the aisle, she felt the eyes of other passengers examining her. She lifted her backpack up, but there was no room in the overhead compartment.

A stewardess in the aisle several rows back was watching her. "Ma'am, let me have that. There some room for it further back. You have to take you seat now so we can take off."

"Of course." The large passenger in the aisle seat stepped out to let her pass. Not having cashed in Hamid's ticket, the middle seat reserved for him remained empty. Her hands trembled as she remained on Syrian soil. Taking her seat by the window, she pulled down the shade, closing her eyes as she leaned into the window to feign a nap.

"Ma'am."

Fearing she'd been identified, she pretended she was asleep.

"Ma'am." The stewardess was more insistent this time.

Sister Helen looked up slightly.

"You have to buckle your seatbelt."

"Yes, of course." She slowly exhaled as the attendant closed the remaining overhead bins before taking her seat up front near the cockpit.

While the plane slowly taxied down the runway, a security guard, delivering flyers with Sister Helen's photo, handed one to the flight attendant closing up the gate.

Locking the terminal door to the jet bridge, she glanced at it. "This looks like the woman who was last to board."

"Did she have a baby with her?"

"No, she was alone."

"Then it probably wasn't the same woman."

"Well, even if it was, it's too late now. They're already taxing, and I'm not calling it back for someone we're not even sure is the one they're after."

While the plane gained altitude, Sister Helen stared out the window as Damascus minimized, falling away from her view. Hamid's small face, phantom-like, haunted her. *So close,* she thought, *so close.* This child stripped from her only hours earlier would be more missed than her own infant taken from her years ago. She loved Hamid. Leaning into the window, she relinquished her grief momentarily to descend into a deep sleep.

Bethshari and Saeed left Danel and Hamid at the apartment while they went to the market. "Saeed, I want to talk to you about something important."

"About Hamid?"

"It's about all of us. Over the last week, your Papa and I have been working on getting your adoption papers."

"I'm scared about what you are going to say."

"Don't be scared. We have them now. You're officially ours."

"For sure?" He hopped up and down, clapping his hands.

"For sure."

She let him finish before taking him by the hand. "But we have decided to leave Syria and go to London where my parents live. We don't believe it's safe here now, and we want to raise you and Hamid in a place free of bombing and killing. That means you wouldn't be back to Syria for many years." She gave him some time to absorb what she had just said. "How do you feel about that?" They had rounded the corner, turning left toward the market.

"Would we all still be together when we go to London?"

"Yes, of course. We'll find a nice place to live there."

Saeed let go of her hand, crossing his arms across his chest to hug his shoulders.

"What concerns you?"

"Do they speak Arabic there?"

"Not so much. My parents speak Arabic, but you'd have to learn English, as would your Papa and Hamid."

"Is it hard to learn?"

"For you and Hamid it'll be easy because you're both so young. For Papa it'll be harder. It's harder to learn a language when you're older."

His pace slackened, dropping him back behind her. "Would we ever come back to Syria?"

She stopped, waiting for him to catch up. "When the war is over, we could come back for a visit."

"How soon would we go?"

"Tomorrow morning very early."

"Is Dr. Abu coming with us?"

She gulped. "No, he's not coming." She hesitated but knew she had to get it all out. "And he can't know we're leaving."

"Is it a secret?" His face scrunched up.

"Yes, especially from Dr. Abu."

He frowned. "I don't understand, he's our friend."

"I know, but he would try to stop us, and we can't let that happen. It's time for us to go." Biting her lip, she said, "Does that make sense?"

"But won't it be dangerous for Dr. Abu to stay behind?"

"Yes, but he'll have to decide for himself what to do."

"Will we say goodbye?"

"No, and if you see him before we go, you'll have to keep the secret. Can you do that?"

"It doesn't seem right." He shook his head side to side.

"But will you do it?"

"Yes, if you ask me to."

"Good boy." They had reached the market. "Now we will need some food for the trip, and we have to make sure we have enough baby food and diapers for Hamid."

"Bethshari, will I like London?"

"It's different from Syria, but it'll be like a great adventure." She loaded several cans of formula into the cart.

"How will I play with other kids if I can't speak English?"

"You'll learn quickly. But let me ask you this. Do you need any language to play football?"

"They play football in London?" He took her hand again.

"All kids play football there."

He smiled, executing an imaginary ball cross over his right toe.

"I don't have a ball."

"Don't worry, we'll get a new one there."

He slowed down, still thinking. "The only thing I don't like is not saying goodbye to Dr. Abu."

"I know. We feel the same way, but that's how it has to be. Promise you won't say anything?"

"I promise."

Sister Helen woke up crying. Rummaging through her pockets for a handkerchief, she realized she must have left it in the backpack. Wiping her eyes on her sleeve, she edged her way over Hamid's vacant seat and excused herself to the passenger on the aisle. Locking the lavatory door behind her, she looked in the mirror. Red blotches covered her face. How different the image staring back at her from the nun who came to Syria two years ago, she thought. She splashed cold water on her face, taking several deep breaths while loading her pockets with tissues. Exhaling deeply, she slid the latch open and returned to her seat. Her sorrow on display, she felt as if an empty wind blew through her heart. She crawled over the passenger in the aisle seat, not even giving him time to let her in.

"Are you alright?"

"No, not really. I'm sorry for climbing over you like that." She grabbed a tissue out of her pocket and dabbed her wet face before dropping into her seat. "It's just that today my heart's broken, and it just doesn't want to behave. I can't seem to stop the water works." She plopped into her seat, fastening her seatbelt.

"I felt the same way when my wife passed. Didn't know I could cry so much."

"It just keeps coming." She spread her hands helplessly in front of her.

"Why are you so sad, if you don't mind me asking?"

"I was going to adopt a dear child that I'd fallen in love with. He lived with me for over two months, but this afternoon he was taken from me. His parents wanted him back. There was nothing I could do. He was supposed to be in this empty seat." She shrugged slightly, attempting a smile.

"I'm sorry for your loss." He pulled a dry handkerchief out of his pocket. "Here, you look like you're going to need this."

"Thanks." Unfolding it, she blew her nose.

He was a big man, perhaps two heads taller than she. A middle age paunch indicated he liked to eat. He wore a flannel plaid shirt even though the weather in Damascus was still warm.

"Do you drink?"

"Well, I haven't in a long time." She blushed.

He pressed the attendant button.

"A glass of red wine perhaps? You look like you could use it. It's on me."

She nodded and blew her nose again.

"Where are you headed now?"

"I'm going to Minneapolis, to my parent's home in Edina to lick my wounds. But I don't think I'll last long there because my mother and I don't get along."

"I always say you can never go home." The attendant handed her a small bottle of merlot and a plastic cup. As he took his, he said, "A glass would have been nicer, but the contents are really what's needed here."

He raised his cup to toast. "To the end of unhappiness."

"Yes, that's a good wish. It's going to take a while." She sipped the wine slowly. "What do you do for a living?"

"My wife and I ran a camp for wayward boys in the Ozarks. I run it without her now." He took a drink.

"What were you doing in Syria?"

"I was visiting my son, trying to persuade him to come home." He unbuckled his seatbelt. "He's married to a Syrian woman whose elderly parents are there. She can't leave, and he won't leave without her. It's very dangerous with this Assad character."

"I know. That's why I'm leaving."

He turned to her slightly. "My name is Henry. Henry Schuster." He extended his hand.

"Helen." She paused, considering if she should give her full name. "McCormick." His hand felt warm as she shook it.

"Glad to meet you, Helen. It'll get better, your heart I mean. With my wife, it was that way. At first I didn't know if I could go on, and then I did. You don't stop missing, but you do stop crying."

"You're very kind." His white beard and mustache made him seem older, she thought, almost fatherly, but the skin on his hands was young. "You never remarried?"

"Not yet. It's not that I would mind, but there aren't many women who'd get involved with the work I do. It's consuming, and whoever I married would have to love that life."

"What kind of boys go to your camp?"

"It's a Christian camp, so a lot of the boys are referred from their churches: boys teetering on the edge of trouble—some already there, and others hanging with poor company, so it's just a question of time for them."

"Is it a summer camp?"

"No, we run it all year round. A boy can stay up to six months if the church can raise the funds. We've turned a lot of kids around. A couple of our hands came to us as kids and returned later to help other kids."

The attendant came by and asked if they needed another drink. Without asking, he ordered two more. "Why were you in Syria?"

"I came over as a nun but have since left my order. I'm a nurse and worked in a Syrian hospital for an NGO."

The second wine arrived and he clicked her cup before sipping. "If you don't think I'm prying, why did you stop being a nun?"

"I just felt it was time for me to stop insulating myself from life. I wanted to adopt, and there was no way I could do that as a nun."

"If you ever want a job working with kids, I've a place for you." He handed her his business card. "Henry Schuster, Director, Beacon Crest, Christian Boys Adventure."

"I may just look you up; I'm going to need a job." Dabbing the corners of her eyes, she shrugged. "Sorry. Just can't help it. I have some unfinished business in Minneapolis to tend to first." She looked at the card again, smiling. "Now I'll know where to mail your handkerchief."

39

Apprehensions

It was still dark out when Bethshari shook Saeed's shoulder. "Saeed, wake up. We've got to leave."

He rubbed his eyes and rolled over. "It's too early."

"You have to wake up now."

"It's too dark. I'll get up later."

"No, you have to get up. We're leaving."

He sat up. "Why are we leaving so early?"

"We have to drive a long way, farther than Za'atari. There'll be a lot of traffic going toward the camp, so we have to allow plenty of time to get to our plane."

Swinging his legs over the side of the bed, he sat up, still drowsy.

"Use the bathroom and get dressed. We don't have much time." She left his room, but the quiet on the other side of the door lured her back to check on him. He was lying down, facing the wall.

"Saeed." This time her voice was more insistent.

"Alright. I'm up."

She stayed until he padded to the door on the way to the bathroom.

"Is Hamid awake?"

"Yes, Papa's giving him his bottle. I've got your breakfast ready, so come as soon as you're dressed." Returning to the kitchen, she found Hamid almost finished.

"Danel, are your things packed?"

"What little I have is in my backpack. What about you?"

"I packed my stuff and Saeed's. I'm getting Hamid's bag loaded right now. As soon as Saeed has his breakfast, we can leave."

"Hamid is almost finished, and then I'll change him."

"Where are the tickets and the visas?" she said.

"In my front zippered compartment. Do you want to check?"

"No, I trust you."

Saeed wandered out and slid into a seat at the table. "I'm not hungry. It's too early."

"Just have some grapes and a glass of milk then. You can eat something in the car when you get hungry."

Laying his head on the table, he rested it on his arm.

"Saeed, do this for me. Please eat something."

He managed five grapes and half of the milk before she gave up.

Danel burped Hamid and settled him into the carrier. "Are you ready?"

"As ready as I'll ever be."

"Let's go. Saeed, come on son, let's go."

As they entered the exterior corridor, Abu's door opened abruptly.

"And where're all four of you going in the darkness?"

"Bethshari, take the boys and get in the car," said Danel.

"I want to stay with you."

"Take them now."

Leaving his door ajar for some light, Abu passed by Bethshari. "Where are you going, Danel?"

"We're leaving."

"Leaving to where?"

"I'm sorry."

He sounded puzzled. "What are you talking about?"

"I put a stop to you and your letters. I notified the authorities."

"No, you didn't. You couldn't afford to have them on your tail. I know what you did, and I have no qualms about telling them."

Two can play this game, thought Danel. "You think you do, but you got it wrong. Hamid's my son. What made you think you could blackmail me?"

"I checked the records. An infant died and yours lived. All the records in your handwriting. It didn't take me long to dig it out. Then you had to tell Bethshari, and she almost bolted. I knew it had to be something horrific."

"The night he was born, we had no other staff to fill out the records. There were snipers and no generators. What you uncovered was a catastrophe, but not the kind you imagined. Now get out of my way. You'll have to reckon for what you've done here and in Beirut soon enough."

He grabbed Danel's arms, shaking him. "What have you done?"

Danel shook him off. "Get your hands off me." He shoved him backwards. "You'll find out. I thought you were our friend."

Abu stepped in front of him.

"Don't try to stop us."

"Danel, listen to me. This situation that I have here, it's lucrative. You could ease right in and the payoff would be more than you could make in a lifetime at any hospital."

"And when the authorities caught up with me, would I flee like a rat the way you did? I have a wife and two children now."

Abu pushed him into the wall, grabbing his shirt. "I'm not letting you leave."

As Danel shoved him back into the railing. Abu started to tumble over, but Danel pulled him back. "I should let you fall."

Abu taunted back. "Let me go, you coward." As the two wrestled, Abu soon had the advantage, now bending Danel backward over the railing.

"Bethshari and Saeed are downstairs with Hamid. What is your plan for them? It's over, Abu. We're out of here." He arched forward, regaining his balance.

"What am I supposed to do now?"

"I really don't care. Run, hide, it makes no difference to me." Danel shoved him back against the wall. "Whatever you do, I am not going to be a part of it." He grabbed his backpack and raced down two steps at a time to the car.

Bethshari had Saeed in the back seat all buckled in, holding Hamid. The engine was running, just waiting for Danel.

"Let's go. Now," he ordered, jumping into the front seat. "Lock the doors."

Bethshari jutted out into the empty street. Unsure of how far Abu would go to stop them, she raced down the block and turned the wrong way.

"That's the wrong direction."

"I know but the right direction was straight ahead. I don't want to be in his line of vision in case he has a gun. Does he know where we're going?"

"No, I didn't tell him. I just said we were leaving." He turned around to make sure that Abu wasn't following.

"Does you tell him you called the authorities?"

"I did, but he'd already surmised as much." She was speeding.

"You should slow down. He's not coming."

"What will happen to him now?"

"If they catch him, the Syrian authorities will extradite him, and he'll stand trial in Lebanon."

"What a waste, but I can't even feel sorry for him."

"Just drive. We've a long way to go and not a lot of time to spare." Unbuckling his seatbelt, he pulled his shirt up to examine his left side. A deep bruise was already forming.

Bethshari glanced over. "That doesn't look very good."

Probing it gently, he said, "I think my rib is broken. Something to remember Abu by."

"I'm pulling over."

"No you're not. We barely have time to make it to our flight. My rib isn't going anywhere. We'll get some ice on the plane."

Back inside his flat, Abu closed the door behind him and dialed Issam Kattani. "Sami, we're blown. Ottawa knows and he's notified the authorities. We've got to pack it in and get out of here right now."

"I've got three infants presold. All we're waiting on is the paperwork. Have you got the documents?"

"Yes, they're in my office at the hospital."

"Are you fucking out of your mind? Why don't you just send a letter to the Syrian police and let them know that the stupidest asshole in the country has left them an incredible evidence trail?"

"I'll have to go up there and get rid of them. The third letter to Ottawa is also there. "

"You're a fucking idiot, Majeed."

"Look, I'll go and remove what's there. You meet me there in thirty minutes, and you can have the documents. I want my cut though."

"You'll get your cut less what my expenses will be for having to set this up in another country, you son of a bitch."

Abu quickly removed his essentials from the flat, stuffing them into his backpack. He grimaced at the four bottles of wine he would have to leave behind. Fifteen minutes later he was unlocking his office, removing incriminating documents and suffng them into his backpack. The third letter was already waiting in Danel's chair. He would have to rifle the lock to get it back. He checked his watch.

"Good morning, Dr. Abu." A night nurse walked by as he was trying to slip the lock open. "Dr. Ottawa doesn't usually get here until 7:30."

"I didn't realize that. I'll just come back later then." He turned back toward his office, listening as she rounded the corner before returning to the door. The old lock resisted his touch, and he had to jiggle it to trip the tumbler. Once inside, he grabbed the envelope out of Danel's chair, left his backpack just inside and closed the door as he exited without relocking.

Back in his office, the phone rang, breaking his concentration.

"Dr. Abu, you have a visitor here in the lobby."

"Yes, I was expecting him. Would you send him up?"

All that remained was the documentation for the three infants that Sami had stashed with a woman who acted as an intermediary. Abu placed them in a manila envelope.

A knock at Abu's door broke the silence.

"Come in."

"Do you have the docs?"

"They're in the envelope." He looked out the window overlooking the parking area in front of the hospital. Four police cars had pulled up, and eight uniformed officers piled out and rushed into the hospital. "Wait here, I've got one more document for you."

"Hurry up. I want to get out of here before we have any trouble."

"I'll be right back." Abu slipped into Danel's office and picked up his backpack. As he opened the door to the back stairwell, the elevator door opened with four policemen. Two others worked their way up the front stairs, and the last two Abu met as he was making his way out. "Good morning, officers," he said as he kept on walking. "I'll show you who's a fucking idiot, Sami," he said under his breath as he opened the door to the outside.

Abu crossed over two streets to hail a cab.

"Where to Mr.?"

Abu jumped in, slamming the door behind him. "Gaziantep."

"Gaziantep in Turkey?"

"It's north of Aleppo." Abu unzipped his backpack and rummaged for a revolver that he laid beside him on the seat.

"I know where it is, but I don't go that far." The driver turned around, draping his arm across the back of his seat. "Look, Mr., I don't want no trouble."

Abu patted the revolver. "Nor do I. I'll make it worth your while. How about double what you make in a month?" Abu counted out the money, adding, "I'll give you half now and the rest when we get there."

The driver grabbed the cash. "Yes, sir. Gaziantep it is."

As the police broke into Abu's office, handcuffing Issam Kattani, the Renault crept at a tortoise pace along M1 Highway toward Jordan. In normal times, the 175 km straight shot between Damascus and Amman would take less than two hours, but the flow of refugees impeding them threatened to turn the journey into a four-hour ordeal. Four kilometers out of Damascus, Danel insisted on taking the wheel.

"We're not going to make our flight at this pace." Staring ahead into the mass of cars, his grip on the steering wheel tightened. "Look, we're not even keeping up with the pedestrians."

Hamid nestled against Bethshari in the front seat while Saeed slept in the back. Her hand firmly gripped the armrest on the door.

"I'm going to ease over onto the shoulder and see if I can move a little faster."

"You can't do that. There're people on the shoulder."

"I can see that."

"No need to snap at me."

"Sorry. How ironic that we snatch Hamid from Sister Helen and escape from the jaws of Majeed, but the traffic to Amman is what's going to stop us." He slapped the steering wheel with both hands. "This is impossible."

"I don't know what to tell you, Danel. Just keep driving."

"This's making me crazy. I can't just plod along here. Stick your arm out the window so people know I'm coming over."

"Danel, there're too many people. It's too dangerous."

"Just do it. Please. They'll move out of the way as we move through. I promise."

She stuck her arm out the window, sweeping it from the front of the car towards the back, as if she were doing the backstroke through a sea of people.

"See, they're getting out of the way." He gradually sped up.

Saeed woke up and rolled down his window. He leaned out the window, mimicking her movements with both his arms, and the crowd opened up to let them through.

"Keep it up. Look at how much faster we're going than the rest of the traffic."

Suddenly, Saeed was screaming. "Sick baby. Sick baby. Going to hospital." The crowd parted faster, allowing Danel to pick up even more speed. Hamid was now fully awake, but Bethshari hesitated calling out lest she frighten him. "What the heck," she said, reasoning if Saeed's shouts didn't scare him she'd give it a try. "Sick baby. Hospital." Hamid watched her intently.

The Renault was now moving about 40 km/hour, more than double the speed before they moved to the shoulder.

"Papa, look, the police are coming."

Danel looked in his rear view mirror. A police car, siren howling and red light flashing, was overtaking them. "I don't believe this." He slowed to a stop.

"Relax, Danel. All our papers are in order. They can't detain us long. Just relax."

Beads of sweat formed on his upper lip.

"Step out of the car. Your identity papers, please."

"They're in the trunk.

The officer followed him to the trunk with his hand on his revolver while his partner stayed behind in the police car.

Danel handed him his papers.

"Where're you going in such a hurry?"

"I have a sick baby that we are trying to get to a hospital in Amman."

"Says here you're a doctor." The officer eyed him suspiciously.

"I am. We have an appointment there with a specialist. Then my baby had a seizure in the car and I knew we needed to get there faster than the traffic would allow."

"What you did endangered a lot of people." The officer looked over his sunglasses, eyeing Bethshari and Hamid in the front seat.

"I panicked when he seized."

"Wait here." While the officer sauntered back to his partner in the vehicle, Danel leaned in the driver window to let Bethshari know what was happening.

"What did you tell them?"

"I told them that Hamid has a seizure and we panicked."

"Did he buy it?"

"I have no idea. We're in Allah's hands now." His own hands felt clammy as he wiped them against his pants legs.

The officer walked back and looked in again at Bethshari and Hamid. "How's he doing?"

"He stopped seizing for now, but I believe he's a little feverish. I'm very worried," she said.

He pulled Danel aside, resting his hand on his revolver.

"Look, Doc, we can accompany you as far as the border. After that the traffic should open up. You promise no more driving on the shoulder?"

"I promise."

"I'm going to pull in front of you. You follow and stay close."

"Thank you so much. May Allah protect you for your kindness." Danel got back into the car and slowly exhaled.

"Danel, are we being arrested?"

He started the ignition in a state of shock. "I hardly know how this happened."

"What's going on?"

"He wants us to follow him."

"Follow him where?" She shifted in her seat to face him.

"To the border. He's escorting us to the border so we can get Hamid to the hospital."

"This is a joke, right?"

"No. It's not a joke. Watch."

The lane of traffic opened up to allow the police car and the Renault into the lane. The siren sounded and the red light on top began to spin. Each car they came upon moved either to the shoulder or to the left lane, allowing them clear passage. An hour later, they reached the border, and the patrol car pulled onto the shoulder, waving the Renault ahead.

Signs to Amman indicated another 80 km yet to go. "We should be able to make decent time now," said Danel. "But Queen Alia International Airport is south of the city. If we're lucky, we can be there in an hour."

Bethshari looked at her watch. "That's going to be close, but I think we can make it."

"Allah made those police come and help us," said Saeed.

"I'm sure he did, because I wasn't getting the job done."

Fifty-five minutes later, they pulled into the airport parking lot. "Come on," said Danel. "We still have to get through security, and our flight leaves in an hour."

"At least we aren't checking baggage," said Bethshari.

Jogging through the airport, they were breathing heavily as they reached the head of the security line. The officer glanced at Danel and Bethshari, hardly paying them any attention. When he got to Saeed's visa, he paused. "Son, your last name is different from the people you are traveling with. Why is that?"

Bethshari's breath stuck in her throat, ready to answer, but the guard had already engaged Saeed.

"Dr. Ottawa and his wife adopted me. My mother, father and brother were killed."

"You had no other family? No grandparents?"

"They were with my mother when the bomb hit our house." Saeed's eyes glassed over telling his story.

"Son, your new family, are they good to you?"

"Yes. My parents would have liked them very much."

The officer stamped his boarding pass. "You be a good son, Saeed, and have a safe journey."

Bethshari walked behind Saeed as he loaded his backpack onto the conveyor to be x-rayed. She bent and whispered to him. "I could not be more proud of you. You handled yourself very well just then."

"All I did was say the truth."

On the plane, they took their seats, Saeed by the window with Hamid in his lap describing the airplanes out the window, Bethshari in the middle seat and Danel on the aisle. A stewardess leaned over and told them that an adult would have to hold the baby on takeoff and landing. Saeed relinquished his charge. "Can I have my brother back after we get up in the air?"

"Yes, you can. You seem like a very good big brother."

"I am." His smiled as he boasted.

As they taxied out to the runway, Danel reached for Bethshari's hand. "We made it."

"Yes, we did. Good job with the police back on M1."

Squeezing his eyes shut, he leaned his head back into the headrest. "I'm not proud that I lied to get us out of that mess."

"I think this time even Ashara would have approved."

He opened his eyes and leaned forward, facing her. "It seems like yesterday that Ashara died and I was so alone." He took her hand in his. "And now I'm married to a beautiful woman and we are a family of four."

"A family of five."

He stared at her, tilting his head, frowning.

"For a doctor, you're pretty slow."

"Five?"

"Yes five, and I'm hoping number five is a girl."

He drew her hand up to his mouth and kissed it. "I don't deserve this much happiness."

"You do indeed. You made a mistake, one from which you couldn't pull back. But your actions were grounded in love, not evil. That counts for something. I think Allah is trying to tell you that you paid your debt and it's time to live your life."

Now airborne, he unbuckled his seatbelt, pushed the armrest back against the seat, and passed Hamid back to Saeed. Then reaching over and unbuckling Bethshar, he took her in his arms and kissed her. "I love you more than you know. I'm never going to let you go."

Saeed turned Hamid to the window. "Don't look, Hamid. Mushy stuff."

Five months later, Danel and Bethshari sat up in bed after the boys had gone to sleep. A pillow was plumped under her knees while she read and Danel worked on his English.

"Ed-u-ca-ti-on. Why's it spelled education and not educashun? T-i-o-n as shun makes no sense."

"Just forget trying to make sense out of the English language. It's got roots in German, Latin and Anglo-Frisian dialects, plus every wave of invader bought a little something extra. Nope, can't be figured out, just has to be learned."

He scrunched up his face. "Arabic makes much more sense."

She rested her book in her lap and placed her hand on her abdomen where their baby kicked. "You know what I did today?"

"What?"

"You remember those earrings that belonged to Abu's mother?"

"I thought you left them behind."

"I just couldn't dishonor her by leaving them. Silly I guess."

"No, not silly. It's actually very endearing, especially knowing what her son tried to do to us."

"Well, I got to thinking that maybe I could sell them and do something good with the money."

"Like what?"

"Well, I hadn't gotten that far. I figured we would figure that out together."

Kissing her cheek, he reached over in time to feel their baby kick. "Feels like our daughter likes that idea."

She smiled, guiding his hand over another shifting bulge in her abdomen. "Anyway, I took them into a jeweler today to find out how old they were and what they were worth."

"What did you find out?"

"They're fake, purple glass and gold plate. He said from the quality of workmanship they were probably bought in some bazaar out of a bin of a hundred more just like them."

"Why doesn't that surprise me?" His head moved from side to side.

"Me either." Removing the notebook off his lap, she set it on the floor with her book.

That's enough studying for tonight." She pulled him close, kissing him sweetly, before reaching over and turning out the light.

* * *

Acknowledgements

Many amazing people, each with a different perspective, have encouraged and helped me through the writing of my first novel. I would like to thank Katy Grant, author of <u>Hide and Seek,</u> my mentor and teacher for all of her patient observations, suggestions and unwavering encouragement.

Martha Kemp, always my dedicated advocate, was true to her usual diligence with scrupulous attention to details. I could never ask for a more thorough editor.

Jean Blomker, a consummate reader, brought big picture expertise, and never wavered in her support. She felt that the war setting and the journey of the characters was a story that had to be told.

Mari Brown offered her critical eye to the manuscript, and kept me honest with her questions and observations.

Kelly MacDonald, who I grew to know and respect through my consulting practice, gave me a broader perspective of the tension in the novel. Her comments were always spot on.

Dr. Wayne Thorburn, author of <u>Red State</u>, whose opinion I have always valued, graciously agreed to read my final manuscript and offer his opinion and suggestions.

Eileen Farrell Kammerer carefully reviewed the manuscript, pointing out discrepancies and offering alternate suggestions which proved to make the whole story more interesting.

Debra Stapleton, whose busy life left little time for herself, managed to read the manuscript and offer invaluable feedback and encouragement.

C. Ashford's detailed reading gave me a thorough analysis of the manuscript's many levels, and her enjoyment of the story further validated it.

My sons, Matthew Heagerty and Michael Heagerty, have always been stalwart fans, and their opinions carry much weight with me. Their encouragement never even flickered for a moment, and their suggestions were invaluable.

My husband Laszlo Marton walked the journey from Damascus to Za'atari and back with me. His patience through my early morning, late night and sometimes all weekend writing marathons never faltered. His belief in me and my writing became a beacon guiding me to completion. He always listened and gave feedback even when I am sure he wearied of hearing about it all.

I would also like to thank Nick at FirstEditing.com for the final professional polish on the manuscript and Andrei Bat for lending his incredible talent and artistic vision to the cover art.

To all of these individuals I am exceedingly grateful.

About the Author

Christine Heagerty Marton was born in Jersey City, New Jersey and educated at College of Notre Dame of Maryland in Baltimore where she received a bachelor's degree in biology. She earned her master's degree in microbiology from the University of Texas at Austin. After raising two sons and a long career in the real estate industry, she turned her attention to her first love, creative writing. She writes stories that she would want to read—that grab attention, transport the reader into the drama and cast a spell not to put it down. Her favorite reader comment is, "That surprised me; I didn't see that coming." Unholy

Innocents is her first novel. She lives in Round Rock, Texas with her husband Laszlo Marton.

If you would like to be on her mailing list, hear about new books and special offers, sign up at www.chrisheagertymarton.com.

Follow her on facebook at www.facebook.com/ChrisHeagertyMarton or on twitter at @Chris_Heagerty

Made in the USA
Middletown, DE
04 October 2015